One of them stumbled out of the grass and into me. I jabbed him in the throat with the barrel of my CAR, and then struck him in the jaw with the butt, knocking him sprawling. He started to roll over. I kicked him in the front of the throat and he gurgled. A second later he went limp, dying without another sound.

I killed him without any thought at all; the moves had become reflexive. That gave me something to think about later, when the killing was over for a few moments.

SLOW DANCE ON THE KILLING GROUND

LENOX CRAMER

AVON BOOKS ◆ NEW YORK

AVON BOOKS
A division of
The Hearst Corporation
1350 Avenue of the Americas
New York, New York 10019

First Avon Books Printing: July 1991

AVON TRADEMARK REG. U.S. PAT. OFF. AND IN OTHER COUNTRIES, MARCA REGISTRADA, HECHO EN U.S.A.

Printed in the U.S.A.

RA   10   9   8   7   6   5   4   3   2   1

Table of Contents

LENOX CRAMER is the *nom de guerre* of a former Special Forces operative. Born in Detroit, Michigan, in 1949, he enlisted in the U.S. Army in early 1967 and qualified as a paratrooper and Ranger. Shortly thereafter he was assigned to the 2nd Battalion, 503rd Parachute Infantry Regiment, 173rd Airborne Brigade (Separate). He served with them until shortly before the 1968 Tet Offensive when he volunteered for and joined the Long Range Recon Patrol (LRRP) element of the 173rd, serving with them for the rest of his tour.

Rotating back to the U.S., he was assigned to the XVIII Airborne Corps' Recondo school on Ft. Bragg before volunteering for the U.S. Army Special Warfare school. Upon graduation, he earned the coveted symbol of the Special Forces, the green beret. He was sent back to Vietnam and served eighteen months with various elements of the 5th Special Forces Group and with MACSOG (Military Assistance Command Studies and Observations Group), a covert operations unit.

Following his medical evacuation from Vietnam as the result of combat with a SOG Recon Team on which he served as assistant team leader, and his subsequent recuperation from those wounds, he was sent to the 10th Special Forces Group in West Germany, where his A Team was detached to an intelligence operation. After a little more than a year in Germany, he was medically discharged from the Army.

Unable to abandon the lifestyle, he worked in the private sector as an advisor and trainer, primarily in close combat and hand-to-hand combat. He asked for and received permission from his Japanese instructor to extract essential fighting and training methods from the traditional martial art that Cramer studied, the first such permission granted to anyone to modify the style. As a result of both his training and experiences in hand-to-hand combat, he wrote a training manual titled "War With Empty Hands; Self-Defense Against Aggression" (1986, Alpha Publications of Ohio) that emphasizes the use of traditional methods in actual combat.

Currently, Cramer writes and teaches the martial arts.

THIS IS AN IMPORTANT RECORD
SAFEGUARD IT.

	1. LAST NAME-FIRST NAME-MIDDLE NAME	2. SERVICE NUMBER	3. SOCIAL SECURITY NUMBER
PERSONAL DATA	Cramer,	R	

4. DEPARTMENT, COMPONENT AND BRANCH OR CLASS	5a. GRADE, RATE OR RANK	5b. PAY GRADE	6. DATE OF RANK			
Army-RA-AGC	SGT E5	E5	DAY 9	MONTH Aug	YEAR 69	

7. U.S. CITIZEN ☒ YES ☐ NO
8. PLACE OF BIRTH (City and State or Country)

7. DATE OF BIRTH — 49

9. SELECTIVE SERVICE NUMBER — NA
10. SELECTIVE SERVICE LOCAL BOARD NUMBER, CITY, COUNTY, STATE AND ZIP CODE — NA
DATE INDUCTED — MONTH YEAR — NA

TRANSFER OR DISCHARGE DATA

11a. TYPE OF TRANSFER OR DISCHARGE: Discharge
b. STATION OR INSTALLATION AT WHICH EFFECTED: Ft. Bragg, NC
c. REASON AND AUTHORITY: AR 27-52
EFFECTIVE DATE — DAY 1 — MONTH Dec — YEAR 71

12a. LAST DUTY ASSIGNMENT AND MAJOR COMMAND: A-222 10th SFG USAREUR
13a. CHARACTER OF SERVICE: Honorable
b. TYPE OF CERTIFICATE ISSUED: Honorable
14. DISTRICT, AREA COMMAND OR CORPS TO WHICH RESERVIST TRANSFERRED: NA
15. REENLISTMENT CODE: 52

SERVICE DATA

16. TERMINAL DATE OF RESERVE/UNIT OBLIGATION — DAY / MONTH / YEAR — NA
17. CURRENT ACTIVE SERVICE OTHER THAN BY INDUCTION
a. SOURCE OF ENTRY: ☐ ENLISTED (First Enlistment) ☐ ENLISTED (Prior Service) ☐ REENLISTED ☐ OTHER
18. TERM OF SERVICE — NA
19. DATE OF ENTRY — DAY / MONTH / YEAR — NA

18. PRIOR REGULAR ENLISTMENTS: NA
20. GRADE, RATE OR RANK AT TIME OF ENTRY INTO CURRENT ACTIVE SVC: NA
20. PLACE OF ENTRY INTO CURRENT ACTIVE SERVICE (City and State): Ft. Jackson, SC

21. HOME OF RECORD AT TIME OF ENTRY INTO ACTIVE SERVICE (Street, RFD, City or Town, County, State and ZIP Code): 152

22. STATEMENT OF SERVICE	YEARS	MONTHS	DAYS
c. (1) NET SERVICE THIS PERIOD	3	9	14
CREDITABLE FOR BASIC PAY PURPOSES (2) OTHER SERVICE	0	0	0
(3) TOTAL (Line (1) plus Line (2))	3	9	14
d. TOTAL ACTIVE SERVICE	3	9	14
e. FOREIGN AND/OR SEA SERVICE	0	0	0

23a. SPECIALTY NUMBER & TITLE: 11D30 Scout
b. RELATED CIVILIAN OCCUPATION AND D.O.T. NUMBER: NA

24. DECORATIONS, MEDALS, BADGES, COMMENDATIONS, CITATIONS AND CAMPAIGN RIBBONS AWARDED OR AUTHORIZED

Distinguished Service Cross, Silver Star with V, Bronze Star w/Oak
Leaf and V, Purple Heart w/4 Oak Leafs, RVN Service Ribbon, RVN Campaign ribbon, Combat Inf. Badege, Senior Para Wings, NDSM

25. EDUCATION AND TRAINING COMPLETED

Ft Knox, KY - Scout
Ft Benning, GA - Basic Airborne
Ft Benning, GA - Ranger
Ft Bragg, NC - USASWC, Light Weapons Spec, HALO

School De Los Americas, Panama-
Jungle Expert

VA AND EMP. SERVICE DATA

26a. NON-PAY PERIODS TIME LOST (Preceding Two Years): NA
b. DAYS ACCRUED LEAVE PAID: 31
27. INSURANCE IN FORCE ☐ YES ☒ NO
28. AMOUNT OF ALLOTMENT: NA
29. MONTH ALLOTMENT DISCONTINUED: NA
26b. VA CLAIM NUMBER: C- NA
29. SERVICEMEN'S GROUP LIFE INSURANCE COVERAGE ☐ $15,000 ☐ $10,000 ☐ $5,000 ☐ NONE

REMARKS

30. REMARKS

Civilian Education Completed: 12 years
Blood Group: ▓▓▓▓▓
Item 23a: Awarded PMOS 14 May, 1967

AUTHENTICATION

31. PERMANENT ADDRESS FOR MAILING PURPOSES AFTER TRANSFER OR DISCHARGE (Street, RFD, City, County, State and ZIP Code): 1322
32. SIGNATURE OF PERSON BEING TRANSFERRED OR DISCHARGED

33. TYPED NAME, GRADE AND TITLE OF AUTHORIZING OFFICER: Patrick L. Keeler LT
34. SIGNATURE OF OFFICER AUTHORIZED TO SIGN: Pat L. Keeler

DD FORM 214
JUL 70
PREVIOUS EDITION OF THIS FORM IS TO BE USED.
ARMED FORCES OF THE UNITED STATES
REPORT OF TRANSFER OR DISCHARGE

+ U.S. air bases in Thailand
o Hanoi's bases in Cambodia

CHINA

CHINA

BURMA

NORTH VIETNAM

Lao Cai

HANOI

Mong Cai

Haiphong

Haian

Dien Bien Phu

Hainan Island

LAOS

Gulf of Tonkin

Louangphrabang

Mekong

Thanh Hoa

Cua Rao

VIENTIANE

Vinh

Udon Thani +

Nakhon Phanom +

Dong Hoi

Demilitarized Zone

Xénô   Xépôn

Quang Tri

Savannakhét

Khe Sanh

THAILAND

Saravan

Da Nang

+ Ta Khli

Ubon

Pakxé

Attapu

My Lai
Quang Ngai

★ BANGKOK

Poipet

An Nhon

Siem Réap

CAMBODIA

Stung Treng

Qui Nhon

U Taphao +

Battambang

Gulf of Siam

Pailin

Pursat

Mekong

Kratie

Ban Me Thuot

Nha Trang

Kompong Cham

Loc Ninh

Cam Ranh

PHNOM PENH

Svay Rieng

SOUTH VIETNAM

Kompong Speu

Bien Hoa

Kimpot

SAIGON

Phan Thiet

Kompong Som (Sihanoukville)

Long Xuyen

Can Tho

Vung Tau

Bac Lieu

South China Sea

Quah Long

Ca Mau Peninsula

Con Son

0   75   150 miles

Foreword

This is a work of fiction. It is based on my experiences while serving in Southeast Asia. The names, dates, times and places have been changed to protect the innocent and the guilty alike, as well as to protect me from violating any National Security Act. To the best of my knowledge, all of the missions of the Special Operations Group (SOG) are still classified. Everything has been kept as close to fact as possible though, even the gist of the conversations.

Information in the Final Roll Call is factual. It represents the fates of the principal characters in this book as best they are known.

Special Forces operatives were the finest the Army had to offer during the Southeast Asian conflict. They paid for their courage, training, dedication, skill and motivation with blood, wounds, death and ultimately the loss of the cause for which they had so valiantly fought. Still, they fought it well. For us, the warriors, it was our *raison d'etre,* or as the ancient Japanese warrior-mystics put it, "The Mission is everything." We danced the slow dance on the killing grounds, to the tune called by others, obedient to the end.

There was a bond, a camaraderie among those men that is nearly unparalleled elsewhere. The green hat became our bond, our symbol. We knew that we could depend on each other, no matter what; and everyone else was suspect. The CIA were treacherous, the grunts or infantry soldiers were sloppy, the Army of the Republic of Vietnam (ARVN) was undependable, and the North Vietnam Army (NVA) the enemy. All of them could get you killed. Green hats, on the other hand, were friends. In a complex war it became the basic reality, one we could rely on.

This was a personal odyssey for me. I was molded by the Army, the war, the jungle, and the other green hats from a wild teenager into a finely-honed soldier by the end of my last tour in Southeast Asia. Somewhere during that time, I found the germinal warrior within, too.

This is a war story. It is not an apology, because there is nothing to apologize for. It's not an indictment of anyone or anything.

We drew the pay, we took the chances. It's not the be-all-and-end-all of covert operations stories or green beret stories. It's just a story.

I would like to thank my editor, John P. Staub, for encouraging me to write this. I doubt this story would have been told without him. It has been like dropping a field pack after a ten-mile run to get all of this out of my memory and onto paper. Just retelling the stories, a few of them for the first time to anyone, has been an exorcism of sorts to me.

I also want to express my love and gratitude to Linda Powell for listening, and for everything else. Oss!

And above all thanks to my comrades, Wooly, Scott, Bertha, and Hoosie, just for being.

Prologue

Central Highlands, 1968

I tried to lie motionless in the dense foliage, but a slight chill caused me to shudder involuntarily. That annoyed me; if the Viet Cong could do it, then why couldn't I stay motionless? Or, maybe the Cong shivered too? The sun would be up soon anyway and I wouldn't have to worry about shivering anymore. My jungle fatigues were wet from the morning dew, but the sun would bake them dry and then my sweat would soak them through again. After nearly a year of this endless cycle it barely mattered to me if my clothes were wet or dry. It was just one of the many little things that used to worry me, but seemed like a part of another life altogether. At this moment, worrying about dry clothes was ridiculous compared to the other things that occupied my attention.

Fifty feet or so below me, a North Vietnam Army (NVA) company was camped in its Remain Over Night (RON) position. We had been scouting them for two days and nights, ever since they crossed the Cambodian border. Watching them from high ground, we saw them move in small cells and regroup into their present company strength in the triple-canopied jungle valleys that hid them from aerial observation. Only ground teams small enough to move undetected in areas that the VC or NVA controlled could find and fix them. Ours was such a unit, known as the Long Range Reconnaissance Patrol (LRRP) element of an airborne infantry unit. I hoped that sometime today we would direct some type of strike against them. Bring in artillery or maybe even air assets like Puff, a cargo plane with mounted cannons, or Huey Cobras, deadly helicopters armed with guns and rockets, on their sneaking-across-the-valley-asses. For now, though, all we had to do was stay out of sight and follow them, reporting their line of march. Our battalion officers would take care of the rest. When the NVA moved out, we would saddle up and move with them.

Dawn broke suddenly. One minute it was gray and foggy, the next it was full day — a strange thing about this part of the world. At home it took about two hours for the sun to come out. I had always figured that the city was such an ugly, filthy MFer of a place that the sun didn't really want to see it. Steam came off my jungle fatigues as the heat dried them out and I wondered if my brain was heating up like that, too. I'd seen guys fall out and have to be medevaced out from heat stroke. That would be a nice way to end my tour. This was my last patrol, then I'd go back to the States — we called it DEROSed for the Date of Estimated Return from Overseas — if I lived through it.

The NVA were packing up. That wasn't much trouble for them. They just put their rice balls in their packs and hauled ass. I sighted my gun, a CAR 15, on an NVA who looked like their officer, and mouthed, "Pow," but then I laid down my rifle. Not today, ol' deadeye, I told myself. Bust a cap on their boss and the whole ant hill would come swarming up and bite all of us to death. It was like the time I'd gotten into a fight with the street gang punk back home. Bad move that day for the Lone Ranger, a taunting nickname given to me by the gang bangers back home because I hung out by myself a lot. Oh well. Today, I'd better just be cool, lay chilly, and wait for orders.

The NVA company finally moved off in good marching order. The NVA always used good trail discipline. Some local VC were with them, probably main force, acting as guides. Peasant porters carried their gear. The porters had huge bundles of gear strapped onto bicycles, and it looked like they were moving south to stay. The company was obviously getting ready for something. Another big offensive? I wanted to know where they were headed, maybe trail them to their staging area and wipe out some VC, too. No. I had to stifle that thought. I was starting to think like an officer or rear echelon-type motherfucker. I had to keep my priorities straight and in perspective. I was a grunt, even though an Airborne Ranger grunt. I didn't know anything that my commanding officer (CO) didn't want me to know, except as it was directly related to surviving this mission. Right? Solid. The last time I had an independent thought I got in trouble for it. A couple of weeks and I would be back to the land of the big PX, back to the World. Round-eyed women. Cold beer, even if I was too young to buy any. Yeah, I had to keep my act together until after this mission and I would be out of the Green Machine.

Okay, the NVA have moved out. I could move now. Fuck, my leg had gone to sleep! Ouch! I had to get moving, find Tully. Biting my lip, I stretched my leg and massaged it until more or less normal feeling returned. Moving back slightly, I caught a glimpse of Tully pulling back through the foliage, too. While three of us had been down close to the NVA camp, the rest of the team were on some high ground with the radio. Linking with Tully, we found our third teammate, Zit, who looked like he had a terminal case of acne, and worked our way back to the field Command Post (CP).

Our team leader, a Korean War vet, gave us our marching orders. I took tail-end charlie, a position at the end of the patrol to watch our back trail. We followed the NVA company, staying on the military crest of a ridge. We flanked them, but stayed under deep cover. Mikey was on point, the lead man in our patrol. That guy was a natural tracker and jungle fighter.

The team leader was on the radio calling in our line of march since the NVA were moving through. The Radio Telephone Operator (RTO) told Zit something about a "hammer and anvil sweep." All of us groaned. They were lifting a grunt blocking force in somewhere ahead of us, and to make matters worse, it was an ARVN blocking force. Another bunch of grunts from our parent unit would then try to sweep the NVA into the blocking force for a classic battle. That was theory, anyway. It didn't work out like that very often, and with an ARVN unit involved, it was a near certainty that it wouldn't. As soon as the NVA hit them, the ARVNs would run through a magazine on full auto with their eyes closed, and then bug out. We would probably get caught in the sweep. It had happened before. Those goofy bastards were determined to get me zapped before I DEROSed, and I knew it. Why didn't they just hit the NVA with artillery or by air? Ah, what the fuck did I know, I was just a dumb grunt and I repeated the grunt's litany to myself.

Ahead, Mikey suddenly flew backwards. I heard a sudden rattle of AK assault rifles. Shit! We were caught cold on the side of a ridge. We all dove for cover, what little there was. I heard voices screaming in Viet. There was movement behind us. Waiting, I let the Viet soldier move again, so that I could pinpoint his location. He was probably the point man for whatever unit was behind us and was moving ahead to check out the AK fire. How did they get behind us, I asked myself? It was too late to wonder now. The NVA soldier popped up for another short advance. I lined my sights on his chest, and evened the score for Mikey a little. The NVA landed on his back, dead.

"They're behind us!" I yelled to my team leader.

He grabbed the mike from the RTO and started talking fast, calling for slicks to pull us out, I hoped. We couldn't stay here. As soon as the NVA figured out what was going on they would rush us and that would be that. When an LRRP team is caught in the field, the only option they have is to outrun their pursuit. We had done that before, too. As our team leader checked his map, the rest of us waited, watching the ridge above us and the bush below us for signs that the NVA were coming. We knew it was just a matter of time.

"Okay, ladies, that's a wrap. Up the ridge," the team leader yelled.

Tully moved forward to pull Mikey's body in, and cut his pack away. The rest of us dropped our packs. I put a few suppressing bursts of fire into the area around the dead NVA just in case any more were lurking. There was no return fire.

All we had with us were rifles; no M60s, an light machine gun, and no grenade launchers. Tully had to leave Mikey's shotgun where it fell. We moved for the high ground in a leapfrog advance. Looking up the ridge, I figured I'd get a burst from an AK47 in my back or chest at any second as I moved, but none came. We all made it to the top and rolled over it.

The team spread out into covered firing positions and looked down where we had just come from. There must have been a hundred NVA swarming up our backtrail. Several squads moved in cautiously where Mikey had been hit. Tully had checked Mikey, but he was dead, his chest ripped open. The team leader checked his map again and had his compass out, orienting himself. I had a lot of faith in him. He was pretty slick in the bush. If we could get out, our team leader would find a way.

Zit and I spotted a squad of NVA skirmishers moving toward us up the ridge. We both switched our weapons to semiauto and dusted two of them. Zit bounced a frag, a fragmentation grenade, in among them as they took cover. I wished for an M79 blooper, a grenade launcher, or an M60, so we could engage them at a longer range.

"Let's go," the team leader instructed.

I took drag again and Tully moved to point. We moved at a jog. Suddenly my mind was filled with the desire for a steaming cup of coffee. Rejecting that, I wished for John Wayne and that .30 cal. machine gun I saw him zap dozens of Japs with in the last war movie I'd seen him in. He'd fired it from the hip. He was my hero. I fell and twisted my ankle. Nice move.

The team leader, taking a position near the end of the team, stopped to check me. "Okay?" he asked.

I waved him on, rolled to my feet and started hobbling after the team. The team leader checked my limp but when he saw I could keep the pace, he went on. It was no problem. If I had just broken my ankle, I'd still be up and running. Fear motivated me real well.

We ran for about an hour, coming off the ridge into a field of elephant grass. Moving by the compass, we found a clearing in the center of the field. Flopping down in a depression in the center of the field, the RTO called for slicks, lightly-armed troop-carrying helicopters. I drained the last canteen of water I had, pouring some water over my head and the towel I wore draped around my neck.

The NVA knew the clearing was there too, and headed right for it. As their first squad moved cautiously into it, we let them move close to us so that no one would miss, and then we blew them away with our rifles. Before another assault could be organized, our team leader moved us into the elephant grass behind us. The NVA were all around us. We could hear them walking right past us on both sides of where we lay. They were talking and hollering to each other. One of them stumbled out of the grass and into me. I jabbed him in the throat with the barrel of my CAR, and then struck him in the jaw with the butt, knocking him sprawling. He started to roll over. I kicked him in the front of the throat and he gurgled. A second later he went limp, dying without another sound. I killed him without any thought at all; the moves had become reflexive. That gave me something to think about later, when the killing was over for a few moments.

The NVA passed and we pulled back into less open terrain, flanking the main force. A small area of woods lay about thirty klicks, or kilometers, west of us. We waited at the edge of the high grass until we were reasonably sure the NVA had all passed, a trick we learned from them, then we pulled further back into the grass as the team leader grabbed the radio again. Sounds of combat came from the south and it was hot and heavy. That was the direction the NVA had taken. They must have walked into our blocking force, or the sweep had caught them.

Over the sounds of the battle came the familiar and very welcome whop-whop-whop of slicks. We moved out into the clearing and secured a perimeter as our RTO talked the helicopters in, telling them that the NVA were all gone. Slick jockeys didn't like hot landing zones (LZs) if they could help it. I didn't blame them either. I didn't care much for them myself. Looking up, I spotted the lead slick as it made a circle over us. I popped smoke to identify us, and the lead slick settled in while another stayed above us, the door gunner spraying various areas just in case the NVA were hiding there.

Our team began pulling back toward the slick, our backs to it, weapons still covering the trees and high grass. Suddenly a loud whoosh filled the air. Behind us the slick exploded, turning into a fireball as a rocket-propelled grenade (RPG) struck it. I was blown face down, shrapnel setting me on fire. I sighted in and opened fire with my CAR on the tree line in front of me.

Two Huey helicopters swooped in and opened fire with their rockets and door guns, ripping the tree line. The second slick settled in and someone lifted me off the ground. It was Tully. He helped me to the slick and tossed me in, then dove in behind me. Mikey's body was thrown in on top of me. I felt the slick sway violently beneath me and we were out of there.

The slick flew us over what looked like a hell of a battle. As soon as we landed at our base camp, the company CO sent for me. I could barely hear after having been so close to the slick when it blew up, but I went anyway. Maybe it was better that I couldn't hear. There had been several times when I wished I couldn't.

"Were you hit?" he asked me after the saluting was finished.

"Sir?" I replied.

"Were you hit?" he repeated.

"RPG went off right behind me cap'n. I can't hear shit," I told him.

He frowned at me. Shit, like it was my fault, right?

"YOUR DEROS ORDERS ARE HERE. WHY DIDN'T YOU TELL ME YOU DEROSED TODAY? I WOULDN'T HAVE SENT YOU OUT. YOU WERE EXEMPT FROM DUTY LAST WEEK!" he screamed at me.

My DEROS wasn't for another two weeks. I was exempt from duty after this patrol finished. It was his fuck up or some other paper-pushing rear-echelon motherfucker's (REMF's) fault, not mine. I grinned at him and shrugged my shoulders, feeling like the luckiest grunt in the country. "Dunno boss," was about all I could get out for a reply.

"HERE ARE YOUR ORDERS, NOW GET OUTTA HERE!" he shouted, throwing my orders at me.

Two days later I landed at Oakland, California. As we got off the plane some goofy-looking MP (Military Police) officer in khakis and a white helmet stood in the back of a jeep, giving us orders through an electronically amplified bullhorn. It distorted his voice so badly that he sounded like an out-of-tune radio. I couldn't understand a word he was saying. My ears were fucked up, ringing and even bleeding once in a while. I'd had the small pieces of shrapnel dug out of me by one of our company medics before I cleared the base camp in Nam. Those wounds were infected, and made me feel very uncomfortable.

"What's he saying?" I asked the guy next to me in formation.

"Not to break formation," the guy mumbled out of the corner of his mouth.

I pointed to my ears. "Can't hear shit man, what did ya say?"

The guy nodded, looked away. He's made it home. He didn't give a fuck if I could hear or not. A green beret staff sergeant was on the other side of me in formation.

"Hey sarge, what's that clown yellin' about?" I asked him.

He looked at me and spotted the scab in my ear. I guess that was why he was a green beret. Putting his mouth next to my ear, he said, "Lay chilly, man, there's VC in the wire."

I frowned at him. What? I started to tell him we were home, but he pointed and I followed his arm to see what he was pointing at. Outside the perimeter fence of the airbase, a huge crowd carried signs on sticks. Most were dressed in multicolored clothes. Their signs read, "Peace", "Love" and something about baby killers.

"What the fuck is all that, man?" I asked the sergeant, a Special Forces Non-commissioned Officer (NCO).

He just shrugged.

After we stood at ease on the airstrip for about an hour, several buses were brought to transport us. I took a seat next to the green hat NCO. As our buses pulled out the front gate of the base, the people in the colorful clothes went crazy. Raw eggs splattered the bus. Since it was late summer and hot, most of the soldiers had opened their windows. Everything that was being thrown by the crowd came into the bus, hitting the guys that were fresh out of the killing grounds. The soldiers were going nuts, too, screaming at the protesters, and wishing they had their rifles back. A few GIs tried to get off the bus to confront those "VC" in the street, but MPs were stationed at the front and rear doors of the bus to make sure that didn't happen.

The green beret sitting next to me said these people were hippie war protesters. A couple of them ran up to the bus and threw bags at us. The bags were filled with human shit. I thought about the VC sappers who tossed satchel charges into our bunkers during the Tet Offensive.

The green beret seemed calm, but as one of the hippies ran alongside the bus, which had slowed as it tried to pull into traffic, he lunged halfway out the window. His left hand plunged deeply into the hippie's hair. Suddenly, the green beret hauled backward, trying to drag the screaming hippie into the bus through his open window. One of the MPs at the front of the bus came running toward us. I stuck my foot out in the aisle and he went facedown.

Two GIs behind us sat on him to hold him in place.

The green hat couldn't get the hippie through the window so he started punching him in the face with his right hand, screaming at him in Viet. As the bus accelerated into traffic, the green beret pushed the hippie away. The MP was released and got back on his feet, his face turning dark red. He said something to me, one hand on his club.

I pointed to my ears. "I can't hear nothin' yer sayin' man, but if you pull that club on me, I'll pretend yer a VC. Get the drift?" I asked him, smiling.

He went away, shaking his head. The green hat grinned at me. "Where are your orders for?" he yelled into my ear.

"Bragg, Eighty-Deuce. You?"

"I'm going to Bragg, too, to the Special Forces Group. I'll buy you a beer when we get there, huh?"

I nodded. "Hey, did those punks call us baby killers back there?"

"Yeah. Pitiful ain't it? You kill any babies?"

"Nah, fuck no. Killed boocoo of their pappa sans though."

We both chuckled. He pulled out a pint of bourbon and we drank.

I enlisted for a three year hitch and that was what I was going to serve. That was okay, since I didn't really have anything better to do. It was painfully obvious that the civilian population wasn't going to welcome any of us back with open arms. Fuck 'em.

Going "home" to my parents' house was out. My old man claimed I was brain damaged and said he didn't care much for the juvenile record I'd compiled. He didn't care much for anything I did. He was still active Army himself, with about one year left before he could retire with thirty years in. He'd made a clean sweep of the wars, having fought all the way through World War II, Korea and two tours in Vietnam before I'd even enlisted. He was Command Sergeant Major Daddy.

He'd kept me in a burr haircut until he threw me out of the house, Ma's house, at the age of fifteen. I'd committed the sin of working enough to buy myself a Triumph motorcycle. The old man had been on his second tour in Nam when I'd bought it. When he came home and discovered it, he also found out that I'd just gotten out of the juvenile detention center for being in a "gang fight." The so-called "gang fight" occurred after I beat up a street gang member who bothered me for being on their "turf" and demanded that I pay protection. Later, I was attacked by four other gang members. When I got away, I was ambushed, and again beaten by a bunch of their roadies. Because of the fight, I had stitches in me everywhere, and then Dad started his shit. "Sell that two-wheel ass skinner, get a haircut, shave, blah, blah, blah."

I picked up a few more stitches for telling him where to stick all that cheap shit.

A few days later, living on the motorcycle, I saw one of the gang members who put me in the hospital during the gang fight. Seeing one of those punks set me off. I shot him in the leg. For me, it was back to the juvenile detention center. Dad made a deal with the judge. In return for a clean slate, I would enlist in the Army for three years. One month later, I was in Basic Combat Training at Fort Jackson, South Carolina.

Seeing the old man again after a tour in Nam wasn't my idea of a good time. And my hometown just didn't have much appeal to me either, after a two-week R&R in Australia.

Life with the "All American" 82nd Airborne Division was about the same as living with my old man. No motorcycles, shine the boots, whitewall airborne haircuts. Airborne all the way, sir. Yeah, all the way up yer ass. There were a bunch of young punks, officers who hadn't been out of their diapers long enough to learn how to deal with other soldiers, screaming at me to act like a paratrooper. I'd been killing armed and dangerous gooks not three months before. Wasn't that how paratroopers were supposed to act? Every once in a while, one of those young officer's faces would start to look different to me, his eyes developing an epicanthic fold, and I'd reach for my fighting knife. Lucky for all of us, I didn't wear it anymore.

Every chance I got I'd slip over to seen the green hat NCO who shared the bus seat with me.

"How's your ears, man?" he asked the first time I saw him at Bragg.

"Good, I'm all healed up now, man. Killed any babies lately?"

We would get real drunk together, or with a few of his green hat buddies, and I'd snivel about how fucked up life was with the Eighty-Deuce. In return, he would tell me how good life was in the Special Forces. Every time he saw me, the green hat NCO baited his hook for me, until I finally swallowed it whole.

"Okay, how do I go about getting one of those funny green hats anyway?" I asked over a beer one night.

"Well now, you know not just anybody can qualify."

I snarled at him. The next day, he took me to see the Post Reenlistment Officer, who filled out the necessary forms. I had to either extend my enlistment or reenlist. I chose to reenlist. Six more years in green. I got a big cash bonus, though.

After what seemed like a lifetime, I put on the beret with a full flash. Trainees wore a 'half flash' on their berets. I was twenty years old, and I had just been crowned "King of the Jungle." I was a fighting soldier from the sky, famed in song and legend.

One of the cadre at Bragg had a big FLH Harley Davidson motorcycle that he let me ride from time to time. For graduation, he let me take it out for a weekend. Riding that big beast gave me a lot of time to think about myself, the war, the nature of man, the dignity of struggle. Most of my thoughts revolved around getting laid, but I did take a minute or two to think about my future. I knew there was little or nothing for me in the U.S. at that time.

The only real ties I had to anyone or anything was in the Special Forces. I was one of their professionals now, like it or not. And the bulk of professional soldiers were where the action was, in Nam.

The way I'd dealt with the NVA soldier who stumbled out of the elephant grass flashed through my mind, too. I was a killer, and now, if nothing else, I was a highly-trained killer. I belonged in Nam, with men like myself who would accept me for who and what I was right then.

When I returned to Bragg, I volunteered for the 5th Special Forces Group, Vietnam.

PART ONE: Forest of Assassins

Chapter One
Back in the Saddle Again

Coming back. I felt a combination of hangover and jet lag as I laid in the reclining seat of the big jetliner. I was groggy, irritable, tense, and feeling hollow inside, like maybe I'd just made a major mistake, but was too stupid to know it. I expected a certain nervous elation about coming back to Nam. I was wrong. So far, there hadn't been any feelings at all other than physical. That worried me.

Earlier in the flight my seat mate had spotted my right front shoulder patch which signified that I had been in combat and tried a line of questions. I didn't want to answer them, so I traded seats with the guy and told him to watch the wings for gremlins while I slept. Guard duty. He could handle that, being fresh out of Advanced Individual Training (AIT) where a soldier learns his skills. He was probably my age or older, but I thought of him as a kid. I felt like an old fart.

The plane carried mostly cherries, guys going for their first tour of duty in Vietnam. A few vets were sprinkled among them, though. Officers were in the front of the plane, in the first-class section, which was fine with me. Most of them were cherries, too. You could tell the West Pointers from the ROTC and OCS (Officers Candidate School) guys. West Pointers were all squared away and straight-backed. They had a look in their eyes like they were going to personally sally forth, slay a dragon or two, then return home and marry ol' Peggy Sue, the cheerleader from high school. The ROTC and OCS guys wanted some Nam dope and sincerely hoped they would get some before the Pointers made them do something stupid or fatal.

"Hey, uh, this your second tour, sarge?" I heard from behind me.

I turned in my seat. A staff sergeant with a big yellow 1st Cav patch on his right shoulder and a crew cut kid in spit-shined jump boots were sitting one row back, opposite me. The kid was talking.

"Third," the vet said.

"What's it like, sarge?" the kid asked.

The sergeant caught my eye and winked. "Ya ever been kicked in the nuts, son?"

"Huh? Oh, yeah, I been kicked in the nuts. I'm from South Boston," the kid said.

The sarge nodded, like that made sense to him. "Well, that's just exactly what a tour in Nam is like."

I turned back in my seat, chuckling to myself. Good line, sarge. Pretty accurate, too. I closed my eyes and began the deep breathing exercise my PAL (Police Athletic League) judo instructor taught me so long ago. It mellowed me out, calmed my mind and let me think clearly, unprejudiced by any external sources. I'd been trying to understand what I was looking for in life and why in the hell I had volunteered for another tour in Nam, aside from wanting to belong to someone or something.

A lot of guys I'd been close to, even some that I hadn't who were just good soldiers or had been in my unit, were killed while I'd served my first tour. I'd felt bad about leaving. It was like I was leaving less experienced guys to do a job that I had started, but hadn't finished. By going back, perhaps I was trying to atone for some sense of guilt I felt. Or, my old man's theory was entirely possible and I was brain damaged. He had fought in three wars and done two tours in Nam. If I had brain damage, it was hereditary.

Maybe I was going because of the beret and the self-image that went with it. Once you got the beret and passed all the mental and physical tests to earn it, you wanted to find out exactly how good you were, what your limits were. The only place to do that was on the killing grounds of Southeast Asia. Working with a team of men who were at least as good as you, beating the enemy at their own game, on their own ground, that was the test. No doubt that had played a large part in my decision to return.

I knew that I liked the excitement of combat. It was scary, but what a rush! The sudden surge of adrenalin, the thrill when your people won the encounter or completed a mission. It would be difficult to satisfy that desire anywhere but in Vietnam. Legally at least. Being an adrenalin junky was rough, especially at the age of twenty, having acquired the habit only two years ago. Once this war was over, I knew that my whole life ahead of me might be devoid of those rushes. That is, if I lived through it.

After mulling it over, I decided most of these thoughts were superfluous. I chose this life, the warrior's path. It wasn't chosen for me. That was why I was going back. After my first tour I could have done anything, gone to Canada, laid down with the Eighty-Deuce. Anything. Instead, I'd chosen to immerse myself deeper in the war. And this time it had nothing to do with Ma, God or apple pie. That was the cheap shit they used to sucker in the cherries. No, this time it was strictly for me, a rite of passage.

When the plane landed, we filed off. My hollow feeling vanished as a wave of heat rolled over me, carrying with it the smell of diesel fuel and shit. It was like coming home. I felt as though a wet blanket had been thrown over me. The humidity was intense and the oppressive heat took my breath for a moment. I heard voices screaming in various languages across the airfield and it was comfortingly familiar. A swarm of ragged, dirty little urchins approached us, wanting to sell their "numbah one cherry girl sisters" and boom-boom pictures and begging for candy or cigarettes. They ducked and dodged the air crew unloading our plane, nimbly leaping aside as the airmen kicked at them, catching a piece of gum or a cigarette tossed from one of us.

One kid grabbed my AWOL bag and I shoved him away. "*Didi mau* ya little varmint!" I growled.

He laughed as he yelled, "Numbah ten GI."

I grinned back.

The base MPs came running after the little hustlers and the band of kids took off. They would pause to yell, "One, two, three, muthafuck MP!" as they ran.

"Hey, all you snake-eaters, over here!" I heard someone yell.

Turning, I saw a green beret NCO standing with hands on his hips, a .45 revolver slung low on one hip. It was my friend from Bragg, the guy who had talked me into joining the Special Forces.

He escorted our group to the processing center. We breezed through that. Then we flew out to the 5th Group Headquarters (HQ) at Nha Trang.

It took a while for the 5th Group to find a position for me. The Forces were short of every specialty except mine, which was light weapons. As an E5 three-stripe buck sergeant, I was a junior weapons man and there were a glut of them in the country. While I waited for orders, I explored Nha Trang both day and night and did some courier work for the Group. The courier work wasn't too bad. I flew pouches all over, hopping rides in slicks or Caribous to various A Team camps. That made me feel better about being, essentially, a clerk. It wasn't like I was sitting around in an office, behind a desk.

Finally, a position opened at an A Team camp. I heard about it from one of the personnel specialists I pestered every day and I had to pester some other REMF to get the job. During my stay at Group, I requested anything that would get me into the field; an A Team, B Team Special Project, Mike Force or Mobile Strike Force, Mobile Guerrilla Force, whatever. I was told that the war was winding down for U.S. Forces, the A Team camps were being turned over to the ARVN troops and the Special Projects were being phased out. Yeah, right. I knew from my courier runs and from talking to some of the guys from the Nha Trang Mike Force that the green hats were still as busy as ever; the Special Projects were still generating major field intelligence, and the Mike and Mobile Guerrilla outfits were still kicking plenty of NVA ass all over the country. I was determined to get out in the field with one of those outfits before the war really did wind down. I hadn't earned the beret to spend the rest of my time in the only war zone around running courier operations. My war wasn't winding down. I pestered another REMF and finally got my orders for an A Team camp.

Packing what little gear I had, I hopped a slick for my assigned camp. I was really looking forward to it. What I liked best about the Forces was that not only were we allowed to think for ourselves in problem-solving situations, we were expected to. No more playing a stupid grunt to stay out of trouble. I could stretch out a little, discover my own capabilities and still be a soldier. It was a situation I hadn't found anywhere else in the Army, and I liked it.

Being a grunt was okay, but there was little tolerance for independent thought in a line unit. You did what you were told, as a cog in the machine. Skill played a small part in whether you lived or died. Even in my airborne unit, which was alleged to be a cut above the regular units, conformity was the order of the day. I knew the A Team camps did things that were effective for their area of operations, and that required each team member to pull his own weight in the daily operation of the camp. That was all I wanted. If that wasn't the way things were the green hats offered more of the same shit I'd put up with before, and I still had six more years to put up with it.

In what we called the World, the green hats were usually real strac, well groomed, so I put on the only pair of starched and pressed jungle fatigues I had. All the patches I'd earned were sewn on them: jungle expert, para wings, combat infantry badge (CIB), combat patch, my new 5th Group patch, and a set of Viet para wings I'd acquired while hanging around Group. I looked pretty sharp, I thought. My new pair of jungle boots still had their shine and my beret was scrunched down over my nose the way I'd seen some of the guys around Nha Trang wear theirs. I wanted to look like a vet and avoid some of the FNG (fucking new guy) trip if I could. My brand new M16 rifle lay across my lap in the slick, patrol harness on, but the belt left open.

The door gunner tapped me on the leg and I edged closer to the door to have a look. We were making an approach over the camp. Smoke billowed up to meet us. From the air, the camp looked pretty ragged, like a dozen other fire bases I'd lived at during my first tour. I didn't see any howitzers at this one, but an airstrip was located just south of the perimeter. The slick came in fast and landed, settling on its skids.

I jumped out of the Huey, gear in one hand and weapon in the other, and the down draft of the helicopter blew grit and red dust all over my clean fatigues. I dropped my gear to keep my beret on, but held on to my rifle.

Then I looked around the camp. The view from the ground

didn't really alter my opinion of the state of things that I'd drawn while in the air. It was a hill that had been leveled off, a bunker line blasted and sandbagged, with more bunkers built inside, forming two concentric rings.

A swarm of indigenous troops surrounded the slick. Most of them wore tailored tiger suits, bush hats with one side pinned up and M16s slung barrel down over their shoulders. I couldn't see any Americans in the bunch. One of the soldiers, native troops usually called indigs, walked up to me.

"You new Cong killer?" he asked in broken English.

He was tall for a Viet, lean with long straight black hair and a wide, white scar from the temple to chin on the left side of his face.

I nodded. He grinned and stuck out his hand, which told me he had been around Americans a while. Vietnamese don't normally shake hands.

"Sergeant Krang. We kill boocoo VC," he said, pumping my hand with both of his.

Turning away suddenly, he barked orders at the other indigs and they snapped to work. I was left alone on the landing strip.

Spotting what had to be the commo or communications bunker by all the antennas sprouting from its sandbagged roof, I headed for it, my boots kicking up puffs of red dust as I walked. Red dust covered every square inch of Vietnam that I had seen, until the monsoons began. Then it all turned to mud. Going into the bunker, I found a big American seated behind a mass of radios.

"Howdy," I said.

He glanced up from his radios, looking over his shoulder at me. "You an officer?" he asked.

"No." Guess he didn't want to get up.

"You a replacement?"

"Yeah," I told him, hoping he didn't start with the FNG trip.

"Commo specialist?"

"Light weapons."

The big guy snorted. "Ain't we all? Name's Bender. You'll find our team sergeant, Randall, in the big bunker over that way," he told me, waving his arm in a general direction.

"Thanks."

Leaving the commo bunker, I headed across the camp in the direction Bender had pointed. The bunker he referred to was easy to find. Three Americans sat in the shade of the bunker's sandbagged wall, drinking beer. One squatted on his heels like a Viet, sharpening a knife. He was shirtless. His bare upper torso was lean, tan, well-muscled, with raised white ridges of scar tissue running over much of his upper body. The other two wore faded, stained tiger suits. One was built like a weight lifter, the other was short and thin.

The one with the scars looked up, then ran his eyes over me from head to foot.

"You a replacement?" he asked.

"Yeah, light weapons specialist."

"Just outta Bragg, huh?" the weight lifter said.

I turned so that my combat patch showed. "Yeah."

They grinned at me, so I grinned back. The guy with the scars stood.

"I'm Randall, team sergeant. The hulk there is Big Dane, intelligence NCO. The little guy is our demolition specialist, Kirby. We've got a good team here son, but they're about to Vietnamize our camp."

"Huh," I replied. I had no idea what he meant.

"The ARVNs are gettin' our camp," Dane interpreted for me.

"Ah," I said, trying to sound intelligent.

"Me, Dane, and Bender, the commo man, built this camp," Randall said, his arm gesturing in a sweep to encompass the dusty camp. His dusty camp. That was lifer mentality. Everything they touched, they owned.

"Now they're turning it over to the ARVNs," he went on.

I detected a Tennessee accent in his voice and the way he said ARVN made it sound bad, like, "I just stepped in some ARVN."

"Well, I guess it is their war, huh?" I ventured.

"You *are* fresh outta Bragg, aren't ya?" Kirby asked.

Settling in was easy. I took a bunk from a guy who had survived his tour and rotated home. After a few days of learning the camp, its procedures, and who was who in the Viet forces we shared the camp with, I was given patrol duty. The camp consisted of two companies of Montagnards and two companies of Viet strikers, a twelve-man Luc Long Dac Biet South Viet Special Forces team, who actually owned the camp, and a Nung platoon. The Nungs were the only operational force in camp that we controlled directly. They were tribal mercenaries paid by the CIA to work strictly for the green hats and act as our bodyguards and strike troops. Randall told me that the Yards or Montagnards were ours to a man, but Big Dane had other ideas. He told me that most of them worked for the nationalist Yard organization FULRO and that their main job was to learn weapons and tactics so they could fight for Yard rights when the time came.

The team A Team leader, Captain Hardin, was on his third tour. He was pretty sharp. Right after I arrived at the camp, he spoke with me and then sent me out on my first patrol. A week later, he sent me with Dane to check on an air strike. We took two "Look Long, Duck Back," as Dane called the Viet Special Forces, a platoon of Yard strikes and six Nungs. It was a walk in the sun for me; Dane let me run most of it. The LLDB NCOs just stayed out of the way. The Yards didn't care much for them, and they were scared of the Yards, so it was good for us.

The next time I went out with Randall, Bender, and the team Executive Officer (XO), Lieutenant Mallen, a young officer just finishing his first tour. Randall claimed to have taught Mallen everything he knew and the Lieutenant backed that up, which told me a lot about the Forces right there. If an NCO said something in a line unit like that, he would have a hard time living with his Lieutenant after that. Dane's intelligence network had picked up some information on a VC tax collector. We were sent out to ambush him at night, take any prisoners we could and collect any further intelligence available.

Our patrol caught him at a bend in the trail we had been told he was following. Krang, the senior NCO in the Nung platoon and his executive NCO, who was named Bao, and I were sent forward to make the snatch. When the rest of the ambush force opened fire, Bao and I stepped out of cover and grabbed the tax collector, then dragged him into the bush as Krang covered us.

Bao sapped him on the head, took his money bag and trussed him
while I searched for weapons or documents. Mallen told us to put
the money in the team fund. We used that for intelligence-related
bribes, needed materials, food or beer.

On the walk back to camp, Randall put me on point and selected
a new, circuitous route so that no one would ambush us. I'd told
him I was good at land navigation, and suspected he was testing
me. I led the patrol straight back home.

When we got back, Hardin debriefed us and sent the prisoner
to the LLDB people after Dane and Krang had a talk with him.
As I headed for my hootch, my private dwelling, Hardin handed
me a package from home. Opening it slowly and hoping for food,
I found instead a long sheath knife inside. It had a black handle
with finger grooves cut into it. I unsnapped the retaining strap and
slowly drew the seven-inch blade from the leather sheath, admiring
its silvery shine and the tapered clip point. From over my left
shoulder Randall said, "That's a Randall Number Four you've
got there, son."

I hadn't even checked the brand yet, but of course he was right.
He had its twin strapped to his web gear. Old Dad was looking
out for me. I guess he knew that I'd need a good fighting knife
working at an A Team camp. That night, I wrote him the first
letter I'd ever written him in my life and told him how much I
appreciated the blade.

I tested it before putting it on my harness and it passed every
test I could think of, and a few Randall showed me, with flying
colors. Randall taught me how to sharpen the knife so that I could
shave with it, then he and Bao, another knife freak, taught me
how to use it. They whittled wooden knives to spar with and after
I had some control with the weapon, we used the knives with
sheaths on them. Later, we sparred with live blades, pieces of tape
covering the edges. I wore the knife on my web gear for more than
a month without blooding it though. Finally, on a hot, humid summer day just before the monsoons started, I got my chance.

We were on patrol to check a trail for signs of recent use and
ambush anything good that came along. To get to the trail, we
moved overland and had to cross a stream. While two Nungs put

out flank security, Bao and I hid and observed the opposite bank of the stream for half-an-hour. When there were no signs of movement, I swam across first and then Bao followed me. I scrambled up the slippery mud bank, slithered under some foliage to reconnoiter the area as Bao reached my side of the stream and worked his way up the bank to me. Pulling him toward me I signaled for the rest of the patrol to cross. Our junior RTO, Blake, started down into the stream, holding the PRC 25 portable field radio out of the water. Suddenly, Bao pushed me down into the foliage.

A pajama-clad VC with an AK slung over his shoulder was strolling toward us, unbuttoning his fly. Blake saw us move to the ground and started back to his side of the stream. If he wasn't carrying the radio, he could have ducked under the water, but he couldn't get our lifeline, the radio, wet. Looking at our patrol which was hidden in the foliage on the other side of the stream, I spotted Randall. He drew a finger across his throat.

I tapped Bao to get his attention and drew my knife. He nodded, ready to cover me. As the VC soldier pushed branches aside to clear a path to the stream, not five feet from us, I made my move. Rushing him as he was looking into the stream and saw Blake scrambling up the opposite bank, I grabbed his weapon from behind and ran my knife to the hilt into what I thought was his kidney. It was the way I'd been trained by my hand-to-hand instructors at Panama and Bragg, who told me it was a quick kill.

They were wrong. The VC ran forward off my knife, spun and charged me barehanded. I was shocked, but my training took over. Hoping that my instructors hadn't been wrong about anything else, I kicked him in his lead knee cap and dove on top of him as he fell. I stabbed him over and over, his blood spurting on me. I'd lost control. The VC was probably dead after my first or second thrust. Bao finally stopped me.

He and I did flank security as the rest of our team crossed the stream. Randall knelt beside me as I frisked the dead VC.

"Wash off in that stream, son. You hurt?" he said, looking me over.

The VC had fought for his life, biting, scratching, and kicking to save himself. He fought hard for what I was trying to take away.

I shook my head.

"That was sloppy. When we get back to camp, I'll work with you some more."

After rinsing myself as best as I could I caught up with the others. We continued the patrol, which turned out to be another walk in the sun for the rest of the guys. I wondered how I'd react to that kill, my first with a knife. It was more personal that way, but no reaction came, other than my wish to do a better job if I ever had to do it again. I guess it was the situation. It was them or us. The bottom line was that it was better for us to do to them before they got the chance to do to us. I had respect for the enemy as brave fighters, but if I had to kill them, so be it. I worked with Randall and some of the others on quick, stealthy killing methods.

I did some other cross-training too, mostly with Marty Bender on his radios and with Big Dane. Blake, the junior RTO, was stand-offish. He never had much to say to anyone, so I worked with Marty on communications. I learned how to repair radios such as the PRC 10 and 25 in the field, and how to talk with people over the radios. I learned how to call in artillery, air and slicks. Dane, on the other hand, taught me the difference between the Nungs, the Rhade Montagnard strikers, and the Vietnamese. There were many differences, too. I worked with a Rhade NCO and a squad of his strikers on a few intelligence-gathering patrols. One or two of the Nungs always came with us as bodyguards. I preferred that side of the war. It was effective. Most of what Dane called humint, intelligence gathered by human rather than electronic or other sources, was gathered by simply walking into Yard villages where the camp strikers had kin, or where part of our A Team had done some civic action project, and ask, politely, where the communists were. Then we went and bagged a few of them.

As I got to know some of the others on the team, I realized there were essentially two cliques at the camp. One centered around the CO, Hardin. All of these guys planned to stay in Southeast Asia until the war was resolved. Some of them liked the action. Some were committed to keeping the Vietnamese free from communist domination. Some liked the Yards and thought that their only hope lay in our continued presence. Some believed in all these reasons.

The green hats who felt this way were more active and I gravitated toward them.

Master Sergeant Randall personified this ideology. I learned from Bender and Dane that Randall had fought with an airborne unit in Korea, had been highly decorated and wounded there. He was on his third tour in Nam and had spent time in Laos with the White Star training team. He was a war horse with a taste for exotic weaponry and for doing unto the enemy before the enemy did unto him or his team. Efficiency was his religion. If that meant bending, or even breaking the rules, fuck it. He and Big Dane ran the camp's day-to-day functions as well as Dane's intel network in the villages around the camp's area of operation (AO). Hardin and Mallen oversaw and suggested what Randall put into practice.

The network Dane ran had been very effective until the Yards found out that ARVN was taking over the camp. Then the intel dried up. Dane didn't push it. ARVN security was notoriously lax. An informer would be found out and tortured to death by the communists before whatever intel he gave could be acted on.

Blake was a quiet, ornery man, about my size, who didn't seem to like anyone or anything not directly relating to killing gooks, the enemy. He was good in the bush, reliable in any situation, and as good as Bender with the radios. Now on his second tour, Blake spent half of his first tour with an A Team and half with one of the Special Projects.

Tex was our senior medic. He made up for Blake's silence with some of the tallest tales I'd ever heard. Just when someone was ready to call him on one, Tex would produce some kind of evidence that proved his story true. Tall, lean and skilled with his medic's pouch, Tex was from west Texas and proud of it.

Brick Anderson was a huge, red-haired soldier who joined the Army just after Korea. He was a heavy weapons specialist. On patrols he carried an M60 machine gun as easily as Randall did his little Swedish K submachine gun, only Brick had several hundred-round belts of ammo slung around his shoulders.

Those were the professional killers. The other clique, all good soldiers, centered around Lieutenant Mallen. He was a good and brave man, and as far as I could determine, he just felt we lost the war in Nam through improper procedure, faulty strategy, and the weakening will of the American people. He didn't want to see any more good men die for no reason. The rest of the team shared his view, more or less, and they were all planning to rotate home as soon as their tours were up.

Curiously enough, these two widely divergent schools of thought didn't cause the slightest bit of tension in the camp. All of the men on the team had proved their ability and courage over and over. It was treated more like a minor family disagreement.

Not long before the camp was to be turned over to the ARVN troops, a Cayuse slick flew in with an Army major and a guy dressed in civvies. Hardin and Randall escorted the men to the team house, disappearing inside with them.

I didn't have much to do, so my LLDB counterpart, who spoke passable English and I took the senior Yard striker, a Nung NCO named Lin, on a tour of the perimeter, inspecting weapons. The senior Nung NCO, Krang, caught up with our party on the edge of the perimeter as I checked the claymore mine emplacement.

"*Dai Uy* Hardin wants you in the team house, *rikky-tik*," he told me.

I nodded and asked Lin, whom I trusted to do the job right, to finish inspecting the perimeter. Krang and Lin smiled. The LLDB NCO glowered, but I really didn't give a fuck if he liked it or not.

Following Krang back to the team house, I thought about our Viet counterparts, the LLDB. Nguyen Van Minh, the camp CO, was all right. He'd go out into the bush and kill communists. For that the Nungs showed him respect, which was rare for them. Even the FULRO Yards liked him. He ran as tight a team as he could, but more than half of his NCOs were lames, political appointees whose families had bought them jobs with the LLDB, thinking they would be safer or could collect more graft with this elite unit. Minh treated the Rhade in this camp's AO well and his strikers were pretty much loyal to him. Even the Viet Province Chief treated the Rhade well as a result of Minh and Hardin using their influence. The main reason our A Team camp was effective was because the people, both Yard and Viet, knew they could get civic and military aid from the camp with no strings attached, no bribes to be paid. When Minh proved that, the camp's strike forces were able to practically neutralize communist activity in its AO.

Lt. Truong, Minh's XO, was a different matter. Randall and Dane hated him, harboring unproven suspicions about his ultimate loyalty. Truong led patrols that were never hit, but never found anything either. He carefully selected the Yards and LLDB or Viet strikers who went on patrol with him and he had his own following among the strikers. Truong was quietly contemptuous of NCOs, no matter what their nationality. He showed some respect and even camaraderie for the officers. Hardin liked him, much to Randall's disgust. Truong wore a Gerber knife, a gift from Hardin, on his web gear.

What worried Randall most was that Truong had a personality cult going among the camp's indig forces, particularly the Regional Force strikers who were Viet, not Yard. It formed the camp into too many cliques, caught between the hard-charging Minh, and the *laissez-faire* Truong. Because there was little contact in the camp's AO, Truong thought it foolish to send patrols further and further afield to hunt for the NVA, only to have them ambushed, sniped at or fall prey to boobytraps. That attitude, one he had widely publicized around the camp, affected the entire camp's morale.

When I got to the team house all of those thoughts were swept aside. Ducking inside, I found Randall, Dane, Hardin and the El Tee (Lt. Mallen). Krang followed me in. I stood near the edge of the table.

Hardin, the Army major and the guy in civilian clothes were seated together, facing the others, a map spread on a table in front of them.

"We are taking a patrol into this area," Hardin said, pointing to an area on the map, "to ambush an NVA cache site and staging area. We'll try to take prisoners, if possible."

I looked at the area he indicated. It was well inside Cambodia.

"The NVA are using an old temple in here for a rendezvous where supplies can be cached, then moved south at will. Elements of the 325th NVA Regiment and a main force VC unit resupply and regroup here," the guy in civvies told us. I noticed he wore sunglasses even in the gloom of the team bunker.

"Wouldn't this be a better job for one of the special projects, sir?" Mallen asked.

"They have their own operations going, Lieutenant," the major said, silencing Mallen.

"We are familiar with this area," Randall said, studying the map.

"Of course, you realize the sensitive nature of this mission. Your LLDB counterparts are not to be informed of this raid, not the intent, location, nor even the results of it. You will launch from a preselected site, not this camp, for mission integrity."

We were lifted by Huey slicks to a launch site a few klicks from the Cambodian border. There, we were outfitted with black pajamas and combloc (communist block) weapons by round-eyed men who didn't wear any uniforms. This was the sort of thing I'd heard about — the sterile covert operations I thought Special Forces were all about.

There were five green hats led by Hardin, and half of our Nung platoon, led by Krang, in our raiding force. From the launch site, we took off on foot over land, skirting the Plain of Reeds. The Nungs took point, all of us round-eyes staying in the center of the formation so that any NVA troops seeing us would think we were a patrol of theirs. Hopefully. Randall gave Krang his suppressed K SMG (sub-machine gun) just in case and several Nungs carried crossbows.

By night, we were within a few klicks of our target area, but Hardin found a RON, and we laagered for the night, eating whatever we'd brought with us. At the launch site we were issued rice balls with fish sauce on them. That way we would smell like Viets in the bush. *Nuoc mam* sauce smelled terrible and it tasted even worse, but the others managed to eat theirs, so I forced mine down too.

Early the next morning, we moved out again. I moved forward with a Nung to the point, taking the slack, or second position. Coming out of a thick clump of bamboo, I saw an ancient Buddhist temple rising from the forest around it.

Hardin and the others moved up and around my prone form.

"That it?" I hissed at Hardin.

He just nodded.

We spread out in an ambush position around the temple while Krang and Randall scouted the two trails we could see leading away from the temple. By midday, there was no sign of any activity. Trail-watchers kept an eye on both trails, but no one showed, even though there were signs of recent travel on both of them. The area had seen a lot of movement, all of it going south. We stayed the night in position.

Early the next morning Bender came crawling past me, dragging the Nung who carried the radio with him. When he reached Hardin, they put their heads together. I couldn't hear anything they said from where I lay. Then, one of our flankers came in. NVA were moving south toward us.

Randall crawled by, giving everyone a quick briefing. "Wait 'til they are all in the killing zone." he instructed. "I'll kick it off by firing a claymore. Got it?" I nodded and he moved on. I laid there, wishing they would come on shortly. Laying out on ambushes sucked.

About thirty NVA came into our kill zone. They were wary, moving at intervals, weapons ready. A point squad moved in and searched the temple before the main body followed them. Randall let the point squad walk right up to his claymore before firing it. Mines, grenades, full automatic rifle and light machine gun fire shredded the NVA. We had demolition ambushes rigged on the open sides of our L-shaped killing ground. As the NVA tried to break out they hit the demo boobytraps, arranged in a series of "breaks." It blew their asses away.

Hardin fired a flare and we began a sweep for a body count, but Randall called us in and hustled us out of the area. We moved almost at a run to our extraction point, where slicks were already inbound.

"What's the rush?" I asked Randall as we ran for the slicks.

"Camp was hit early this morning right after we left," he told me.

"No shit! Any of our team down?"

He shrugged.

The black slicks that extracted us flew us to the camp's airstrip. A Nung Mike Force was already there, deployed around the camp, the tiger-suited tribesmen spread around the airstrip for security as we came in. Hardin was off the slick before it landed, running to join three other green hats I'd never seen before.

I followed Randall and Bender to join the pow-wow.

"Have any of your people been inside the camp yet?" Hardin asked a green hat captain.

"Gustav went in with Sergeant Chan and reconnoitered the area. When he exfiltrated, he came out through one of your escape and evade routes he said had been used. That was about two hours ago. Paul, fill Captain Hardin in," the green hat captain said, turning to a tall, lean, darkly-tanned green hat NCO.

Gustav spoke with a European accent I'd never heard before. "Most of the inner perimeter bunkers have been hit with satchel charges, sir. The Strike Force area was hit also. The strange thing is that there are no bodies in the wire. Your camp was taken from the inside, cap'n."

Hardin was livid. His neck began to swell and veins bulged from his neck and forehead.

"What?" I gasped incredulously. They just ignored me.

A Nung from the Mike Force ran to Sergeant Chan, a Mike Force green hat, and began speaking rapidly. Chan translated quickly to the officers.

"Tim," the Mike Force captain said to Hardin, "I've got some good news for you. Some of your people showed up. One of our patrols spotted them and brought them in," he said, pointing to the far end of the airstrip.

Four green hats came toward us, two of them carrying a third. As a group, we moved toward them. Blake and Tex carried Kirby, the little demo specialist. Brick walked behind them, cradling an M60.

"Sorry 'bout this cap'n," Brick said, looking first at Hardin, then at Randall.

"What happened Brick?" Hardin asked, his voice low and dangerous.

"That cocksucker Truong, sir. He fragged Lt. Mallen and Mayo, killed them in the CP, blew the commo bunker and gut shot Kirby there. Some of the strikers were gooks, sir, and they tossed satchel charges and frags in on their amigos. I guess some more sappers or somethin' came in through the wire while the camp was running around shootin' at each other and they blew up most of the bunkers. It was wild cap'n. Big Dane was right about that cocksucker," Brick said, leaning on his M60.

"Who made it out?" Randall asked in the silence when Brick stopped talking.

"Cap'n Minh bought it. He and a few of his men tried to fight back, rally some of the strikers, but they got the shit shot out of them. Some of Truong's boys had a gun bunker turned in on the camp. They cut Minh in half with an M60. The Nungs saved our ass. They got hit pretty hard too, but they fought a rear guard action for us while the rest of us E&Eed through the wire. We brought ten Nungs out with us, Bao's leading them. They're pretty fuckin' mad cap'n. Blake and I trailed the gooks when they pulled out, but we had casualties, sir."

Hardin stepped forward and put his hand on Brick's shoulder. "You did all you could, Brick. I'm just glad you men made it out."

Kirby made a low rattling noise in his throat and died. Tex had been working on him, but it was too late. Someone from the Mike Force spread a poncho over his body.

"Truong's gone?" Hardin asked Brick. His hands were white where they clutched his M16.

"Yes, sir. Some NVA came in through the wire, like I said, and helped finish off the wounded strikers. They looted the camp and hauled ass for the border," Brick answered.

I glanced around at who was left of the team. Their faces were hard, jaws clenched, eyes were glaring. We all wanted to kill something.

"Carl," Hardin said to the green hat captain, "let's take the camp. Can you get a reaction force after those NVA?"

The Mike Force airlifted out two days later, leaving a platoon of Nungs with Gustav and another green hat NCO to beef up our security. A reaction force of grunts tried to catch the retreating NVA force before they got across the border into Cambodia, but lost them. To keep our minds off what had happened, or at least give us something to focus on, Hardin and Randall made us rebuild the camp so we would have something to turn over to the ARVN unit when the time came.

The camp was a mess. Some Yard strikers had E&Eed through the prepared routes in the wire and were drifting back to the camp a few at a time when they saw we had it under our control. We sent for more body bags. Our supply was used up the first day, and we hadn't dug out all of the bunkers yet. Truong and his boys had mutilated the bodies of the green hats and LLDB they killed, making it difficult to identify them. Mallen had received a lot of Truong's attention.

None of us spoke much. We all wanted the same thing. Rebuilding the camp was only a temporary act of defiance to what Truong had done. All of us looked forward to the day when a heavier payback could be arranged for Truong and any other NVA who got in our line of fire. Using our team fund, Dane put out a big reward for intelligence on Truong or his unit. We sent patrols to watch the border for movement, hoping to get a line on Truong that way. Word went out on the Special Forces "old boy" network to other A Teams, the Special Projects, as well as covert operations guys to look for Truong or any intel about him. He had killed one of theirs, through betrayal, and the green hats looked out for their own. It was a matter of pride.

Two weeks later, Hardin, looking as grim as the day the camp had been overrun, told us we were ordered back to 5th Group for reassignment. Our camp was being turned over to an ARVN Ranger unit.

That night in the team house, we all gathered to drink our nightly beers, except Bender, who had the radio watch. Randall couldn't sit still, pacing back and forth. Finally, he stopped in front of Hardin, who sat by himself at one end of the bunker.

"Cap'n Hardin?" he said.

"Master Sergeant Randall?" Hardin replied, looking up from his beer.

"Sir, it seems to me we have some unfinished business here. Is there any chance of us getting another camp?"

Hardin looked at all of us, each waiting for his answer. Even the guys who planned to rotate home were talking about extending their tours if they could find some way to stay in the field, at least until someone greased Truong.

"You know how it is, sergeant. We're being phased out. Besides that, some of our team are ready to DEROS."

Randall swept us with his gaze. "How many of you would extend if we could get another camp?"

My hand shot up simultaneously with Dane's. Blake just nodded, and Tex grinned. Brick even stood, saying, "You gotta ask?" The rest of the guys made various affirmative gestures.

"You wanna stay, do you Hammer Head?" Randall asked me. I was the junior member of the team. Hammer Head was Randall's nickname for me ever since I'd head-butted him one day during our hand-to-hand training.

"I'm stayin' 'til the job's done, sarge," I said quietly.

"Well, there it is, sir," Randall concluded, sitting down.

Hardin nodded. "You men know that I want Truong's head as badly as anyone, but I can't control what the Group will do when they close this camp. Believe me, when I get to HQ I'll do my best to find us a camp. You men are the best team I've worked with, I'd be pleased to continue working with you. But don't get your hopes up. Questions? No? See you men in the morning then."

Everyone said their goodnights and drifted off, one by one. I walked over to the commo bunker to tell Marty Bender what had been said. I asked him if he would extend his tour.

"Yeah, I got an in with Delta." It was one of the Special Projects.

On the day before we were to leave, an ARVN Ranger unit airlifted in. They looked pretty sharp compared to some of the ARVN units I'd seen. Our Nung platoon warily watched them from a distance. Krang understood what was happening, but few of the others did. None of them liked it at all. The ARVN had offered them NCO slots. I didn't know if Krang had accepted one or not.

The Viet LLDB and their strikers who had replaced the former camp team were drawn up for review, but the Viet Ranger CO breezed by them and headed straight for our team. He and Hardin shook hands like long-lost brothers and Hardin took him on a tour of the camp. We found out later that Hardin had been an advisor to the ARVN Rangers on his first tour and that the Viet colonel had been a Ranger captain then. They had been through some hairy shit together.

The next morning, three slicks came in to pick us up. The Nungs went into formation and gave us their version of a twenty-one gun salute. All of them fired in the air on full auto until their rifles were empty. It scared the shit out of the slick crews. Hardin, Randall and Dane all said long goodbyes to each Nung, while the rest of us shook hands and gave the Nungs personal mementos. I gave Bao my machete and little Lin got my Zippo lighter with the Special Forces crest which I'd bought at Bragg. As I headed for the slick, I saw Randall hand Krang his prized Swedish K submachine gun and a sack of magazines.

Little Lin, Bao, Krang and the rest of our Nung platoon were good fighters. I had grown to respect them, even like them as some of the others did. When the shit got deep, they didn't bug out like most of the ARVN and even some GIs would. I'd seen that on my first tour. Once three guys ran during a fire fight down in the Iron Triangle. They had been running their lips about how bad they were, personally, at the fire base. They told anyone who would listen that it wasn't their war. They said it was the rich man's plot to kill off the poor and on and on. I'd known one of them in AIT and jump school and he wasn't spouting all of that political rhetoric bullshit then. It was only his way of covering up the fact that he was a stone coward. We got hit real hard one day in the Ho Bo Woods and these three bugged out when it looked like the VC might overrun us. Somebody greased all three of them. We found their bodies after the fire fight had been resolved in our favor. I didn't know, and didn't care, if it was the gooks or one of our people who got them. I hated cowards, no matter who they were, and conversely, I respected the valiant. Anyone who has the guts to fight for what he believes in has my respect. For the grunts, it was a matter of fighting for each other — that was what you believed in.

Turning to take one last look at the camp, I bid it and the ghosts of Lt. Mallen, Kirby and Mayo a last farewell, then climbed aboard the slick. Minutes later, we were off.

True to his word, as soon as he hit Nha Trang, Marty left for Project Delta. The rest of us sat around in the transit barracks, hating Truong and no way to find him.

Chapter Two
The Team

Randall had been on the prowl for two weeks, calling in every old favor he could to find us a team slot somewhere. The rest of us were pulling various duties around Nha Trang. None of us saw Hardin more than once or twice during that time, so we were somewhat surprised when he strolled into our quarters one evening. I was relaxed on a bunk, reading a Conan paperback. I never claimed to be an intellectual. The big barbarian didn't fuck around. He cleaved and hewed with a broad sword that never dulled like my machete. His sword must have led to those cowboy movie six-shooters that would fire at least thirty rounds before they needed reloading. I was wishing for a rifle like that when Hardin walked in.

Blake was doing isometrics at one end of the room, Brick was sharpening his knife and Dane was asleep. Hardin cleared his throat to get our attention. We sort of stood up, but he motioned us down. Hardin wasn't too involved in boot camp style formalities other than what it took to run his team or keep the REMFs off his ass.

Sitting on the edge of an unclaimed bunk, Hardin pulled his beret off and rubbed his hand over his face. Then he looked at us. "Sergeant Randall found a way for us to stay together as a team, if you men are willing. It involves working for Intelligence."

"What do you have in mind, sir?" Dane asked, sitting up. Of all of us in the room, he had been in the Forces the longest.

All of us had checked around Nha Trang for something we could do as a team. Bender said he would put in a good word for us with the people at Delta, but we never did hear anything from them. What we discovered was that a lot of the teams losing their camps were either rotating home or being turned into REMFs. I had a phobia about that. A green hat wasn't trained for a year to push papers.

"There is a special operations group that will take us as a team, but there's no guarantee what Corps area we will be assigned to. The missions will be reconnaissance, strategic interdiction of enemy forces and intelligence-related operations," Hardin answered.

"SOG," Dane said.

Hardin nodded. Dane had a sour look on his face.

"What . . . ?" I began.

"It's a spook outfit man, a real meat grinder," Dane said, looking around at all of us.

"They want a team with diverse skills that has worked together for covert operations. Sergeant Randall found out about it first. An old friend of his named Stone tried to recruit him for his own team. Randall could have been team leader, but he said he'd have to check with us first," Hardin went on.

I thought that was nice of Randall. The man was loyal.

"Stoney. It figures," Dane said.

"If Stoney's in it, there's got to be a catch somewhere," Brick said, grinning at Dane.

"Who . . . ?" I began again, wanting to know who Stone was.

"Later," Dane said.

"We can recruit some of our Nungs from the A camp if we go to SOG and we won't be working with the Viets. We won't be working for the Group or even the Army for that matter," Hardin told us, standing. "It's the best chance we've got of finding Truong. Maybe the only chance."

He turned to leave, then paused at the door and put his beret on, scrunching it down over his nose. "You all think it over. I'll be over at the BOQ," he said and left.

"Hey Dane, if we aren't working for the Group or the Army, who in the fuck are we working for?" I asked.

He grinned at me. "Figure it out man. If it isn't the Army, who's left?"

"The Agency, the CIA," I said.

"Bingo."

There wasn't much debate. Randall came in about a half-hour later and looked around at us. It was clear he was waiting for our answers. We were all doing more or less the same things we had been doing when Hardin came in.

"You going over to the BOQ, sarge?" I asked.

Randall nodded.

"Tell Cap'n Hardin I'm game," I told him.

Randall grinned his approval at me. One by one the others told him the same. We had all volunteered for the Army, then Airborne, the Forces, Nam and now this. It seemed like the right thing to do and the only way to stay in the war. Spooks, intelligence agents, didn't mean much to me then other than a slightly romantic image I had from watching a few James Bond movies. I was still naive in the ways of double-dealing. If SOG was a "meat grinder," what was being a line grunt? Nothing could be worse than that or so I thought at the time.

Krang's seamed, scarred face split into a huge grin when he spotted Randall and me in the deuce-and-a-half truck at the airfield. He, Bao, Lin and seven other Nungs who survived the camp's seizure and who had been hand-picked by Krang had just deplaned from a C123, a twin-engine cargo plane, that had transported them from our former A camp. They had all taken jobs as NCOs with the ARVN Ranger unit we turned the camp over to, but all ten of them tore off their ARVN rank and hauled ass when Randall told them they could work with us again. Randall flashed an ear-to-ear grin back at Krang.

The Nungs instantly lined up for inspection. They wore brand new tiger suits and patrol harnesses, each carrying a new M16 rifle. Krang had his K SMG slung over his shoulder. He inspected his squad, did a sharp about-face and saluted us.

I noted Bao was still wearing my machete. As Randall and I walked to greet them, Krang and Randall suddenly embraced and the formation broke up. I shook hands all around, nodding and smiling as they barked at me in their sing-song language and pidgin English. I shook Lin's hand last. Bowing, he said, "Now we go kill VC!" With that, we loaded into the truck.

After our reunion, we flew to a SOG base camp for training. The cadre there, all green hats, taught the six of us round-eyes the essentials of bush survival in covert operations. The training was specialized for Southeast Asia and taken directly from lessons learned by teams that practiced their brand of warfare daily, unlike some of the lessons I'd learned in the U.S. The rest of the team was familiar with these principles and procedures, but they went through the course, taking it as a refresher. I learned to handle air assets of all types, what their capabilities were and how to use them to their fullest. We were told we would operate beyond the range of artillery fire most of the time, so air control was a mandatory skill. Having the ability to call in and direct air assets from any source in Southeast Asia and to personally control them was a real rush. The rest of the course focused on small unit tactics for covert insertion and extraction and tips from guys who had been on recon teams before.

After finishing the course, we were flown to our Forward Operating Base (FOB) in the Mekong Delta. I'd heard about the Delta on my first tour. Its name was used to threaten us, the same way the Germans threatened their troops with the Eastern front during World War II. If the highlands were bad, the Delta was worse. For volunteering to fight, I'd gotten the Delta.

Two Army Intelligence officers briefed us on the Target Area (TA). Our team received its code name, Recon Team Iron. Our primary mission was to interdict enemy supply, troop and infrastructure movement in our TA acting on humint from our control sources. We were under the authority of Command and Control South and the Phoenix Program. I'd never heard of them, but that didn't matter to me. Our secondary mission was to identify and neutralize the Viet Cong infrastructure in our TA at village level. We all liked hearing that at the briefing. It had been our mission with the A Team, more or less, but then we had been trying to win the hearts and minds of the indigenous people. This time we could just go kill the enemy. Before there had been too many rules, too much bullshit bureaucracy to cut through. With a light team whose sole mission was to kill the enemy, we could expect more success.

We were given a license to do something that might actually affect the war effort. The Civilian Irregular Defense Group (CIDG) program we had been in was a start, but to hunt and kill the enemy on equal terms for a change, and as our main priority, was the only way we could conceivably make any headway against them.

Leaving our initial briefing, Brick looked at me and grinned. "Let's rock and roll!" he said.

We drew our weapons at the launch site. They had any kind of firearm we could possibly want in the arms room there, so Hardin told us to draw what we thought we might need for the TA. Brick found an M60 with a modified box on it like the door gunners used. Blake picked up one of the new M16/M203 combinations. It was an M16 rifle with a 40mm grenade launcher mounted under the barrel. I found a short 12-gauge pump shotgun and a CAR 15. Hardin and Randall both found themselves Swedish Ks and Hardin got an M16 with a night scope on it as well. It paid to be an officer. Tex and Dane both picked up CAR 15s. We all had our personal weapons too, mostly .45 autos or Browning 9mms. Randall, the lone exception, wore a .357 Colt magnum with a six-inch barrel. While we were there, Dane picked up an M79 40mm grenade launcher for one of the Nungs and a High Standard .22 auto pistol with a suppressor attached.

Hardin and Dane received other goodies while we were there, like a kit containing a variety of drugs for putting prisoners to sleep, getting them to talk, or killing them without any medical trace. Blake got a new radio called a burst transmitter. All of us were issued maps of the TA and a variety of intelligence reports that covered just about every aspect of the enemy, terrain and situation in our TA.

Our spook control didn't waste any time. The next day, he briefed us for our first mission. As we sat in the briefing room at the operations base, listening to an Army officer give us a political orientation on the area, two civilians came in. The term "civilian" is used loosely. One was short and stocky, fat, with a graying crew cut and a cigar stub clamped between his teeth. He wore a safari-type suit and sunglasses.

"Spook," Dane muttered from behind me.

Turning to look at Dane, I saw he had his face all scrunched up as though someone had just forced him to eat some *nuoc mam* sauce. I mentally shrugged it off. Dane had been an intelligence NCO on several tours. No doubt he'd had his share of problems with the non-military intelligence services. Fourteen years later, they would terminate Dane in another war, another hemisphere, but of course we didn't know that then. Too bad, we could have evened up the score some.

The second man was tall and lean. His long black hair hung to his waist, tied in the back into a pony tail. A drooping mustache fell on either side of his full-lipped mouth. He looked Indian, maybe Mexican, with a hint of Oriental in his features, too. It was hard to distinguish. Looking into his eyes as they swept over us, I saw them linger on Dane and Randall. His eyes were hard and shiny black. The olive drab (OD) jungle pants and sleeveless black T-shirt he wore were stained and faded.

Glancing over at Dane again, I saw that his face wasn't merely scrunched up this time. It was hard and set, jaw muscles bunched. A vein throbbed near his temple. Randall was impassive, though he nodded slightly to the man.

The man in the safari suit took over the briefing. We were to raid a village and snatch a commisar, an NVA officer who traveled a circuit of villages preaching communist propaganda. He was a major, which made him a legitimate and desirable military target, not to mention his value as an intelligence source. A ten-man NVA unit traveled with him as bodyguards. They dressed like VC. The major felt safe enough to stay in our target village overnight, which was where and when we would take him. He would probably sleep in the headman's hootch.

Our intelligence source was the village schoolteacher, according to the man in the safari suit. This teacher was tired of seeing his village taxed to feed the NVA and VC, its young people drafted by force as local guerrillas or coolies, its local women raped by marauding bands of VC. I snorted. Like the ARVN didn't do the same thing, right? I understood why the spook put this sweet glaze on the men of this mission, pointing out that our target was an NVA officer and not a civilian and how bad these dudes were, but we didn't need that kind of psychological edge. We already knew he was a bad guy. He was a communist. The village source was probably someone who gave information on the communists for money, not idealism.

That worried me. The briefing wasn't over yet and I already suspected that the fat man was lying to us. I didn't like to trust my life to habitual liars, which I strongly suspected the spooks were, just as a matter of policy. He didn't *need* to lie to us. We weren't stupid. I learned later that the schoolteacher was putting out the local VC propaganda rag and that the spook leaked his name to everyone in the hopes that someone would leak it back to the VC. That way, the VC would know that the schoolteacher was our informant after we snatched the major. The schoolteacher would take the blame, the NVA would grease one of their own and the real informant would be covered. Devious bastards.

At the end of the briefing the tall, lean guy got up. "I'll be your field control. I am familiar with the AO and the target village. Questions? No? Brief back in one hour."

We were left alone in the briefing room to make our own plans, working out the details within the team. I put my two cents worth in after looking over the aerial photos of the village. Randall liked it, but before we got any further Hardin stopped us.

"Dane, is there some personal problem there?" he asked, nodding at the door to indicate the two spooks who had briefed us.

"No sir, nothing that will affect the mission. I can work with the Cat on this, so long as he stays out of the way," Dane said.

" 'Stays out of the way?' Dane, he's our field control, not some strap hanger," Hardin began.

"Well, who the fuck is he?" Brick interrupted, unable to restrain himself. He beat me by only a few seconds. Something like this that could affect the mission, and potentially endanger our lives, needed to be out in the open.

"They call him *El Gato*, the Cat. He was one of us, a green hat, before he went with the Agency. I knew him in Laos with Bull Simon's team, then the Bull brought him along to SOG when he took it over," Randall said.

"I met him in the I Corps on my first tour," said Dane. "He was running a team of Road Runners across the border in Laos off the A Team camp I was on. He found out one of his team was a double, but he couldn't determine who it was, so he set up the whole team. He sent them into Laos dressed like VC, sterile so their equipment couldn't be traced, and then put another SOG team, like us, on them. Greased the whole team."

"Set up his own team?" Blake asked. He didn't sound outraged or angry. Actually, there was a note of admiration in his voice.

Randall shot him a hard look. "Yeah, set up his own team. The Road Runners were all indigs who reconned the Ho Chi Minh trail early on. The thing was, the team Cat had blown away wasn't Viet, they were Yards. Men Dane had recruited and trained himself, then handed over to Cat."

Hardin nodded. "I see the problem. We have to work with him Dane."

"Yes, sir. But I promised him a long time ago that if he ever fucked up, his ass was mine."

"You think he will? Fuck up?" Brick asked.

"No," Randall said, his tone indicating that the discussion was over.

A lot of the green hats who had gone to Nam in the early days had worked very closely with the various Yard tribes, and grown close to them. The green hats had recruited them out of their mountain villages, trained them, lived with them and fought with them. The NCOs were particularly close to them. I knew Dane had a great deal of respect for the Yards he had worked with. The story about the Cat wiping his team, men Dane had recruited and trained, wasn't all that hairy to me, but I could see how Dane might have felt about it. Here it was cover your ass everywhere, wasn't it? If the Yards were naive enough to trust *anyone* else to cover their asses, I felt sorry for them.

Those kind of relationships were new and strange to me. I'd had a friend during my first tour. I was his A-gunner (assistant machine gunner) when I first came in-country and he'd shown me the ropes. His name was Calucchi, and he was from Queens, New York. Caluch was a real psycho, too. While teaching me what a grunt should know to survive in the bush, he ignored his own lessons one day while in the Ho Bo Woods. He stood up during a fire fight, firing his M60 from the sling to try and suppress an ambush. A single AK round took him right between the eyes as I was hooking another belt onto his weapon.

Pieces of his head splattered on me. He was the first, and last, friend I'd made in Nam. I was fighting that feeling for the guys I was working with now, but there wasn't much danger of me getting tight with any of the indigs. They were still dinks to me.

After that, we worked out an operations plan and speced it out from every angle. When the Cat came back, we ran it by him. He sat silently, listening, and when Hardin was through, he nodded. "Fine."

We moved by truck to a jump-off point south of the target village then worked our way north and east, staying under deep cover. We came to a knoll overlooking the village just before dark and three of us slipped down to reconnoiter the target area. I led two Nungs up an irrigation canal, chest deep in water, so that the village dogs wouldn't catch our scent and bark at us. Crawling into the village at about 2100 hours, we heard a speech in Viet coming from the schoolhouse, a cinder block building that the United States Agency for International Development (USAID) had built.

One of the Nungs told me it was a political harangue. I heard Uncle Ho mentioned several times. Even though he had recently died, Ho Chi Minh's name was still evoked in the communist catechism in Vietnam. We crawled under the headman's hootch and waited. It seemed like a month passed while we lay there sweating, waiting for the speech to end, praying that no bamboo vipers would crawl up our pants. I had to find out for sure where the major went, what hootch he slept in, and where his bodyguards would be.

Finally the meeting in the schoolhouse broke up. We pulled further back under the hootch. A group of armed men came toward us, the political officer leading them. He was easy to spot, still fired up from the speech. He was talking, gesturing with his arms, pausing every few steps to make a point to his men and the few villagers who accompanied his little group. Every time the headman, a short, stooped little old guy, tried to speak, the major would listen to the first few words and then cut in with a stream of rhetoric. Typical politician. I could just imagine some of the ones back home if they had an armed escort of bodyguards. If the audience didn't listen and respond enthusiastically to the clown when he gave a speech, you were strung up and disemboweled. I bet Nixon was eating his heart out over that! The thought of Nixon ordering some hippie protester strung up to the front gate of the White

House, his belly slit and his intestines pulled out nearly caused me to burst out laughing.

I could picture it in my mind. Nixon in his classic pose, jowls shaking, both hands raised in the Victory sign. Behind him some hippie kid hanging from the gate. "Trust me," Nixon saying. I bit my finger to choke off a laugh. The Nungs were eyeing me rather strangely. They probably thought I was going crazy over here.

Just in front of the headman's hootch, the little group stopped. The bodyguards were ordered off, but one sat at the top of the steps leading into the hootch above us. The others wandered off to another hootch. Above us, we heard more speechmaking and then a woman's giggle. Footsteps from the booted feet of the major were heard as he walked to the front corner of the hootch. Lighter, shuffling footsteps, which I took to be those of the headman's, led to the rear of the hootch.

We had what we came for. Easing back from the hootch, we moved quietly to the canal. Just as we slid down the bank, the NVA guard who had been sitting at the top of the steps of the headman's hootch came toward us. He opened the fly of his black pajamas, AK rifle slung over his shoulder.

The Nungs were in the water, I was on the bank. If I moved, he would see me for sure, so I froze. He stood on top of the canal bank and urinated over the edge, splashing me. You're mine when we come back, asshole, I promised him silently. Then he squinted at the canal and leaned forward.

He said something, unslung his rifle, and took two steps down the bank. Then he looked back to the village, back in the canal and back to the village again. I guess he thought he saw something in the canal, but wasn't sure and was trying to decide whether or not to call one of his friends. He took another step down the bank.

I decided not to let him do anything else. Forcing him down, I snapped his neck with a violent tug, then lowered him down the bank to one of the Nungs. We hauled his body until we left the canal, then weighted it down with stones so that it sank. It was another first for me. He was the first man I'd killed with my bare hands, but I didn't pause to contemplate it just then. The Nungs enjoyed it though. When we rejoined the rest of the team, they made a point of showing the others how I'd turned the NVA's head around.

I briefed Hardin on the situation. As I did, the Cat appeared out of the darkness and stood right beside me. I jumped. The guy moved like a cat. He wore all back web gear, a black pajama top over his T-shirt and a long knife or short sword was strapped over his back. Another knife rode his hip and he carried an old M2 carbine from either World War II or the Korean War in a paratrooper folding stock.

"You IDed the target?" he hissed.

"Yeah," I hissed back.

"Let's do it then," he said.

Hardin grunted and passed the word to move in.

Randall and three Nungs, including Bao, went to the north end of the village and intersected the trail. They gave the rest of us time to get set and then began walking in toward the village, talking to each other in Viet. Blake, Andrews and three other Nungs went to the west side of the village so they could take the hootch where I'd seen the bodyguards go. I led the rest of the team up the canal. We needed to hit the village before the NVA missed its sentry.

One of the villagers was standing guard on the north end of the village. He heard Randall and the Nungs coming in so he ran and woke one of the NVA bodyguards, who came out fast, challenging Randall's group. Bao did the talking, telling them they were moving south and had stopped in the village looking for food and a dry place to sleep. Another NVA joined them less than a minute later.

Our group slid up the bank and circled the headman's hootch. When Randall saw us come out of the water, his group silently killed the two NVA and the villager with their knives. As we deployed around the hootch, Randall and his Nungs took the guards' places. Cat, Krang and I went into the headman's hootch.

The NVA major laid in the front room on a bed made of mats. A Viet woman was cradled in his arms, both of them naked and asleep. Cat pulled something out of his pocket. A sap. He leaned over and struck both of them behind the ears with it. Then we dragged the major out of his bed and tied him quickly. Krang gagged him as I snatched his clothes and a pouch he had been carrying earlier that evening. Taking him outside, we handed him over to two Nungs. As our part of the team began to withdraw to the canal, Hardin and I stayed behind as rear guards.

Randall noted our progress. When Hardin and I fell back to the canal, he and his Nungs walked out of the front of the village.

All three groups rendezvoused at a predesignated point and called for extraction slicks. We laid in a circle, facing out, in a clearing until the slicks were in-bound. Then Randall and I set up a strobe light to guide them to us. They were, I noticed, all black without any service markings at all. Cat personally loaded the major into one slick. We landed at our launch site just before dawn. The fat guy in the safari suit debriefed us.

As we unloaded from the slicks, Cat took the prisoner to a blue jeep that was waiting for him. A guy in commercial style polka dot camouflage was sitting in it, an Uzi SMG in his lap. That was the last we saw or heard of the major. I never learned if they got anything good from him or not. Intelligence never filtered down in the Army, so it was only logical to assume that it didn't with the spooks either.

We got a few days off then were hustled back into the briefing room. The team had gotten a pat on the head for its first operation. This briefing would be a step up for us. They had been checking us out, breaking us in easy to see what we could handle.

Church, the tubby little CIA officer who had given us our first mission, was waiting in the room for us. "We have agent reports that a large force of NVA are moving south through Cambodia into a staging area in the Delta, our AO."

What's this "we" shit, I thought to myself as Church droned on. He passed out maps, aerial photos of the area and other reports including weather projections. There was a choke point on their jungle highway. We were to insert and stay on the ground as long as possible, find the NVA, then direct air assets to blow them away. If a large enough force was found, our team would split in half. One group would stay with the trail at the choke point while the second half would stalk the NVA to its staging area. We wouldn't be taking any spooks along this time and we didn't have to worry about taking prisoners either. It was a straight search and mangle mission, just finding and killing gooks.

We had two days to plan this mission, draw what extra gear we might need and rehearse the operation. Randall, Blake, Krang, two Nungs and I would form the mobile element if it came to that. I drew forty magazines, ten frags, a claymore and sacked up a bag full of rice balls dipped in honey. They were my idea of Lurp rations and much tastier than *nuoc mam*. We planned on a five-day maximum stay. On a Lurp patrol, the object was to stay concealed from the enemy while observing them. If we were forced to resupply in the field, the slicks would give away our presence, if not our exact location. The enemy would then either vacate the area or hunt us and either way our mission would be compromised. For a small team, it was much better to be the hunters than the hunted.

SOG had its own air assets assigned to it, elements of both the U.S. and Viet Air Forces flying slicks and fixed-wing support for us. We would have on station an O-1 FAC, a small plane armed with phosphorous marker rockets that would act as our radio relay for further air support and be our eye in the sky. In addition, fast movers, C-130 Spectre gunships and Skyraiders were all on call. There were also two artillery fire bases that could hit our AO once the NVA crossed the border. A Mike Force and some grunt units were also waiting for us to tell them where the enemy was concentrated. I felt important, having the full might of the combined U.S. forces at my beck and call. I truly hoped to be able to help some of those forces spend some of their ordnance.

The local VC had LZ watchers all over our AO because SOG recon teams had visited them with destruction before. The terrain was going to be hard to hump, being mostly dense jungle and mangrove swamp. I was weighted down with so much equipment that any terrain would be hard humping for me. Still, the ammo and food were vital. I decided to add a machete to my load as well.

On the second day of planning, we delivered a briefing in the morning. Later that afternoon, we loaded on slicks. My adrenalin was pumping as soon as the slick lifted off. This was serious shit.

Despite the pre-mission jitters I was having, I was proud to be part of it. Working with this team was worth all the hard times I put in to get where I was at this moment. This mission was worth all those nights I'd spent with the grunt unit laying out on ambushes that never panned out, the hours spent sitting beside some trail for nothing. This operation would trap and destroy an NVA unit, not a small patrol, but something worth hitting, something that would be felt. If I got wasted during this mission, well, tough shit. I would go down doing something worthwhile. This was what soldiers did; took risks, fought battles and tried to win wars. So far, I felt I'd just been taking the risks, especially with my grunt unit. The only real battle I'd fought was during the 1968 Tet Offensive and I'd lost that one. Something had been missing. But on this operation, all the pieces seemed to be fitting in place for a change.

The slick I was on had the rest of my half of the team on it. We would be the second slick into the LZ. Hardin was going in first. There were six Hueys in our flight, four of which were gunships. The flight in was cool. We were above rifle range and the air was actually chilly. As we approached the LZ, the slicks would drop down low, just above the tree line, so that we could observe the area before being set down.

Our Nungs were all dozing. They amazed me. All of them were tough, good under fire. I respected them as soldiers, but still wasn't sure how they felt about me. Glancing at Randall, I saw him looking at his patrol map. Blake was staring out the door. Krang was looking at me.

When we made eye contact, he smiled at me. "We kill boocoo VC!" he yelled, grinning.

I nodded and grinned back. Krang told me once that both his job and his religion were killing VC. He took the trigger fingers off the men he killed personally and when he got drunk, he wore a necklace made of their finger bones. The communists had done something bad to Krang years ago. They might have been Viet Minh back then. He never said what it was, and I didn't pry, but he truly hated the VC. Motives were like a prevailing wind to me, subject to change, as the politicians in Washington proved on a daily basis. Krang wanted to kill VC and not me; I couldn't care less about the reason for it.

The slicks dropped suddenly, making my belly lurch up toward my throat. Randall held up a magazine as a signal and we all locked and loaded. Two of the gunships veered off and swept in low to our east. One of them dropped a mechanical fire fight simulator as the other hovered low over an LZ. It was a fake to draw off the LZ watchers. The other two gunships circled high above us while Hardin's slick dove for the LZ. As we watched, the door gunner saturated the tree line with M60 fire while Hardin's team leapt out of the hovering slick. Suddenly it was our turn.

Hitting the ground, we waited a moment to see if there was a reception committee. The slicks circled overhead, then moved to the south to swoop another LZ in another feint to draw any potential heat off us. When we didn't take any incoming fire, we moved quickly into the tree line. Hardin oriented us and we moved out at as fast a pace as we could, Blake on slack to a Nung's point, Krang and I as tail gunners, trying to cover our tracks as we marched.

The terrain was as bad as we had anticipated. Worse. It took us three hours to move four miles. We chopped our way through wait-a-minute vines, bypassed or slithered through bamboo thickets and fought the dense foliage. Our RON position was in a clump of bamboo. We crawled in and pulled the bamboo stalks back into place to cover us. As dawn broke, we were up and moving again. Hardin and Randall worked over the maps and had a fix on our position from our Forward Air Control (FAC) which was flying above us. We moved out of the bush and into a stream, making a lot better progress in the water staying close to the overhanging foliage on one bank. It kept us cooler, too. Leeches and snakes shared the stream with us, but they were everywhere; I'd gotten used to them.

Finally, Randall led us out of the water and into the jungle. We skirted clearings, moving through man-high and taller elephant grass. And then we were on station. A slight rise in the terrain gave us a view of the jungle below us so we moved onto it, breaking for chow for the first time that morning. After eating, we rested in the shade. Randall and half of the team moved down to the trail to reconnoiter it. We found another "jungle highway" almost immediately. The agent reports that the spook had presented gave us a good fix on it. We walked in to be sure that we didn't alert the local VC that we were headed for their infiltration route and it worked so far. We deployed along the trail, sending a Nung to guide Hardin down to us. They would join us after sunset.

The coolies who cut the trail out of the jungle had done a good job. It was hard-packed earth, rutted where carts had come south along it and wide enough for three men to walk side by side. The trees were tied together at the tops for cover from above. While we watched that afternoon, we saw some movement, but not enough to warrant any kind of strike. We saw a few cells of VC or NVA pushing bicycles. One pair of them stopped right in front of us for lunch. Later, one of them wandered over by us to urinate. We all just stayed very still and the enemy soldiers went on their way. Just before dark, Hardin's team joined us and we pulled away from the trail to eat and sleep.

Before dawn, we were at the trail again. According to reports, we were positioned just below an intersection where three trails merged into one. If a big move came, this was where they would be forced to slow down. Randall decided to take Krang and another Nung to the nearby intersection and scout around. We had been on the ground nearly two days. While Randall was gone, Dane came crawling to me.

"Hardin says to take a prisoner, NVA," he whispered to me. I passed the word.

Dane, a Nung and I moved slightly south to a bend in the trail and sat, waiting. Around 13:30 three NVA came ambling along, pushing bicycles. One had a pouch slung from his left shoulder. As they rounded the bend in the trail, I shot the lead man with my silenced CAR. Dane and the Nung sprang on the other two, the Nung knifing the second bicycle-pushing soldier. Dane snatched the soldier with the pouch, jerked him off balance with one arm and struck him in the side of the head with an elbow strike. He then pulled the man's AK off his shoulder and tossed it to me. The Nung helped Dane tie and gag the prisoner and I hustled him off the trail. Dane and I covered up the signs of blood, dragged the two bodies into the bush and then pushed the bicycles even deeper, using loose foliage to cover them. As Dane and the Nung took the POW to the rise where Hardin and the radio were, I rejoined the guys beside the trail.

Randall came back about an hour later and I briefed him on what happened while he was gone. He just nodded and told me he hadn't seen anything significant during his recon of the other trails. That night, when Hardin moved down to us, he told us that the POW was part of an NVA HQ unit for a battalion. The POW had been moving south ahead of the battalion to catch up with an advance element with orders from the battalion CO. The advance element had passed through our AO the day before we reached the trail and the battalion would be moving through that night. The NVA considered the trail secure.

Our whole team stayed alert beside the trail that night, but the NVA didn't move by us. Early the next morning, they did. They came down the trail in good marching order, keeping their intervals, but we could tell from the casual way they moved that they felt secure in the area. As soon as we could, we pulled back to the rise and called in the air assets.

I was sitting behind a tree when the first fast movers dove in. One moment it was quiet and the next the air was ripped apart as two fast movers came hurtling down from the clear blue sky, diving out of the sun. They were guided in by our FAC spotter, which had made a pass moments earlier, firing a marker rocket. The two fast movers, F4 Phantoms, dropped napalm canisters and it set the jungle on fire. I felt the heat roll over me, the sudden vacuum as the napalm ignited sucking up all the area's oxygen. The two jets circled and began another run, dropping cluster bombs and strafing with their cannon. A Spectre gunship arrived behind them and opened fire as soon as the jets were clear, ripping up the smoldering jungle. We could see the surviving jungle foliage fall apart as the multibarrel cannons tore it up. It was an awesome display. There were secondary explosions along the jungle trail as ammo carts were hit or caught fire. I felt a pressure wave from the blasts wash over me.

As I sat watching, two more Phantoms came on station. They

dove in and dropped more napalm and cluster bombs. The Spectre's miniguns hummed their tune of death up and down the trail. We couldn't see much because of smoke so we pulled back. It didn't matter much now anyway. We had done what we went here to do, and had grabbed a prisoner on top of it.

We took a different route out of the area just in case any surviving NVA, now surely aware that a ground team was around, spotted our trail in. It led us to another stream, this one with more densely covered banks. When we couldn't follow the stream anymore, we cut across country, staying in deep cover, moving slowly toward a predesignated extraction point. We had to ford another stream not far from the LZ.

Putting out flank security, we sent one of the Nungs across the stream and then began crossing it in pairs. I was in midstream with the POW, Blake and Krang the last two behind me on the bank, when the NVA opened fire.

The POW spun away from me and sank quickly under the shallow water. Blood blossomed from multiple chest wounds, so I left him and dove as deep as I could, swimming for the opposite bank. Blake and Krang opened up with everything they had to cover me as did the guys who had crossed before me. My equipment dragged me down as I scrambled up the bank to join the rest of the team and a bullet grazed my leg. I fell flat, but kept climbing. Bullets were whip-cracking past me, thudding into the dirt around me. The guys returned steady suppressing fire. The grenade launchers were blooping. Digging the toes of my boots into the slimy mud bank, I pulled myself over the top. Brick yanked me up by my patrol harness. An RPG exploded behind me on the bank, showering both of us with clods of mud.

Looking across the stream, I saw Krang and Blake rip off bursts from their weapons and then dive into the stream. NVA appeared on the bank right behind them. I sprayed them, seeing one fall backward as another pitched forward and rolled into the stream. Krang and Blake swam hard, bullets cutting the water all around them. We fired everything we had. Brick was up on one knee with his 60, Bao fired another one from a prone position. Suddenly, Andrews spun and fell on top of me. I put a pressure bandage on his left arm, then went back to the firing line.

Glancing upstream, I saw a small force of NVA crossing the stream to our flank. Just then, Blake burst out of the water and scrambled straight up the bank. I reached out for him, grabbed his weapon and hauled him to me. Krang was right behind him. As I reached out my hand for him, he took it, and jerked as a bullet hit him. Krang fell back down the bank.

"Goddam!" I yelled and without thinking leapt down after him. Blake went up on one knee to cover me, firing over my head.

I grabbed Krang and hurled him halfway up the bank. Bullets smacked all around us. Two NVA ran out of the tree line on the opposite bank, rifles leveled at us, and Blake got them both. Krang tried to crawl up the bank. I grabbed his patrol harness and tossed him up the bank and over the top.

There was more lead in the air than ever. A frag went off in the stream behind me and shrapnel hit my back and legs. Rather than slow me down, it supercharged me. I bounded over the top before they could throw another frag at me and pulled Krang in behind cover. Randall dashed over to help pull us in. As I pulled Krang into cover, Randall worked on his wounds. I laid panting beside him, then rolled over, retrieved my CAR and rejoined the firing line.

Randall flopped down beside me. "Good job," he said, slapping me on the arm. When he spotted the blood on me, he started to pull a bandage out of his kit.

"Not yet, sarge, I'm all right!" I said.

He nodded. "We've got to get out of here. They're flanking us."

Just then, one of the Nungs at the other end of the firing line got up on one knee and fired his M79 into the woods on our side of the stream. Screams sounded after the explosion. Firing a second round, the Nung suddenly jerked upright, then toppled over backward. Dane pivoted and brought fire on the tree line.

Hardin was on the radio to a new FAC. I had just raised up to fire again when a bright light went off in my head and my world went dark.

I woke up with a powerful headache. Brick was lying near me and I heard fast movers zooming around nearby. Then the noise of inbound slicks overwhelmed all other sounds.

"Shit," I growled. There was sporadic firing around me. My mouth tasted like shit, too.

"Wha' fu' happened?" I asked Brick, slurring the words.

"It was gettin' deep, but the zoomies brought smoke on their asses. We're at an extraction LZ," Andrews answered.

"Huh," I mumbled.

We were taking some sniper fire, but that was it. The slicks came in under gunship covering fire and we went back to our base camp.

The local evac hospital wasn't bad at all. There were lots of round-eyed nurses to lust for and plenty of cold drinks. I had six pieces of shrapnel dug out of me, but they left a few little pieces in for some reason. Bullets had creased my leg and the top of my head, causing some blood loss but nothing serious. Just what I needed, I thought, another head wound. Andrews was okay, too. He had a clean in-and-out bullet hole in his arm. One Nung, the guy with the M79, had been killed after breaking up the NVA's flank attack. Krang had been hit by a ricochet and he was okay. A few of the others had been dusted with shrapnel, cut by rock chips or ricochets and had lesser bruises and cuts.

A grunt unit later swept the area to assess the damage. They counted more than two hundred bodies on the trail and found thirty-four more around the banks of the stream. That wasn't a bad trade in my book. We'd taken a heavy toll on that NVA battalion. Of course, the body count around the trail was based mainly on parts of bodies found since the napalm and the Vulcan cannons in the Spectre gunship hadn't left much in the way of whole bodies.

I laid around a few days at the hospital with Brick and then the nurses threw me out. Dane came and got me.

"C'mon, I've got someone I want you to meet, man," he told me.

I borrowed a set of fatigues from the hospital since their staff cut my tiger suit off of me. Picking up my field gear and a brand new beret which I crushed down in front, we hopped a ride to Saigon on a medevac slick.

"So who are we going to see? Abrams?" I asked, naming the new Military Assistance Command, Vietman (MACV) commander.

Dane grinned at me. "No, it's his bastard son, the guy who got us into this. Stoney."

Madame Xhian's House of Floating Petals was in Cholon, a Chinese suburb of Saigon. It was off-limits to GIs so we appropriated a blue jeep from MACVSOG on Pasteur Street, not far from where we were going. Blue jeeps were CIA, and no MP in his right mind would stop two green berets in a blue jeep. Dane drove us to an ornate colonial French house set behind a brick wall. A huge ethnic Chinese let us in the front gate. Parking beside another blue jeep in the side yard, Dane led me to the front of the house. Another, much larger Chinese let us inside. This guy was about the size of an M60 main battle tank. He wore a long, drooping Mongol style mustache and except for a braided scalp lock, his head was shaved bald. As we entered, I heard someone singing "The Ballad of the Green Berets" in broken English. I looked at Dane, but he just smiled at me, then bowed to the Chinese who had let us in. When he returned the bow, Dane asked him something in Chinese.

"Yes, Stone and Lee Hung are in parlor," the big guy replied in nearly unaccented English.

After the two bowed again, Dane led me into a large side room that I guessed was the parlor. It was decorated in traditional Chinese style, but a bar ran down the length of one side of the room. Young women of various oriental nationalities, all impeccably dressed in embroidered *ao dais,* long, tight-fitting dresses worn over pants and slit up the sides to the hips, traditional dress of Vietnamese women, brought us drinks. They waited on us hand and foot.

"Well, Dane Trail, heard you were dead, son," a gruff voice announced from the center of a pile of cushions on the floor.

"Not yet, asshole, but you sure have made it hard to stay alive," Dane replied.

A blond-haired bodybuilder stood up out of the cushions. He was about my height, five ten or so, but built like Conan himself. He was bigger than Dane. He wore a pair of tiger-stripe pants and nothing else. Like Randall, scars crisscrossed his torso and arms. Steely blue eyes blazed out from under his bushy, sunbleached eyebrows.

"Me? I didn't force you to join the Forces," he said, smiling at Dane.

Dane sighed. "You didn't tell Randall SOG was looking for a team either, huh? Well, that's why I'm here — to let this guy punch you in the snout for what you got him into," Dane told him, grinning. I'd wandered over to the bar to look at the cuties.

"Hey," Dane called.

I turned around. "What?" I asked.

"This is Stone, the guy who got us into SOG's clutches," Dane said to me. He turned back to Stone. "That's Hammer, the only man to head-butt Randall and live through it."

Stone smiled at me. "Is that what happened to your head?"

I grinned, but before I could get into it, Dane explained about the fire fight at the stream and my attention wandered back to the cuties.

Mike Stone, or Stoney to his green hat buddies, had been a California biker before enlisting in the Army. Joining the Forces in '62 he had been in Nam since '63, off and on. Mostly on. He was the leader of a team known as RT Steel, working the same general AO we did with two other green hats and ten Nungs, based out of Ban Me Thuot. The guy was pretty well known to both sides in Southeast Asia.

"Shit, Stone, he pulled one of your stunts. Went over a river bank under heavy fire to pull in a green hat and a Nung. Stopped a bullet with his head. So where are Wong and Cisco?"

Stone sat quietly for a moment, his face clouding over. "Ain't heard, huh? Cisco went down."

"No shit. Damn, I thought he'd be one of the survivors."

Stone shrugged. "We hit a camp over inside the Fan Tail, man. I thought it was too good to be true from the intel reports and it was. That Chinese cocksucker set it up and when we hit the camp looking for POWs, he blew our asses off. Cisco got hit right away leading his Nungs in, then he got hit again before they could extract what was left of us."

Dane turned to me. "Me 'n Cisco went through Bragg together. We were on an A Team camp up in I Corps. He was a good man."

I nodded, "Sorry to hear it."

Stone shrugged again. "*C'est le guerre* as Bear would say. But

Wong is around here somewhere."

As we talked, Stone told me about Madame Xhian. She'd been Chiang Kai-shek's mistress for years. When his power started to collapse, Chiang Kai-shek sent her south to Saigon with a chest full of gold and a company of his Kuomintang. Settling in, she opened an exclusive bordello for the French and Viets, then later for the Americans. She also ran an efficient intelligence network in South Vietnam, Cambodia, Laos and the Golden Triangle. In return for her help and intelligence sources, the Agency ran a secure smuggling operation out of the Triangle for her opium. She, in effect, ran a Tong in Cholon with Agency protection.

Her house was now open only to green hats and intelligence people since it was a sideline to her main business, opium and spying. Her intelligence network was run by her lieutenants, trusted sons of former Kuomintang officers who had accompanied her to Cholon. Stone told us she had fallen for a young French officer of the paras who had been killed at Dien Bien Phu and so she preferred the company of Americans who actually killed communists rather than REMFs. I smiled at that. Good lady.

While Stone was talking, my eyes strayed to a beautiful woman in a red *ao dai*. She was Eurasian. I felt an instant lust. Stone saw my attention wandering and grinned at me.

"Michele, my friend would like to speak with you," he told her.

Oriental women are wondrous people. I love them and hold them in awe. Having played back seat love games in the States with girls who popped gum in my ear as I grunted away on top of them, the women I met in Southeast Asia were a whole new experience, a real conscious raiser. Michele was trained to be a man's slave and yet, through her total submission, she gained a type of mastery over men. She and her sisters of the shadow world gave me an education I'll never forget. Eventually she married a green hat officer and moved to the United States.

The next morning, I wandered downstairs for breakfast, a traditional Chinese meal of *dim sun* and juice. A dark brown Oriental in Army fatigues sat at the table with Stone and Dane. I joined them.

"This is Hung Lee Wong," Stone said, introducing me.

Lee Wong was an ethnic Chinese of Hawaiian descent. He was

Stone's one one, his number two man, on RT Steel. "Heard you saved old Krang's ass," he said by way of greeting.

"I gave him a hand," I said, being Mr. Modest. I felt humbled in this company: fence jumpers, guys who fought every mission in a foreign country, long-time Cong killers. I was damn near a cherry compared to them.

"Yeah, Dane gave us a blow-by-blow, man," Stone started.

"Freeze it, Stone. He's on our team. Don't try stealing our guys before breakfast, huh," Dane cut in. Stone put on a "Who, me?" face.

We spent the morning telling war stories. I had a few grunt stories from my first tour, a lurp story or two. I mentioned I had been on a firebase in the Iron Triangle during the '68 Tet Offensive. That brought all of them up short. Only nine GIs survived that. We were all left for dead. The combined NVA/VC force had overrun us and pretty well dusted a heavy platoon of grunts as well as a lurp team that had been operating from that firebase. My lurp team. I'd been butt-stroked and bayoneted in a close encounter with the NVA, all of whom died as a result of it.

It turned out that one of Stone's friends had been a lurp team leader with the same outfit. He had come in with the relief force the next morning. I didn't remember much about that following morning though.

After lunch, I visited Michele again while Dane and Stone talked with Madame Xhian. When I came downstairs, Lee Wong and the large Chinese who had let me in were in an enclosed courtyard, fighting like mad dogs.

I watched, fascinated. Kung Fu and karate movies hadn't made their way to the U.S. in very large numbers back then and there were very few martial arts schools at home. I'd played judo, a grappling art, but those two weren't playing judo, the gentle art. Their kicks and punches flew so fast that it was hard to tell what they were doing. Suddenly, Wong flew backward and landed on his ass. As the Chinese moved in for the kill, Wong spun on the ground., sweeping the big guy's legs out from under him. Wong kicked him with his heel as they both lay on their backs, then he kipped up and drove a heel into his opponent's throat, screaming horrifically as he struck. Wong's heel stopped less than an inch short of impact.

The Chinese hopped to his feet and they bowed to each other. Several of the girls rushed out to them with towels and juice. Wong saw me watching and flipped a salute. I nodded back.

"Nice," I told him.

"My father was a *sifu*. He taught me from the time I could walk. I don't get to practice much like this, though. Stone spars with me a little, but he's, uh, like a boxer. This is the real thing."

I looked at the Chinese and could believe it was like the real thing. "Is Stone into karate?" I asked.

"Well, he can fight. He has been stationed with the Forces in Korea and Okinawa, so he probably trained in the local styles and other guys have shown him moves. He's unpredictable and a hell of a fighter, but I wouldn't say he's exactly into karate."

I grunted something. My chief claim to fighting was judo, what I'd been taught at Bragg, what Randall had shown me and the street brawling I'd done before enlisting. I wondered what I would do if I was unarmed and several opponents attacked me. It gave me something to think about. Maybe I could get some of the others who knew martial arts to teach me.

Dane came downstairs, collected me and we split. My recuperation was over.

"Get any leads on Truong?" I asked.

"You catch on fast. No, not yet, but Xhian said she'd put the word out for us. Stone, too. We've gotta keep our ears to the ground for a Chinese intelligence officer, the one who set up Stoney's team on that raid."

I nodded, satisfied. No problem. Truong and the Chinese major's time would come sooner or later. It was a small world.

Chapter Three
The Special Zone

The Rung Sat Special Zone was the foulest piece of real estate I had ever seen and I had only flown over it. It was a densely foliated swamp with open canals and small islands dotted throughout it. I knew from reports that it was all ankle-breaking mangrove swamp with thick, partially impenetrable forests and bamboo groves on the islands. It was home to a variety of snakes, poisonous spiders that could snare small birds in their webs and quick mud. It was also home to the remnants of the hard core Viet Cong, the black clad guerrillas who had survived the 1968 Tet Offensive in Saigon and then our counteroffensive.

These VC retreated into the fever swamps of the so-called Forest of Assassins to regroup, but they came out often enough to make their presence felt. Our team had been transferred to help hunt them down and either kill or capture as many of them as we could, disrupt their terrorist activities and make life as difficult for them as possible. We knew from briefings that the Navy had counterinsurgency teams, the Seals, denying the VC supplies by aggressively patrolling the waterways, interdicting their sampans that brought food, water and ammo. Seal units often ran recon and ambush patrols in the southern areas of the Zone, too.

Even though I had been in-country since '67, I had never actually operated in a swamp before. I didn't really want to either. During our first over-flight of the Zone, I let my imagination run wild about what a patrol would be like. Taking bits and pieces from all the old horror flicks and Tarzan movies I'd seen growing up and from the facts I'd learned from our briefings on the area, my mind created horrible scenarios. In one, I was patrolling in knee-deep swamp water beneath a triple canopy jungle and the Creature from the Black Lagoon popped up right in front of me. This was my normal reaction to a new operational area. I let my imagination go, conceiving the worst possible scenarios. Then when I had to face the reality of the situation, it was never as bad as what I'd thought up. Certainly nothing I couldn't rationalize away anyway.

The Rung Sat was to teach me a lesson, though. It was worse than anything I could ever imagine.

They moved us from our fairly comfortable quarters up at one end of the Delta to a launch site just outside of the Zone. It was humid, muddy and filthy and we lived in hootches like an A Team camp. Since the monsoons just started, all of our hootches were constantly half-filled with water. That gave us something to look forward to when we came in from patrols in the swamp. All our gear and parts of our bodies started to rot immediately.

Our first patrol in the Zone was a fine introduction. The Nung walking point went into some quick mud waist deep and we couldn't get him out. That was about an hour into the patrol. We finally had to call a slick to drop a line to the guy and airlift him out. The helicopter blew any chance we had of operating covertly so we scrubbed the patrol and pulled out before any contact was made with the enemy.

That first patrol educated me about the Zone. We had inserted by slick, then humped through the dense forest, cutting into the streams and canals from time to time. It was so hot and humid that I could barely breathe and I had to keep my sleeves rolled down and my collar buttoned. Any exposed skin was a target for the mutant mosquitoes that droned like Skyraiders when they passed close to my head. Those suckers were huge and thirsty. Then there were the leeches, big black bloodsuckers that fell off trees and slithered up my legs out of the mud and the water. It felt like I was breathing water inside the forests, where no breeze ever rippled the leaves. It rained during the entire first patrol, cutting visibility down to just a few yards, even when the foliage gave way far enough so it was possible to see further than that. With every step I took and every breath I breathed, I felt I was about to trip a boobytrap or be shot from ambush.

As if to confirm my fears, on our next patrol one of the Nungs, moving slightly on our flank, tripped a snare trap. It picked him up by his ankles and swung him into an upright bamboo frame that held sharpened bamboo stakes. He died slowly, painfully, hanging upside-down on that rack. The guy never made a sound! We kept strict noise discipline on our patrols. The Nung never broke it, except for a low grunt that he made when he hit the stakes. He didn't want to give us away to the VC. Tex inserted a syrette of morphine into his chest, just below his heart and injected it. It was an act of mercy, a last kindness to a brave man. I helped Bao pull him down and we hid the body so we could pick it up on the way out.

We found the VCs' sign, but we didn't find them. We battled the mosquitoes, burned leeches off of every conceivable part of our bodies (whenever we would find anything dry enough to light) and twisted ankles in the hidden mangrove roots. We didn't find any Cong. At the launch site, we were pretty rough to get along with, even Hardin and Randall displayed uncharacteristic bursts of temper at any REMFs who got near them. We came in late from a patrol one night and the cooks wouldn't give us a hot meal. Hardin stuck his CAR barrel in the head cook's nose and he personally fixed us whatever we wanted from then on, anytime we wanted it.

We were frothing at the mouth for a contact after nearly a month of fruitless patrols and losing another Nung to a boobytrap. The VC had left a U.S. .50 caliber ammo can in plain sight. The Nung walked over to it and opened it. A homemade claymore inside the can took most of his face off as he bent over to look inside it.

As if the swamp and the boobytraps weren't bad enough, about then we picked up a sniper. Beginning with our second month of patrolling in the Zone, an invisible killer with a crossbow began stalking us. We never saw or heard him until one of his arrows struck. He usually didn't shoot to kill either. He shot for the lower stomach, which was a painful, nasty wound, prone to infection. We found out from the medics that the arrows were dipped in dung to spread infection faster.

It became a war of nerves. We countered the crossbow by obtaining more suppressed weapons. We could return fire silently that way, possibly flank him, pin him down and then kill him. If he didn't know where the suppressing fire came from, he might not be able to evade us. None of us wanted to go back in, but none of us could admit it to the others. It would have been admitting defeat, psychologically. So, we rethought our tactics.

He hadn't killed any of us yet. His arrows had hit stomachs, hips, legs and gear and a few had even missed altogether, though not by much. The guy wasn't perfect. The first time he appeared we lost another Nung to him by an arrow in his hip. Tex took one in the thigh two days later. One hit my magazine pouches and knocked me down. His bow was powerful, at least at close range. The day he hit me, I found the position he fired from and his tracks as he moved out of the area. From then on, we split into two- or three-man groups on patrols and worked pincer patterns, trying to encircle the sniper.

The next time he fired at us, I again found where he had fired from, following the angle of the arrow back to it and then his tracks. Brick and I followed them, but he went into one of the canals and lost us. Then I thought I found his lair. It was a hootch someone had made by pulling brush together. A sheet of plastic lined the inside like a ground cloth and the brush that covered the front of it was pulled aside. I lay in cover for over an hour, Brick covering me, waiting for whomever lived there to come home, but nobody did. Finally I got up and moved toward it. Tracks led into and away from it. They were the same sandal prints I'd seen around the ambush sites. Moving back to Brick, we decided to get the rest of the team and set up an ambush.

"One of us has got to stay and stake the place out, man," I said.

He shrugged. "Go get the guys. If the cocksucker comes back, I'll take care of him," he said, patting his M60.

I got about ten yards from Brick, moving slowly and quietly, when I heard someone crunch a branch near the hootch. I moved back to Brick. He pointed toward the hootch as I crept up to him. I nodded and stopped crawling, pushing my CAR forward through the foliage I used for cover. Brick had his M60 up, too. Another branch cracked. I exhaled, took a deep breath, then held it, squinting along the sight.

A monkey broke through the foliage. I sent a five-round burst into it, blowing the monkey back into the foliage. The silenced CAR 15 hadn't made more than a loud "pop" on full auto, but if the sniper was around, I knew he'd heard.

"Fuck," I hissed. Then I heard Brick laughing quietly behind me.

"Hey asshole, it ain't that funny. I'm gonna go fuck his hootch up," I hissed, raising up from a crouching position. Pulling a frag from my pouch, I began moving toward the hootch.

"Freeze," I heard Brick hiss.

I froze.

"Back up real slow man," he called to me. From the sound of his voice, he had changed positions. He was flanking me.

"Okay, back up. You didn't touch the wire," he said.

I backed up. The sniper had boobytrapped the hootch. When I was safely in the bush beside Brick and the adrenalin had worn off a little, we lay there like two kids chuckling quietly. Whoever this guy was, he was one sharp gook. I wanted to meet him. He was taking on a whole Special Forces strike team and doing a damn good job of it. We strung a few frag boobytraps around the hootch, just in case he really did live in that dwelling and found our way back to the rest of the team.

A pattern was beginning to develop as to the way the sniper was hitting us or at least the area. Before we went in again, we plotted the areas where he had hit us on Hardin's patrol map. Then we plotted where he had led us after each strike. Randall said he had a hunch about what was going on. The sniper would pick us up shortly after we would insert, then hit us and lure us off in a specific direction. It was a different direction from the insertion point each time. While we tried to insert in different locations in an effort not to become predictable, he always kept us from patrolling one area. The sniper had given us a pattern to work with. We tried a new approach. Using three Hueys as a distraction to swoop one LZ, we came in by boat, then split into pairs. It worked. We found one of their base camps before the sniper could find us and lure us away from it.

It was just a clearing not far inland from a canal. They had built some bunkers in the tree line and a few hootches to keep their ammo dry. We rigged a demo ambush on one side, then called for the Cobras. They tore the place apart. There were plenty of secondary explosions from the bunkers. A small force of VC, perhaps fifteen of them, tried to run. We shot at them, funneling them toward the demo ambush. None of them survived our claymores. After the ambush, we stayed in place and caught a squad of VC as they came in that night to scrounge anything left after the air strike.

The Seals had been through that area not long before us and hadn't found anything there, so it was a fair bet that the VC moved their base camps frequently. The sniper kept us away from that one for weeks.

Coordinating with the Seals, we had a Navy patrol boat run up and down the canals, while three slicks swooped the LZs to confuse and distract the enemy. We inserted by rappelling down lines from two slicks that weren't swooping LZs, crashing down through the thick jungle canopy so we wouldn't be spotted on an LZ. That worked too. Spreading out on the ground, we reconnoitered an area that appeared to have some kind of small building on it, pinpointed for us by aerial photos. We found the building without making any contact. It was a small Buddhist shrine, set in a clearing that served as a hub for several trails radiating out from it like spokes on a wheel. Several of the trails were freshly cut. The Cong tied the treetops together over the new trails to shield them from aerial observation. It worked since they hadn't shown up in the photos we had been shown.

The Viet Cong, being communists, had little use for religion. In fact, their doctrine opposed religion of any sort. If a religious shrine was out in the middle of communist-dominated territory, or Indian country as we called it, it was a fair bet that the shrine was a ruse. It was left there in the open as a cache site for weapons, food or munitions. We set up an ambush around it.

I laid behind the exposed roots of a huge old baobab tree. We learned that by taking huge quantities of two water-soluble vitamins, which produced an oily film on the skin, mosquitoes wouldn't bite — not even the mutant monsters that inhabited the Rung Sat. They would still buzz around us, but they wouldn't sink their needle-like nose in our skin. I was fairly comfortable as a result of that discovery, despite the smothering, almost liquid heat of the swamp. I was more or less dry for a change, not having to wade through any water so far on that patrol and it hadn't rained that day. Due to that, there weren't any leeches on me yet, either. We were on dry land so the big bloodsuckers wouldn't be crawling on me right away. They would be there sooner or later, but they hadn't found me yet. I settled in to wait, with Brick and his M60 to my left.

After about an hour of lying quietly, I heard a low whistle from my left. Looking over at Brick, turning my eyes and head only enough to see him, I saw that he was pointing up, over my head. Rotating my head slowly back, I looked up to see what he was pointing at. Only inches from my face was the huge head of a python, its tongue flickering in and out, "tasting" me.

My mind flashed to what I knew of snakes, while my body froze into immobility. Pythons weren't poisonous I knew. Were they man-eaters? I didn't remember. This one was big enough to be if he wanted to. It was like a flashback from one of the Tarzan movies I'd been thinking about when I first saw the Zone.

We stared at each other, his head swaying slightly from side to side. I could see more of his body as it hung from the tree above me. He looked to be more than ten feet long, his body thicker than my thigh.

I laid my silenced rifle slowly aside and began moving my hand for the Randall knife that hung upside down on my web gear suspender. It hung handle-down for a faster draw, which was what I needed right then. I moved my right hand very slowly. I seemed to remember someone telling me once that snakes only struck moving targets. I wondered how fast a moving target had to be moving. Just as I popped the snap release to free my knife, the snake struck, answering my question about movement. Its huge head darted forward too fast for me to evade and it clamped its serrated teeth onto my hand like a vise.

Even though I'd managed to pop the release on my knife, I couldn't get my hand around the hilt while the snake was trying to swallow it. I took a deep breath and with my free hand tried to pry its jaws off my hand. Suddenly, the snake dropped its coils on me from the tree and began wrapping itself around my body.

It began to squeeze. It was a heavy snake. I felt like a ton of bricks had fallen on me. It coiled around my left arm, too.

Just then I heard voices and they were speaking in Viet. A grenade went off somewhere in the clearing in front of me and the roar of automatic weapons fire shattered the stillness of the swamp. The distinct popping of the AK47s, the main weapon of the VC, sounded close to me. Bullets thudded into the roots I lay behind and I couldn't even return fire. The snake and I were fighting our own war.

I began beating the snake's head on a root with my right hand as it squeezed me tighter and tighter. I couldn't draw a breath and what I had in me was being forced out. My vision was getting hazy. I heard my own ribs crack and a roar began in my ears. Lurching upward, heedless of the fire fight raging around me now, I drove my right hand down in a hammer fist strike, all of my weight behind it, bullets whip-cracking past my head, and smashed the snake's head down onto a tree root. It let go and my right hand streaked for the hilt of my knife. The snake drew its head back to strike again as I grasped the hilt. The snake lunged forward. I met it with the razor-edged Randall, cutting its head off.

Its death throes nearly killed me, but I finally untangled it from around my torso. It had crushed two of the four canteens I carried. I lay on my back, gulping air, listening to the fire fight that still raged, though with lessening intensity. It peaked and then stopped abruptly. There were a few scattered shots, then silence returned to the swamp.

Brick appeared beside me, prodding the still twitching snake with the barrel of his M60. His presence beside me meant that we had won the fire fight.

We included the snake in the body count; it was obviously VC. From then on, I carried the Randall knife in a custom-made python-skin sheath.

We didn't get the sniper, whom we nicknamed Cochise, in that ambush. He picked us up sometime before we extracted and as we loaded up on our slicks, he fired an arrow into one.

Still using indirect methods of insertion, we timed it so that we were on the ground and in position around the phony LZs when the distraction flights came in. Once, the helicopter crews slid dummies down rappelling ropes. We ambushed a small, ragged band of VC as they laid their ambush for the dummies, but we didn't see the sniper. One of the dummies had an arrow through its midsection though.

Word of Cochise's exploits began to spread among the jungle fighters. The Seals contacted us several times with reports of a bow sniper. They were hunting him with a three-man scout/sniper team, but even they hadn't been able to do the job. Hardin and one of the Seal team leaders worked out a plan of attack. Our team would come in from the north, split into two main elements and sweep south. The Seals would come in from the south and work toward us. We'd have Navy patrol gunboats and Huey gunships on call in case we ran into a VC concentration, but our main objective would be to kill the sniper. In our eyes, anything else would be a bonus. To sell the plan to our respective high commands, we presented it as a coordinated sweep of a specific sector of the Zone for the purpose of killing many gooks. They wouldn't let us spend their resources just to kill one man.

The VC relied heavily on psychological warfare both to garner popular support from the peasants and to keep the American military off balance. Their terrorism kept the line units confused and edgy. It also ensured that the government of South Vietnam would grow more and more repressive to combat the terror, fulfilling the VC's prophecies that their propaganda preached, that the regime was a dictatorship. Hell, it was bad enough without the VC's help. It was a sound ploy by the communists and one they exploited to the fullest. This sniper was becoming a symbol to them of their invincibility. After their shattering defeat in the 1968 Tet Offensive and the failure of the "Popular Revolt" their leaders had called for and predicted, the surviving VC needed such a symbol. The longer the sniper lasted, the stronger the morale of the VC in the Rung Sat became. It was our mission to shatter that myth.

We inserted by boat, split into two-man teams and began our sweep early in the afternoon. We varied our operation times so that the VC wouldn't know exactly when or where we might show up. Brick Andrews and I worked together. Moving slowly, we traversed the tangled foliage, canals and occasional clearings, keeping a careful eye out for any movement in the surrounding jungle.

I was scared. Not the same kind of fear that I was used to, a normal fear of events that I had little or no control over. No, this was the kind of fear that almost makes your body freeze up, your mind cease to function rationally and lets the "flight" part of your "fight or flight" reflex take over. Brick didn't look too happy either. The thought of an arrow dipped in shit going into some part of my body was a worse prospect than a chance of getting hit with a bullet or tripping a boobytrap had ever been. Part of it might have been that I was buying into Cochise's mythos too. I knew from experience that our team was good in the bush, but this one lone VC was doing a number on us and the Seals too. Accurate, untouchable and silent, he was a killer who spoke only to those who dared violate the Zone.

As we got further into the Zone, my attitude began to change. We had not only dared to violate the Rung Sat, we were making it our home. Our operations had lasted a little longer each time we had gone in and gradually we were becoming more and more effective against the VC who lived in it for years. We were hitting them where they lived. A sniper had hit a few of us, but we paid him back tenfold, at least. Cochise wasn't perfect. His arrows didn't always find their targets and he had missed me once. One of us would get him. If not me, then Randall or the others. We would bring superior firepower to bear on him, pin him down, close and send him to that big commune in the sky. Reassuring myself, I moved forward into the Zone, eyes sweeping every inch of swamp ahead of me. I was slightly ahead and to the right of Brick.

Climbing out of a chest-deep canal through a clump of bamboo, I thought I saw movement ahead of us. It was just a flicker through the brush. Signaling for Brick to go left, I moved right crawling until I found a depression in the mud where someone had recently lain. Small shoots of grass were just beginning to pop back up. Following the familiar sandal prints I found behind the depression, I saw Brick closing on me from my left. He pointed at something ahead of us. Still ahead and to the right of Brick, I moved deeper into the swamp. I thought I saw a flicker of movement again and I quickly stepped behind a tree. Turning to look for Brick, I couldn't find him. A sudden ball of ice formed in my stomach. Brick was reliable and really good in the bush. Whatever caused him to not be on my flank hadn't made a sound. It might have been a boobytrap, but I doubted that. I knew I had to find him, quickly.

Scanning the area around me with both my ears and eyes, I moved from cover and backtracked. Brick was down with an arrow through his heart. Only the feathered end of the arrow protruded from his shirt. He had folded back on one leg so that his body was arched upward, a look of surprise still on his face. I circled the spot where he lay, slowly, staying under cover, trying to find the sniper's sign.

I sat behind a tree and felt my eyes well up with uncontrollable tears. "Ah, fuck, Brick," I hissed. I was alone with the sniper in the middle of the swamp, far from friends or support. Now it was just me and him. There wasn't any choice to make, like trying to break off and rejoin the team. Not with Brick down right in front of me.

The Brick's M60 was lying at his side. Any VC in the swamp would want this big machine gun and a lot of the other gear Brick had on his body. If Cochise hadn't seen me yet, maybe I could lure him in to loot the body and grease him. Waiting, staying very still, I kept a watch over Brick's body for an hour. When no one showed up, I moved up to his body, covered it with a poncho, then dragged him off into the bushes so I could pick him up later for extraction.

I began searching for the sniper's tracks again. Moving from point of cover to point of cover in a dash, I paused to observe the area, trying to get the feel of it. Once I'd done that, I'd get up and dash again. Halfway to where I thought the sniper fired the arrow that killed Brick, I crawled into a thicket of thorns, pulled myself behind a fallen log and began searching for any movement around me. Suddenly, I knew Cochise was watching me. It was just a feeling, but I *knew* he was near. And watching. This time,

I pushed myself up slowly instead of jumping up from my place of cover and dashing as I had been. Something swished over my head. If I had jumped to my feet, that arrow would have taken me in the heart. I fell flat and rolled in behind a branch. Raising my CAR, I ripped through a thirty-round magazine, hosing the area where I thought the sniper fired from. Ammo wasn't a problem for me. I carried thirty-five thirty-round magazines for the CAR. Reloading quickly, I moved at a run to my left, quartering the distance where I thought the sniper was. I still felt him nearby. Taking cover again, I stopped to listen and thought I heard footsteps ahead of me. I ripped through another magazine, reloaded and moved forward at a run to a tree. Just as I stepped behind it, a second arrow whizzed by me, inches from my face.

I fired as I advanced, charging the spot where I thought the arrow came from. I'd seen it fly from a clump of foliage from the corner of my eye, just an impression more than a recognition of an arrow. I found his sandal print in the mud behind a clump of bushes.

The game began in earnest then. We circled each other, my full auto firepower against his silent, single shot. He was good in the bush and he was showing off. I figured that whoever won this duel, neither would ever have to doubt his ability to stalk and kill the best the enemy had ever again. It was a rite of passage into the fraternity of the warrior, both of us reverting to our most primitive state, intent only on hunting down and killing the other. Both of us had opportunities to break it off, go our own way, but neither of us would. I lost track of time and it grew dark.

We were close to each other. I still felt his presence, but there was no purpose to hunting him in the dark. I'd probably fall into a canal or get stuck in quick mud. So, I found a dense clump of foliage, crawled inside and went to sleep.

Before dawn broke, it started raining. I crawled out of my little hootch and crept down to a canal bank for water. Lying in the foliage right at the edge of the bank, I spotted a sandal print not five feet from me. He'd done the same thing I was doing. I eased back from the bank, found his tracks as they led away from the bank and followed them. They led to a tangle of vines. I sprayed it with my CAR. An arrow struck the ground inches to my left and from its trajectory it hadn't come from the vines. As I left the area, I walked backward in my own tracks trying to confuse him when he followed me and found a bamboo grove to hide in and wait for him. He didn't go for it, but I got my first sight of him. He looked like a Nung. Some Nungs worked for the communists for pay, but they were rare. The Nungs, as a rule, didn't care much for the communists or any Viets really.

I was beginning to wear down from the heat and the tension, the constant adrenalin pump. It wasn't enough to slow my movement or dull my reflexes, but it was a warning sign. I promised myself that the next time we went out on an extended operation like this, I would take some of the speed they doled out on the launch site. I think it was benzedrine. Just before midday, I heard a fire fight break out to my southeast. Claymores boomed and machine guns rattled. It was a pretty good fire fight. Some of the team must have swept up a VC unit while the sniper and I were playing. That also meant that the team was ahead of me and if I lost, the sniper would be behind the team when they came back through this area looking for Brick and myself.

I began to quarter his area, cutting off his running room, leaving little boobytraps for him behind me, trying to push him toward a canal. He slipped past me as I hoped, into a space I left open for him and I went into the canal myself. Using my Randall, I cut a bamboo shoot and submerged, breathing through the hollow tube. I swam underwater up into a bamboo thicket, crawled up onto the bank and waited.

He came for me. I knew he would. We had spent too much time together locked in our duet for either one of us to abandon it. It had become a personal contest, Cochise's and mine. Ideologies, governments, eastern and western, all distinctions were gone. We had been stripped to man's elemental state, that of the predator, the hunter. We felt the nobility of the ancient warrior within us. It was a transcendental feeling for me, far beyond the adrenalin rushes I'd come back to Nam for. No, this was the real thing, a high beyond narcotics, a reality totally divorced from any civilized state. I found it exhilarating.

I raised my CAR slowly as Cochise crept along the canal bank, silently, examining my boot prints. They looked like they led to a tree. When he was twenty feet away, I think he realized he had been had. Perhaps he felt me. He turned and looked into the bamboo where I was hidden and for a split second we were staring into each other's eyes. He smiled at me. I sent a three-round burst into the tip of his nose.

As the first round hit, his head jerked back. His body shuddered as the next two rounds impacted, pushing him over backward. His knees buckled and he crumpled to the ground.

I waited to see if there were any more VC around. When I detected no sign of them, I crawled out of the bamboo and approached Cochise from an angle, then knelt beside him. He wore black cotton pajamas and Ho Chi Minh sandals. A large crossbow was still clenched in his hands; a quiver with only one arrow left in it was strapped to his waist. I took the bow and the quiver.

When I got back to Brick's body, I hefted him over my shoulder and slowly worked my way to where the team was to rendezvous. Three Seals were there with our team. A few of the guys were eating C-rations. The others were cleaning their weapons and talking. It was obvious they considered the operation over.

Silence descended when I came limping in, having turned my ankle on a mangrove root crossing a canal. I laid Brick down gently and walked over to where Hardin and Randall stood, talking. Everyone was staring at me, the question unspoken but in their eyes: Did you get the sniper?

Hardin and Randall looked at me, then at the arrow in Brick's chest and the bow in my hands.

"We were getting ready to come look for you this morning when the Seals alerted us that they were in pursuit of a VC force coming our way. We ambushed them and wiped them out," Hardin said. "I'm glad you made it back."

"Thanks, cap'n. The sniper got Brick yesterday," I replied.

One of the Seals walked over. "Got him, huh?" he asked, eying the crossbow I held.

"Yeah."

Hardin put his hand on my shoulder. "Take a break, soldier,

get some chow."

When I walked over and sat beside Brick, Randall joined me, squatting beside me. I was still off in another reality.

"You've been there now, son and there ain't no going home."

I shrugged. I knew what he meant, but it didn't matter if things were never to be the same for me again. I'd been on a plane of existence I never knew existed and that was good enough for me.

We extracted by slick shortly and our team was rewarded with an R&R for cleaning up the Rung Sat.

Dane and I decided to take our R&R together. Hardin was flying to Hawaii to see his wife and kid, Randall was going to Thailand, Blake and Tex were headed for Japan. We talked it over and at first we decided on Australia. I'd been there for two weeks on my first tour and vouched for the loveliness of the women, all round-eyed, that could be found there. The prospect of speaking English to our dates, even if it was the barbarous Australian version, was inviting. Being able to eat food that didn't swing from trees before it was cooked or try to crawl off the plate while you were prodding it with your fork would be a pleasant change, too. Then Randall told us some tales about Bangkok, Thailand. The name alone, Bang-kok, drew mental images of pleasures I could only begin to imagine. Dane had been there several times over the years and was more than willing to go back.

By some miraculous exception to the Army's version of Murphy's Law, our orders were cut right away. Putting on the least ravaged pair of jungle fatigues we owned, we hopped a slick with Randall for Tan Son Nhut airbase. Arriving there, we found that the next flight we could catch would be the following morning. We would spend the night in Saigon-town.

After months in the Zone, a city was a truly welcome sight. The three of us signed in at the transit barracks, then went out for a good meal. It was the beginning of R&R, which meant rock-and-roll to me. When it was close to curfew, Dane and Randall caught a cyclo back to the barracks. I wanted to party in rowdier surroundings than Xhian's. I'd been raised in the City, its rhythms were mine. Hell, I'd lived through the '68 Tet, Saigon-town surely couldn't hurt me.

I remember hitting some bars, running into some other green hats, fighting with some MPs and racing through the darkened streets with Viet bar girls in our laps in a speeding jeep. I woke up the next morning in a hotel room, alone, naked and hung over. Seriously, horribly, head-poundingly hung over. It must have been that formaldehyde beer I drank. Groaning, I rolled onto my back and promised myself that never again would I touch Ba Mui Ba beer. I raised my arm to my face, squinting, trying to read my Seiko diver's watch.

It wasn't on my wrist. Letting out a long sigh, I heaved myself out of bed in uncoordinated, jerky motions. Searching for my clothes, I couldn't find my fatigues anywhere. Only my beret and jungle boots. Since those were all the clothes I could find, I put them on. It seemed appropriate.

About then, I remembered the plane. There wasn't time to fool around, get a uniform or anything else. I *had* to catch that plane. I was on a mission. Once my feeble mind accepted that, I was okay, no more fumbling around. The first thing was to find some kind of clothes. Hell, this was like part of the survival course in Panama. I looked out the window of the room, knowing some places hang clotheslines out the windows. Maybe someone had washed my fatigues and hung them out to dry.

No such luck. There was a clothesline outside the window, but the only thing hanging there was a woman's *ao dai*. It was purple. Well, I decided, it would cover me, more or less. I had to inch along a ledge, a narrow ledge, on the outside of the hotel and then go hand-over-hand along the clothesline out to the dress. Snaring the *ao dai,* I started back, four stories up. Looking down I saw a band of little dirty-faced Saigon street urchins staring up at my naked, white body, giggling.

Back in the room, I pulled on the *ao dai*. It was made for a Viet woman. I was 5'10", 130 pounds or so, definitely bigger in every way than the average Viet female. I got it on, but it tore in several places and the waist was cutting me in half. Designed to hang to a woman's ankles, the *ao dai* stopped just below my knees. Well, I was clothed. The next priority was transportation. Running downstairs and out the front door, I paused to look up and down the street. Just as I looked to my right, an MP jeep drove by. They spotted me, then burst out laughing. I said some very uncomplimentary things about their parents, then took off running as they both leaped out of the jeep to chase me.

I hid, they ran past me and I doubled back to the jeep. I left rubber as I headed for the airbase at Tan Son Nhut. Somewhere along the way, another MP jeep pulled in behind me. The sight of a white man wearing a purple *ao dai* and a green beret must have offended their sense of style or color coordination because they chased me all the way to the airfield.

Rounding the last turn by the hangers on two wheels, I spotted the C123 I wanted. Its props were turning. Sliding the jeep sideways to a stop, I leaped out and ran for the plane at full speed just as it started to taxi out. A hatch swung open in the side. Dane and Randall stuck their heads out. I stretched a hand for them to grab and pull me aboard.

Randall fell back out of sight laughing, but my friend, Big Dane, instead of grabbing me, focused his 35mm camera and snapped a photo.

"C'mon, asshole, gimme a hand!" I yelled as Dane nearly fell out of the hatch in a fit of laughter.

Behind me I could hear the wail of the MP sirens, growing louder.

Randall reached out and grabbed me just as the C123 started to pick up speed, pulling me in the hatch. I listened to them laugh all the way to Bangkok.

My first week in Bangkok I passed in a drunken haze. Randall stayed in town a few days, introduced me around, then skied up for parts unknown. He and Dane took me to their favorite bar in the city, a gathering place for green hats and freebooters of all sorts.

Bear's Lair was a sprawling place out towards the river that bisects the city. Decorated in cheap oriental, practically all of the furniture was made of bamboo. Dane told me it was to cut down on the breakage after a rowdy Saturday night. A rough and ready crew hung around the Lair. I spent a lot of time there, feeling right at home and was quickly adopted into the Lair's extended family.

The owner, Bear, usually stood behind his bar, towering over

it like a bronzed Colossus of Rhodes. He was six feet four inches
tall, weighing in around two hundred sixty pounds of mostly lean
muscle that stretched the fabric of the flowery print shirts he habit-
ually wore, especially when he flexed his shoulders or arms. His
dark tan was offset by a tracery of thin, white lines of scar tissue.
They covered his bronzed forearms, chest, the knuckles of both
hands and were etched around the ridges of both eyes. His red
hair was cut close, streaks of gray barely visible. When he grinned,
which was often, his blue eyes lit up, the scowl he normally wore
lightened and he gained an almost boyish look.

A huge glass case was located behind the bar. It enclosed all
sorts of military memorabilia. There were old black and white
photos of a younger Bear wearing camouflage bush fatigues and
a bush hat with one side pinned up. Other photos showed him
in the *kepi blanc* of a Legionnaire, in boxing trunks and in jeans
with a remarkably beautiful Oriental woman.

All of us who were "family" at Bear's knew his story from the
nights when he ran out all of his non-combatant customers, locked
the doors and drank all of us "young troopers" under the table.

Of Irish descent and Aussie by birth, he had boxed a bit, then
joined the Australian Army at sixteen, just in time for World War
II. By the end of the war, he had been with the Australian OSS
Strike Force Z for two years. He fought in Korea next, where he
was wounded and given a medical discharge. Bear quickly grew
bored with peace. Buying a ketch, he smuggled among the Islands
until he was caught by the French. Growing bored with prison,
too, he escaped, reaching the recruiting office of the French Foreign
Legion just ahead of a pack of gendarmes. He decided to enlist
on the spot. Arriving in Indochina a month before the fall of Dien
Bien Phu, he was one of the last of the reinforcements to be par-
achuted in. Wounded again, he was captured. He wasn't able to
escape from the Viet Minh POW camp, so he waited for repatria-
tion. The Viet Minh were hard on him and consequently he hated
them with a passion. From Indochina, he went to Algiers with the
Legion, fighting there with the 1er REP, the Legion paras, until
the mutiny.

When his enlistment expired, he returned to Indochina, a land

of enchantment for him. He married Mamma Bear, the beautiful
Eurasian woman in the photos and opened the Lair. That was in
the early sixties. Some of the old green hats, like Bull Simons and
Hardin contributed to the collection in his case. Hardin's green
hat was in it. Some of the other souvenirs included a necklace of
finger bones, jump wings with the combat star, an Ek fighting
knife and some locally-made SOG Recon Team patches.

When Dane wasn't there, I often sat alone at one end of the
bar, studying the glass case. I was neither looking for nor wanting companionship at times like that. I was mentally reliving the
Rung Sat Special Zone or the little firebase I'd been on during
the '68 Tet Offensive. I guess I had the thousand-yard glare. Other
warriors saw it and knew what it was, knowing also that I wanted
to be left alone. I had to tell some of the non-combatants, but
looking into my face when I did was usually enough. A Korean
officer didn't take it too well, but I figured he'd get over it. One
day toward the end of my R&R, I was sitting alone, eyes unfocused,
hands clenched tightly around a frosted mug of beer, when a rough
Australian voice brought me rudely back to the bar.

"Hey mate, have ye seen this?" Bear boomed at me from down
the length of the bar.

Looking up, I saw Bear shaking a newspaper he had clenched
in one huge, hairy paw. I shrugged in reply. I didn't read the news-
papers very often, other than the Pacific Stars and Stripes.

He came down the bar and spread the paper out in front of my
face. It was a Paris paper, written in French.

"I don't read French, Bear," I told him.

Slapping a hand to his forehead in mock astonishment, he barked, "A green beret what don't read French? What's the bleeding
world comin' to?"

"Leave me alone man, I'm on R&R," I growled.

He laughed, a big, booming laugh, pearly white teeth flashing
in his tanned face. Then he read the lead article to me in perfectly
accented French. I turned my back on him. He lifted me off the
stool with one hand, grabbing my collar and turning me back
around to face him.

" 'Ere, I'll translate for you. It says twenty thousand frogs,
which is Frenchies to you, gathered in Paris to protest you Yanks

killing Viet women and kids. How can you blokes kill women and kids?'' he asked, slapping his forehead again, eyes wide.

"Ya don't have to lead 'em so far,'' I growled at him, flashing back to those protesters at the airbase when I'd gone home in '68.

Bear howled in amusement. Drawing himself a beer, he raised it towards me.

"Vive le morte!" he intoned.

I knew this ritual. Raising my glass to him I replied, *"Vive le guerre!"*

Then, in unison, we barked, *"Vive le sacre Legionnaire!"*

We downed our beers and smashed the mugs on the floor.

Reaching over the bar, he gave me a rough slap on the shoulder. "Too bloody right, mate,'' he growled, then wandered off down the bar, paper still in hand and began humming some Legion marching song.

On the last day of R&R, I went to the Lair to say my goodbyes to Bear, Mamma Bear and their son, Bear Junior. A Korean officer, one I had told to leave me alone at the Lair one day, was sitting where I normally did at the end of the bar. The only open stool was the one next to him. BJ, Bear's son, was at the bar, so I told him I was leaving for Nam that day. We shook hands and he went to get Bear.

The ROK officer was drunk. He looked me up and down, then said, "You green beret?''

I smiled at him. "No sir, I'm a sergeant. This,'' I said, pointing at my beret, "is a green beret.''

He blinked several times at me. "What? What?''

"It was a joke, sir. See, we don't call ourselves green,'' I tried to explain.

"You rude, round-eye mu'fucah. First tell me to leave 'lone, now make fun of me,'' he said, getting up, and to my surprise, grabbing my shirt front.

I knocked his hand off me. We pushed each other away from the bar to where there was some clear floor. He stepped back into a fighting stance, barking at me in Korean.

This is great, I thought to myself. I'll go to jail for beating up an officer and be court-martialed. "What's your problem? It was a joke," I told him, hoping to defuse the situation.

"Round-eye mu'fucah, you coward," he said, spitting at me.

I snorted. "Okay, asshole, I'll show you a round-eye mu'fucah," I told him and squared off. Sliding my right foot forward, I launched what I thought would be a killer jab.

I saw him slip it, then a blur out of the corner of my eye and my lights went out.

I woke up propped in a chair at a table. Mamma Bear was patting my face with a cold rag. Bear was towering over me, too.

"You all right, Yank?" Bear asked.

"Wha' fu' hap'ned?" I gasped.

"Captain Sung whopped you upside the head with his boot is what. Knocked you straight out mate," Bear told me.

My right eye was swollen shut. I could barely focus out of the other one. "Bummer. Who was he?"

"Korean Marine Captain, comes in here from time to time."

I grunted. "Well, I came to tell you all *au revoir*. I'm headed back to Nam today. Thanks for everything."

I'd left Vietnam for my R&R in a dress. I landed at Tan Son Nhut in khakis, with the whole right side of my face swollen.

Hardin smiled when he saw me, shaking his head. "Glad to see you got some rest, young sergeant," he said.

Chapter Four
The Raid

The first person I saw back on the launch site was Marty Bender.

"Well, I see you had a good time on R&R," he laughed, pointing at my eye.

We shook hands. "What happened? Delta get too tame for you?" I asked. "Heard we were having too much fun without ya?"

Marty just shrugged. "I heard about Brick. He was a good soldier."

Tex walked out of a hootch, grinning at me. "Put some raw meat on that eye, son"

"Jesus. Is that what they taught you in medic's school?" I asked. "How's the leg?"

He slapped the spot where the arrow hit him, making me wince. "Like new. I'll be busting broncs again as soon as I get home."

"Well, if you get the urge before then, Marty and I'll gladly corral ya a water buff," I told him, heading for my hootch.

When the whole team reassembled, they moved us to Ban Me Thuot. From there, we were moved closer to the Cambodian border to another launch site. Unlike most other units I had been with, there was no rumor mill, no idle speculation to indulge in. We knew that when we had a need to know, our handlers would brief us on the changes. It didn't take a rocket scientist to figure out that our next TA would be in Cambodia.

I thought about that when we were in our billets back at the FOB at Ban Me Thuot. Cambodia was totally denied to us. U.S. troops were not allowed in there according to the Geneva Accords the U.S. had signed. We were also not wanted in Cambodia by the Cambodian government. The Agency, however, had both indig tribal-political groups and out-and-out mercenary units on its pay roll at FOBs inside Cambodia. Air America flew supplies to them. SOG had cross border teams working inside Cambodia too, doing both reconnaissance and raiding. Most of those units, both CIA paramilitary and SOG teams, were trying to interdict the communist

supply lines that ended in South Vietnam. That, as far as I could
determine, was a real good idea, but an ineffective strategy. It was
like trying to dam a river by throwing pebbles into a flood. If there
was really a major effort to deny Laos and Cambodia, then *that*
would have an effect on the NVA's ability to wage war in the south.
I always thought that the major effort should be to choke off the
supply line in the north at the North Viet border with Laos, but
that was my opinion. No one, Church least of all, was particularly
interested in what I thought.

But working in Cambodia would be a start, I thought. If we
were captured over there, the communists would torture us to
death. No POW status for us. They hated the Recon Teams. I
couldn't blame them either, as many of them as we killed. Stone
told me that there was a bounty on fence jumpers. The prospect
of capture was alien to me; I just didn't accept it. Like being badly
wounded, losing a limb or my nuts to a boobytrap, capture was
always a possibility, but not one I chose to dwell on. I carried
enough weaponry and ammo to be sure that I wouldn't run out
at a crucial moment and be taken that way. I'd been knocked un-
conscious by concussion and a glancing bullet wound, but I knew
my teammates would drag me off or kill me before they'd let the
gooks get hold of me. I'd do it for them.

The main reason that I wouldn't accept capture as an alternative
was that the VC had taken me in 1967. The grunt platoon I served
with had been ambushed. Our squad was cut off from the rest
of the platoon after we overran the initial ambush and the VC
closed the jaws of their real ambush on us. About half of the platoon was hit right away, pulling back, leaving us to cover them.
I was trying to cover my M60 gunner, Calucchi, while he worked
to clear a jam in his weapon. The VC were all around us. When
Calucchi saw we were surrounded and that all the GIs anywhere
near us were down, he told me to trash my rifle and raise my hands.
I did it.

The VC overran us. They bayoneted or shot the badly wounded,
beat us with rifle butts and boots, then finally hustled the survivors
into the bush. There were about ten other GIs from our platoon
at the VC base camp when they led us in. We were tied with our

elbows together behind our backs and then beaten to the ground.

I was pretty scared when they first captured us, but as soon as they began the casual beatings my fear turned to hate and contempt. When they brought us into their jungle camp, they searched us, taking our watches, lighters, anything they could steal. Then they beat us to the ground next to the other prisoners. When any of us tried to talk, one of the VC who was more or less guarding us would curse us in Viet and beat the offender with his rifle butt.

We were captured in the late afternoon. They left us tied, arms behind us, on the ground until just before dawn the next morning. Then an NVA officer came and looked us over. He pointed to a black soldier named Harris, a squad leader. Two NVA hauled him to his feet.

"Why you fight for white masters?" the officer asked Harris.

We hadn't had food or water in hours. Harris was really scared. His legs were trembling and his eyes rolled. He couldn't seem to get any words out. So the NVA officer pulled a pistol and shot him at point blank range in the chest, twice.

I tried to work up some saliva so I could talk if they hauled me up. Or to at least spit at the little gook before he killed me. He was just another street gang bully to me.

They hauled up a white GI I didn't know and this guy was ready. Before the gook officer could say anything, the GI spat in his face. The two VC beat him to the ground with their rifle butts, then the officer stopped them and barked some orders. They lifted the soldier to his knees and bent over him. The officer shot him in the back of the head.

He lectured us on the evils of capitalism, how we were fighting an imperialist aggressor's war, colonizing Vietnam for the rich elite. If any of us didn't seem to be paying enough attention, one of the VC clubbed or kicked us. When the little gook finished his song and dance, he just strolled off, wiping sweat and GI spittle off his face.

The next morning they were gone. We were left alone, tied, beaten and thirsty in the jungle. Sometime that afternoon, some GIs found us. They were from our company and were sweeping the area. We were medevaced, or flown out. After that, I promised myself that the gooks would never take me alive again. I'd go down fighting first.

Having settled that with myself, I put it away. If the time ever came where I had to make the choice, it had already been made. I didn't even have to think about it.

Dane and I ran into Stone and another green hat whom he introduced as Edwards a few days after we got to Ban Me Thuot. Both of them were filthy and still wore their tiger suits and patrol harnesses, so we figured that they had just come in from a rough patrol and were about to be debriefed. They were burned out; their eyes had the thousand-yard glare. They just nodded and mumbled as they went past us.

Two days later, we were briefed for a cross border operation. RT Steel, Stone's team, had found what looked like a temporary POW camp about five miles inside the Parrot's Beak, an area of the Cambodian border that dipped into South Vietnam. RT Steel was going back in to recon the site again and if it was still in use as a POW facility, RT Steel would serve as pathfinders for us. We would insert and raid the camp with our full team, rescue as many of the friendlies as we could and wipe the garrison.

The bulk of that briefing was delivered by an Army Intelligence officer. Just as he covered the general outline of what was going on, he paused, and Church, the CIA case officer who had run us down in the Delta, came in. The Army officer left.

"That camp is under the direct command of a Chinese major, an intelligence officer on loan to the North Viets. He specializes in interrogation and trapping small elite units. He is directly responsible for the deaths of many of the SOG operatives killed in Cambodia and for several of our paramilitary (PM) teams being trapped and wiped out. I want him, gentlemen," he told us. I thought back to what Stone had said at Xhian's about a Chinese officer setting his team up for a POW camp raid.

"There may be one or two of our PMs in there," Church went on, "and we want them out if possible. If not, they must not be interrogated. It is vital to mission success that not only are the POWs rescued, but that the Chinese officer, Major Yuen, be terminated with extreme prejudice."

"Sir?" Randall asked.

"Sergeant?"

"If we assault that camp, won't the NVA kill all their prisoners? That is their standard operating procedure."

"Work that out organically. We do not want the POWs killed if it is possible to rescue them, but it is essential that you terminate Yuen. Questions?"

There were none, so he left us alone with a stack of maps and a model reconstruction of the camp. Randall and Dane tried to find Stone, Wong, or Edwards, the third member of the team, right after the briefing, but they were already gone. We read over his debriefing report for a description of the camp, the area it was in and how many NVA might be there. We wouldn't go in until RT Steel positively identified American POWs in the camp or at least until they were sure that Yuen was there. That might take several days, but as soon as they knew POWs were in the camp, we would have to move fast. The NVA were infamous for moving their POWs around. We studied the maps, formulated a general plan of attack, cleaned our weapons, readied our gear and settled in to wait. Early the next morning, we got the word. It was a go. Loading into three black slicks, we lifted off for Cambodia.

We deployed quickly from the slicks, Stone's team offering security on the ground around the LZ. They led us on a fast march deep into the jungle, taking us to their RON and gave us a fast briefing on what they had seen inside the camp. We discussed our plan of attack, working out a coordinated plan for later that night. We wanted them to get some sleep before we moved in.

Their RON was in the ruins of an ancient Khmer temple. It filled me with awe, these ancient ruins and the jungle that was slowly reclaiming them. I wondered what my home city would look like if nature took it back from man or if nature would even want it back. Would I hear wild animals calling across Mulberry Street? Well, come to think of it, I'd already heard wild animals on Mulberry Street. Those street gang punks qualified for that.

Just before dark we moved out, taking a circular route to the camp in case we were spotted. They might think we were headed for something other than the camp. One of Stone's Nungs led us in. Finding some high ground that overlooked the camp and provided us with good cover, we moved into it. Our luck had been good to that point. We had inserted cleanly and made it to the camp without any contact. Krang, Randall, Stone and I crept down from our high ground to scout the camp, spending most of the remaining daylight watching it from different locations.

There were three bamboo cages, two of them occupied, in the compound yard. A bamboo fence had been hastily erected around the outer perimeter of the camp. The camp had been built in the cover of a stand of trees to hide it from aerial observation. Inside the fence, we counted three thatch hootches standing along one wall of the fence. There wasn't much movement in the camp during the day. We counted a total of twenty NVA both inside and out.

Crawling back to the rest of the team, we planned the raid itself. It would be fairly simple. Three of us would infiltrate the compound, release the two POWs in the bamboo cages and get them out of the camp. The rest of the team would assault the camp and kill everyone in it.

Edwards, Krang and I would infiltrate the compound. As the sun set, the three of us moved down from the high ground, where the rest of the team was concealed, to take our position. As we approached the clearing around the bamboo fence, Krang grunted us down. Moving forward, he knelt and then turned to show us the wire Edwards had almost tripped. Stepping over it, we moved on. I marked it so that the rest of the team wouldn't trip it when they followed us during their assault.

It was a cloudy night, but a full moon swam in and out from behind the clouds. Sometimes the clouds would part for several moments and the cloaking night would be ripped apart as though by a celestial spotlight. When that happened, we froze in place. Finally, we found a clump of brush that gave us cover as well as a good view of the fence we planned to breach.

The next time the moon lit up the camp, we saw movement. A man was being dragged by his arms, feet trailing in the dirt, from one of the hootches to a cage. His guards threw him inside and locked the door. Putting my lips next to Edwards' ear, I said, "Bingo."

The prisoner was probably American. The NVA never took any-one else north as prisoners. The only Americans they would have there would be troops captured nearby or airmen. Because of teams like ours, they moved their prisoners frequently and killed them when a team assaulted one of their camps for a rescue. The only chance these guys in the cages had was if we could sneak them out before the assault. I'd never done anything like this before, infiltrating a compound, but now I had to do it and I was game. I damn sure hoped someone would do it for me if the situation was reversed.

We hadn't spotted any roving patrols and there were no guard towers up. The three of us moved forward, crawling on our bellies to the fence. Krang cut an opening for us. I wriggled through first, silenced High Standard pistol thrust out in front of me. We opened a hole as close to the cages as we could. Edwards crawled through the hole behind me, staying prone, covering me as I crawled toward the cage.

The prisoner in the cage closest to me was slumped in the small cage, knees pushed up around his ears, and his head lolling for-ward. They must have really fucked the guy over, I thought as I crawled up to his cage.

"Hey man, I'm an American and I'm here to get you out," I said, shooting the lock off his cage.

Reaching in to get him, I felt his skin. He was ice cold. Pulling him forward, I checked his pulse. He was stone dead. Grunting, I pushed his body back in the cage and moved to the next one. Pausing to look around, I saw that the camp was silent.

I reached into the cage and touched the POWs ankle. This one was warm. "I'm an American. I'm here to get you out."

The silenced pistol coughed again and the cage's lock fell away to my touch. I pulled the cage door open slowly. "Can you walk?"

Suddenly the POW dove on me, screaming at the top of his lungs.

"Shut up, man! I'm an American!" I hissed in his ear as we wrestled on the ground. "Shut the fuck up!"

The guy was all over me. I tried to club him down with my pistol, but he had me wrapped up. Then he kneed me in the groin. I heard

Edwards yell something, then several Viets were shouting. Edwards opened fire over us with his rifle. I was fighting for my life, but the POW had me tied up tight, arms and legs all around me. I bit, kneed, clawed. He broke my nose with a head butt. Blood gushed down my chin.

"Cocksucker!" I snarled. "Yer dog food!"

I got one arm free, twisted his head around, head butted him so hard it stunned me, but his grip slackened. Rolling over on top of him, I slammed the butt of my pistol down on his head. Looking up, I saw Edwards stand and dash toward me, firing from the hip at an angle into the camp.

"C'mon!" he yelled.

He flew over backwards and landed in a heap near the fence. I started to rise and my head exploded. I remember falling, hitting the ground hard and then everything went black.

I woke up tied to a chair. I had no idea where I was and only a vague recollection of what had happened. My whole body was screaming "I hurt" at me. They must have worked me over while I was out. For a change, my mind was clear. Looking down, I saw that I was naked and that a wire was attached to my penis. Following the wire with my eyes, I trailed it with a kind of fascinated horror to a table where an American field phone sat. I groaned to myself. If I hurt now, it was only a warm-up. The real pain hadn't even begun yet.

Just then a tall man in American jungle fatigues walked into the room, came over to stand in front of me, then circled me so that I could no longer see him. He laid a hand on my shoulder expecting me to flinch I think. I didn't.

"I do not have time for games. How many men were in your team, what is its designation and who is your team leader?" he asked in a strangely accented voice. I didn't recognize the accent.

I tried to speak, but my lips were swollen and crusted together. Licking them, I got them to separate. As I opened my mouth to speak, there was a sudden sharp pain in my jaw, one I recognized from past experience. My jaw had been broken. Great, I thought, now when he cranks me up I won't even be able to scream.

"Tell me what I have asked you."

"Fuck you, asshole," I finally got out.

The hand on my shoulder tightened, fingers clawing into my muscle. They felt like steel pincers closing through my trapezius. Suddenly he hit the brachial plexus nerve and I screamed, and that *really* hurt. He kept squeezing until I ran out of wind.

He barked a command in Viet and an NVA officer entered the room. The man behind me spoke again and the Viet officer cranked the handle of the field phone. My world lit up.

I don't know how long that went on. When I passed out, they woke me up. They alternated the electroshocks with squeezing pressure points and occasionally old fashioned beatings. They changed shifts on me once. One NVA NCO kept stepping on my feet, grinding his heel on my bare toes. After an electroshock, they could beat me all they wanted. I was numb. Another one burned my chest hairs and skin with a zippo lighter. I could handle that a lot better than when one of the goofy bastards decided I needed recharging and gave the field phone a good crank. I hallucinated for a while, thinking it was my old man beating on me. Then it was the street gang punks.

Finally the guy in fatigues called it off. They dragged me outside to the cage I'd been trying to pull the POW out of and locked me in it. Karma, I told myself. I probably deserve this for beating up and shooting those gangbangers the day before. Then I realized I was hallucinating again. Just what I needed.

"You," a voice called. I knew the voice. It was outside of the pain, so it wasn't part of the hallucination. It must be that street gang punk who made me feel like this.

Focusing on the source of the voice, I saw it was the gook in the OD fatigues. Big fucker, I thought. I didn't remember the gangbanger being a gook. Whattafuck, over? I asked myself. Then, just for general principle, knowing that this gook had something to do with the pain I felt, I spat at him, but it didn't clear my lips. It just rolled down my chin.

"You are strong, you did well under the torture. But you *will* tell me where your team is. Save yourself further pain. They ran away and left you. Tell me how many they are, what they are called so that I may punish them for leaving you," the gook said.

"Yer momma," I croaked, but I felt better. The gook had just told me that I hadn't broken, yet.

I'd noticed the gook had a big lump on his face. As he left, I saw that his fatigues were muddy. He'd been the POW in the cage. I felt even worse. I'd been suckered. After Stone's team spotted this place, they must have been seen themselves and this Chinese clown waited for the next team to come in for a rescue. It was a sweet setup and it worked. They didn't get the team, but they had me and Edwards. A cold rage swept through me. Church set us up for this. He knew there weren't any PMs in this camp, only the Chinese officer. He knew that if some of us were captured, Yuen would hang around, waiting for another rescue attempt so he could bag some more green beanies.

The gook stood and watched all of that run across my face. He smiled at me.

"Your pain has only begun," he told me and left.

I worked on my bonds, but my arms and legs were numb from the contorted position I had been forced to assume in the cage. My elbows were pulled together behind my back. I found that by rolling my shoulders and flexing my arms I could restore some of the circulation, as painful as that was. I'd need both arms and legs to escape, which was foremost in my mind.

After about half a day, judging from the position of the sun, an NVA soldier cut my arms free. He opened the cage and dragged me out, throwing me to the ground, then kicked me around until I stood. As soon as I was on my feet, he beat me to the ground with his fists. Looking around as he screamed at me, I saw that he was alone. I downed him with a leg scissor kick as he tried to kick me again and rolled on top of him, hitting him with an elbow as I landed on him. I went incoherent and beat the guy with my fists, elbows, anything I could think to hit him with. When I stopped, I couldn't see his face. It was just a mask of blood. I had killed him. I stripped his belt from around his waist. A holstered pistol and a bayonet were on it, but he didn't have a rifle with him.

I crawled out of the hole in the fence Krang had cut for us. They hadn't bothered to patch it yet. Feeling something sticky on my back, I rolled over and looked up. Edwards' dead, mutilated body was hanging from the fence. They had cut on him. His intestines were hanging down. I had crawled through them. It was a challenge to the team. Come back and I'll do it to you.

My mind snapped. The thin veneer of civilization that normally kept me on an even keel left. At that moment, all I wanted was to kill gooks, as many as I could before they killed me. I crawled along the fence toward the front of the camp and had almost reached it when Randall grabbed my ankle. I spun on him, the little Russian pistol I had drawn from the belt's holster in my hand. Before I could turn all the way to him, he tackled me, putting a hand over my mouth.

"Let's go," he hissed in my ear.

"Kill," I croaked back at him, nodding toward the camp.

When he looked at my face, he winced. I must have looked pretty fucked up. "The team's about to hit the camp, let's go," he insisted.

I pushed him off me. "Kill!" I growled, pushing myself to my knees, then crawling for the front of the fence.

Randall followed me.

At the front gate, I peeked around the corner of the fence, but no sentries were in sight. I stood and turned the corner into the camp. An NVA soldier lounged in the shade of the fence. I walked right up to him, stuck the little pistol in his eye and dropped its hammer. Taking his rifle, I staggered into the compound. The man I shot had been the NCO with the foot fetish.

One of the officers, the one who cranked me up the first time, and an NCO were coming out of the nearest hootch to me, talking to each other. When he saw me, the NCO made a grab for his rifle. I blew both of them off their feet with a long burst from the AK. Bullets cracked past my right ear and I pivoted right, but Randall was covering me. He cut down two more NVA.

Suddenly two of the hootches blew up, showering me with debris. Randall tackled me and threw me to the ground. A heavy fire fight was raging around us. I kept trying to get up.

"Lay chilly, goddammit!" Randall screamed in my ear and I relaxed beneath him.

The fire fight was over fast. Nungs in tiger suits walked the camp shooting NVA corpses. I got up slowly when Hardin came over to us, extending his hand to help me. My adrenalin rush was gone and I felt weak and sick.

"Where's Krang?" I croaked through my broken jaw.

"Sit down," Hardin said.

"No, fuck that. There's a big gook here somewhere. I gotta have his ear."

"He's *dinky dau,* crazy in the head, cap'n," Randall said to Hardin.

I guess Hardin thought I was really out of it. I can imagine what I looked like right then, all bruised, burned, naked and generally fucked up.

"We've got slicks in-bound. We'll have you out of here ASAP," Hardin told me as Dane walked up.

I turned on the three of them, the AK still in my hands, and waved the barrel at them, but my eyes weren't focusing right. "Get Krang over here," I told Randall.

He turned and yelled to the Nungs in their dialect. Krang showed up a minute or two later.

"No Chinese among dead, *dai uy.* Chan see big man in fatigues run north," Krang reported. "You want?"

I staggered over to Krang, toppled forward, then caught myself. "Was he big, tall?" I asked.

He couldn't understand me with my jaw fucked up, so Randall asked him for me. Krang nodded and rattled off something in his dialect.

"Yeah, was that Yuen?" Randall asked me.

I nodded, looking north. If I'd been able to walk, I'd have taken off north right then.

Before the slicks arrived, Stone and his team came in. Two of his Nungs carried a body between them, a tall man in OD fatigues. Stone trotted up to me. "You gonna make it, dude?"

I grunted. "Is that Yuen?"

Stone grinned at me. "You ID him."

The Nungs threw the body on the ground. They had riddled him. I kicked his body over and looked closely at his face. Turning to

Stone, I nodded. Stone pulled a camera from out of his pack and snapped a picture of Yuen's face.

"For ID. Church'll want double proof," he said, putting the camera away.

"When you got hit inside the camp, we pulled back," Hardin told me. "Krang got back to us and told us what happened, but we didn't know if you were alive or not. Stone took his team north to block Yuen if he tried to make a run for it. We called slicks in and faked an extraction, then we came back for you."

I sat and stared at the dead Chinese officer.

"We let him run right into our ambush," Stone said, then he kicked Yuen's dead body. "For Cisco, you Chinese cocksucker."

"You knew this was a setup, didn't you?" I asked Stone.

He looked up slowly. "Yeah."

"You let me and Edwards walk right into it?" I asked, not fully believing it even as Stone confirmed it.

"Church ordered this."

I looked at Hardin and Randall. Dane stood off to one side, his neck swelling up and face coloring with anger.

"They didn't know about it, it's on me," Stone told me. "Everyone thought it was a legit raid to save some Agency POWs. Church briefed me separately. He knew there were no POWs in camp, that the whole camp was a ruse to lure a rescue team in. It was the only way we could be sure that Yuen stayed in place until we could kill him."

We all stared at the dead man.

"Look, I didn't mean for this to happen to you man. Church lied to me, too. I lost one of my own, man, and I gotta live with it if that means anything to ya."

Dane took a step forward and knocked Stone off his feet. Hardin grabbed Dane, pulling him away.

Stone sat up, rubbing his jaw, then climbed to his feet. "I had that coming. You all right?" he asked me.

I nodded. "I'll live."

Stone looked down at Yuen again. "I owe you one."

"Fuckin' aye you do." My energy reserves had finally given way. I stretched out until the slicks came.

Hardin came to see me in the hospital first. "How are you?" he asked.

I shrugged. "I'll be back as soon as the shrinks say I'm sane enough to rejoin a recon team."

Hardin smiled. "Sane enough to rejoin a recon team? Well. The rest of the team sends their regards. They'll be down as soon as they can."

They kept me in the hospital a month, three weeks for my physical recovery and a week further for evaluation. I was healed physically, other than a few bruises and cuts. Some goofy officer came in and pinned several medals on me, both for the last mission and others that were past due. I took them off and sent them, along with the presentation orders, to my father. Maybe he'd be impressed, but I wasn't.

I was in an emotional vacuum. I felt betrayed by people I thought were trustworthy. I felt betrayed not by my team, but by the structure. After I thought about it, I decided I could trust my team to look out for me, regardless of who ran us. They had saved my ass at the camp. Together, we could survive and possibly even conquer.

Once I worked it out for myself, I told the shrinks I was okay, which was basically all they wanted to hear, and they sent me back to the team.

The guys weren't sure how to take me when I showed up. I didn't talk much and when I did it was only in response to direct questions. To break the ice they threw me a party at a bar downtown. Dane filled me in on the two patrols they had been on while I was away. Both had been easy ones, with little or no contact. I grunted in reply. Probably the only easy patrols the team would ever have and I missed them both. Is that karma, or what?

Hardin and Randall took me for a walk the next morning. They wanted to know how I felt about them, Church and things in general before they let me have a rifle again. I couldn't blame them. If the situation was reversed, I'd damn sure want to know if there was a nut on my team. They began with a short patriotic speech, how I was fighting for a noble cause, for mom and apple pie.

"Cap'n, sarge, let me save you some wind," I said, cutting into the speech. "I asked to come back to *this* team. What happened is over. I learned a lesson and I'll leave it like that so long as we aren't used like that again. Hell, all they had to do was to ask. I might've agreed to be bait in a trap. I don't like it, cap'n, but it won't affect my performance."

The three of us stared at each other a moment, Hardin and I making eye contact. Then the two long-time vets exchanged a glance between them and Hardin stuck out his hand.

"I'm glad you are back, sergeant," he said as we shook hands.

Randall grinned at me and the ceremony was over.

Later that morning we were put on alert to act as a reaction force for another team that had stepped in it across the border. We loaded up all the ammo we could carry, drew our weapons, cleaned them, then sat around waiting. We didn't know whose team it was that needed us. It didn't matter. Green hats needed help. That was all we needed to know.

Orders finally came for us to go. We had a quick briefing from Hardin. An RT, a Special Forces team, was trapped at their extraction point in a valley by an unknown NVA force. Air assets were on station, but ran out of ammo and fuel, so they needed to rearm. The fly boys had been able to keep the NVA off the RT, but the slicks could not get in close enough to pick them up because of ground fire. Our reaction force would land behind the enemy force in a second valley, ascend the high ground and take the enemy force under fire. A squad would break through the enemy lines and link with the RT, supporting them with our added weaponry and ammo.

The reaction force was made up of all the RTs who were on the FOB, and whoever else was not doing anything. A green hat who was on courier duty from Nha Trang was there when the call came, so he grabbed an M16 and a bandoleer of ammo too. When a call came for a reaction force, everyone grabbed an M16. We were all looking around at each other. All of us had been on hot LZs before, unable to extract with the NVA trying to overrun us. We had all needed help. I could see the guys' faces tightening as they thought back to those moments, when a bunch of green hats and Nungs came to help them, and how bad the situation had looked before the reaction force had gotten there. Then we boarded the slicks.

As soon as I got in the slick, my mouth went dry immediately. I clenched my jaw subconsciously and only became aware of it when I felt a sudden stab of pain from where the break had been. Leaning back in the slick as it took us toward a fire fight somewhere in Cambodia, I tried to relax, but that was futile. I noticed Randall and Dane kept glancing at me. The next time I caught Dane looking at me, I flipped him the finger. He flipped one back, grinning. No one else paid me any attention. They had their own demons to deal with.

Then it was lock and load time. The door gunner began firing and when we didn't take any return fire, the slicks went in. I was diving out the door, then lying prone on the ground. Our team was the first one in. We moved out and secured a perimeter as the rest of the slicks came in and unloaded. Hardin was the only officer present, so he was in charge of the reaction force. When all of the teams were on the ground he moved us out, our team on point. We moved almost at a run along the floor of a river valley near the Srepok River. Turning, we moved on line up a ridge, more carefully now. If the NVA were trying to lure another team in and hit us with a counterambush, the ridge was a good place for it. Hardin moved half of our team ahead to recon the area. We heard a major fire fight on the opposite side of the ridge. Smoke drifted up above the top of the ridge in columns, like dark pillars, from the napalm and rockets the fly boys had dumped on the NVA.

Cresting the ridge, we swept it. The NVA were below us to our left. We could see them moving in the trees, see their muzzle flashes. The RT was holed up in a small clearing with their backs against a river. The NVA must have cornered them there. There was nowhere to run. NVA dead were scattered all around the RT's position. The NVA had tried to overrun the RT and paid a heavy price from the way it looked.

Randall sent a Nung to bring up the rest of the reaction force. I spotted what looked like a route down to the RT and pointed it out to Randall, who briefed Hardin when he came up.

Hardin studied the situation quickly while Blake made contact with the RT below us on his PRC 25. The other RT leaders, all NCOs, gathered around Hardin when he talked to the besieged RT leader.

"They need ammo, whatever we can send. And there's a heavy machine gun over there," Hardin said, pointing to our left. "They would like us to do something about that too."

I grinned. No doubt they would like us to do something about it. I could see its muzzle blast when it fired. While all the team leaders and Randall made their plans, I made a few of my own.

"Hammer," Randall called.

I joined their group.

"You and Tex take six Nungs down that route you showed me and reinforce the RT. Take all the spare ammo you can carry and at least one '60. We'll cover you," Randall briefed me.

"Sarge, let me have two LAWs and I'll get that MG for you on the way."

I quickly outlined my plan.

"Okay, go with it," Hardin said.

I took Tex, Bao, Lin and four other Nungs from our team. Bao and I each bummed a LAW, a Light Anti-tank Weapon, while the others took extra 5.56mm magazine bandoleers or belts for the RT's M60. Briefing them on the move, we pulled back from the crest and followed the ridge line northeast toward the river. The ground sloped gradually upward.

When we had climbed to a high point near the river, we crawled where the ridge curved in toward the RT, then moved to the crest, finding cover behind some loose rocks. I dug my field glasses out, finding the gook's heavy MG through them. We were at a better angle now to hit it than we had been with the reaction force. I could see the gun crew as they fired their MG.

Letting Bao spot the gun through the glasses, I told him to hit it with the LAW. He grinned, opened the firing tube and sighted in. Tex took the rest of the patrol down the back of the ridge. When we fired, they would make a dash across some open ground, under enemy fire, to the RT. Giving Tex time to get in place, I opened the second LAW tube and laid it beside me.

I gave the signal to fire and Bao let it rip. Watching the gun through my glasses, I saw the rocket impact beside the gun, blowing it over and killing the crew. Letting Bao look through the glasses, I watched Tex and his squad run, firing from the hip, to the RT.

"Look, they set up gun," Bao said.

"My turn," I told him, shouldering the second LAW.

I zeroed in. I couldn't see the gun because of the smoke from the first rocket's impact. Peeping through the flipped-up sights, I waited. Then I saw two NVA with the gun and carriage. I drew a bead and pressed the switch. The two NVA were obscured by the explosion.

"Hit gun!" Bao yelled, grinning so widely I thought his face might break in half.

He passed the glasses back to me so I could take a look. I'd hit the gun all right. Putting the glasses away, we smashed the empty LAW tubes and moved down the ridge. Bao and I took a longer route than Tex had, moving below the bank of the river until we were behind the RT. Alerting them that we were coming in so they wouldn't shoot us, we crawled up to their perimeter.

As we crept down the river bank, we heard the reaction force hit the NVA, hard. They were sweeping down off the ridge line with covering fire from above, rolling the NVA's flanks up out of the tree line. The RT, with the ammo Tex brought them, were taking their other flank under fire.

Suddenly, a large NVA force burst out of the tree line, charging the RT. I'd just crawled in beside Tex when they came at us, screaming and firing. We were on one end of the RT's perimeter, closest to the ridge. The RT's green hats were at the other end of the line, both of them wounded but still firing. I rolled a few feet away from Tex, behind a clump of dirt that gave me a little cover and opened fire with my CAR.

Swept by fire from the ridge, from part of the tree line where the reaction force had secured positions on their flank and the RT in front of them, the assault wave was hit hard. It was a desperate maneuver on their part. They must have really wanted to inflict damage on the RT to charge them like that, knowing there were more of us all around them. They managed to overrun the far end of our perimeter. The RT were all wounded. Some of them were hit again and went into shock or were killed. I saw one of the green hats stand, fighting hand-to-hand with two NVA.

I sprinted across the clearing to fill the gap in the perimeter, firing from the hip as I ran. Bao sprang up behind me and was following. Bullets cracked past us. I ran at an NVA soldier who was trying to bayonet a prone Nung, firing, putting a five-round burst into him. As another NVA ran at me, we fired at the same instant. I shot straighter. He staggered and I hit him with another three-round burst. Someone hooked an arm around my throat from behind. I dropped to one knee and bent forward. An NVA soldier fell over my shoulder. Before I could kill him, I looked up and saw another one coming at me. I fired, my CAR barrel almost touching his stomach when I pulled the trigger, emptying the magazine into him.

The guy on the ground rolled over and leaped for me. I took him over backwards, rolling under him, my right boot in his stomach, a throw I'd learned in judo as a kid. As he hurtled over me, I jerked down with my arms so that he landed face first. Doing a back roll, I landed on top of him, drew my knife and stabbed him in the throat. I quickly reloaded the CAR, looking for targets.

It was over. A few NVA were running around, trying to figure out which way to go, but the assault had been wiped out. I sank down to my knees, suddenly very tired, my CAR held in a ready position just in case. I was a few feet behind the RT's perimeter line where I'd first encountered the NVA who had broken through. One of the two RT green hats was in front of me. As I watched, he rolled over and sat up, pushing two NVA corpses off him. He was the one I had seen in hand-to-hand combat. Turning, he looked around at the rest of his team.

It was Stone.

I slowly raised my CAR. Glancing around, I saw that most of the Nungs were busy searching or looting dead NVA. Tex was patching wounds. Then I saw someone move behind Stone, a body in the grass. I snapped the CAR up to my shoulder.

Stone saw the sudden movement I'd made out of the corner of his eye and spun toward me, the pistol in his hand coming up.

He saw me, recognized me, and I fired at roughly the same time. Behind him a wounded NVA shuddered and dropped the AK he had been raising as my three-round burst hit him.

When Stone realized that I'd been firing at something behind him and not at him, he turned to see who it had been. The NVA was off to one side of him, but the rounds had come close. Lowering his pistol, he turned to face me. My CAR was pointing at his face. He just stood and looked at me. After a brief moment of staring at each other, I jerked the barrel of the CAR up. Stone walked over and squatted down beside me, wiping his hand over his face. We looked at the carnage around us. The reaction force was moving in to the RT from the ridge and the tree line. We could hear inbound slicks.

The two of us sat side by side until Randall and Hardin came.

When we were back at Ban Me Thuot, Tex waited until no one else was around, then sidled up to me while I was sharpening my knife.

"You were gonna grease Stone, weren't ya?" he asked.

I didn't say anything. How could I answer that? Americans, or green hats anyway didn't off each other. Ever.

"I figure you had a right to, if anyone ever did. Why didn't ya, hoss?" Tex persisted.

I put my knife down. "He lived through that fire fight, man. It didn't seem like it was up to me to grease him."

That was the last that was said about it. I saw Stone several times after that and once we even went out drinking together. War was a bitch, but we had asked for it, so we took the cards we were dealt and played them.

PART TWO: Command and Control North

Chapter Five

Laos

We were moved to Da Nang without any warning a few days after the rescue mission. The SOG compound there was much better, with more modern, drier billets. One end of the compound ran out onto a beach that overlooked the South China Sea. We all assumed that Church wanted the team and me in particular out of his face, so we were sent north. No one on the team seemed to mind, though. All of the green hats had done part or all of one of their earlier tours in the I Corps area. The second day, an Army Intelligence officer gave us an orientation briefing, handing out maps of our projected TA. It was the border region of South Vietnam and Laos, but the maps covered a good deal more of Laos than just the border.

According to the situation briefings, the bulk of men and materiel that moved south along the Ho Chi Minh Trail came out of the southern region of North Vietnam and passed through the Aideo Pass in Laos before it dispersed into the many infiltration routes that made up the Trail. Highway Nine, which ran through the Khe Sanh area, also cut through that pass as the highway wound its way into Laos. The NVA could use trucks on much of the drive. Further south, the Trail cut the Se Kong River in two places, one branch of the Trail angling east toward Da Nang, cutting through the Ashau Valley. Our operations were to interdict movement along the Trail and gather intelligence on the NVA's movement into South Vietnam.

The topographical maps showed southern Laos, our projected TA, to be an area of heavy forests and rugged hills. Mountains which reached up through the jungle paralleled the border. West of the mountains were large, open plains. It didn't look promising as a TA as far as marching went. The high ground was difficult to move through at the best of times. For us, it meant that the NVA would be confined to the valleys and we'd know where to find them.

Our first mission came a few days later. The 101st Airborne were catching hell in the Ashau Valley and they wanted an assessment of who and what they were facing. Our team would go in at full strength and recon the known infiltration route into the Ashau area from the Laotian side of the border. Specifically, we were to guide air assets to any targets of opportunity we found. If nothing big enough for an air strike came along, we were to stay in place for five days, keep our FOB informed of what we saw and then rig an ambush along the route as we exfiltrated the area. The last RT who went into that area, code named Charles Seven, was shot off the LZ. The NVA had LZ watchers all through the Charles Seven grid. We planned our insertion based on our experiences in the south, using distraction slicks, and got ready for the operation. Early the following morning, loading up on all black slicks at a launch site near the border, we went in.

Our slicks were escorted in by black gunships. They all flew close to the ground, tossing us around as though we were on a roller coaster. I wedged myself against the rear bulkhead, using the heels of my boots to keep me in place. Bao sat on one side of me, Lin on the other. Tex was on the far side of Bao, in the door.

Randall held up a magazine, slapped it on the heel of his hand to make sure all the rounds were seated right, then inserted it in the magazine well of his K gun. As he locked and loaded, the rest of us followed suit. Adrenalin hit me with a rush. I felt my pupils dilate, energy surge through me.

The slick swooped in sideways, skidding in the air, and Tex went out the door. We were only a few feet from the ground. Lin went out the opposite door. I was just about to leap to the ground when Tex blew up. His body cartwheeled in the air right in front of me. The concussion threw me back into the slick as the ship rocked violently. Shrapnel hit my legs, setting them on fire with pain.

Bao tumbled halfway out the slick, then caught himself. Crawling to him, I grabbed his web gear and pulled him back inside. The door gunner was slumped in his harness. Looking down at the LZ as the pilot pulled up the slick, I saw Tex writhing on the ground, most of one leg gone and what was left only a bloody wreck. Lin was kneeling beside Tex, weapon raised, looking up at me, afraid to move.

The gooks had mined the LZ.

I heard Randall screaming at the right seater, the command pilot, telling him to take us back down so we could lower a line to our men who were on the ground. Small arms fire began crackling below us, some of it hitting the ship. I pulled the door gunner, who was only stunned from the concussion of the mine, out of the way and took over his M60. As I opened fire with it, everyone in the slick aimed their weapons at the tree line below and cut loose.

The pilot screamed something at Randall and in reply, Randall pushed the barrel of his K into the pilot's neck. Below me, I saw Lin go down, his body twitching as he took repeated hits from small arms fire. Then our slick pulled up and away.

As it did, one of the escorting gunships dove on the LZ. Rockets and miniguns blazed. I watched as Tex and Lin vanished in the explosions. That was our introduction to Laos.

Dane came to see me in the hospital. I had shrapnel all through my legs. They picked the bigger chunks out, but left a few of the slivers in. I could feel them buried in my flesh.

"How you feeling?" he asked.

"Better than Tex," I said.

We both sat silently for a few minutes, neither of us looking at the other.

"Listen man, we couldn't get him out. That was SOP, not to leave anyone or anything for the NVA. We can't leave our people for the gooks, man," he said.

I deflated a little. "I know man, I know. It's just..."

"Yeah. There it is, man, there it is."

When I rejoined the team, there was already a replacement for Tex on the compound. He had been with the Army's Riverine Force in the Delta as a lurp. When they sent the Riverine Force home, he volunteered for the SF Recondo school at Nha Trang so he could stay in Nam. It turned out that he had been in the Rung Sat before we worked the area. When he graduated from the Recondo school, he went to the 5th Group and then to SOG. He wasn't a real green beret, but he was the next best thing for Nam. He had combat experience with a small unit and he liked it. Just what we needed.

When I first met him, I was putting my gear away in the hootch. He strolled in and introduced himself.

"Hey dude, what's happening?" he said.

Most of the GIs I'd met in Nam seemed to communicate in clichés. They were unique at that time to the war's arena, although some of them could be heard wherever GIs who left Nam were stationed. I fell right into that mode of speech on my first tour, but it began to wear thin and by the middle of my second tour, I avoided all but the most appropriate cliches for a situation. The favorite, and most often used word in the GI vocabulary, was fuck. I'd heard it so often, I just knew that one day I'd read it in a training manual. "Take the fucking claymore..." Not too many of the older green hats talked in the cliches, so when I heard what sounded like a California surfer accent in a SOG compound, I immediately thought an REMF had wandered into the area.

"Who the fuck are you?" I growled, turning to look at him.

"I'm, like, a replacement, dude. Name's Billy, but they call me The Kid," he said, holding out his hand.

He was tall and thin with longish blond hair and a bushy mustache. A pair of round, blue tinted glasses were perched on his sunburnt nose. He wore a pair of jungle fatigue pants cut off just below the thigh pockets and a flowery print Hawaiian shirt. A hippy in SOG.

I grinned and shook his hand. "Have you met Sergeant Randall yet?"

The Kid was twenty years old, an insane surfer from Venice Beach, California. He wired a track commander's helmet up to a huge Japanese eight-track tape player and at night he would take his tapes, a bottle of wine, a bag of weed and his helmet out to the beach and party by himself, sharpening a huge Bowie knife as he sat alone.

Our next attempt to infiltrate the Charles Seven area met with more success. The flight of slicks we used coordinated with an A1 Skyraider just after we locked and loaded. The pucker factor was extremely high. I still saw Tex's body flying upward past

me as I stood in the door of the slick. I could barely breathe for
the adrenalin pumping through me. The look on Lin's face as he
knelt on the ground beside Tex, staring up at us waiting to die
was still with me, too.

The Skyraider dove ahead of us and dropped a 750 pound bomb.
It blew an instant LZ. The lead slick, Hardin's this time, flew in
sideways and his half of the patrol unassed, moving out of it. Ours
slid in behind it as the escorting guns circled above. We cleared
the slick in seconds and hit the ground, spreading out.
When no one fired at us, we regrouped and headed for the bush.

Randall told me to keep an eye on Billy, so I stayed close to him.

We worked in the Annamese Cordillera, a range of mountains
that marched through Laos, Cambodia and both Vietnams. Our
team spread out in single file as we humped the hills, steadily climbing. It was rough country; a pair of jungle boots lasted only one
patrol. Fatigues were shredded. Sometimes we couldn't see the sun
at all when we moved into dense forest, but then we would break
out on the side of a ridge and nearly run to make better time.

When we reached the area we had chosen for our field CP, we
hadn't seen any signs of the NVA at all, which meant that they
didn't patrol the high grounds too often. They moved through
the valleys and left the ridges and hills to the H'Mong Montagnard
tribes who lived throughout the Laotian mountains. We settled
in to wait and watch. Bender checked in with our electronics relay,
some huge Air Force electronic intelligence plane flying high above
us. When we had a target for air assets or needed an extraction,
the plane would relay our request and guide a FAC and fast movers
to us. From our vantage point, we could see several trails that
wound through the jungle below us into the hills. We were facing
east so that the NVA moving into South Vietnam along those routes
and into the Ashau Valley area would have to pass right by us.

By evening, we hadn't seen anything so Randall, Dane, three
Nungs and I crept down from the CP closer to one of the larger
trails and established a listening post (LP). Somewhere around mid-
night, a large group of NVA moved through and we followed them
to their RON. They set it up not a mile from the border. One of
the Nungs carried a PRC 25. He and Randall called the sighting

in to the team, who sent out the contact report to the relay. A few minutes later, we were told to guide an air strike in on the NVA in the morning.

As we waited for dawn, we heard a low growling coming up the trail.

"Trucks," Randall said.

I recognized them too. They were a dull drone in the distance. We called that in, too. Our orders were amended to hit the trucks when they caught up with the NVA unit and if possible snatch one of the truck drivers. We thought we could probably do that under the cover of the air strike.

Billy, Krang and two other Nungs found us a half-hour later, just as the trucks were coming up the trail to the NVA unit's RON. They were loaded with supplies of some kind. Dane produced a camera and began snapping photos of them.

"Air is due on station in oh-five," Randall said, rejoining us.

Five minutes later, we heard the drone of an OV-1 FAC and Randall talked him in. He had four F4 Phantoms on station with napalm and 500 pound bombs. We decided that would make a fine wake-up call for the NVA, who were just beginning to stir in their RON. They were taking their time saddling up. The FAC guided the fast movers onto the target.

One moment it was fairly quiet in the dense forest, a few early morning birds were chirping, and the next moment two Phantoms were diving out of the sun. I sat behind a tree overlooking the RON where the NVA were, watching their reaction when the jets dove on them. A few tried to run, others turned their faces upward and then the jets dumped their ordnance on the NVA position. Napalm swept through the soldiers, incinerating them, men, clothing and equipment. Within seconds, the lush jungle where the NVA camped was turned into an inferno as the second pair of Phantoms dove in on them, dropping more canisters of the jellied gasoline. Then the first pair came back for another run, dropping bombs and strafing.

"Let's go," Randall yelled and we swept down on the trucks. The drivers pulled off the trail when the air strike began, leaping out of their trucks and running for cover in the forest. Billy and I ran after one of them while Randall and Dane began booby-trapping the trucks. The Nungs covered the demolition party. We followed the fleeing NVA driver by the path he left through the foliage. I hadn't seen him carrying any weapons so we ran after him at full speed. The path led us toward a cliff.

"There, to the left, man," Billy panted, pointing.

I saw the man as he broke from the tree line and tried to scramble up a rock face. Putting out all the speed I had, I caught his ankle just as he heaved himself up onto a small plateau and dragged him down to me. He was fighting with everything he had, but it wasn't much. Obviously the guy wasn't one of the hard core NVA because he couldn't fight worth a damn. I hit him in the forehead with a palm heel thrust and knocked him cold.

"Hey, dude, I caught him. You carry him," I told Billy.

We rendezvoused with the team at the field CP. Billy dropped the tied NVA driver at Hardin's feet, grinning like he had done a fine job. Bender looked down at him.

"Kinda small to keep, ain't he?" he asked.

"Fuck that, just call the slicks," I said.

We pulled back to our extraction point and were lifted out without contact.

Three days later, we ran another operation in the same TA. Inserting from a small launch site near the border run by an A Team whose only purpose was as a covert operation's launch site, we flew in behind an air strike that another RT had called in. Staying off the trails and the ridge crests, we managed to make pretty good pace. Our TA had been seriously bombed and napalmed. The craters formed small ponds or lakes where more bombs had fallen, making one huge pockmark on the face of Mother Earth.

Where it hadn't been bombed and burned, Laos was beautiful. Lush tropical foliage thinned to forest as we climbed. Black, ancient granite mountains thrust their peaks skyward through the forests. A variety of colorful, exotic birds lived in the trees, flapping their wings and squawking at us as we moved through the forest below them.

Command and Control North (CCN), our control in Da Nang,

wanted an NVA officer to talk to. Several RTs were on the ground trying to capture one. We were a field control team. Our job was to relay any intelligence that the other, smaller teams uncovered and coordinate their extractions. Bender had a PRC 77 transmitter for the occasion.

Hardin and half the team, with Marty carrying the big burst transmitter, moved to the high ground for better reception and established a field CP. Randall and the other half of the team, including me, reconnoitered the area, hoping to find an NVA unit on the move. We didn't, so Bao and I went hunting along the trails ourselves, armed with suppressed weapons.

Sneaking through the forest, looking for signs that the NVA moved through the area, we found what must have been a RON for a small unit. It hadn't been used recently. A network of small trails led off of a larger, more frequently used trail that ran north and south, so we paralleled the main route, checking along the side trails, too. I liked working in Laos, in the forest like that. There weren't any judgment calls, no civilians to get in the line of fire. Anyone we saw was the enemy.

Just before dark, we rendezvoused with Randall and the others. They hadn't had any luck either. Moving to a RON Randall found, we fell asleep, taking shifts on guard. Around zero-dark-thirty someone shook my foot and I came instantly awake.

NVA were moving into our RON. Krang spoke to them and after an instant of clanking bolts and scuffling boots, when we all thought we would have to shoot it out with an enemy force at point blank range in the dark, I guess they believed whatever Krang told them. Who else but other NVA would be there at one of their RONs? Whatever he said satisfied them, because they moved into the RON with us and sacked out. I'd counted twelve of them. We all acted like we were asleep and gave the NVA plenty of time to be sure they were all sound asleep. One was lying right next to me. I could smell the *nuoc mam* on his breath, the odor of sweat from his uniform. I slowly unsnapped my knife and drew it, lying on my stomach.

Randall crawled to me, drew his finger across his throat and moved on. Giving him a few minutes to be sure that everyone got the message, I rolled on top of the NVA and killed him quickly. All around the small RON, our team killed them, suddenly and silently. The smell of blood and feces, the smell of death, drifted through the small clearing. I saw someone stand and run out of the clearing. Grunting, I grabbed by CAR and took off after him.

Following him wasn't hard, even in the patchy moonlight. I listened for the sound of him crashing through the forest. If he ran into another NVA unit, our mission would be compromised. If it was a large NVA unit, we could be surrounded and chopped up, so this guy had to go down. He moved toward the main trail. I cut off to my right, moving through an area that Bao and I had scouted earlier that day and began to run. I moved parallel to the NVA's noisy flight and finally moved ahead of him.

Hitting the main trail, I turned left on it, guiding myself by the clearer moonlight on the main trail. When I heard him coming right at me, I sat in the middle of the trail and raised my CAR. The NVA soldier burst out of the forest just a few feet in front of me, but he didn't see me because I was seated. He looked up and down the trail.

"Chao," I said, greeting him in Vietnamese.

His head snapped around. I put a five-round burst in his chest, driving him back into the foliage.

After I hid the body, I crawled deeply into a clump of foliage and went to sleep. I knew it would be easier and wiser to wait until daylight before trying to find my way back to Randall. If I crept into their RON at night, I might wake up with my throat cut.

As dawn broke, the birds woke me. I retraced my path to Randall's RON and found them in place, having slept among the dead, waiting for me to show up.

"You get him?" Randall asked.

I just nodded for reply.

"Git some, dude," Billy said, grinning.

"We got us a captain," Dane told me, gesturing at the only body in the clearing that wasn't cut open somewhere.

"Good deal," I said, thinking we could extract, mission accomplished, forgetting all about the two other RTs we were controlling.

We stashed the dead NVA, cleaned up the RON as best we could and dragged the tied NVA officer to Hardin's field CP. Krang alerted Randall that one of the group of NVA who wandered into our RON had been an officer. When the killing began, Randall knocked him out. The group at the CP had been awake all night, monitoring the other two RTs' broadcasts, both of whom had made contact, but neither taking any prisoners. One team was under pressure and was trying to extract. Bender relayed their request for slicks and was waiting for a response to send back to the RT. He sent out confirmation that we had a live officer as soon as we pulled in. It brightened Hardin's morning to see us dragging the Viet officer in with us.

While we waited for orders from CCN, I ate, slept a while, then relieved one of the Nungs downhill from the CP. We had security out because we didn't know how often, if at all, the NVA patrolled the high grounds around their infiltration routes. It wasn't long after that Dane came by and ordered us in.

"We're pulling out," he said.

Both RTs we were coordinating had already extracted. We moved cautiously off our elevated perch and reached the extraction site without the NVA seeing or detecting us, though we saw several of their units. I suspected that the unit we ambushed hadn't been missed yet.

I was really pumped up on the flight back. We were some bad hombres in the bush. We could sneak in, grease eleven gooks, sneak out with their officer as a prisoner and then walk out like what we had done was legal. Of course, I knew we had combined battle luck with personal and team skill, but it was a real rush. I grinned at everyone in the slick and they grinned back. I guess the mood was infectious.

I got an Army Commendation medal for greasing the NVA runner. An Arcom. It didn't mean anything at all. It was more like a gesture, a pat on the head. Considering that I was already well on my way to having a chest full of medals, the Arcom was kind of a goof to me then.

They gave us a two-week break after that. Then the CIA control officer who briefed us on the prisoner snatch called in half of the team. Hardin, Dane and I were alerted for a mission briefing. It was fast and simple. The Air Force, SOG RTs and CIA-funded air and ground units were seeding Laos with electronic sensors for years. These sensors registered various things, such as body heat, then burst transmitted the information to a satellite, which down-linked it to the National Security Agency (NSA) facility near Hue for analysis. It was disseminated from there. Basically, those sensors could tell how many men passed them at what period of the day and which way they were going.

One group of sensors recorded massive troop movements through a grid that RTs found to be devoid of any sign of enemy troop movement. The troops the sensors reported never showed up anywhere else. RTs waited several days on the report of the sensors that troops were in the area, but there was never any sign of them coming out of those grids. RTs combed the grid over and over, looking for some kind of tunnel complex, but didn't find anything vaguely like one of those either. It was a mystery that the CIA wanted solved.

Three of us, with five Nungs, were to insert, recon the area and then with some special equipment that a spook strap hanger would carry, check the transponders. We all winced when told that a spook strap hanger was coming with us, but the guy, who had been sitting in the back of the room all along, stood up.

He wore a faded pair of tiger stripes with his web gear buckled on. "I'll keep the pace men. I've worked with RTs in the field before," he told us, grinning as we turned to look at him.

We went in on one slick. The strap hanger told us to call him Harry. He had his gear strapped to his webbing so that it didn't rattle or clank and he carried an old M2 carbine. He had a certain air of competence that I found reassuring. A Nung whom he brought along, his personal bodyguard, sat with him. This guy was old. His hair hung down to his waist and it was almost entirely gray. His left hand was missing. To show how long he had been fighting the communists, he carried a French MAT grease gun, the weapon the French paras and Legionnaires used when the conflict had been in Indochina, not Vietnam. Krang, who we took with us as a matter of course, showed the old Nung great deference. The two talked quietly in the corner of the slick.

The insertion was fast, with no contact. Krang and I were to keep an eye on Harry and his Nung, but they didn't really need it. Harry could and did keep the pace as he promised. We moved through the bush and then began climbing for the high ground where the sensors were located. They were seeded along a series of trails that led up from a deep valley floor into the hills. Dane took point with Harry behind him on slack, an electronic locating device in his hands. It took half a day of climbing before we found the first one. Dane and Harry checked them for calibration and whatever else they had to do. We moved along, locating them one by one. Two of our RT Nungs and I did point and security once we hit the hills. As they finished testing each one, we radioed in for a confirmation that NSA was receiving the test signal. That night, in a RON on the high grounds, we received confirmation that all the sensors we checked that day were still sending.

An hour later, we got a report that a large group of what the sensors said were men were moving through our TA. According to the sensors, they were moving along the line of the sensors we had just checked. Hardin, Harry and I crept down from the RON to the area where the sensors pinpointed movement. There was very little moonlight, but Hardin had a night scope. As he unlimbered it, I moved a little closer to the trail. We waited, looking and listening for any clue that enemy troops were moving along the trail. There was no clank of equipment, no crunch of feet on rocks, nothing. After about half an hour, I pulled back to Hardin.

He and Harry, the spook, were laying on their sides, laughing.

"What the fuck, over?" I asked them.

Hardin handed me the night scope and pointed down the trail. I put the scope to my eye and scanned the trail where Hardin indicated. There were shapes moving along the trail all right. They were monkeys. Big monkeys. Some of the guys called them rock apes. I burst out laughing. We were still laughing when slicks brought us back to our FOB.

The debriefers had a hard time with our story. If it hadn't been for Harry, they might have sent us back in, thinking we had just laid around and fucked off. Harry backed our story and they finally accepted it. We told the story to the rest of our team. Every time

Billy saw a spook after that, he made monkey faces at them.

Our next operation was in response to an alert. A spook electronics plane had gone down in Laos. Three teams were pulled in for the alert, plus whoever was hanging around the compound.

"One of our aircraft went down in this area," the spook briefer said, slapping a map of Laos with his collapsible pointer. "Find it. Destroy it. Bring any of the surviving crew out that you can find. Do not, and I repeat, *do not* allow any of the men or equipment from the aircraft to be taken by the communists. Clear?"

"When do we deploy?" Hardin asked.

"An hour ago, captain," the spook said.

An Air Force Search and Rescue team was already in flight and searching for the location of the plane. Other air assets were standing by in Thailand, waiting for word that we found the wreckage. If we couldn't get to the craft from the ground because of enemy activity, we would call in an air strike on it. The spooks wanted an on-site recon of the area regardless. It didn't take long after that before the reaction team was in the air, aboard an old Air America Dakota. It was all black.

We deployed in a stick jump formation at low level. That was the fastest deployment I'd ever made. They wanted us on the ground and in action fast. I hadn't made a jump in a year, but like sex, once you knew how you never forgot. Jumping was almost as good as sex to me anyway and almost as good as riding a motorcycle. When we landed and everyone pulled their chutes in, we found a CIA paramilitary unit on the ground waiting for us. They put security out around the Drop Zone for us. They were a wild-looking bunch, wearing a blend of uniforms and carrying mostly Combloc weapons. They split up, a few of them going with each team, acting as guides. We got an Australian and two Cambodian indigs. RT Sink went to the east and RT Kitchen circled to the north, while we went straight north so that our three teams would encircle the Target Area.

When we were about five klicks from where we thought the wreckage was, we heard a fierce fire fight break out north of us. Hardin got on the radio and found out that an NVA force had been looting the wreckage when RT Kitchen stumbled upon them.

Following orders, RT Kitchen opened fire on the NVA and the wreckage with LAWs, grenade launchers and small arms. The NVA took off with one prisoner, heading east, directly into RT Sink, who as soon as RT Kitchen got ahold of them on the radio, spread out in ambush position to act as a blocking force. They would try to stop the NVA until the rest of us could close on them.

When we heard firing from our east, we moved at a run, but the firing began to taper off quickly. Rather than try to overrun RT Sink, the NVA were trying to disengage and extract from the area. The NVA made good their escape while we were still closing on RT Sink. There was a sporadic fire fight going on when we arrived, but it was a rear guard the NVA had left to hold off pursuit as long as possible. We flanked them and RT Kitchen, who had joined the fight just after we had, overran them.

After a quick field conference between the three RT leaders and Randall, half of our team went in pursuit of the NVA, while the other half returned to the site of the wreckage and put out security for RT Kitchen while its demo man planted charges around the plane. We found four bodies in and around the plane, which meant that one of the five-man crew was missing. That would account for the prisoner the NVA dragged off. When all of the demolition charges were set, we all backed off and RT Kitchen blew it up. Then, we called for extraction.

The plan was for Hardin and his half of the team to follow the NVA to its camp or staging area. When they found it, Hardin would alert us at our launch site and we would land on them with both feet. When the slicks came, all of us who weren't in on the pursuit lifted out and they took us to a little camp just inside the Thai border instead of to Vietnam. The first person I saw as we loaded off the slicks was the Cat. He waved, but kept going. I knew better than to ask questions about where we were and the purpose of the camp, but I was burning with curiosity.

The camp had a fair-sized runway. Black slicks, C123s, even a few old DC 10s were parked around it. Men in a variety of camo uniforms with all types of firearms strolled around the camp. They fed us in a prefab corrugated tin building and the food was pretty good. That was the final clue that told me the compound was definitely *not* under U.S. military control. I drank about a gallon of their coffee.

I was sitting in the shade of a hootch, watching some indigs unload a bunch of crates from a Chinook helicopter and then load them on a C123 when Randall found me. Hardin had tracked the NVA force to a small field CP in a stand of timber. We loaded up in our black slicks and flew into Laos. Our force inserted behind a valley, Hardin and the CIA PMs putting out security for us. They guided us to the NVA camp.

The NVA picked a good site for its base camp. It was in a small stand of woods at the base of a ridge line. Two sides of the camp opened into a field, giving the NVA clear fields of fire. They dug bunkers just inside the tree line on three sides and two small hootches were set up under the protective cover of the trees. They were concealed from the air and a patrol wouldn't see them until they walked into the bunker's killing ground. Hardin and his people already had reconnoitered the area and led us to a concealed vantage point from which we could observe the NVA camp from the ridge line above and behind it. I could see someone in a flight suit tied to a tree inside their compound.

The three RT leaders and Randall put their heads together while the rest of us kept an eye on the camp. When a plan had been worked out between them, they briefed the rest of us. RT Sink and Kitchen would hit the camp with small arms fire from the ridge line while the CIA PMs moved around one flank and brought it under fire too. While all of that was going on and the NVA would hopefully be rushing to defend two sides of its camp, our team would sneak in from the opposite end of the camp where there was some cover for us to move through, free the POW, search the camp for any pieces of the plane the NVA might have made off with and plant demo boobytraps. When we exfiltrated, Hardin would call in an air strike on the camp, directing it from a safe distance back. When we all understood our role in the plan, the respective teams moved to their fighting positions. When we were in place, Bender broke squelch twice, our signal to the others that we were ready.

Almost instantly, all hell broke loose from the ridge line and to our east, fire pouring down into the NVA camp. Seconds later, from the CIA PM position, a wave of small arms fire washed over the bunkers and the camp. Grenade launchers, M60s, SMGs and rifles poured steady streams of fire into the bunker line. Inside the compound, the NVA scrambled for the bunker lines on the flanks from which the fire was coming, leaving our flank open, just as we had hoped. A few headed for the area we had to infiltrate.

We moved in quickly. Randall, Billy and I, with three Nungs, led the infiltration. Crawling up to the bunker line, using high grass and rocks for cover, we passed the bunkers. We checked all of the bunkers to make sure they were empty before we moved past them and all of them were. As the rest of the team moved in, they mined the bunkers and then established positions around them to cover the six of us who would actually move inside the compound. If the NVA was able to close off that side of its perimeter by manning the bunkers, we would be trapped inside the compound.

My job was to search the hootches, while Randall and Billy went for the POW. Crawling up to the nearest hootch, with Bao behind me covering my rear, I set a claymore behind it, then crawled under the hootch's stilts. Going in fast, I found it empty. It must have been an officer's hootch because there was nothing in it but a spare uniform and a can of shoe polish with a Russian label on it. I pocketed that. I also found a pouch with some maps and papers written in Viet so I stuck that in one thigh pocket of my tiger suit. Moving to the other hootch, I found a case with a combination lock on it, obviously of American manufacture. The lock had been forced. Opening it and scanning its contents, I knew it came from the aircraft. It was an SOI, signal operating instructions, with codes and other instructions for the aircraft to use in communications or monitoring. I doubted the NVA could win the war with the SOI, but they could compromise some of our communications or agents in the North with it. I couldn't carry it, so I took a claymore from Bao, taped a white phosphorous grenade to it and set the claymore inside the case.

Hooking the wire to a clacker, a hand-held electronic detonator, I left the hootch to check on Billy and Randall. Krang trotted up to me as soon as Bao and I exited the hootch.

"Prisoner safe, we go," he said.

We pulled back to the bunker line where Hardin and the rest of the team were waiting for us. A few NVA had tried to get into their bunker there and had never heard the suppressed weapons that killed them. The team hid their bodies in the empty bunkers until we rejoined them. We exfiltrated as a group. Bao and I did rear guard, waiting until the others were clear before firing the claymores we left. A cloud of white smoke drifted up from the white phosphorous grenade.

"Tell the flyboys to put their ordnance on the white smoke," I told Marty, who was already calling in an air strike when Bao and I made it to the team.

We pulled back to the ridge line and gave the signal for the other teams to rendezvous with us as a flight of Skyraiders came roaring in. They blew the camp apart. It drove the surviving NVA out of cover and into our guns. As we pulled back for extraction, I got a look at the POW Randall had rescued. He was an Oriental.

"I almost knifed him, after what happened with Yuen," Randall said as I walked up to him and the prisoner.

"Is he a Nung?" I asked. The man was definitely of Chinese extraction.

"Chinese. He's from Formosa, one of their regular Air Force officers," Hardin said, joining us. "Of course, none of you men saw this."

"Of course, sir," I said, smiling at him.

As the inbound slicks reached us and we started loading up, Billy looked over at the destruction we caused in the valley, then back at the Chinese crewman from the electronics plane.

"Wow," he said.

I decided I needed a week at Madame Xhian's after our operations in Laos and I took Billy with me, deciding he needed some culture, too. Despite his brilliant conversational abilities, he and I shared a deep and abiding love for rock and roll as it was being expressed in the late Sixties.

When we got to Saigon, we partied for seven days and seven nights straight, though we weren't straight much of that time. We

rocked, we rolled and we did some things best left unsaid. I had
to carry him out of Xhian's when our week was up, but I was barely
moving myself. Some chopper jocks felt sorry for us and poured
us into a Chinook that was flying a load of something in the general
direction we were headed. When we got aboard, I saw that it was
a load of rubber tree plants. The crew chief told me they were
headed for a Yard village in the central highlands.

Billy passed out, leaning on my shoulder as the ship took off.
I just hoped that he wouldn't throw up. On that thought, I nodded
out myself. I woke up feeling something crawling on my shins.
Looking up, I saw a four-foot-long black snake slithering over
one of my outstretched legs. I wasn't afraid of a four-foot black
snake. I kicked it off me.

It landed a foot or so away from me and raised its head, a hood
spreading out on each side of its neck.

"Oh, fuck," I muttered, freezing in place.

It crawled away.

"Billy, wake up, man. There's a fuckin' cobra on board!" I
screamed into his ear.

He sat up and rubbed his eyes, then drew a Browning 9mm from
beneath his shirt. "Far out," he said, drawing a bead on the snake.

"Don't shoot in the ship, man!" I yelled, grabbing the hammer and slide.

"Chill out, dude, I'll catch it," he mumbled, giving me a hurt
look. Putting his pistol away he started to get up.

"Just leave the fucker alone, man," I said, trying to crawl up the
cargo netting that had been suspended from one wall of the ship.

About then, the door gunner spotted the snake as it crawled
forward. "There's a cobra on board!" he yelled.

The pilot looked out the window for the Cobra gunship he
thought the door gunner was talking about. "Where? I don't see
any Cobra," he said.

He glanced back at us and saw the snake, which wasn't far from
him. He yelled something and jerked the nose of the ship up. The
snake slid back toward the door gunner. He stepped out the door
and hung by his safety strap.

"Get this fucker on the fucking ground, fucking now!" I screamed, pointing down. The pilot nodded, one eye on the snake and one on the controls.

He landed in a deserted field near a small village. We all piled out of the chopper, except Billy, who chased the snake out of the ship. The door gunner hopped back into the ship and revved up his door gun, some kind of multi-barreled minigun. As the snake tried to escape and evade, all of us opened fire with whatever we had. The snake crawled through it without even a single hit being scored and vanished into a hole in the ground.

We all just looked at each other, then loaded into the chopper and took off.

When we landed at some A Team camp in the central highlands, the pilot told some of the other green hats about our adventure. One of them grinned at me and Billy. "Hell, you boys weren't scared of that snake were ya? We used to eat 'em for breakfast on Bragg."

"You ain't ever been on a chopper with one, have ya?" I asked.

"You shoulda seen them, trying to crawl up the cargo net," the door gunner chimed in.

While I was trying to think of some witty comeback, a chore because of all the partying we had done the previous week, Billy beat me to it.

"Fuck off, asshole."

We ran a few more patrols in the Charles Seven area, most of them at half-team strength. When one half of the team went in, the other half stood by on alert as a reaction force, just in case. After one patrol, Billy, Dane and I wandered down to the Enlisted Men's (EM) Club for a few beers to unwind after our debriefing. Even when we didn't make much contact, the patrols were always highly stressful. When we got to the club, it was almost full of REMF types. As Dane and I stood outside, pondering on the wisdom of going in, Billy just wandered in, drawn no doubt by the pulse-pounding music blaring from the smoky interior. Dane and I looked at each other, shrugged and followed him in.

He was seated at a table with two other guys in tiger suits. They had new clean suits on, while ours had fungus growing out of them. I thought they might be ARVN Ranger advisors or maybe some

SOG types because I hadn't seen them around the compound before.

"Hey dudes," one of them greeted us as we stood behind Billy, looking around the club. "Hang out. Wanna pop some tops?"

Dane and I sat and ordered some beers. "Who're you guys? I haven't seen you around the compound before," I asked with my usual diplomacy.

The two looked at each other. "I work for AFN at the Mountain," one said.

I choked on my beer. Armed Forces Network? In tiger suits? "Covert radio broadcasts or what?" I growled.

The other one turned out to be a clerk of some sort. They bought us beer all night and I traded the clerk my old sawed-off shotgun with notches cut in the pistol grip as an REMF sales incentive for a case of whiskey and two new sets of tiger suits. The other one promised to take me to meet Chris Noel, the most desired disc jockey around, but that never panned out. I had deep lust in my heart for that woman. As far as I was concerned, she was what I was fighting for.

During the course of the evening, the clerk asked me if I'd hit the Terrible Twenty yet.

"The what?" I slurred.

"The Terrible Twenty is like when you grease twenty gooks, man," Billy translated for me.

I thought he was asking if I had turned twenty years old yet. I'd heard of clubs like that, the Dirty Thirty, Filthy Fifty. I never kept track personally. Missions were a blur to me during the combat phase and then during the debriefing I'd remember enough of the details to fill in a report. The killing didn't stick with me. I dreamed about some of the things that happened, usually the deaths of friends, but not killing the enemy.

After I thought about it for a few minutes, I said, "I've killed boocoo communists, but you'll be my first REMF."

The guy split. I didn't care much for REMFs. Most of them lived in their own little air-conditioned worlds. Their traumas came from cramped hands when they typed too much, running out of cold soda pops, having their air-conditioners break down. It was a rough life, but someone had to fill out the forms, right? Clean clothes, shined boots, dry socks, no leeches, snakes or NVA. One of them got a Purple Heart for cutting himself with a safety razor while shaving as the NVA launched a mortar attack on his compound.

The next day, Billy talked me into going out on the beach with him to get some sun. Actually, what he said was, "Let's cop some rays, dude." My skin was snow white from wearing my sleeves rolled down, my shirt collar buttoned all the way up and living in the deep jungle out of sight of the sun for days at a time. While lying on the blanket Billy had issued me, wearing only a pair of OD Army issue boxer shorts, some goofy REMF clown came trotting over to me.

"Hey man, you can't lay out in the sun like that," he said.

I shaded my eyes with my hand and sat up. It was the beach lifeguard. He wore a pair of cut-off Levi shorts, unlaced jungle boots, a boonie hat, sunglasses and white goop smeared on his nose. Dog tags and a Hawaiian surfer medallion hung on a chain around his neck.

"Get the fuck away from me," I growled and laid down.

"No, man, we got a dress code on the beach here. There's nurses out here, don'tcha know? Plus, like you might get a burn."

"My God, not that, not a sunburn!" I snorted at him, but he wouldn't go away.

"For real man, they'll article fifteen you if you get sick from a sunburn."

I rolled over, got up and started for him. He danced back, seeing the evil intent in my eyes.

"If you don't get away from me, ya rear echelon mutherfucker, I'm going to..."

He held both hands out toward me, still backing away. "Hey dude, chill out. I paid my dues man. I was a grunt. I ain't no REMF bro."

That was too much. "Bro?" I snarled and caught him by his neck chain. I had him down and was ready to do him when Billy pulled me off.

Hardin called me into what he used for an office in the briefing area. "Sergeant, this is the first discipline problem we've had in this team. I don't blame you, but try not to scare the REMFs like that. Especially around here where all of us have to live."

I grinned at him and he grinned back. "Sorry about this, sir. Is that it?"

"I think the next time we are between missions, we'll try to get a separate R&R center for the RTs. Some of the Control officers have been talking about it. This might be just what was needed. That is all, sergeant."

I went back to my billet and tried to relax. It made me mad that I couldn't kick back and enjoy myself around other Americans without some stupid REMF fucking with me. I didn't have those problems out in the bush. Some of the slick pilots called the bush the Void, but the RTs called it home. It was where the adrenalin pumped, where the enemy lived and where we were the sole rulers of our own fates. It was getting to the point where the bush was the only place I felt right and I felt terrible in the bush. That was a paradox I didn't know how to cope with. It scared me. Was I some kind of deviate? It worried me so much, that I stopped thinking about it. I just waited for the next mission, stayed drunk in between and put all of my efforts into avoiding REMFs of all ranks when I was at the FOB. It was a covert war within a covert war.

Chapter Six
The Snatch

Blake slowly reached up, pulling his camouflage headband off his forehead. Then he slumped back on the cot, muddy boots and all. I sat on my footlocker, trying to pull a mud-caked knot loose on my right boot.

Both of us were mentally and physically exhausted. We had gone into a hot TA in Laos, north of the Charles Seven area, on a bomb assessment patrol. Hardin, Blake, me, Krang and five other Nungs inserted by slick and took small arms fire before we got off the LZ. A running fire fight ensued until we reached the highlands and we simply outran them. Our mission was compromised, the gooks knew we were in the area and we had two wounded Nungs.

Hardin called a Medevac for the Nungs and used it as a distraction so we could move out of the highlands into our TA. Blake took the wounded to the LZ, loaded them in a slick, jumped in one side and then dropped out the other. He and two Nungs he had taken to pack the wounded joined us moving down a slope. We reached our patrol objective without contact. Our ruse of calling in the slicks worked. They thought we'd *didi*'ed or were still in the highlands. When we started reconnoitering the TA, we found bomb craters but not much else. Climbing back into the highlands, we made contact at sunset with an NVA unit. Another running fire fight began and we took off into the hills. After dark, we finally lost them and found a RON.

The next morning, we went back to our TA and combed it again. This time we found a platoon of NVA regulars and a small group of black-clad peasant porters moving toward us, skirting the area of the bombing. Following them, we found a bunker complex with shelters behind the bunkers in a tree line for passing troops. Hardin called in air. The fast movers went in with five hundred pounders, napalm and cannons, strafing the area after they dropped their heavy ordnance. There were several small secondary explosions, then one big one.

Our team moved quickly back toward the highlands, but we were cut off by several NVA units on the move. We made contact with one crossing a narrow trail, ran for the high ground and ran through another NVA unit. The recognition was mutual and we shot it out at practically point-blank range. One of the Nungs fired at the same time as an NVA, only a few feet apart, killing each other. Hardin was hit in the side, but it was only a flesh wound. Blake was on the radio to our relay.

We moved for the high ground again. Climbing, we found a level area big enough for a slick and we spread out to form a perimeter, setting our claymores out. I fastened a white phosphorous (WP) grenade to mine. I saw a lone NVA soldier emerge from the tree line below me, look up to our position, then motion for someone to follow him. He walked toward us. Then I heard the slicks coming in. Hardin was talking them in.

I went to Hardin, the clacker for my claymore in one hand, as he popped smoke for the slicks. Two Cobras circled overhead. The others fell back on us, still watching the perimeter, the edge of the clearing. The lead slick started down.

Gunfire erupted to our left and Blake blew his claymore. AK rounds came from several directions. I blew my claymore when I spotted movement near it and told Hardin to put the Cobras on the smoke from the WP grenade. They came in firing miniguns. A Huey gunship equipped with rockets made a run as our extraction slick settled in. We ran for it. An RPG barely missed it, exploding on the opposite side of the slick. The door gunners were both firing their M60s over our heads. One of the Nungs went down. Randall grabbed him, slung him over his shoulder and we all headed for the slick. Randall tossed him in, dove in behind him and I piled in behind Randall. The slick lurched, swayed, then accelerated out of there, the door gunners still firing, hanging out of the doors to make sure they got as many as they could.

Arriving at the FOB, we debriefed for what seemed like a day. Hardin was taken directly to the hospital, then Blake and I went back to our hootches.

"Hey, you want a shot of whiskey?" Blake grunted from his cot as I gave up trying to untie the knot and sliced it open with my knife. I hadn't slept in three days or nights. I was so tired and still wired up, I couldn't sleep.

"Yeah, I would," I said, going to work on the other boot.

Blake was an aloof man who didn't have much to say to anyone. He was competent in the field, he never got shaken no matter how bad things got, but he had a cold streak in him. He really didn't care about other people at all. Some guys tried to cultivate that as a survival mechanism, but with Blake it was for real. His offer of whiskey was the first time in the year that I'd known him that he ever opened a conversation with me that wasn't mission related.

He fumbled in his footlocker, then handed me a half-full quart of Jack Daniels. I took a drink, then coughed as it burned its way down my throat. He grinned as he took the bottle back and took a long swig.

Pulling my boots off, I went to work on my shirt.

"What are you going to do when this ends?" he asked, out of the blue.

"Will it? I can't see that far into the future, man," I told him. It was true.

He took another long pull from the bottle. "Wars build up an energy of their own, a momentum. That burns a lotta fuel. One day this'll just burn out, man, just fizzle to a halt. Or at least the American involvement will."

I nodded. One side always gave up, a nation could only stand so much loss. From what I'd read about Nixon and Vietnamization, ours was throwing in the towel, our energy expended, bled out by the war and the social unrest at home. The will to win is a fragile thing, nationally.

"What are you gonna do, Blake? Stay in the Army?" I asked.

"Nah, I'm going private sector man. You ever know Jim Sanders? No? He's doing private sector work in Africa now. He wrote and said it's great."

"Keep fighting?"

"Yeah. What else is there?"

I shook my head. "Man, I'm moving to Key West and watch the round-eyed women on the beach."

He smiled at me. "Yeah, for a while, but you'll come back if the war lasts long enough. Or you'll find another one."

"Not me, man."

"Yeah, you. Yer into it. Yer on yer third tour now, right?"

I nodded.

"Why? 'Cause you like it man. Same as everyone else on this team. Well, I'm out front with it is all. The rest of the guys have a rap about fighting communist aggression and all. I like the fighting and I'm going to another war when this one fizzles out."

I fell asleep on that thought.

We were briefed to return to our last TA several days later to conduct a follow-up on the air strike. Randall would lead the team in while Hardin was gone. After briefing our handlers, we inserted by slicks a few klicks east of the bunker complex. We moved cautiously. Reaching the area of the strike with no contact, we approached the blown-up tree line very carefully. The NVA often left boobytraps after evacuating its jungle forts. Staying in the tree line as much as possible, we moved through the area of devastation. It was a walk in the sun. We didn't find any weapons, bodies, or live NVA.

Our team stayed on the ground for another day, scouting the area, but no enemy came near it. We extracted.

A week later we were called in for another mission briefing. Hardin had returned to us the day before. A spook was waiting for us when we filed in and took our seats.

"We know that on 12 November a general of the North Vietnamese Army and a high level commissar in the National Liberation Front (NLF) will leave this area of North Vietnam and proceed south along this route, through eastern Laos," the spook began, tapping an area of the map. "We do not know their exact destination."

The NVA would depart from a city in North Vietnam named Xom Ca Trang, drive down highway 12, cross into Laos through the Mu Gia Pass, leave the highway at Na Phac in Laos and proceed south out of the mountains on foot.

As the briefer paused for breath, we sat studying the area of the map he indicated. Billy, I noticed, was making monkey faces at the spook.

"We want both of those men taken alive," the spook told us.

He waited for a reaction from us, but he didn't get any. We all sat stone-faced, except Billy, who stopped making the monkey faces at him, but was smiling instead. The spook let a slight smile flit across his face too.

"There is a twelve-man bodyguard. They travel in an old jeep and a truck and from this point south," he paused, again tapping an area of the map, "they will have to walk. Work out your plans and I'll arrange insertion and extraction."

After the spook left, we poured over the folder he left with us. It was very complete. It provided photos of the two targets he wanted, aerial photos of the entire route of their march, weather forecasts and other details of the area of operations. We studied the material and our options for an hour, then began to work out a plan. It didn't take long after that to work it out, detail for detail.

We inserted by helicopter a few miles south of the North Viet border inside Laos. Fanning out in the LZ as the slicks zoomed away, we moved into the tree line fast. I took point. We followed the Se Bank Fai River for over an hour, then cut away from it and headed north into a long, deep valley. It gave us cover, but turned out to be mainly mangrove swamp. We finally emerged from it, none of us having broken or wrenched our ankles on the treacherous roots.

Billy took over for me on point. He was as good as me on land navigation and trail-blazing. About two hours later, we moved into a RON in the upper end of the valley. Making a cold camp, we ate and laagered for the night. By my estimation, we still had half a day's march to reach our ambush site. All of it was uphill since we decided to take the prisoners before they left the mountains.

When I woke, the sun hadn't exploded into the sky yet. The cool night air held dampness and made me shiver. My fatigues had grown stiff overnight from the salt in my sweat, but the dew moistened them. They felt cold and clammy and I flashed back to my last patrol in '68 with the Lurp team. Pulling on my head-band and web gear, I walked over to Hardin, who was doing the same thing. He had his map open on the ground beside him.

Squatting beside him, I nibbled on a rice ball as he quietly outlined where he wanted me to take us. I nodded, checked my compass and we moved out.

It was a hard march. We were in a totally denied area and had to maintain stealth. Anyone we saw was a potential enemy. If they didn't go straight to the communists, they might attack us themselves and collect a bounty. If a peasant saw us, we had to wipe him out for mission integrity. All of our movement was uphill diagonally along a broken ridge face. I moved from point of cover to point of cover in a running crouch, then paused to look and listen. I scanned for boobytraps on the move. When I was so many feet ahead of the team, I gave them a hand signal to move up. They advanced in a leap frog pattern the same way I did.

Descending the opposite side of the ridge was just as bad. There were several exposed areas which took an effort to skirt. Then, finally, we were off of it and back in the jungle.

We were close to our ambush site and had to cross a dirt road. Moving up to it in the cover of some dense foliage that grew down to the edge of the road, we lay and watched it for half an hour. Hardin motioned me across. As I rose for the dash across and took my first step, two men on bicycles came toward me. None of us saw where they came from, they just appeared about thirty feet away.

I froze. Their heads turned toward me and they increased their speed. One called out to me in Viet. As they got closer, I saw they were NVA soldiers. When they clearly saw who I was, they stopped, reaching for rifles they wore strapped across their backs. Three of us with suppressed weapons opened fire. It bowled them over.

The flankers went further out immediately to cover us as we carried the bodies into the woods. Two Nungs carried the bicycles off too, hiding them in deep foliage. The team moved quickly across the trail.

The site we had picked for the snatch from the aerial photos looked good from the ground when we reached it. We studied the area from concealment, then moved in and selected our position. We would catch them on their flank as they came uphill, rounding a bend in the trail. Big Dane took a radio and two Nungs a mile down the trail to serve as a listening post.

We laid around for several hours until Dane alerted us by breaking squelch twice on the radio. The men we were here for were
coming our way. My pulse started pounding. Dane and the Nungs
rejoined us shortly. He told us they were moving in a staggered
column with our targets in the middle of the file. There were twenty
in the group, not the fourteen we'd been briefed to hit. Five of
us doubled up on our targets.

As the NVA unit moved into our killing zone, they came along
confidently. They were slightly bunched, with their weapons slung.
When Hardin triggered the claymore that signaled the ambush,
I shot my first target in the ear, switched to my second just as
he started to react and caught him in the chest and neck with a
three-round burst. A brief moment of fury raged along the trail.
When it ended, Dane and his two Nungs dashed forward, running
for the general and the politician.

The two Viets were frozen with terror and shock. The politician was on his hands and knees, the general standing erect, gaz-
ing at what was left of his escort. All of his men were dead, or
about to be, lying scattered on the mountain trail. Blood and bits
of the nearest soldiers to them had splattered their uniforms.

Dane screamed in Viet for them to surrender. The politician tried
to stand. Krang flattened him with a boot. The Nung leader knelt
beside him, frisking him before tying his hands tightly behind him
and looping a strand of det cord, explosive detonation cord, around
his neck. Dane did the same to the general while the rest of us covered the trail, sending flankers out on each end to make sure that
the capture party wasn't surprised before they could get their prisoners moved out. Bao and I made sure that all the NVA were dead.

When Dane had the prisoners secured, Hardin pulled the flankers
in and we moved out. Billy took point and I took tail gunner with
Bao. The prisoners cooperated; they knew we wouldn't hurt or
kill them if they obeyed us. Perhaps they would be rescued or could
escape later. We made good time. All of us had gotten used to
surreptitious movement in the hills on the way in.

Our extraction point was in the valley to our southwest. We
moved fast along a ridge line, then down into a valley. Our LZ

was a natural clearing near one end of the valley. Blake, carrying the radio for this patrol, talked to our relay as we worked along the ridge, insuring contact before we got down in the valley. He passed the word that slicks were on the way.

The NVA hit us as we moved out of cover toward the LZ. Billy was killed instantly, nearly cut in half by an RPD MG. We fell back, unable to recover his body, and we began taking heavy automatic weapons fire. Dragging the prisoners with us, we ran. Dane, Bao, a Nung who carried an M79 and I fought a rear guard action. We brought their first wave of pursuit to a halt in the middle of our intended LZ, laid a quick demo ambush with claymores and took off to catch the rest of the team.

We knew where the secondary LZ was located so we headed for it. I led, taking compass bearings almost at a run. A heavy fire fight broke out ahead of us and we humped up a ridgeline to get a better view of what we were running toward.

Our team was pinned at the exposed base of a low ridge below us, taking heavy fire. We identified our team from the sound of their weapons. An NVA unit was laying suppressing fire on them from cover while another group of ten tried to flank them. The four of us moved in behind the flank element and wiped them out in a charge. We flanked the stationary element as Randall and Blake laid down a rapid fire barrage on them. Our Nung took out an RPD with his '79 and we assaulted them. The fighting went toe-to-toe for a minute. There were more of them in the tree line than we thought. Hardin led a breakout that took the pressure off us before they could get organized.

We were fighting so close that I killed one NVA by ramming the end of my suppressor into his throat as he turned toward me. A frag went off near me, burning me up with shrapnel as the NVA tried to rally. The fighting went hand-to-hand. I used my .45 after the CAR clicked empty and when the pistol locked back on an empty chamber, I drew the Randall knife.

An NVA ran at me with his bayonet extended from an SKS. I smacked it aside, stepped in close and sank my blade to the hilt under his armpit. He blew a bloody froth from his mouth on me and fell away. I reloaded my .45 quickly. Looking up, I saw Hardin slam an NVA soldier head first into a tree, killing him. He sidestepped another one who lunged at him, sidekicked the guy, then spun and drove his boot heel into the NVA's crotch. Another NVA stabbed him in the side with a knife and Hardin grabbed him by the head with both hands and twisted it. The soldier's neck snapped. Just then, another NVA shot Hardin twice with an AK, blowing him over backwards. I dropped the shooter with two rounds from my pistol.

The NVA were withdrawing and we sounded off, gathering our team and went back to where Bender kept the prisoners. If we'd been wiped, he would have ignited the det cord around their necks before the NVA could rescue them. He had Blake's radio too. Dane and Blake dragged Hardin to cover, quickly patching the two holes in his chest, then carried him as we moved out. Randall took over automatically as team leader. He moved us back to high ground. As we climbed, we could see the NVA patrols below us.

Bender got our relay on the radio once we hit the high ground. An extraction was set up, with heavy air cover. Once we confirmed that we had the prisoners, alive, they were willing to send in a B52 strike if we asked for it.

Finding a place where we could laager, we waited while wounds were dressed. All of us were wounded in varying degrees. The NVA hit Hardin in the collar bone, shattering it, and blowing a chunk out of his trapezius muscle. He was bleeding, in tremendous pain, going into shock, but he was conscious. Randall sat beside him, giving him a situation report.

They'd killed Billy, the cocksuckers! One minute he was walking along and the next he'd been riddled. Now Hardin was down. I shook with a rage I didn't know I could feel, couldn't understand why I felt. Goddammit, they were my friends! I admitted it to myself. These guys were more than friends, they were brothers.

"Slicks in-bound," Dane said, passing the words.

They came in fast. Gunships ran cover, flitting around above the slicks like dragon flies. We loaded up quickly, wounded in the first slick, the rest of us in the second, and we were out of there.

After we had been debriefed, I looked at myself in the mirror. Stained from hair to waist with a dead man's blood, my tiger suit muddy and torn, eyes hollow and staring, I felt as ragged as I looked. When I got to the hospital to have the shrapnel dug out, I collapsed on a bed, sleeping a day and night after they dug out what they could.

Our reward for snatching the NVA general and getting our asses shot off was another R&R in Bangkok. I saw Hardin off when they medevaced him to Japan and then hopped an Air America flight to Sin City alone. I changed into jeans and my only black T-shirt, which had my hometown logo on it, a fist holding a smoking revolver. After checking into a hotel and satisfying my various desires for good food and sex, I took a cab over to Bear's Lair. The food there wasn't bad, but I'd wanted the full spread, not Mamma Bear's Thai junk food. Bear didn't let the high class hookers work his place either. Most of them wouldn't go there anyway. The guys who frequented Bear's bar wouldn't pay their prices.

Sitting alone at one end of the bar, I watched the other drunks come and go. Bear came over once, but he caught the thousand yard glare in my eyes and left me alone. He kept me supplied with beer, however. Most of his regulars wore civilian clothes. They were Air America pilots, some soldiers or paramilitary types, smugglers, mercenaries and a few other expatriots like Bear. There were also some spooks from various intelligence agencies, both ours and theirs. It was an eclectic kind of place.

A half dozen Aussies sat in one corner, telling stories in their heathen English, laughing, yelling at Bear and fondling his bar girls who laughed and slapped their hands. I barely understood them. Aussie is a dialect of English I've never mastered.

I drank alone, seeing Billy being stitched with the RPD, Brick down with an arrow through his chest, Hardin being shot to pieces and Tex hurtling through the air again and again. I felt the dying breath of that NVA hit me in the face, nerves shrieking as we fought the NVA in the woods, hand-to-hand and toe-to-toe, again in my mind. That had been a close thing, damn close. Hardin shipped home with two bullets in him as a result. All of us were wounded repeatedly, fighting our own bodies so we could still fight the enemy. As I lifted my beer, my hand shook so badly I spilled beer in my lap.

"Here mate, I want you to meet some blokes," Bear growled, appearing in front of me after watching me use both hands to raise my beer.

"I'd rather drink alone," I replied, grabbing my glass with both hands again.

"Son, I've bloody well been where you're at. Let's go meet these fellas," Bear told me, leaning over the bar and clamping his vice-like grip on my forearm. He more or less dragged me down the bar and over to the table where the Aussies sat.

Bear introduced me and gave one of them, a large, beefy red-faced man with a crooked nose, a signal. Each one told a short war story that the others listened to with great solemnity and respect. They were all pretty heavy stories. It turned out that one of them was a Brit, another a Kiwi, a New Zealander. The Brit was former Special Air Service (SAS). He told a story about Kenya during the Mau Mau insurrection, about a friend captured by the Mau Mau and found by his patrol in a cold Mau Mau camp a week later. The guy had been tortured to death, mutilated in a ceremony. The Kiwi told a story about Malaya and the jungle fighting there.

Then I told my story. By the time I finished it, I was drunk, but my mind had returned from the mission. Talking it out to these men had done it. I sat there, hoping my brothers, Randall and the rest of the team, would find a way to work it out for themselves too. Randall probably didn't need to though.

When I finished, I slumped back in the chair. The group at the table simply stared with glazed eyes into their private memories of war and death. Looking around, I noticed for the first time that Bear had locked the front door and our group was alone in the bar.

"Well, lad, I've got one for you," the big Aussie beside me said.

The others at the table groaned. "Not about your sheep ranch again is it, Muldoon?" one of the others said.

Muldoon grunted, "Bloody hell! Had to pen up the sheep whenever Carl here came to call, else they'd all try to follow him home."

We all chuckled. Then Muldoon continued.

"Me mate MacEntaeger, whom I shall call Mac from this point on, and I were a bit broke. We'd been in Korea, Kenya, the Congo and a few lesser spots together over the years, but there was a bloody nasty outbreak of peace going on in Africa right then. So we were in Salisbury, having a pint, when in walks old McWhirter, the flying fat man..."

"Pig McWhirter? Bloody hell. I saw him in Hong Kong just a month ago!" the Kiwi chipped in.

That started a brief discussion about mercenary pilots in general, Pig McWhirter in particular, until Muldoon cleared his throat loudly.

"Ahhhemmm. Now, as I was saying, the Pig walks in dressed rather well, for him. He spots us and between pints he tells Mac and me all about his new job in the new Republic of, mmmm, ahhh, well, let's call it Bunga. He had more or less stepped in it and come out ahead. He had been flying poached ivory out, the bobbies had got onto him and pinched him with a load. While the Pig was in the nick, the government changed hands several times. Turned out that the most recent new president of Bunga was the head poacher Pig had been flying for. So he got Pig outta the nick and made him chief of the Bunga Air Force, such as it was.

"The Pig had his own Dakota, one old Brit Spitfire and a seaplane of some sort and that was his total air force. The country is landlocked, so the seaplane hasn't moved in years. It's floating on a small lake. The new pres gives the Pig carte blanche to go build him a good air force though and in six months the Pig has some Yank surplus light bombers, a few old fighters, has an airstrip built and both merc pilots and ground crews for the whole outfit. He also has himself a fat Swiss account.

"Just as the first planes are being given shake down flights, one of the pres' old cronies who he had promoted to general of the army tried a coup. The Pig was flying one of the fighters when he heard what was happening from one of his ground crew on the radio, so he goes and strafes the Bungan troops that are attacking the palace, single-handedly breaking up the coup. He becomes a national hero, at least to the pres and the tribe he is from.

"After the coup, he feels that he can only trust the mercs he has hired and he wants to rebuild his army with officers he can trust, so he turns to the Pig and his witch doctor. The pres is a very superstitious little fellow and he keeps a witch doctor in the palace with him. The Pig tells the pres he knows some professional soldier blokes, the witch doctor says the gods favor the white man and the Pig favors the juju man with a few quid. That is how the Pig had come to land in Salisbury.

"Mac and I sign straight aboard. The situation in Bunga is a bit rough, as far as the army went. They were using their bolt action Enfields like cricket bats. The army was the police force also, so a few had uniforms, most just wore old clothes and a few wore loin cloths. The president's tribe had taken over the country, naturally, and the other tribal groups had the status of slaves. A revolution was brewing. It was easy to see. As soon as we did a thorough reconnaissance, we got ahold of some of our mates and we reformed the bloody army from the ground up. Old Mac was a pretty sharp medic so he set up a hospital and a medic's school. I ran the infantry, a bloke named Hodge and Luke Keyes ran the artillery and training camps.

"About the time we got the troops in pretty good fighting order, the rebellion broke out in the northern provinces. We drove north in a column of trucks and armed land rovers, feeling a bit like old Popski and his Long Range boys and stamped it out. We took a few prisoners for his holiness, the pres, burned a few villages, let the troops loot a bit just for their moral and killed a few of the bad guys. It was more a show of strength than anything and the revolutionaries weren't organized. The pres promoted me to Hero of the Republic, too.

"Keyes, who was an old para, convinces the pres that we should have an airborne unit as a mobile reaction force. His holiness buys the gear and we set up a jump school. Only a handful of the trainees graduate without breaking something and all of them had to be pushed out the door on their first jump except this one captain. He was great, a real bloody hero. He had a swagger stick. The man stood in the door, swagger stick under one arm, and when Keyes, who was the jump master, tapped him, he just stepped out. Bloody beautiful. On graduation day, the pres and all his cronies come to watch his paras do their thing. We put on a stick jump with the captain first out the door and then Keyes does a bleedin' great free fall. The pres and his juju man go crazy. They want men that can do that. So we outfit a squad, but only the captain graduates without hurting himself or refusing to jump. On their graduation day, the pres and all his mates show up again for the ceremony. Our boy jumps from thirty thousand feet. Bloke never pulled his rip cord. Fell all the way, hit the runway, he did. A bit messy.''

I fell over the table laughing. The others, more restrained, let out a guffaw or two.

"So what happened to Mac and your blokes?" the Brit asked.

"We stayed on a time. The pres got to be a bit flaky so we looted the national bank and headed back to Salisbury," Muldoon said, leaning back in his chair.

I woke up the next morning slumped over a table. I'd passed out where I'd sat. My mouth tasted terrible, my head hurt, but basically I felt alive again. Or, at least human. Later that afternoon, an Air America pilot I knew told me they wanted me back at Danang ASAP. I caught a hop back with him.

Chapter Seven
Fire Bird

"You two are being transferred," Randall told Dane and I.

"*What*?" I barked, cutting Randall off. I couldn't believe it. Leave the team?

"To an intelligence outfit," Randall finished. He looked at the two of us.

Dane muttered something and slammed his fist down on a table he had one hip perched on.

"All of us are being shuffled around," Randall went on and then paused, waiting for a response.

"It's Church. I heard he was being transferred up here to Danang. That's why we're being split up," Dane finally got out.

Randall nodded with sudden comprehension. "Uh huh."

"Can we put in a fix somewhere? We've been pretty effective as a team," I said hopefully.

Randall grinned like he knew something that we didn't. "We'll see. In the meantime, do what they tell ya."

Dane and I showed up at the SOG building on Pasteur Street in Saigon as ordered. We were sent to another building by car, a luxury for me. I had really gotten used to jeeps and open trucks. The other building turned out to be an old walled-in villa on the outskirts of town, by the Saigon River. Armed Nungs opened the new steel gates to let us in, then quickly secured them behind us. Everyone we saw inside the walled compound wore civilian clothes or safari suits, which were uniforms of a sort.

Our driver escorted us into the villa. It had been left seedy on the outside, but inside the main house was modern. Passing through the ground floor, we saw a huge electronics commo room and another room crammed full of filing cabinets. We were led upstairs to a fancy office. The driver turned us over to a male secretary and left.

The secretary took us into a big office without knocking.

"Welcome to project Fire Bird, sergeants," a tall, trim man

147

dressed in jeans and a white open neck shirt said.

He wasn't the average spook. His hair was longish, dark, with a tinge of gray at the temples and he had a tan. He held a briar pipe in his left hand. He looked a little like Hugh Hefner. Gold-rimmed glasses lay on his desk. A definite patrician, he was no doubt a high level career officer with whatever agency he worked for.

"I'll be frank with you men. You were transferred to me on the recommendation, and request, of your control. Usually, I recruit my own people, not have them forced upon me. Do you men know why you were sent to us?" he asked, indicating seats to us as he spoke.

We took the seats. Dane began to speak, but I cut him off.

"A CIA case officer named Church used our team for bait without telling us he was doing it. One green beret was killed and I was captured and tortured as a result. He had our team moved from his command and control authority to Danang. Now I hear he's being transferred there, so our team's being kicked out," I told him.

He nodded. "That's not exactly what our reports say, uh, sergeant."

"No, sir, I don't reckon it is if Church wrote 'em."

The guy smiled at me. "You don't have a problem expressing what is on your mind, do you? Well, do you have any problems working here?"

"No sir. We are trying to reassemble our team. Until we do, this'll be fine," I said.

"Thank you. You'll be working for some of our people. No indigs and no uniforms. Do you men have any mufti?"

"Well, Dane here bought a safari suit up in Danang," I told him and the guy burst out laughing.

We were quartered in a hotel, given new ID and told to go buy some clothes. The big PX at the MACV complex took care of that. We were issued a variety of weapons. I kept my reworked .45 but Dane got a Browning 9mm. Then we were briefed.

The Fire Bird network was extensive. It collected *all* incoming intelligence, sorted through it with the aid of a computer, a first in the intelligence war, and acted on that intelligence in various

ways. The strong arm of the Project was the Provincial Recon Unit.
They were often run by two Navy Seals and composed of platoons
of indigs. The PRU teams struck at the communist infrastructure
at province level, raiding villages, ambushing NVA/VC tax men
and political officers, performing any task that required paramilitary force. Dane and I were a step up, working on a more covert
level. We infiltrated an area by blending in with it, not charging
into it.

In the secure compound, Dane and I were led to a room that looked like the ones at the Command and Control North (CCN) areas.
Four other men in civilian clothes were in the room as well as a
spook in a safari suit. No introductions were made, though Dane
nodded to one of the men and the guy returned it. When we were
seated, the spook passed out folders with "TOP SECRET"
stamped on them in red letters. I hesitated before opening mine.

"Open your folders, gentlemen," the spook said, apparently
noticing my hesitation. We all obeyed his order.

"The photos inside are of your target. He's one of ours and
he has gone rogue. We want him terminated with extreme prejudice," the spook told us and left.

All of us read the files silently. I knew why the spook left as
I thumbed through mine. It was so thorough that there wasn't a
damn thing he could add. It was also up to us to work out the
method of termination. The target was an American named Caffrey, who was a former U.S. Army NCO. He had worked for the
Agency in 1966 as a PM. He was not just a former NCO, but a
former green hat NCO. He had a long and deep involvement with
the Agency's Asian paramilitary operations and knew a lot about
them. During an operation for Fire Bird the previous year in Cambodia, he vanished for two weeks. It was suspected that he'd been
doubled, but when the mission was accomplished successfully, he
came in, turning himself in to a Thai border patrol unit. Returning to RVN, the Republic of Vietnam, he went completely rogue,
recruiting a mixed band of thugs.

He was still of use to the Agency though. For the Agency, he
dealt drugs, guns and information to the highest bidder. Some of
the intel he sold was good and some was disinformation. He was

an asset of sorts and they used him accordingly, especially for wet work (murder) on "civilians." That meant non-communists who got in the way of the Agency's plans. Opium warlords who wouldn't deal with them, for example.

But the guy had gone over the line. He'd smoked a CIA case officer. The Agency wanted him taken down and badly.

Hitting an American was a first for me and I didn't much care for it. I reread the file, trying to find a single thing that leapt out of the pages that would make me think this guy *should* go down, but there was nothing there to rationalize the hit. Not after working for the spooks myself. In the end, it came down to orders. We had our orders and that was that. If we didn't do the job, someone else would.

"Either of you two been on intel ops before?" the guy Dane had nodded to asked.

He was a big man, like Stone and Dane. In jeans, work boots and a short-sleeve khaki shirt, he looked like a construction worker until I looked into his eyes. There was a gleam there, a look of total concentration as though he could read my mind.

"SOG," I said.

He grunted. "This ain't much different. Yer wearin' yer cammo now instead of tiger suits is all."

Getting up, he walked over and stuck his hand out to me. "Name's Janca. I'm a marksman. Caulderson there," he said, pointing to a thin, hyper-looking guy with red hair and freckles, "is my spotter."

"They call me Hammer, light weapons specialist. Dane here is intel and ops."

The other two were Kile and Landers. All of us were green hats. We worked out a tentative plan. Kile actually knew the target. He would make contact, saying he and his partners had hijacked a load of weapons from an ARVN warehouse and then try to sell them to the target. If that approach failed, we would follow him until we found a spot where Janca could get to him. If the first approach worked, we would lure him to us, Janca would snipe him, I'd cover Kile and Landers' exfiltration from the hit site and Dane would handle the vehicle we would leave the area in. It sounded pretty simple. When we briefed our spook handler, he liked it too, so we set it in gear.

Kile knew a whore who worked at Xhian's who could carry messages to anyone. She was sort of Xhian's find-anything girl, so we sent her to find a black market buyer for stolen automatic weapons with the stipulation that the buyer had to be a round-eye. Then we set up an office in Xhian's and waited. Pretty soon, a Frenchman came wandering in, looking for us. He was a friend of a friend, he told us, and would inspect the merchandise to be sure it was worth buying. If it was, then the head man would make the transaction in American dollars. We had a place set up, if it was needed, but Kile got the Frenchman drunk, showed him an M16 and the guy *didi*'ed back to Caffrey. A meeting was set for the next night at Xhian's. It was a neutral place and she enforced her own security.

Dane and I went in several hours before the meet and partied, making it look like we were legitimate customers. Xhian's Chinese main security guard greeted us like long lost friends, inquiring after Lee Wong. Janca and Caulderson staked out on a rooftop to ID the target. Landers would follow Caffrey, if possible. Kile came in right before the meet.

Caffrey arrived a few minutes late. His indig bodyguards spread out on the grounds. One tried to come inside armed with an M3 grease gun, but Xhian's guard stopped him. No flunkies allowed. He and Kile talked briefly, drank a beer, then Caffrey went upstairs to see a whore. Kile split and we followed a half hour later, staggering out like we were drunk. Caffrey stayed the night.

Our team reassembled early the following afternoon. Landers had followed Caffrey to a small, run-down villa on the Saigon River.

"This is too easy," Dane said.

All of us nodded in agreement.

"Let's do it and get it over with," Landers growled.

There really was something wrong. The question was, should we try to find out what, or just carry out our mission? None of us liked the feeling we had about this operation. If Caffrey was a rogue and had killed a CIA agent, why was he still wandering around Saigon? Only a fool would do that and he didn't act like a fool. That was the danger of the CIA using fairly elite troops for goons; we thought about more than just how to perform the mission. We had a fairly rigid code which we lived, fought and sometimes died by. Caffrey didn't look or act like a man who had broken faith with his code and, rightly, feared for his life as a result. No, to me he seemed more like a security-conscious operative running a covert op. I think we all felt that way, except maybe Landers.

"Do we go?" I asked.

"Shit," Kile muttered.

"Yeah, there it is," Dane summed up for all of us.

Caffrey walked up to Kile, who was silhouetted in the glare of a streetlight, and the two turned and walked into our warehouse. Caffrey brought a truck and four indigs with him, all of them staying outside with the truck. Dane and Landers took the four of them with quick bursts of suppressed M3 grease gun fire as soon as the door closed behind Caffrey and Kile. When our target stepped through the door, I stuck my .45 in his ear and Kile disarmed him quickly.

"You guys tryin' to rip me off? Yer fuckin' up if you are," Caffrey told us, not sounding too concerned.

We injected him with sodium pentothal. Dane knew its use. It took us several hours to get the whole story out of him and be satisfied that what he was telling us was the truth. Caffrey wasn't a rogue. He was working for the Agency on a covert op. Someone decided that he knew far too much about their drug running ops and decided that he should take a long walk off a short pier for their own security. He was just a man doing his job. The curious thing about it all was that Church had been the guy's control on the Cambodia mission where he had allegedly turned.

Dane revived him with some drugs, stimulants that came from the same black case he had taken the sodium pentothal from. When he was up and around, our whole team, except Janca, assembled in the warehouse. He was around somewhere.

"You listenin'?" Kile asked Caffrey, who was tied to a chair.

"Uh huh," he mumbled, looking up at Kile.

"The Agency wants you whacked man," Kile told him.

"Shit," Caffrey responded.

"As far as we can tell, they have a file on you that says you wiped one of their case officers, that you've gone rogue. We know you aren't. So it must be you know something that they don't want you to."

"Huh," he said. Caffrey didn't know exactly what was going on and he didn't trust us. I couldn't blame him on that point.

"Tell him," I said to Kile.

"Look, can you E&E if we let you go man? Just fucking vanish?"

Caffrey looked up, his eyes searching our faces.

I nodded to him. "He means it."

"Yeah, I got a back door."

"Then git," Kile told him as Dane cut him loose.

Caffrey stood, rubbing his wrists and looking at us. "You boys cover yourselves?"

"Just go, man," I told him.

As Caffrey walked toward the front door, Landers snapped the barrel of his M3 up. "Freeze. No one goes anywhere. I thought you assholes might get goofy about this."

He covered us, then moved slightly to one side of Caffrey.

"You weak punks," he said, smiling at us. I smiled back.

"What did the spooks offer ya? A drug run you could skim?" I asked him.

Landers was still smiling as he swung the barrel of the M3 from us to Caffrey. He was smiling when he flew forward, blood gushing from the exit wound the souped up .308 hollow point made as it blew the front of his face apart.

Behind his corpse, Janca dropped down off a stack of crates across the warehouse, his modified, scoped, suppressed M21 rifle in his hand. He trotted to us.

"We're covered now. Caffrey, put your jewelry and ID on him and haul ass. And don't forget who saved yer ass, man," Janca told him.

Our report reflected that after we'd killed Caffrey and his four bodyguards, a fire broke out in the rear of the warehouse, possibly from a stray round fired during the hit. Five bodies were recovered from the ruins, one of which had been IDed by a ring on it as belonging to Caffrey. Janca's bullet had blown too many teeth out for a dental ID. We got a pat on the head for that.

Our next op was a cakewalk for us. Dane, Kile and I posed as the bodyguards for a CIA guy who was known as a black market arms dealer. We sold a load of rifle ammo and some mortar rounds to a VC who posed as an opium warlord's soldier. Every third bullet and every mortar round was boobytrapped with enough C4 plastic explosive to kill the rifleman or to demolish a mortar crew. We heard later that the buyer was executed as an American agent by his own people.

I'd mentioned to several of the spooks around that I wanted to find an NVA officer named Truong. They must have checked up on it and decided Truong would make a nice reward for us. Dane and I were called in for a briefing not long after the rigged ammo operation.

"Here are your travel orders. Report to our office in Can Tho. Wear uniforms," our handler told us with no further explanation.

We did all that, wearing jungle fatigues and our web gear, carrying CARs. At the Fire Bird office in the U.S. compound at Can Tho, a small city in the Delta, we were briefed by another spook and a Navy Seal officer. He led the PRU team for that province.

"One of Major Truong's men is in the village of Con Long. He was a sergeant on your A Team camp," the spook told us.

"Which one?" Dane asked.

"Suon," the Seal answered.

"Heavy weapons specialist. Little fat-faced guy who thought he was a real cowboy," Dane told me. I nodded. He had been Brick's counterpart.

"Capture him alive and he might lead you to Truong. We think that the major is operating out of Cambodia, just north of Con Long, and using that village for a staging area when he moves south," the spook said. "You'll be working with Lieutenant Nielson's PRU team on the snatch."

Con Long was a small hamlet on the Song Hau Giang River. The villagers farmed rice and fished the river so they were rich by their standards. The VC had been taking their various harvests in tithes, so the villagers informed the green berets who ran an A Team camp near them. When the camp was turned over to the ARVN forces, the head man tried to inform them about the NVA. ARVN security was like a sieve. The next ARVN patrol that went through the village found the head man tortured to death, mutilated, hanging from a tree near the village.

The Fire Bird people had several informers inside the village, though. Nielson and his PRU team had gathered then acted on several solid leads generated by the villages' informers. The PRU team caught sampans, small covered boats, full of ammo coming down river to the village one night and had taken out two NLF politicos and their escort a few weeks later.

Nielson and his XO, an enlisted Seal, briefed us on the village, then showed us a series of aerial photos. Since we were strap hangers, we couldn't plan the mission ourselves, as badly as we wanted to, but Nielson let us put in our two cents worth.

When we met his team that afternoon, I was surprised. Dane and I had worked with some pretty good indigenous troops, but the PRU team looked like a bunch of thugs, a street gang or something. Nielson assured us they would perform in the field, based on prior experience and a threat he held over them. If they didn't do what he told them and do it well, he would put them back in the jails he recruited them from.

Dane and I exchanged glances at that and the Seals laughed at us. I didn't think it was all that funny.

"We've got Nung NCOs though," Nielson said.

That night, we all piled into two big sampans, our faces patterned with camouflage paint, and headed upriver to a point a half mile south of the village. The PRU team consisted of almost fifty men. The Seal NCO took half of the team north, then spread out as a blocking force around the village. The rest of us went in from the south, infiltrating the village from the river.

Dane, a Nung NCO who spoke passable English and I would hit the hootch where Suon and his bodyguards stayed. Nielson and a squad of Nungs would cover us while the rest of his team deployed around the other hootches.

Dane and I crawled up into the village from the river bank, looking for sentries as we moved toward our target hootch. Around us we saw the shadowy shapes of the tiger-suited PRU team moving in, covering the hootches with their weapons. Suon must have felt very secure in the village. Only one sentry had been posted, and the PRU team got him quickly.

We moved into Suon's hootch. Suddenly, gunfire erupted outside. At first it was just a few shots, but it quickly escalated into long bursts of full auto fire. Many of the weapons we heard firing were AKs. Dane and I crouched, looking around the hootch. There was no one there.

Nielson burst in the front door. "It's an ambush. Fall back to the river," he said.

It wasn't much of an ambush, but it drove the PRU team out of the village. They weren't combat troops; they were the thugs that they looked to be. The Nung NCOs kept them in line and maintained a sort of fire discipline, but a lot of them were just spraying with their weapons, not hitting anything. We pulled back to the river bank, followed it to the sampans and loaded aboard them. The boats pulled into the PRU team's launch area at dawn. We were debriefed by the spook over a large breakfast.

Nielson caught us outside as we headed for the slick pad to catch a hop back to Saigon.

"Why don't you two hang around a day or so, see what turns up," he suggested.

"You think something will?" I asked. I was tired, sleepy and very pissed off about the failed raid.

He shrugged. "It'll take a few days to sort out who set that ambush up and why. Then we'll have some intel on Suon."

We agreed and Nielson sent us into town to a fancy colonial French hotel one of the spooks had a half interest in. We slept most of the day. When I woke in the late afternoon, I was starving, so I found my way downstairs to the dining room and ate a big meal. While I was eating, the Seal NCO joined me.

We talked about the raid and the Delta in general, how fighting there was different than fighting anywhere else in Nam. The Delta was the only area he had been, so I told him about the hills and mountains, the paddies and the rivers of the central highlands.

We started talking about the Rung Sat. He had been there too. Just as I finished my meal and ended my story about the Rung Sat, Dane joined us. Hearing us talk about the Zone, he told the Seal that I was the one who greased the crossbow sniper.

After that, the Seal NCO, whose name was Ernie, couldn't do enough for me. He found out I liked rock music, so he loaned me his portable 8-track tape player and a box full of tapes. That night, after supper, he lined me up with a pretty hooker. While he and Dane went to see the spook, the girl and I went back to my room.

Before either of us began undressing, I hooked up the tape player. Looking through the box of tapes, I found several by the Doors, my favorite band at that time. The first time I heard Jim Morrison, the band's lead vocalist, sing, I was hooked by the hypnotic, erotic quality of his voice. One of the band's songs, "The End," just about caused me to run into a mortar barrage. That was my introduction to the band. I'd been sitting in a gun bunker on a firebase in the An Loi Forest during a mortar attack when that song came on the radio of one of the other guys in the bunker. The End? Holy shit!

Nam was a rock 'n' roll kind of war. It seemed incongruous to me that professional killers like us were rocking to the same music as the hippies, who obviously hated us. But a lot of the younger green hats were. And when I say I was "into" rock, I mean to the point that I could name every song on any given album, knew the words to most of them by heart and knew the name of every band member for any band I liked and their history. It was my release, an escape of sorts.

All of us had our little vices, except Randall whose only known vice was exotic weapons, but they were never talked about as long as they didn't interfere with our performance on a mission. I drank, smoked weed on occasion and ate benzedrine in the field when I needed it. It was issued to us. Some of the others did the same and some didn't. As long as I didn't get drunk on a mission, light a joint in the field or become addicted to anything other than the combat itself, no one gave a fuck what I did to survive between ops. It was an unwritten rule of the war. Some of my other vices

were eating good food, making love to tasty women and listening
to loud rock 'n' roll.

"Do you like rock 'n' roll?" I asked the girl.

She just smiled.

Taking that as an affirmative, I pushed the tape in the deck.
The room was filled with the eerie, haunting sound of the organ
and then Jim's voice. The girl squealed something and dug into
her purse, coming out with a huge joint. Waving it at me, I nodded,
and she smiled again.

We smoked it sitting on the bed, making it a sensual experience,
touching, slowly undressing each other as the warm, mellow high
washed over us. We made love slowly, tenderly, on the big soft
bed while the Doors sang us a metaphysical lullaby. While we lay
sated and panting, the tape began to replay. I got up and dug
through the box of tapes and found several more by the Doors.
Plugging one in, I went back to the bed. The girl gave me a mas-
sage and my mind drifted.

I woke to the ripping snarl of full auto weapons fire. My mind
identified them immediately as AKs. I pulled my jungle fatigue
pants on, laid my Colt pistol beside me on the bed and thrust my
bare feet into my jungle boots. The girl stood by the bureau where
the tape player was, naked, washing herself in a basin. She looked over her shoulder at me and smiled.

I crossed the room to a pair of shuttered doors, cracked one
open and peeked out into the night. We were on the second floor
of the hotel. I couldn't see the street below so I pulled the door
open further and edged out onto the small veranda. Below me,
I saw a Viet MP jeep with two dead Canh Sats (South Vietnamese
National Police) in it. Across the street, two black-clad VC were
climbing a steel ladder up the side of a building. Looking up, I
saw another one on the roof of the building, almost directly across
from me. He turned and looked down at me.

I dove for the open door as the VC fired a long raking burst.
The doors splintered under the bullets' impact. I rolled inside the
room and came to my feet. As I rose, I saw the girl fall sideways
off the bureau. Her blood was splattered on the wall and had
puddled on the bureau. Jim Morrison sang something about

touching him.

Peeking around one of the corners of the door sill, I saw the VC on the roof looking down into the street. He was pointing at my room and yelling instructions to someone below. Taking a steady two-handed grip, I double tapped him with the .45 and the VC fell back. I fired two rounds at another one on the ladder, saw him sag, then ducked back into the room and made a dash for the telephone. It was dead when I lifted the receiver.

I heard a long burst of AK fire inside the hotel, the sound of running feet in the hall and my door suddenly burst open. The VC fired at the sound of the music when he came through the door, screaming in Viet. I let out an incoherent roar and hit him twice in the chest with the .45. The goofy fucker was not only trying to kill me, he was shooting at my music, too! He staggered, bounced off the door and fell inward.

Moving quickly, keeping the door covered and staying close to the wall on the opposite side of the room from the tape deck, I reached the VC and took his AK. I was down to my last pistol round, but I had a rifle and some spare magazines from his bandoleer now. I could hold the little fellas off for a while now.

From the hallway, someone called out in Viet. I took a peek around the door sill and saw two VC creeping toward my door, nervous, weapons covering the doors to the other rooms as they came. I stepped halfway out the door and hit the closest one with a burst from my captured AK. It threw him back into the other one and they both went down. As the fallen VC tried to untangle himself, I riddled him. The AK clicked empty.

Dropping the magazine, I pulled a full one from the pouch of the dead VC in my room and chambered a round. I heard something thump in the hall and dove away from the door. A grenade went off, blowing the door off its hinges. I rolled behind the bed, pulled the mattress down in front of me and waited. Morrison was singing about digging a grave for the Unknown Soldier. Great.

I'd make my last stand listening to rock 'n' roll. That should be good for a footnote in *Rolling Rock* magazine, maybe make the Rock 'n' Roll Hall of Fame someday. I started giggling.

A VC tossed a frag in the room. I tucked myself under the mattress as it blew, deafening me. Shrapnel cut through the mattress, burning me. I could still hear the Doors, though. Incredible. A VC jumped through the door, firing, spraying the room. Then another stepped in behind him. I ripped the first one from the groin to the chest with the AK, rolled over once to my right as the second VC sent a burst into the mattress where I'd been and I put him down too.

I could hear a fire fight going on outside. Standing, I staggered over to the shredded porch doors and peeked outside. I saw men in tiger suits advancing, firing as they moved along the street below. It was Nielson's PRU team. Then I heard a bolt slam shut behind me.

Whirling, I saw the last VC I'd shot sitting up, trying to clear his AK. I'd fucked up and hadn't made sure they were all dead before turning my back on them. I pointed my AK at him and barked, *"Cheiu Hoi!"*

He looked up. It was Suon.

I walked over to him and he threw the AK aside. I'd hit his weapon and not him.

"You remember me?" I asked, standing over him.

"Yes."

The guy had fancied himself a cowboy. He'd worn his .45 auto in a low slung gunfighter rig on the camp and I saw that he still wore it that way. I guess that was what we got for showing too many John Wayne movies to the Viets. For some reason that I could never understand, American Westerns were really big with the Viets and the Duke in particular was a cult hero.

"Where's Truong?" I asked, moving the barrel of the AK I held close to his face.

He ignored my question. "May I smoke?" he asked.

I kicked him in the face. "Where's Truong, you gook cocksucker?" I snarled.

He spat blood on me.

"You fight me fair, big nose? You and me, fast draw. You win, I tell where Colonel Truong is."

Morrison sang, "The music is your special friend, dance on fire until the end."

I thought about his offer. If I won he would be dead and he couldn't tell me shit. I was a fair hand with any weapon, but I'd never practiced quick drawing a pistol. If he won, I'd be dead and I didn't care much for that idea.

Suon laid a hand on his pistol butt, releasing the snap that held it secure in the holster. "What say, green beret? Fast draw?"

"I say, fuck that!" and ripped him with a long burst from the AK.

The PRU team greased the rest of the VC raiders. I was sitting on the floor, smoking a cigarette I found on one of the dead gooks when Ernie the Seal and some of his PRU team came in, looking around at the damage and the bodies.

"When the music's over, turn out the lights," Morrison sang.

I hit the light switch as we left the room.

A few days later, Dane and I got orders for CCN, Danang.

Chapter Eight

The Village

Dane and I landed at Danang and were met by Randall and a jeep.

"How'd ya pull this one off?" I asked him after we all shook hands.

"I made Church a deal," he said grinning, leading us to his jeep. I didn't like the way he grinned at us. "A deal?"

"None of us will kill him if he doesn't try to kill any of us."

"That was it?" Dane asked, suspiciously.

Randall grinned at us again as he wheeled the jeep around and headed toward our compound. I got a sinking feeling in my gut.

"I volunteered us for a training op in Laos. As soon as we're all back together, we'll be briefed on it."

I sat back in the jeep. A training operation in Laos? That was a major portion of the Special Forces' mission roll, that of force multiplier, training indigs to fight so that Americans didn't have to. Not exactly what I thought SOG did. Laos was off limits to U.S. troops. As far as I knew, the Agency ran its PMs, not green hat teams, in there to train the mountain tribes. It didn't really matter to me, though. I was game for anything.

When Randall pulled up at our compound area, the three of us went inside. Marty Bender, Blake, and a huge hairy guy in a tiger suit were sprawled on the bunks, drinking beer. We all shook hands and grinned. Randall introduced the big guy as Griz, a contraction of his Polish name which Randall couldn't pronounce and no one in the Army could spell. Someone had named him right. He looked like a grizzly bear.

The next day a Lao general named Ving Tao briefed us on the situation with the Montagnards in Laos. There were four tribal groups being paid by the CIA to disrupt the flow of supplies coming down the Ho Chi Minh Trail. Most of them were trained by CIA

PMs, led by Royal Lao Army officers and supported by Air America planes that brought the villagers rice and weapons. The Royal Lao Army hadn't been very successful in those operations because the Yards hated them. The Agency decided, based on the success of the White Star teams led by Bull Simons in the early Sixties, to run a U.S. Army team, troops that were specialists in training and leading insurgency forces, into Laos. It was tailor-made for green hats.

Our briefings from General Tao, a Montagnard himself, and several Agency people went on for several days. There was a huge amount of information to ingest, so they briefed us, then gave us short breaks while we thought it all over and tried to make sense of what they were telling us about the region, the people and the situation. One evening after a long day of briefings, Dane and I were crossing the compound on our way to the NCO club when we saw Gustav. He had been with the Mike Force that had helped secure our camp after Truong had sold us out. Now he headed toward us.

"Paul Gustav?" Dane asked the tall man, dressed in tiger suit and patrol harness.

"Dane, good to see you! I didn't know you were up here," he said shaking Dane's hand by clasping it with both of his.

"You remember Hammer here?" Dane said, nodding towards me.

Gustav shook my hand the same way, making me feel that he was really glad to see me. "Hammer, a curious name, one from my homeland. You were on Hardin's A Team," he said, stating fact, not asking a question.

"Yeah, and his recon team."

I couldn't place the accent. It wasn't German, something I'd heard at home all my life. And it wasn't Pole or Russian, other familiar accents from my old neighborhood. Gustav was tall and lean, his pale blond hair cut so short I could see his pink scalp. His eyes were a striking blue and had a piercing quality that was hard to meet for long. Dane invited him to join us. We found Blake and Griz already at the club when we arrived.

Gustav greeted Griz like a long lost brother. Then we all got

drunk and war stories started flying. Griz told Gustav stories and
vice versa. Paul Gustav had been born Paal Gustavsson in Finland.
At fifteen, he fought the Russians for three months in his father-
land's ill-fated Winter War. Later, he joined the German SS, fighting on the Eastern Front until the end. He enlisted in the Legion
with many other SS veterans and fought in Indochina. Wounded
before Dien Bien Phu, he missed that debacle. Sponsored into the
U.S. by an ex-SS officer who worked for both the Gehlen Organization and the CIA, he Americanized his name. When he heard that
the U.S. Army was looking for men of Northern European extraction who spoke their native languages, he enlisted and became one
of the first of the green berets. He was on his fourth tour in Nam.

"I have been among the H'Mong most of my time. Some Katu,
but they are treacherous and uncontrollable. The H'Mong are fine
gentle people. Fierce in battle, but they only fight to defend their
opium," he told Griz between mugs of beer. He swallowed them
whole, in a single gulp.

"I worked with them once. You see?" Griz said, holding up
one huge forearm. Clasped around his wrist was a beaten copper
bracelet.

Gustav grinned. "Yes, but I have been there in this decade!"
he said and emitted a low rumbling laugh.

Gyrzabowski, Griz's real name, had led a Meo force during his
tour in Indochina with the Legion. They were similiar to our Mobile
Guerrilla Forces; lean, mean and mobile. The French had disarmed
them, leaving them to the not-so-tender mercies of the Viet Minh
after Dien Bien Phu, a fate Griz had never forgiven the French
for. He joined the OAS, a French terrorist group, years later for
revenge on the government he felt had betrayed his efforts, but
hadn't gotten that either and eventually drifted to the U.S. and
the Special Forces.

The more they drank, the more war stories came forth. Late
in the evening, they began singing Legion songs. I joined in, having learned a few at Bear's. The rest of the evening was a blur.

Four days later I saw Gustav again. He was dressed for an operation. Two other green hats and six Nungs were standing around
with him at the edge of the helipad. Behind them two black slicks

were warming up. He spotted me and waved. I threw half a salute. They loaded up and were gone. I watched their slicks disappear into the distance, mentally wishing them well.

Gustav's RT hit its LZ and lost the second slick as soon as it touched down. An RPG, a light machine gun, killed the pilot and wounded the copilot as the team members cleared the slick. It crashed straight down. Small arms fire pinned the team to the ground. An RPG hit the slick and it fireballed, spewing bits of molten aluminum over the LZ. A shattered piece of rotor blade cut a Nung in half as it flew away from the ship. Then the NVA assaulted the team.

It only took one wave to overrun Gustav's team. One of the green hats rose to his knee, firing his CAR 15 into the front ranks of advancing NVA while a Nung tried to put out M79 rounds, but they were both hit repeatedly and fell back. Gustav fired from the ground, throwing a frag, before enemy soldiers were all over him. He kicked one in the groin, beat another over the head with his CAR 15 and felt the stock shatter. Jamming the flash suppressor in another's eye, he squeezed the trigger and shot off a three-round burst. Bits of the NVA splattered on him. He killed several more in quick hand-to-hand combat.

As quickly as it had started, it was over. The first slick came back on station, both door guns blazing. It took several hits from ground fire and veered away, calling for gunships.

Gustav crouched among a pile of dead NVA. Blood ran from his multiple bayonet wounds from the hand-to-hand fighting and the back of his uniform smoked where pieces of hot aluminum from the burning slick struck him. Roaring a battle cry, he charged the nearest tree line, snatching up an AK 47 as he ran, spraying it on full auto.

Suddenly the LZ was hit by a rapid series of explosions as two gunships dove, firing their rockets. An explosion right behind Gustav picked him up and threw him through the air like a rag doll into the foliage at the edge of the LZ.

At Danang, we got a sudden alert. A team needed help; a Hatchet Team or reaction force for covert operations, was being assembled. There was a sudden rush for the arms room, drunks became sober and we scrambled into all of the available slicks. Our team would go in first to secure the LZ.

There were gunships with us; they would fly cover and a FAC was already on station. Spectres were getting the word too. Our slicks dove in for the LZ and we hit the ground. Regrouping, we moved in a sweeping skirmish line for the LZ where the RT was down.

When we got there, we found a massacre. Part of the reaction force put out security while the rest of us closed on the LZ. The wrecked, smoking carcass of a slick and the sickly sweet stench of burnt flesh greeted us. Then we found the stripped, mutilated remains of the RT spread around the small clearing. One of the green hats on the reaction force was sick. We counted the dead and called for an extraction with thirteen body bags. It was all over for that RT.

When we had been briefed, Randall took Dane and I out onto the beach.

"One of the green hats is unaccounted for. Krang and I found a set of jungle boot prints leading away from the LZ, fresher than the NVA tracks. I think it's Gustav. The other American bodies weren't tall enough," he told us.

"You think he's alive?" I asked, incredulously.

"Yeah and I'm pretty sure where he'll go. I told Church my thoughts on this. I want to take a team in and try to bring him out. You game?"

Dane and I both nodded.

When we approached Church about it, he said no. Our launch date for the operation in Laos was being pushed up. Some of the higher ups in the Agency and the Pentagon wanted the project in operation ASAP to gauge its feasibility. If it was successful, more teams would be sent in. Our final briefing was on air support that we could call on. There were covert air base FOBs in Laos, flying all sorts of prop-driven combat aircraft that we could control. Fast movers were available from bases in both Nam and Thailand. In addition, Air America would supply all of our ground supply needs.

That night we were loaded onto a C130 and flown to Thailand.

I sat next to Randall during the flight. He studied a map for most of the trip.

"What about Gustav?" I asked.

Randall shrugged. "We'll do what we can. He may work his way out by himself. I think he'll look for a H'Mong village and hide out 'til he feels like humping on down. Right now we got our own thing to do."

"Maybe we can send some patrols out," I started.

He made a chopping motion with his hand. "We'll do what we can. Look, I don't like it any more than you, but we've got our orders. Gustav's got more time under the gun than our whole team together. If anyone can make it out, he can. Case fucking closed."

I slumped back in my seat, knowing Randall was right and hating it. Missions superseded individuals. I knew the logic of that. It was the personal side I had some problems with. We landed an hour later at a small FOB in northern Thailand, got some sleep and then boarded an Air America Caribou for our insertion. It took us to a small jungle airstrip hacked out of the woods in a valley deep in Laos. When we cleared the plane, it turned around and took off immediately. A small group of H'Mong tribesmen in OD jungle fatigues met us at the field with a white man in a camouflage uniform. He carried a Swedish K SMG. I didn't recognize the camo pattern he wore.

"French," Griz told us, referring to the camo as the small group of men walked toward us.

The white man introduced himself as Marcel. Griz and Krang spoke to him briefly in French. He grinned at them, led us to two small trucks that were hidden under some camo netting and we were off. Our next stop would be the village.

It looked like something straight out of a movie. Peaked, thatch-roofed long houses built of logs were on stilts around a small clearing in a valley. The people looked like the Yards we had worked with on the A Team camp in Nam, but these people wore brightly colored clothing and smiled more often. As we drove into the village, the workers stopped working and the long houses emptied as H'Mong tribespeople gathered around us.

An old white-haired man forced his way through to us, bowing. He spoke a rapid stream of French to Marcel, who rattled something back at him. Griz began translating to Randall in a low voice that I couldn't hear. I thought that curious since I knew Randall spoke French as well as several dialects of Yard and Viet. Perhaps he didn't want the H'Mong to know that he could understand them yet. I let my attention wander to the smiling faces surrounding us.

The women stood in the front ranks, staring boldly at us and smiling. Most oriental women wouldn't meet a man's eyes or show a smile in public so boldly. I decided right then that I liked these people. I noticed that many of the women had blackened teeth from chewing betel nut, a mild, natural amphetamine. They were mostly short, stout people, but they looked both happy and healthy, a real contrast to the people, both Yard and Viet, I'd seen in Nam.

When the head man finished his speech, Randall made one of his own, which Marcel translated into French. There was a lot of grinning and clapping when Randall told them about the free rice and guns they would get just for helping us out. After that, the head man introduced his three sons to all of us. After a brief tour of the village, we broke up and went to our assigned long houses. That night, after we stashed our gear, the village threw us a feast. We drank some of their fermented rice wine and partied with them until Randall called us away from it. Our team retired to a long house we appropriated for our field CP, put our Nungs out as security and held a team conference.

"They grow poppies sarge," Dane told Randall. "There's a field on the hill behind us."

"Yeah and some of the old men smoke it, but I saw no sign of wide use among the young," Griz added.

"I hate fuckin' opium," Bender grunted.

"They trade it for weapons," Dane said, "for food and for protection."

"They've got us now," Randall told us, then gave us our individual briefings and job assignments.

Blake and I were to set up a range and instruct our first platoon in small arms. That platoon would form the cadre and train others. Griz would teach mortars, Dane the M60s. Bender would set up a commo bunker in the village, then train platoon and company RTOs. All of us would have several Nungs working with us, too. Randall and Krang would recon the area around the village with one of the head man's sons and several of the son's cronies.

We had to build a small airstrip, too, one capable of handling a Caribou. Our first load of supplies, weapons and ammo, would be sent in by helicopter, but all of our resupply would come in by plane. While Dane, Griz and I built our range, the others would start the strip. Perforated Steel Plates (PSP) were coming in slung underneath the helicopter that was bringing our weapons. The manual labor made me feel better physically, and the H'Mong pitched right in. We'd tell them what we wanted done and they would just go and do it.

The big Sikorsky helicopter came in and dropped our weapons and PSP that afternoon. Randall and Krang had security patrols out, but they saw no sign of the enemy at all. We kept working with the villagers and within a week we had begun actual training with the rifles and M60s. A plane came in on our tenth day in the village, bringing in rice and medical supplies from USAID. Two weeks later, we had the basis of a trained strike company consisting of sixty H'Mong villagers. We began sending out patrols further and further from the village.

At the end of our first month there, a patrol of ten H'Mong led by one of the head man's sons, three Nungs, Blake and I, drew first blood. Randall had given us the okay to hit the NVA wherever and whenever we found them. We found them on that patrol, moving along a trail about ten miles from the village. We were on a three-day patrol to find them and check for troop movement. Bao had been leading us along a heavily forested ridge line, with me on slack, when he held up a fist. We all froze in place in response to his hand signal. I turned to watch the H'Mong to check their reactions. They froze and slowly sank to one knee, all behind cover. Perfect. Just as we trained them.

Bao gave me a hand signal. Fifteen NVA, two Pathet Lao guides. I flashed a signal back to Blake and the others. They spread out and watched me. Blake came crawling up. I briefed him quickly and we decided to blood the patrol.

The enemy force was moving past us at an angle, walking down the face of the ridge into the valley below them. We moved behind them after they passed, dropped down into the valley, then stalked them until they stopped for food.

I spread our team out along the trail ahead of the line of march we hoped they would take. Moving among the H'Mong, I made sure that they all had their weapons set on semi-auto and told them to wait for me to fire before they took any targets down. Blake spaced the Nungs with the H'Mong, making sure that a battle-hardened soldier was close to every other tribesman. Then we took our places at opposite ends of the firing line. I was carrying a pump shotgun. After I was sure that we were set up right, I settled in to wait.

A half hour crawled by and then one of the Pathet Lao came strolling down the trail on point. Not far behind him the other Lao guerrilla led the NVA squad. I blotted sweat out of my eyes, pulled two extra shells out of my pocket, cupped them in my left hand and hefted the shotgun. As the point man got slightly past me, I blew his head apart, spun and caught the second one in the chest. A wave of single rifle shots sounded, so close together that they sounded like one long shot. NVA dropped, hurled off their feet. A second barrage began. Blake yelled a command and the firing stopped.

We'd wiped them all. Blake called in a contact report, we stripped the bodies of weapons, ammo and personal affects to make it look like bandits had done the job, then hid the corpses. H'Mong troops put security out for us as we worked. They had done well. Blake rounded up all of our people and we moved off.

In the following three weeks, we took turns running patrols. All of us made contact. Randall even found enough NVA to merit an air strike. He caught a company of NVA moving with six trucks full of ammo. While one patrol was out, the rest of us did security duty at the village or visited other H'Mong villages, trying to recruit them. We also did Medcaps, medical missions into villages where we offered free medical treatments. I was learning H'Mong as fast as I could and learned enough to engage in simple conversations.

Dane and I brought in a second village. They lived above us, on the side of a high hill. Our H'Mong helped train them and we brought in another load of weapons, rice and medicine for them. By the middle of our third month in place, we had two companies of strikers. The Agency loved it. They sent us tiger suits, boots and whatever we asked for. Our operations began to expand, too. We took out three or four platoons at a time for raids, our best one wiping out the headquarters element of an NVA regiment, then controlling an air strike on the rest of the unit. Later, that same strike force ambushed a large NVA supply convoy and wiped it out also. Blake took a round through the forearm on that operation and had to be Medevaced out when the strike force made it back to the village.

Things were going well. The H'Mong troops were, for the most part, excellent soldiers. They fought hard and well, showed initiative in the field and were tireless on the march. I was so relaxed living among them that I had put on ten pounds. Dane ran intel patrols to other villages and began gathering better and more immediately useful information. He worked on setting up a regular network. Randall or I usually accompanied him, along with three Nungs and a squad of the H'Mong. At one of the villages south of us, a H'Mong smuggler from another village even further to the south told us about big battles around his area. A Meo tribe was kicking boocoo NVA ass, according to this smuggler and they had a foreign warlord leading them. We tried to get more information from the guy, but he clammed up and wouldn't say any more after the local head man made a hand sign to him. We wanted a better description of the village so that we could locate it on our maps.

When our patrol got back to its HQ village, we told Randall about what the smuggler told us. A big grin split his face.

"Gustav," he said.

"We can check it out, see if another RT is in place. If not...," Dane said.

Before any of that was accomplished, we got an order to have the head man bring his opium harvest down to the airstrip for pickup. We gritted our teeth, but we did it. None of us wanted

to touch the shit. We kept our involvement peripheral. The two
villages we ran brought their harvests of raw opium in together.
It sat in bales, covered by tarps and camo netting at one end of
the strip with a guard of villagers around it. The patrol we had
planned was canceled so we would have plenty of security out for
the pickup. Our orders had been specific. We were all to be in
the village when the plane came.

We were all there. The plane landed, opened its hatches and
Church hopped out. Naturally. Opium seemed to attract scumbags
and Church fit that bill perfectly. As the H'Mong tribesmen began
loading the bales of O, Church and two round-eyed PMs with Uzi
SMGs dangling from their shoulders came jogging toward us.

"Where's your CP?" he barked at Randall, who led him to it.

The rest of us trailed along. Randall called Dane and Griz in
and left me outside with the two PMs who wore dark glasses and
didn't speak. Marty was with his radios. I got tired of waiting,
so I took Bao and went on an inspection tour of the village's
defenses. I stayed away until Church briefed Randall, visited the
head man, then got back aboard the C123 and flew out. Then I
went back to the CP.

"You're not gonna like this, son, but listen to all of it 'fore you
start barkin'," Randall told me when I climbed the notched log
that served as a front stairway into our team house.

I frowned, puzzled, and sat down next to Dane, picking up a
gourd of water. "Sure, sarge."

"There's a village about fifty miles southeast of us that's been
hitting General Ving Tao's villages on a regular basis, according
to Church. They're bandits, maybe in the NVA's pay. They've
hit a coupla RTs too, for the bounty. Church wants us to take
a full company of our strikers and wipe the place," Randall said.

I didn't say a word.

"After that, we'll start rotating out two at a time for two week
R&Rs in Bangkok," Randall went on.

"Can I talk now?" I asked.

Randall nodded at me.

"You believe that bandit shit?"

"What do you think?"

We were transported from our HQ village to our TA by black slicks flying out of Thailand. They set us down in a valley far enough from our TA that we hoped they wouldn't see us when we inserted. I was on the lead slick in. We unloaded, secured the LZ and brought the rest of the slicks in. Very few of the H'Mong had ever been on a slick before and they were having a ball. We even had a hard time getting some of them off. They wanted to go back up and come in again. Finally, we got all of them off. I took the squad I had drawn first blood with, who were acting as the recon element for the strike force, and led the way off the LZ and up onto a ridge line.

Bao and I took the point and led the way to the village. We moved cautiously and quietly. If the people in the village were really bandits, they probably would not have any LPs or roving patrols out. If they were run by the NVA or Gustav, it was almost certain that they *would* have extended security of some kind around their village. I didn't want to run into any of their people before we could establish just who controlled this ville.

Around midday, we spotted the village by the smoke from its cooking fires from up on the ridge we had been following. I halted the strike force and briefed Randall. He sent my squad down closer to check out the place. Dane came with us. We worked along the ridge to get a better view of the ville and found that it was screened by patrols. We couldn't get closer. Roving patrols crisscrossed each other, weaving a pretty tight net around the village. Our squad pulled back to the strike force after getting as close as we dared. I briefed Randall on what we had seen, which wasn't much.

Calling in, we told our relay that we couldn't hit the ville that day. We'd make a move that night. The confirmation was a simple affirmative and we were told that the extraction slicks would be staged right across the Thai border, waiting for our signal to come and get us.

We ate and rested. That night, Krang and Randall led us down off the ridge.

We found an LP and quietly killed the two men in it. None of the patrols we had encountered earlier were around. They had been pulled in for the night. Closing on the village, we halted and spread out in the tree line just beyond the bunkers that surrounded the village. We waited. It took several hours after we were in place before the inhabitants quieted down and went to sleep.

I crawled over to Randall and put my lips next to his ear. "This place is set up like an A Camp."

He grunted. "You see any tall white men in there?"

"No."

"Let's do it then."

We moved in on the ville, each of us taking a platoon of H'Mong strikers. Griz and his platoon worked their way to the south edge of the ville as a blocking force. I led a ten-man infiltration squad to clear a path through the bunker line for Randall's and my platoon. Dane and his platoon would follow Randall in, but act as a reaction force and mobile reserve in case we met too heavy a resistance. As I crawled across the killing ground, the clear space between the tree line and the village, a flare went up from the village.

Right then, I knew how the VC felt when they tried to infiltrate our perimeters. I don't know if I tripped the flare or someone heard me moving and popped one. I tried to dig a hole with my shirt buttons when it went up, though.

My squad froze in place, burying their blackened faces in the dirt. I held my breath, my heart pounding so strongly I was sure they could hear it in the village. We waited. The flare began to sputter and fall to the earth. When it went out, I waited a minute, then signaled the squad to move in. As we started forward, a second flare popped and an M60 opened fire on us from the village. Bullets cut through the air inches above our prone bodies. Suddenly the M60 stopped firing and something landed with a dull thud ten feet in front of me.

Just as my mind recognized it, the frag went off, stunning me. I'd covered my face and head with my arms, but that was all I'd had time to do. The next thing I knew shapes were running past me, hands were on my body and I was being dragged somewhere. A big man stood over me. I realized I was inside the ville.

Looking up, I flashed back to the big Chinese major and the POW camp, but I knew that guy was dead. My heart skipped a beat. Then I looked up into the man's face.

It was Gustav.

"Hey, Paul Gustav! You're fuckin' alive, man!" I shouted, trying to stand.

The man leaned over me when I'd fallen back to the ground, then he poured water from a canteen over my face and wiped at it.

"Hammer?" he barked in surprise.

"Yeah."

"Is that your team out there attacking my ville?"

"Yeah."

"Why, for god's sake?"

"The CIA told us you were a bad guy, a gook."

"*What*?"

"A spook told us this ville was run by bandits or NVA, man."

"Stay here, I'll stop this madness," he told me, when wheeled and stalked off into the night.

I heard him yelling for his troops to stop firing. Then he yelled to Randall. Soon both men were walking across the killing ground toward each other. When Randall saw Gustav and recognized him, he slung his rifle and embraced the big man.

Our strike force came in when Randall called each platoon on the radio. Griz just about ran in. Gustav's village threw us a feast. None of them seemed to hold it against us that we had knifed to death two of their men just a few hours earlier, or that we were trying to catch them asleep and slaughter all of them. Gustav explained to his ville's head man that it was just a big mistake and all was well. It was time to party.

I'd been hit with shrapnel in the head and arms and blood poured down over my face. That was what Gustav had wiped off of my face when he was trying to recognize me. His village medic patched me up, picking out a few of the bigger chunks, cleaned the wounds, then sewed me up while the feast was going on. Around noon, Bao came and woke me for a team meeting. The party was still going.

All of our team were seated in a hootch which obviously belonged to Gustav. He sat cross-legged on a mat in one corner of it.

"Why's the Agency want your head, Paul?" Griz asked as I

came in.

Gustav grinned. "Because, *mon ami*, I have five villages under my control and none of them bow to the expoiter, Ving Tao. I have stopped the cultivation of the poppy for Ving Tao's coffers and replaced it with rice. These people feed themselves now. They don't need handouts from USAID or any opium warlord."

"They told us you'd hit two of our teams, man," I said.

"No, I wiped out one of their PM bully boy outfits that tried to convince one of my villes to grow poppies again. Wasn't much of a fight. They shot the head man when he refused to plant poppies. I arrived the next day and shot them," Gustav told us.

"Seems fair," Griz said.

We talked for several more hours. At the end of it, we made a deal and a plan. Gustav would move his village up into the mountains. We would claim another village under our control and supply them with food and weapons. When he evacuated his village, we would torch it, claiming mission success on our raid. All of us liked the idea.

"What're ya gonna do Paul, stay in the bush?" I asked later that afternoon.

"Yes."

"Forever?"

He smiled. "I have been fighting communists since, well, for over thirty years. It began when the Bolsheviks unleashed their Mongols on my homeland. I was only a child, yet our children fought. My homeland survived, but many of my kinsmen did not. This is my revenge. I will fight the communists until I no longer have breath to power my body."

I nodded. That guy knew how to hold a grudge. Thirty years of war. I was into my third. I could feel myself dying inside from it, from the cruelty inflicted on my comrades not only by the enemy, but by our own people as well, like the hippies who greeted us at the airport, and Church, flip sides of the same coin.

"How the fuck did you get off the LZ man?"

"When the gunships made their run, the NVA broke off their assault. I ran into the nearest trees, taking what I could from the dead NVA. By that night I'd made it into the mountains. My uniform had been practically burnt off my back and I was wounded, so I chanced a fire to boil water and warm myself.

"The next day I found a group of NVA. Following them, I snatched one from the trail and got his food and ammo. I made a shirt from mine and his together. Then I struck out for a H'Mong ville. I knew that if I stayed in the highlands I'd find one eventually. So instead of going east toward Nam, I went west into the Cordillera.

"Finally, I found this ville. I don't know how long I'd been on foot. Days, weeks, I don't know. As I approached it, a band of Pathet Lao came jogging into the ville. There were about ten of them. They shot the head man for growing poppies for Ving Tao, then dragged his wife and daughter into a hootch and began gang raping them. I snuck down to the ville and took their sentry out. Then I went into the hootch after them. The ville elected me its head man that night.

"Since then, we've been training and organizing. I don't dislike Ving Tao as much as I say. He does some good things for his people. I hate the drugs though. They are stealing the soul of these folk as the communists steal the souls of the people they rule. I try to show the H'Mong that they don't need the poppy, that they can survive as warriors and hunters, with dignity, without being anyone's pawn."

We had been walking as he talked. He stopped, clapped me on the back and turned back toward the long houses.

"My sermon for the year. Let's rejoin the party," he said.

When our extraction slicks returned to our village, Church and his two bodyguards were waiting.

"I want a full report," he told Randall, his eyes darting to me nervously. I looked pretty wild, bandaged and bloody and not very happy to see him.

Randall told him more or less what really happened until I was captured. Then he told Church the version we had concocted. When he was through, Church questioned all of us carefully about whether any Combloc bodies had been found in the ruins of the village.

"Combloc?" I asked.

"Yeah. Russian, East German. Combloc."

"Nah. Jus' gooks."

We stayed in place, with two weeks of R&R in Bangkok as promised, until just before the next poppy harvest was due. Our strike
force was doing well, hitting the NVA and Pathet Lao deep in
what they considered safe territory. We took casualties, but they
were comparatively light for the amount of action we saw. I was
made a member of the tribe in a drunken ceremony, waking up
the next morning to find a beaten copper bracelet around my wrist.

Gustav and his village arrived in the mountains above us two
weeks after our meeting, establishing a new ville. He and his strikers
raided with us several times and went out on their own also, killing NVA and Pathet Lao north of us. We saw each other briefly
a few times, but he stayed in the mountains, working with other
villages and tribal groups.

A month later, as I arrived to catch a plane for my R&R, I saw
Blake getting off the plane that was to pick me up.

"Hey, asshole," he said, greeting me.

"Nice to see you, too," I said, grinning at him. "Where'd you
get those *shineeee* boots?"

He wore a brand new pair of jungle boots. Mine were so old
they were almost worn white.

"Fuck off."

I waved goodbye, climbed in the plane and took off for Bangkok. It wasn't the kind of R&R I had expected though. As soon
as we landed at the FOB airfield in Thailand where our supplies
were ferried out from, Church and another spook grabbed me and
kept me stashed there for three days, debriefing me. They mainly
asked about the series of villages in the mountains to our north.
I told them that our team hadn't been up there. We didn't know
what was going on with them if anything. He finally let me get
on with my R&R, but that was a lousy start.

When I landed back at the village ten days later, the guys were
real hot about something. There was none of the usual ribbing
that one of us got after returning from Sin City.

"An undetermined force hit Paul's village, man," Dane told me.

"NVA?" I asked, puzzled about their reaction to what was an

occupational hazard.

"Coordinated air and ground strike. Skyraiders, Hueys, the works. All black Hueys," Randall growled.

I told them about Church debriefing me for three days.

"What about Paul?" I asked them.

"Dunno. The place was napalmed. Ground teams ambushed the survivors and threw the bodies in the village, then it was napalmed again. We got an eyewitness account from some Meo who were nearby when the attack started. They hid and watched," Dane said.

"That fuckin' Church," I snarled.

"Yeah," Randall muttered.

Right on schedule, the C123 landed to pick up the poppy harvest. Church and his bodyguards hopped out and strolled toward us. We more or less closed around them, escorting them to our team house. When Dane and Randall took Church inside, Griz and I took the PMs out with sucker punches. Disarming them, several of our Nungs tied and guarded them while Griz and I walked into the team house, the PMs' Uzis in our hands. Church saw the weapons and his mouth fell open.

"What," he began.

Randall knocked him down. When he tried to get up, reaching inside his safari suit jacket, Randall kicked him several times, then took the nickel plated Colt Trooper Church had been trying to dig out.

"Ya got two choices, shithead. Transfer yer ass outta this hemisphere and be damn sure you don't come back or I turn the Hammer loose on you. Choose," Randall told him.

"You, you wouldn't," Church gasped.

"Kill a spook? No. Your plane would go down somewhere. None of you would survive, of course. But we got the dirt on you. I don't need an excuse if we do ice your scum-sucking ass."

Dane kicked Church in the side. "You signed the agent report sayin' one of *your* PMs had turned and gone rogue while he was on an op *you* sent him on in Cambodia. Guy named Caffrey. He wasn't a double and he wasn't a rogue. He knew something on you, didn't he?"

Church coughed. I saw the color drain out of his face.

"That's right, motherfucker," I spat at him. "Dane and I had him under sodium pentothal for three hours before we killed him. The team that took him down knows all the gory details and so does this team. You gonna kill us all, scumbag?" I snarled, kicking him too.

Randall hauled him up by the lapels and slapped his face several times.

"What's it gonna be?"

Church started crying.

"I'll transfer. But I need time to."

Randall slapped him again. "No. Nothing. If I see you again, I'll kill you and turn over all the evidence we have that *you* are the rogue."

"Okay, okay. I'm gone. Just keep *him* away from me!" Church wailed. I'd drawn my knife and started toward him.

We tried to get the villages we controlled to plant rice instead of poppies, but they thought that was stupid and politely refused. Why grow rice when USAID gave it to them and traded weapons for the flowers?

A week after Church was sent out of our village in tears, a recall order arrived. We knew we were through, but none of us cared anymore. We had done the best we could as soldiers, and as men, to put a dent in what we believed truly to be the enemy. Only time would tell if we'd been the least bit effective.

Another green hat team arrived to replace us. Lee Wong was one of them. We spent several days briefing them on the strike force, the AO and the people. I took Lee Wong out and introduced him personally to the H'Mong squad I'd drawn first blood with. They were a good Lurp element and I wanted Lee to know it.

The night before we left, both of the villages threw us a feast at the HQ village. It went on all night and even after we left the next day, welcoming the new team in. We flew to an FOB in Thailand and were debriefed for five days by a team of spooks and Army intel guys. We asked, rather innocently, where Church was and why wasn't he debriefing us? He had been our handler, after all.

They told us that Agent Church had taken a sick leave.

"Damn, that's too bad. I hope he gets better," I told my spook debriefer.

He just nodded and went on with his questions.

We all got another two-week R&R before we had to report back to Danang. I headed for Bangkok, my home away from home, and Bear's Lair, where my extended family lived, and partied with them.

The dreams began as soon as I went to sleep the first night after the mission. I couldn't sleep, so I drank and drugged while I was in Bangkok and talked to some of the guys in Bear's Lair. It didn't work this time. I couldn't shake the images of my friends being mangled and killed or the thought of what had happened to Gustav in his village. When I finally got back to Danang, I looked like a zombie and I couldn't sleep there either. Perhaps, I told myself, when we get another mission, I'll be able to sleep again. I was looking forward to anything that they could come up with. If the rest of the team noticed, they didn't say anything to me. I performed all of the duties required of me around the compound efficiently. But I couldn't sleep at night.

Then I began to have the dreams during the day. I'd be sitting around spacing out from lack of sleep, and I'd see Church, about ten times his real size, reaching out for me with a claw hand, going for my throat. As in all my scary dreams, I was powerless to respond or defend myself. I'd wake up with a growl or a scream, jump and scare the shit out of whomever was around me. It worried me, but I didn't know what to do about it so I just drank more when I was on the compound.

Chapter Nine
The North

I spent several days alone in a hotel room in Bangkok, thinking about what happened during our operation in Laos. We had bluffed Church, although we knew what we had told him was true. Church *had* done the things we accused him of and more. He was one of the old school of Cold War spooks, a throwback to the hard-drinking, cigar chomping, Wild Bill Donovan types who set the pattern for thirty years of covert operations. A new breed, like the guy Hardin and I had taken out to check the sensors, was on the rise in the Agency, but our efforts in Nam were largely directed by the old school Cold Warriors.

Actually, I was paranoid. I knew that Church would strike back at us in some way some day. After three days of lurking in the hotel room, not sleeping because of my dreams and feeling like there were spooks in the woodwork watching me, I finally shook the worst of the paranoia and ventured out. For the first time since I had been going to Bangkok, I went out and saw some sights. Then I gorged on food and expensive whores until I was sated. After that, I dropped over to Bear's Lair to see what was happening.

Hardly anyone was there.

"What's going on Bear, people finally figure out what's in your beer?" I asked, downing a pint.

"It's the fights mate. One of my home boys as you Yanks call 'em is fighting a challenge match against the Thai Army champion over at the Pit. Me 'n' the missus are goin' in a bit. You like the fights?"

"Boxing?"

Bear grinned. "Muay Thai. A bit like boxing. This, bein' a challenge bout, has no rules though. A fight."

"The Pit, huh?" I knew the place. We called it the Pit because there were always bizarre combats staged there for the rich or bored to gamble on. Man against man, man against beast, beast against beast. Nothing was too bizarre or grizzly. It was a huge night club on the outskirts of the city, owned by an old Chinese. I'd gone there once.

There had been an Asiatic brown bear in the boxing ring there, declawed and muzzled. For five U.S. bucks anyone could climb in the ring with the bear and if they could stay there for one full minute, they won a prize of five hundred dollars, U.S. I wanted that money. I watched one guy, a Thai, try to evade the bear with fancy footwork. The bear lumbered down on him and smacked him with a paw, knocking the Thai out of the ring and breaking his face.

Then a big, muscled U.S. Marine NCO tried to go up under the bear and slam him. The bear scooped the Marine and beat the shit out of him before it tossed him out of the ring. After watching those two, I plotted my strategy, thinking about a movie where I'd seen ol' Dan'l Boone down a black bear, paid my money, and climbed in the ring.

The bear shambled toward me. I waited for it. I could hear the audience, a mixed group of Anglos and Orientals, calling out advice or insults. The bear thought it had me pinned in the corner and attacked, trying to hug me. I slipped under its encircling arms and spun away from it. A smattering of yells and applause came from the audience. I kept that up, letting the bear come to me and slipping away from it as it rose on its hind legs to grab me. The bear got mad and started howling through its muzzle. Glancing at the time clock, I saw I only had fifteen seconds left. When I looked back at the bear, he was about three feet from me and closing fast.

The audience hooted and laughed. As the bear reached for me, I acted like I was going to slip it, leaned back and nailed the bear on the tip of his snout as hard as I could with my right fist. It snapped the bear's head back. As it shook its huge head, I hit it again, then ran to the far corner of the ring, eyes on the time clock. With one second left, the bear was coming for me again and the big bastard was mad too. A bell rang. I vaulted the top rope. I won.

The bear didn't know it was time to quit though and climbed out of the ring too. He beat up half the audience before the handler could tranquilize him. I got my five hundred, U.S., though.

When Bear and his wife left the bar for the Pit, I went with them. The place was packed, but Bear had his own table and I sat with them. When the fight began, a big, beefy Aussie came trotting out with his fists wrapped with strips of leather instead of gauze, wearing combat boots and fatigue pants. The Thai Army champion wore baggy satin trunks and no shoes. His feet and fists were wrapped with what might have been white tape. The bell rang after the Thai performed some type of ritual dance and the two men began fighting. Boots and fists flew in almost continuous motion. When the bell rang ending round one, they kept thumping. After a one-minute break that fighters normally take, they rang the bell for round two. The fighters had never paused.

Around the five-minute mark and several bells later, the pace began to slow. There was a considerable amount of blood flowing from both of them and they were panting, but neither would stop at round bells. They began circling a bit more, throwing fewer kicks and punches, but the ones they did throw would kill bulls if they landed. The audience grew restless.

The bellboy rang the bell again and kept ringing it at the owner's orders. The two fighters broke, the Aussie holding his open hands out to the Thai for a moment. Then he leaned over the ropes, raised the bellboy up by this throat and glared at him through a mask of blood.

"You ring the bleedin' bell one more time, me 'n' Siri over there are going to pinch yore bleedin' head off. Eh?" the Aussie fighter growled.

Releasing the boy, he went back to the fight.

When Bear took his wife and me back to the bar after the fight, all he could talk about was the action in the ring. Neither of the two had won, but certainly neither man had lost. They had beaten each other until neither could fight anymore. I could understand his enthusiasm. That fight had truly been a stirring event. Two men who enjoyed the combat, both finely tuned and well trained. There had been no retreat and no surrender. They had fought with skill and courage until their bodies simply could no longer drive their blows.

Bear and I strolled in the front door, hooking and jabbing at each other. An Air America pilot I knew strolled up to me and told me I was wanted in Danang right then. He said that he would fly me back in the morning and since we only had a few hours to wait, we both decided to drink them away at the bar. I sat with Bear, another old Aussie friend of Bear's, the pilot and another American I didn't know, telling them about the fight. The drunker we got, the more involved Bear and I got into the retelling of it. About midway into my third version, I looked up to the bar and saw a Korean officer leaning on it, watching us.

Smiling, I shoved my chair back and stood up, then staggered over to the bar.

"Hello," I said to the ROK officer.

His eyes narrowed as he looked at me. He grunted something I suspected was a word in his language.

"You like carrots?" I asked him.

He was still staring at me, eyes narrowed in concentration, brow furrowed. The expression he wore said that he knew he had seen my face before, but he just couldn't remember where.

"What?" he asked.

"I said, do you like carrots?"

I had him there. I could tell that his mind was racing furiously, trying to decipher the drunk round-eyes's question.

"Cawwots?" he said.

"Yeah, cawwots. You like 'em?"

Seeing no obvious joke at his expense, or threat, and not knowing that he was dealing with a dangerous sociopath, he nodded.

"Yes, like cawwots."

I knocked him off the bar stool with a right lunge punch, then as he started to get up I kicked him in the face. He collapsed, bleeding from his nose and mouth. I looked around at Bear and winked. He was grinning.

"You really hate carrots, don'tcha mate?" he asked.

When I arrived at our compound, I slept most of that day after telling Randall I was back. Waking early the next morning to Randall's standard wake-up call, a hard thump on the bottom of one foot, I raised up on one elbow to see the entire team standing around my bunk, staring at me.

"Hey, you like cawwots?" Dane asked me.

"The pilot ratted me out, huh?" I groaned.

They all burst out laughing.

After a big breakfast at the PX cafeteria, Randall came and got us for a briefing, driving us over to the briefing area in a jeep. When we filed into the secure room, I actually expected to see fat-assed Church sitting behind the podium. To my surprise, though, the first person I saw was the Cat. Standing behind him was a scruffy-looking guy, his head down as he looked over some papers, wearing faded jeans and an old bush fatigue shirt, the kind with epaulets. When he looked up, I saw that it was Harry the spook. I made a monkey face at him and he grinned back.

As we all took our seats, I asked Harry where Church was.

"I guess you men know more about that than I do. He's been transferred from this command structure, though. Permanently," he said and paused for a moment.

"You'll be under my direct operational command and control from now on. We are working under a different operations plan. No more strategic recon in Laos. Our area of operations will be strictly North Vietnam."

He gave us a moment to let that sink in. No one visibly reacted.

"I asked for your team specifically, several months ago while you were in Laos. Our section had been handpicking its operatives over the past several years for missions into the enemy's home country. Do any of you have a problem working with me or going into the north?"

We shook our heads no.

"Good. Good. Okay, here's the deal. I know a little about what Church put some of you through and I know a whole lot about your actions as a team. I want you to trust me. That'll be very important in future missions. The best way I know to gain your trust is to go out with you."

Someone let out an audible groan.

"He went out with us before. I can vouch for him," I said.

"To check the sensors," Randall said. I nodded to him.

"I'm not a useless strap hanger, men. Sergeant Randall will still be the team one one. Cat and I will be extra guns if needed and we both have some intelligence gathering experience you guys don't.''

Early the next morning, I got up for a run along the beach and a practice session with Randall. I tried to stay in condition between drunks, bouts of sleeplessness and the missions. Randall had been working with me on karate. Early in the morning the REMFs hadn't hit the beach yet either, so we were able to practice without the goofs staring at us. As I hit the soft sand of the beach, I heard a scream from further down the beach and a strange, swishing whine. Jogging down the beach to a stand of trees, I snuck through them until I located the sound's source. I stood motionless in the stand of trees, watching with fascination the deadly ballet being played out before me.

Harry and the Cat were fighting with short swords in prearranged drills. One would attack the other, then the defender would parry and whip one or two counterstrikes at the attacker, the live blades stopping only fractionally short of lethal contact. As they struck, they screamed. I watched for some time, until they took a break and toweled off. Then the Cat turned to look right at where I was standing, screened from their view by the trees.

"Join us?" he called.

"I didn't mean to spy, I heard the *kiai* and the whine of the swords and I...," I apologized, walking toward them.

"The song of the katana," Harry said, smiling, wiping his sword blade with a piece of silk cloth.

"These are the *wakazashi*, the companion swords. The great sword is impractical for the bush," the Cat told me.

"Uh huh, " I said. Swords? In an age of jet fighters, machine guns and frags?

They were both smiling. Not at me, but just because they were happy. I excused myself and took off jogging down the beach. Later, after our karate workout, I mentioned what I'd seen to Randall, making a joke of it.

"Don't laugh. They practice a warrior discipline that was old when our ancestors in Europe were still clubbing each other. Like the knife, the sword is a tool of personal combat that goes beyond modern warfare. Like you stalking Cochise in the Zone."

I just grunted. I'd have to think about that. In the meantime, I practiced karate.

We didn't have long to wait for a mission. Harry alerted us and we assembled in the briefing room. Army intel people delivered the initial day-long briefing. It was on the terrain and situation of our projected TA. The next day, Harry met us in the briefing room and assigned us our mission objective.

Three Controlled American Source (CAS) agents, indigenous agents run by American Intelligence, had to be extracted from North Vietnam. One of them, Le Dao Van Nguyen, had been in place in Hanoi since before Ho Chi Minh's ragged army had taken possession of the city. An old revolutionary, he felt the communist faction Ho led had betrayed the cause. He had also been a highly placed mole for the Agency since the late 1950s. He was code named the Hawk. The other two were part of his agent net. Alerted to his imminent arrest after one of his net had been detected photographing a Russian trawler unloading something secret in Haiphong Harbor and captured by Russian intel people, the Hawk pulled the plug on his net and fled west with two of his people. He was bringing some real hot intel out with him as well, to make sure that his handler came and got him. Harry stressed that it was vital to mission success that we bring him out alive.

"Where exactly are they, sir?" Randall asked.

"You can call me Harry, sarge," the spook told him.

"Yes, sir," Randall replied.

"Okay. Well, they are holed up in a safe house in the city of Viet Tri right now. About here," Harry said, tapping the map pinned up behind him.

"Jeez," I hissed. Viet Tri wasn't far from Hanoi, a bit northwest, right on the Red River. It was deep in hostile territory.

"If you decide to insert by parachute, I can arrange an air strike against the MIG jet fighter base at Phuc Yen to cover the insertion," Harry said.

"Uh huh," Randall agreed.

"The secondary rendezvous point for them will be further west in the Truong Song mountains, closer to the border. Movement will be difficult and dangerous for them though and their safe house net may not stay safe for long with one of their people in KGB hands. I can have them move, but it has to be soon.''

"Yes sir, we're on it," Randall told him.

Harry left. We brainstormed for several hours, working out all the scenarios we could from the data available. The final option we decided on was to HALO parachute jump in behind the air strike Harry promised, send Krang and Cat into Viet Tri to meet the three CAS agents, while we secured a sampan big enough for our team, two if necessary. We would then move the CAS people downriver from Viet Tri to Cho Bo. From there, we would go overland west to Laos where we would be extracted from the mountains by slicks.

If complications arose, we would head for the coast, following the Red River out to the delta it formed and call for Swift boats manned by Seals to pick us up. We worked out a few other options also in case we had to split up before we extracted or whatever. It was good to be prepared.

While we were in the process of working all that out, Harry came bursting into the room.

"Okay, new deal. They had to move into the mountains. Our last contact was less than an hour ago from a burst transmitter, but we lost their signal. NSA thinks that it was due to equipment failure from the cached transmitter they are using. If we can get an extraction team into them soon, we've got a chance.''

Randall looked up from his map. "Are you sure it's them calling sir?''

Harry didn't hesitate. "Yes. They relayed a series of codewords that confirmed their identities and that they weren't being forced to make the transmission. If it will put your minds at ease, I'm going with you men.

"Me too," the Cat said from where he stood, leaning against the doorframe.

We went to work on an alternate plan and several variations in case one or all of the CAS agents had been doubled. That was always a possibility. A double would be able to alert the NVA in some way when a rescue team made its move and not only would the real CAS agents be taken, but so would an American covert operations unit. If any of the CAS people had been captured when we got there, we would try to break them out. It seemed like it was worth a try. Harry told us that a reaction force would be standing by from the time we inserted just in case we ran into a reception committee on the ground.

Our team, Harry, the old Nung who had accompanied him when we had gone out to check the sensors and the Cat all loaded up into a black C130 around 1500 hours that afternoon. We were planning a stick jump from one thousand feet. Parachuting was a thrill to me and I tried to jump every chance I got, which wasn't very often in Southeast Asia. The stick jumps were all right, but I much preferred the HALO free falls. More time in the air. As we flew toward our TA, I thought to myself that since we would be working in North Vietnam, I might be able to get a few HALO jumps in. It was a hell of a way to go about getting some more jumps in though.

Randall acted as our jump master. After our equipment check and hook up, we trotted down the open ramp and were airborne. It was night outside the aircraft. Hurtling through space for five seconds, I assumed the position and then the modified TIO Army parachute deployed above me with a sharp snap, lifting me up a foot in the air. We came down fast, steering with the risers of our parachutes as best we could. Jumping into the mountains was tricky. I'd done it in training several times and once had gotten in an updraft that carried me almost a mile from my drop zone (DZ). On this operation, that could be fatal. If I felt the parachute start to rise, I had to spill air fast and get to the ground. It was even more dangerous to HALO into mountains. One miscalculation and the whole team would end up smeared onto the side of a mountain. That was why Randall chose a stick jump as our method of deployment.

All of us landed safely. We dropped in on the Lao-North Viet border, perhaps a little on the Lao side. Regrouping on the ground, we dropped our parachutes and moved out on a forced march for high ground. Randall and Krang led us. It was a hard march in the dark, with loose rocks underfoot and cliffs to contend with.

Randall wanted to get us up high, fast, in case anyone had seen our parachutes coming down.

When he called a halt, we were on a plateau that made a good RON. Settling in was easy, we just fell down and crawled under cover so that the dawn wouldn't catch us exposed. I sat sipping water not far from Harry, Cat and the old Nung. Randall sat down beside me and called Harry over.

"We're ten klicks out from where your people should be. We'll ascend to this next plateau here," Randall said, pointing to a spot on his map in the dim light of predawn, "at first light. From there we'll reconnoiter the area. If we find them where they're supposed to be, we'll be back in Danang for supper tomorrow."

Harry nodded. "They'll be there if they haven't been taken, sarge."

Randall grunted and turned to me. "You and Chang take the point in the mornin'. Keep yer eyes open."

I grunted an affirmative to him and Randall moved off. I went to sleep.

Chang was a stocky Nung who had been in the A Team camp, one of the few survivors. He was tough, quiet and competent. When Randall told us to hit it, he and I scouted for a trail, then we moved off slowly uphill. It didn't take long to reach the next plateau. The only problem was that an NVA patrol of six men were already there. I sent Chang back to alert the team. The NVA were all still asleep, feeling secure this close to their own border. A sentry had been posted, but he had nodded out on his post.

When Randall arrived, he crawled forward to take a look. When he came back he said, "We gotta do 'em."

I drew my knife, but the Cat stopped me. "Harry and I can do this."

Before Randall could say no, the two crawled off. They moved well, staying low and moving quietly among the rocks. Reaching a clear space on the edge of the plateau, they skirted it until Cat was only a few feet from the sleeping sentry. Cat stood, one hand reaching back for his sword hilt. Its blade flashed in the sun as it whirred through the air. The sentry didn't move. I thought the Cat had missed, but Harry and the Cat were suddenly among the sleeping NVA. Harry had his sword too. It was quickly done and they signaled us to come forward.

When we joined them, I prodded the NVA sentry with my rifle. His body toppled forward, his head falling the other way.

"Jeez!" I yelped. It had startled me.

"Finest blades in the world, the Japanese," Blake said, standing near me. The admiration shone from his eyes.

"Shit," I heard Dane bark.

The NVA had a radio and there was a voice coming from it, calling someone who had not answered so far. No doubt it was a call for the squad we had just wasted.

"Plan's changed. Hide the bodies. Hammer, Blake, take two Nungs and recon this area," Randall said, showing us on his map where he wanted us to go.

"What are we looking for Harry? A cave, a building, three guys out wandering?" I asked.

"A building, possibly a temple. Take Cat," Harry replied.

We moved out.

It was a temple. An old Buddhist temple. We circled the area around it and found no one watching, so we moved in closer. There was no sign of movement around the temple at all. Birds fluttered in and out of the domed roof, which was about all that was left of the building. The walls had caved in here and there and one side had caved in completely. There were statues in front that were crumbling and faceless. Taking point, I moved in closer.

Then I smelled *nuoc mam*. Waving the others down, I crept close to a hole in one wall, taking a quick peek through it.

Three Oriental men were eating lunch inside. They all wore civilian clothes. I brought the others forward and the Cat peeked inside.

"That is the Hawk," he said.

Cat said something in Viet. I heard a clatter inside, feet rushing around, then a rifle bolt being pulled back. Cat rattled off more Viet. After a few tense seconds, one of the three men from inside appeared at the hole, answering Cat. Cat showed himself to them and one of the Viets inside laughed in relief. One of our Nungs spat, obviously disgusted by how easy the Viet "spies" had been to sneak up on. I smiled at the Nung and shrugged.

Moving inside, we sent one of the Nungs back for the team. They arrived at the temple quickly.

"We gotta get out of this place," Dane said, paraphrasing a popular song. "There are boocoo NVA coming up from the valley down there." He waved in the direction of the temple front.

We boobytrapped the temple and pulled out, taking a direct route down off the high ground, heading toward Laos. We made good time too, moving almost at a run. Stealth wasn't our major concern right then. The Viet agents, dressed in civilian clothes, were having a hard time making the pace, but they tried their best. As we marched, we heard a series of explosions behind us. The NVA had obviously found the ruined temple.

We moved out of the hills and down into the jungle, making for an abandoned Katu Montagnard village on a ridge side. We had to cross some low hills, a forest and then a river. We estimated it at ten miles, a four-hour march.

By rotating the point man, we were able to keep a steady pace. Just after I'd taken over, I walked us into an NVA patrol. We were a klick away from the river we had to cross, the Song Ma, at one of the natural fords marked on the patrol map. I guess the NVA patrol had just crossed the river and were coming toward us to check out the noise where the other NVA had triggered our boobytraps. Their point man and I nearly collided.

I shot him, freed a frag and waited for his squad to show up. When they did, the Cat, who was walking my slack, and I both hit them with frags. We overran them after the grenades detonated among them. There had been six of them and we got them all. The Cat and I put out flank security for the river crossing, then crossed last, trying to cover the team's tracks. Harry fell back with us. The NVA would be on us hot and heavy after that; they had a sign of our location and which way we were heading.

I laid a claymore ambush with the Cat, while Harry covered us at the ford, then we ran to catch the team.

"Harry, stay with your CAS agents, man. Cat and I can handle this," I said as we ran, giving him a little shove.

"Damn green berets. Think they can do it all," he said to the Cat, grinning.

"We can," I said, pushing him ahead of me again. "It's what we get paid..."

My words were cut off by the claymore's blast behind us. We weren't fifty yards from the river. The NVA were hot after us and closing fast.

"Git," I told Harry. This time he got.

Cat and I kept moving as Harry ran after the team. We readied frags. When I heard the Viets closing behind us, we dropped off the trail we had been following and tossed a frag apiece at the lead element of our pursuers. I tossed a second one for good measure, then we hauled ass up the trail.

The ground began to rise. We were getting close to the village. If we made it there ahead of the NVA, we would be lucky. This would be a close call. As we caught up to the team, firing erupted from the point. We scattered into the bush and moved forward. Three NVA had been on the trail and the Nung on point dusted two of them. The third was raising hell. We flanked him and blew him away. Randall took point and led us up a ridge out of the bush and into the village. We were there before I realized we were even near the village.

"Slicks and guns are in-bound. ETA three zero," Blake yelled. Randall nodded and gave us our deployment orders.

Cat, Marty and I went out to lay boobytraps. We spread two claymores and ten frags around the trail and in the bush on the single approach to the village. The village itself consisted of four Yard long houses that were dilapidated. Located in an artificial clearing cut from the foliage on the side of the ridge, we controlled the high ground in the village for the moment.

The three Viets from the temple were huddled together behind a stone wall where Randall thought they would be safe. The oldest one, Nguyen, had a Makarov pistol in his hand. Seeing me stare at him when we came back from laying the demo ambushes, he stood, bowed and spoke to me.

I returned the bow. "I'm sorry, I don't speak Viet," I said in English.

"Pistol for me, them. No surrender," Nguyen said in broken English, waving the pistol at his friends.

I nodded. "Don't worry, man. We won't let 'em take you."

He bowed again. "No capture. Please," he said, pointing at my CAR 15.

I returned his bow again. "I promise. No capture." He wanted me to grease him if it looked like the NVA would overrun us. I could dig that. I felt the same way. "Hang tough, man," I told him.

He smiled and returned to his friends. I strolled over to the Cat and sat beside him, telling him about the encounter.

"Nguyen's a tough little guy," Cat said.

Watching him out of the corner of my eye, I asked Cat something that had puzzled me since I saw him and Harry with the swords back at Danang. "Why do you do this man?"

Cat smiled at me. "The same reason you do. You thought I was some cold motherfucker, huh? Some spook in love with the game and nothing else. Randall told me," he said when I began to protest.

"We do it for the people, man," he went on.

I was surprised. Dane and his love for the Yards, Randall and his ideals of self-determination and basic freedom. I could see those guys having their ideals to fight for, but I didn't give a fuck about most of that and I couldn't see any ideals in the Cat either.

"What people?" I asked him.

"Us. Each other. The *real* people. Randall, Dane, Harry, your team, now Nguyen, a tough little guy who will kill himself and his friends rather than be captured and go back as a slave."

I grunted. My assessment of Nguyen was a little different, but I could deal with that. He didn't want to suffer the indignities that the NVA and their KGB masters would inflict on him. That was basically how I felt about it. I could handle the pain of torture, though not willingly, but it was the indignity of having it inflicted that I resented.

"What else've we got, Hammer? Our war, our identity as green hats, spooks, elite warriors in a hot war. Our brothers in arms. That is why we do this. It sure ain't the pay," he said grinning.

"Here they come," someone said.

The NVA were advancing cautiously. The boobytraps had slowed them down along our back trail and they were looking for more.

Their point element was coming up the trail slowly, with flankers out on either side. I laid two magazines out beside me for faster access.

One of their point men tripped a claymore. It blew the NVA back down the trail. We heard screams of pain. Then they moved toward us again. I knew that as soon as they found us in the village that they would try to flank us, going up the ridge above us and then sweeping in from the side and our rear. We could hold the village until they worked a force around behind us. I didn't think it would take them long to figure that out either, once the fight really got started. C'mon slicks, I prayed.

They sent a squad forward to probe us. Another claymore took them all out. We had another respite while they regrouped again. Then they hit us in force. I guess they figured fuck the cheap shit. An assault line came at us.

"Must be a company of 'em," Cat said, sighting in his carbine.

When they were close enough, I tossed a frag and opened fire with my CAR. It was a handy little weapon, but it didn't have much range or stopping power. Our team rocked, pouring out an awesome amount of firepower. The assault line died. A second one came for us while an RPD back in the tree line and slightly downslope on the ridge raked our positions. Being downslope, the bursts were either just short or passed over our heads. I saw Blake hitting them hard with his M203.

Bao popped up beside Randall, a LAW on his shoulder. He fired into the tree line. I guess they spotted the RPD's muzzle flash. After the LAW round exploded, the RPD was silenced. The second assault wave died too, but they had gotten closer and we had expended a lot of munitions stopping them.

We got another respite. The NVA were satisfied to wait in the bush a while and I suspected they were sending scouts around us, up the ridge line, to find a way to flank us. Blake and Randall patched a few minor wounds.

"We can't stay here much longer," Cat said as Randall crawled past.

"If we can hold 'til the slicks get here," I began.

Randall shook his head. "Slicks can't land. They'd be blown

away as soon as they hovered. We gotta E&E."

"Wait for dark, work up over the ridge," Cat said.

Randall nodded.

That was how it worked out too. The gunships arrived and kept the NVA off our asses until it was dark. We beat off three more assaults and then the sun set. We boobytrapped the village and headed up the ridge. As we moved out, Randall stopped and looked back at the long houses.

"You want a rear guard, sarge?" I asked.

He didn't answer.

"I'll stay. I've still got ten mags left. That'll hold me."

The Cat strolled by. "Leave us one Nung."

Bao walked up. "I stay."

Randall shook our hands and told us where to meet him when we broke contact. He said "when," but he meant "if." Our team couldn't go over the ridge in daylight even with gunships suppressing the NVA. We had a chance at night, but as soon as the NVA realized we had pulled out they would move in and the team would be caught on the downslope of the ridge, like fish in a barrel. The three of us would stop the NVA's advance long enough for the team to get clear of the ridge and into the bush.

As the team pulled out, Nguyen stepped up to the three of us and bowed deeply.

"Hang tough," he said. We shared a smiled and he vanished into the night.

The first probe came minutes later. They had brought in reinforcement. As they began to advance, we sniped at them in the moonlight, picking off any of them who looked like they were giving any kind of orders to the rest. We would fire and move to another firing position to make it appear that there were more of us than there actually were.

The second probe overran us. They came at the village screaming and firing. I let one close right up to me, pushed his barrel up with my barrel and shot him in the heart. As he fell, I shot another one right behind him and then I fell back to the ruins of a long house, mindful of the boobytraps.

Cat and Bao were already at their secondary positions, doing selective damage as the NVA came screaming into the village. More of them were advancing up the trail. We gave ground slowly, using the long houses for cover, drawing them toward us.

Then we broke for the ridge and the bush that grew up its side. The NVA came for us. They ran in among the long houses. The claymore boobytraps detonated. They blew them away. Halfway up the ridge, I saw Bao fighting three NVA hand-to-hand. I ran for him, below me and to my left, shooting one of the NVA off Bao as I closed on them. The other two had him down. I kicked one in the head, but the other shot him, then I shot the NVA.

Reaching down I tried to pick Bao up, but he pushed my hands off him. "Go," he wheezed.

"No. I carry," I said, trying to lift him again.

NVA were pouring into the village, firing up the ridge line.

"Go!" Bao gasped, fighting me off. He knew that I'd have a hell of a time packing him up that ridge.

He pulled two frags out of his web gear. "Kill VC," he grunted, his face suddenly contorting in pain. He pulled both pins. "Go!"

Tears suddenly flooded my eyes. Cat grabbed me and hauled me up the ridge. We were just over the top when I heard Bao scream "*Sac mau!*" and then two frags went off. Cat and I ran for our lives.

We rejoined the team at the rendezvous point Randall had shown us. The NVA were still after us, so we didn't get any rest. We ate a handful of benzedrine. As the sun came up we moved out.

The NVA hit us again just as we crossed an open field. We had skirted open places before, but with the NVA in hot pursuit we crossed this one on the run. An ambush patrol laid across our route as a blocking force and opened fire on us too early. We charged them, firing everything we had. It was our only chance. Suppress and overrun them quickly or be killed out in the open. There was a pursuit force not far behind us.

I saw Dane stagger as I dropped an empty magazine and slapped a fresh one in place, charging the weapon. He was still moving forward when I glanced at him again, so I went on. Spotting movement in the tree line ahead of me, I raked it with a long burst from my CAR. A frag went off behind me and the shock wave of its detonation pushed me forward. A sudden stinging, burning pain in the back of my legs told me I'd been hit with shrapnel, but not much.

Then we were in among the NVA. One stood up right in front of me, raising his AK. I shot him, turned and shot another in the back as he stood to shoot at someone else. A third lunged at me with his rifle barrel. I crescent-kicked it aside, spun and kicked him in the bladder with my heel, then slammed the butt of my CAR into his head. The CAR was shattered. I picked up an AK, but it clicked empty.

Glancing around, I saw Harry moving among the NVA who were trying to shoot him. He had his sword in a two-hand grip, slashing and thrusting as he danced through them. Bodies fell away as he passed, the sword singing its song of death. It was like something out of a movie. At point-blank range, the sword, in skilled hands, was an awesome weapon.

Drawing my .45 auto, I went to cover, looking for a target as I moved, but the action was over. I heard Randall calling us in and the guys sounding off.

"Anyone low on ammo, pick up an AK and a bandoleer off a dead gook. Where's Dane?" Randall yelled, standing amidst a pile of dead NVA.

I picked up another AK, checked the load in the magazine, threw it away and picked a bandoleer off a dead NVA soldier. As I inserted a full mag in the AK's magazine well and chambered a round, I saw Dane. The frag that had stung me had dumped its force into him. I took off running toward him.

"Oh, man," I hissed when I reached his side.

His boonie hat had been blown off. A chunk of his skull was gone. I could see his brain pulsing through a clot of blood. I got a sterile bandage and tied it around his wound, then checked him for any other major holes. A bullet had opened a huge, fist-sized hole in his upper chest, but as far as I could tell it hadn't hit any major organs. It had glanced off a rib, expanding and doing major tissue damage. Using his first aid kit, I plugged the holes and put pressure bandages on them. Then I heaved him across my shoulders.

When I caught up to Randall, he looked me over, then Dane.
"You're hit," he said

I just grunted.

"Dane's hit hard."

"Let's move out, sarge. I've got him, let's go," I growled. I'd
just lost Bao. I wasn't going to lose Dane, too.

Randall nodded. When we moved out, he stayed right with me.

We humped. Our rate of march into the Cordillera was fast and
hard and we seemed to be outrunning our pursuers. From time
to time, I heard a single shot on our back trail as the NVA trackers
followed. We hadn't lost them. We had just outmarched them.
Randall and Griz fell back to plant boobytraps as we climbed into
the hill country, Blake on point.

Sometime during the climbing march, I turned completely inward. All of my concentration was solely upon making one more
step and willing Dane to live. If I'd been hit right then, I don't
think I would have felt the bullet. I was frothing at the mouth
when we ascended to a wide, flat plateau high above the jungle
floor.

The whole team had given that hump their all, yet none of us
flopped down. I wouldn't give Dane to anyone else to carry, but
all of them, at one time or another, had pushed or pulled or just
held me up when I needed it. The Cat, a man Dane hated intense-
ly, had changed Dane's bandages while we were on the move and
then helped haul me up a steep incline. So, for real, all of us shared
the burden of carrying one of our own, even the Nungs, who had
taken my gear. When we reached the plateau, each man carefully
picked a spot, laid his gear out, sat, then sipped his water. The
three Viet CAS agents approached me shyly and then helped me
lay Dane on the ground.

Relieved of my burden, I laid my gear on the ground, then sank
to my knees, head falling forward, exhausted. Randall approached
me and poured a little water over my head. Then he tilted my chin
up and poured some of his water between my lips. I looked around
at the team. All of us were wounded to some degree and each of
the guys were checking the others. Even with our wounds, we had
just scaled a mountain. The guys were inspecting each other's

weapons as they had their wounds dressed. The Cat dragged Dane behind some rocks where he might be covered if the NVA attacked us here. There was no complaints, no bitching, no orders given. Everyone knew what they had to do and they just did it. I smiled at the guys and then up at Randall.

"Ya did good, son," he told me.

"We all did," I said as he walked off to find Marty and the radio.

While Randall called for extraction slicks, I found a slight rise on the edge of the plateau that gave me a clear field of fire down our back trail. Cat and Harry were laying claymores and booby-traps below me. I straightened the pins of the grenades I had left, laying them out around me and then stacked the AK magazines in front of me for faster access. Blake, a much better medic than I, was working on Dane.

With all my defensive preparations finished, I looked around at our position. It wasn't really a plateau, but more like an outcrop of rock that had been flattened out so that it was accessible from the way we had come and from the other side only by a fairly steep climb up an open ridge. It was a good defensive site. We had the high ground, forcing the enemy to climb to get at us, and we had an open killing ground. Now it would be a race between the slicks and how willing the NVA were to spend men to overrun us. I fell asleep on top of the AK rifle.

The sound of the Huey's rotors woke me up. We were about to be extracted. I tried to stand, but my body refused to cooperate. I was drained completely, mentally and physically. I saw Griz and Cat lift Dane, gently, and put him in a slick and then Harry and one of the Viet agents were helping me into one. Seconds later, we were airborne.

I was sitting across from Nguyen. He looked at me, smiling a little, funny smile, then nodded. I returned the nod. He showed me the little Russian pistol, then tossed it out the open door of the slick.

We all got time off after that mission. Dane was shipped out from the big evac hospital in Danang to a Naval hospital ship and then back to the U.S. for his long, long recovery. He was pretty

fucked up from what one of the doctors would tell us. All of us
had some repair work done, but none of it was serious. They dug
some new pieces of shrapnel out of my back and legs and left a
few in for good measure. I never did know why they did that. A
doctor told me once that they would work themselves out and that
they didn't have the time with all of the other casualties coming
in to dig every little sliver out. Well, that was all well and good,
but I could feel the foreign matter inside my body and I didn't
like it. They didn't give a fuck though. They stuck some bandages
on me and told me to hit it.

I asked them for something to help me sleep at night and they
gave me a glass of warm milk.

I flew to Thailand, but went to Chiang Mai this time, taking
in the ancient Imperial Capital and the temples that were scattered
throughout the city. It was amazing and beautiful. The CIA had
a safe house there, so I had a place to stay. On my second day
there, I ran into Stone at the safe house. He was coming back from
an operation. We went out to eat and I told him the latest about
Church and Dane and asked about Lee Wong. Stone told me that
he was still running a team in the Annamese Cordillera, training
and advising H'Mong villes. Stone had been doing special ops for
the Agency without a team, but he was on his way back into Vietnam to put a new RT together, probably in Danang. They hadn't
told him much beyond that.

The two of us flew to Bangkok and partied at Bear's for several
days and then flew back to Danang together. On the way back,
Stone moved over closer to me in the plane.

"Hey, why didn't you shoot me that day when you had the
chance?" he asked.

"What've you got on your head?" I said, flicking my eyes up
to take in his green beret.

He grinned at me. "I owe ya one, son and I always pay my
debts."

"Don't sweat it Stone. I always collect mine," I told him,
grinning.

My dreams were getting worse and more frequent too. Randall
taught me to meditate right after I woke up from one. After med-

itating, I'd fall back to sleep for a while, but then the dreams would return. When I'd found that the meditation and the warm milk the doctors offered didn't work, I went back to drugs and booze. They got me through the nights while I waited for another mission.

Chapter Ten
Red River Valley

Harry grinned at us as he stood at the lectern in the front of the briefing room. We had only been back twelve days from our last mission to extract the CAS agents. In my own way, I was mourning Dane, which was to sit alone on the beach drinking whiskey. I was sober when they alerted us for this briefing. All of us knew that a mission would be assigned to us soon.

"I got my ass in a sling for going out with you guys. I can't go out and play anymore," Harry told us.

Case officers were career men, not field operatives. They were too valuable to lose in the bush on missions, unless it was vital. Besides that, I'd never met one that liked humping the bush before, but it was obvious that Harry liked the thrill of combat. It had been his stated intention to earn our trust by putting his life on the line in the same way we did and he had pretty well accomplished that. I held the personal opinion that he liked the bush and used us as an excuse to get there. After the operation, our team had gotten together for a meeting just to talk about Harry and his participation in the mission. We knew that he would spend us, just like the Army would, in the pursuit of a valid mission objective, but we all agreed that he wouldn't sell us cheaply or sell us out.

"Join the Army, Harry," Marty quipped.

We all grinned. Harry flipped the cover off the briefing map, timing his move pretty well and our grins vanished. Our TA was an area around the North Viet-Chinese border. Taking a pointer off the lectern, he slapped its tip at a village named Lao Cay right on the border. I felt a surge of adrenalin rush through me.

"We learned from our agent Le Dao Van Nguyen that a shipment of chemical agents is being shipped south from Peking. They will be transported by rail to a point in Laos and they will be transported over land to South Vietnam. At an undetermined time and place, very probably at Cam Ranh Bay, they will be detonated, causing massive casualties. The casualties will be especially heavy among the civilians. The NVA and the VCI, the military and political leaders of VC cells, will blame it on the U.S. military, claiming that in a last-ditch effort to win the war we are storing chemical weapons in RVN. You can imagine the political repercussions at home, what concessions it will force on our negotiators in Paris.

"Gentlemen, these chemical agents *must not* be allowed to cross into North Vietnam! We will be sending the entire communist hierarchy a message through the actions that your team will take to prevent this. *We will not tolerate any use of chemical or biological agents in this theater*!" he said, a vein bulging in the side of his neck. Harry was emotionally involved in this one.

He paused for breath, gauging our reactions. All of us were hunched forward in our seats, expectantly. I felt the adrenalin thundering through me. We were going to the Wall, our slang for China. This was some heavy shit we were being briefed for.

"The train will leave Mengtse, China, on a certain date and cross the border into North Vietnam on a railroad bridge over the Song Hong or Red River. We want you in place and ready to interdict the bridge forty-eight hours in advance of the train's arrival at Hokow, here, right across the border from Lao Cay," he said, slapping the map with the tip of his pointer again. Then he slid the tip to the southwest slightly. "The road bridge here will be dropped simultaneously to ensure that any rescue effort from the garrison here, at Chapa, will be delayed en route. This will allow us a plausible denial also. If two of their bridges collapse under what we'll assure the rest of the world was an earth tremor, the North Viets will have a hard time pointing the finger at us publicly."

Pausing again, he turned and began tacking a series of photos up on the board beside the map.

"The Cat and an indigenous agent will accompany you in. Gentlemen, this is a mission of total unit closure. You will go in sterile. Work out an extraction scenario using any assets you may need. I'll take care of that. Here are your briefing packets."

Harry came out from behind the lectern to hand us each a fat manila folder that was sealed with a blob of wax and some tape. TOP SECRET was stamped all over the folders in big red letters.

"How long do we have for mission preparation?" Randall

asked.

"Approximately two weeks. You'll be issued any equipment and have a chance to check it during the second week. We have ongoing Big Bird and Black Bird surveillance, so if the train moves any closer than Mengtse, where the line to Hokow begins, you'll be alerted. Well, fellas, I'm outta here. There will be a guard on the door. If you need to leave or need anything at all, call him and he will get ahold of me. Good luck."

We nodded a goodbye as Harry left the room, but all of us were already engrossed in the briefing packets. I began with the train itself, the focus of the mission. There was an entire file that was thicker than my military personnel file just on the train. It was an old Russian engine that had been manufactured just after the turn of the century, but had been rebuilt two years previously by the Red Chinese Army. It was in excellent condition and was not expected to break down during the journey. That was what I had wanted to know. Would we be on the ground, deep in enemy territory, waiting for a train on a timetable, when the train would break down somewhere north of us? I wanted a shot at a clean mission-in/mission-out with no hanging around deep in enemy territory. The longer we were on the ground, the greater the chance that we would be discovered lurking around Lao Cay.

The railroad cars that made up the rest of the train were a mixed bag. There were four boxcars behind the coal car that would carry the actual chemical weapon containers. They were armored on the roof and sides, with sandbagged MG emplacements on the roof. Behind them were two troop-carrying cars with an undetermined number of troops, probably Chinese, aboard. Since we were not expected to engage any of the troops, just blow up the train and drop the bridge from beneath it, the security personnel aboard weren't really a factor.

Behind the troop carrier was an officers' coach car that doubled as the radio center. According to a cross reference, there were several technicians who were not Chinese, but European, traveling in the officers' coach. We were to insure that after the train went, they went too. I began looking over the coach design. A couple of well-placed rockets in the coach car and it was AMF, adios motherfucker. Or maybe we could place some souped-up shaped charges directly below the tracks and wait for the coach to roll directly over them. I began to get excited. Yeah, I told myself, use the charge to take out the coach and double it as a trigger for the main charges that would drop the bridge.

Pulling a small pad and a pen out of my fatigue shirt breast pocket, I began jotting notes. Randall and Griz were doing the same.

I flipped back to the specific orders about how the chemical cars were to be taken out. They couldn't just be dropped in the river. The NVA could salvage them that way. I flipped through the report on the actual chemical agents involved. If we blew the containers, would the chemical agents then spread and kill us or half the civilian population of Lao Cay? That could be just as damaging politically as if the agents were detonated in South Vietnam. Reading on, I found the answer. The chemicals were inert in their containers for safety during transport and storage. They had to be mixed in a certain way and then deployed by a certain method before they became dangerous. If they were destroyed in an explosion, they would vaporize harmlessly. Okay. That meant a *lot* of boom in the charges. Heat would kill the shit. I wrote "heat" and "vaporize" in my notebook and underlined them.

I had a general idea of what would be required of us by then. Just dropping the bridge and the train at Lao Cay wasn't enough. We would have to destroy the train either before we dumped it into the river or simultaneously.

Going on, I flipped to information on our route in and the area surrounding it. Lao Cay was a small city, not a village and it sat right on the Viet side of the border. We had an excellent series of SR 71 Black Bird high altitude photos of a wide area around both the city and the bridge. It was directly across the border from Hokow. I stood up and walked to the display board where Harry had tacked up the Big Bird satellite photos alongside copies of the SR 71 photos. Lao Cay was approximately two hundred twenty miles from the capital of Laos, Luang Prabang, and roughly the same distance from the North Viet coast in the Red River Delta area to the TA. It was too far from the Delta where we could land surreptitiously via Navy Seal boats to make it worth the effort to walk in.

Walking in from either direction was out of the question. We would be seen somewhere on the mission-in phase and our mission compromised. There was a large NVA military base just outside Chapa, to the southwest of our prime TA. Moving past them on foot, covertly, would complicate what was already a complicated affair. The simplest answer was obvious. A HALO insertion somewhere between Chapa and Lao Cay at night. The area around both Lao Cay and Chapa was mountainous, so we would need a more thorough photo recon of the area and I noted that on my pad as I searched the photo display for an area that might possibly be suitable for use as a DZ. I found what looked like an abandoned village in the foothills slightly west of Lao Cay and marked that on my pad also.

I had some ideas for insertion and the attack on the train itself. Since Griz was our demolitions specialist, he would work out the final specs on what charges we would use, where they would be placed as well as when and how we would detonate them, all subject to Randall's approval, of course. The HALO insertion was obvious. Returning to my seat and the briefing packet, I checked for information on North Viet radar. How much was deployed around Lao Cay and where was it pointed? What about Chicom or Chinese communist radar? Most of it was pointed toward Thailand, where we had air bases with bombers. Could we avoid it by flying in from the sea? From Laos? More notes went into my notebook.

I flipped over to the secondary target, the road bridge at Chapa. It crossed a gorge approximately ten miles southwest of Lao Cay. The NVA garrison force was two miles further southwest. Harry had said he wanted both bridges dropped, but not when. For the most effectiveness, if the Chapa bridge were dropped just after the Lao Cay bridge, the demolition party might be able to catch an NVA force on the bridge. That meant that the demolition party would have to be on-site in both places to detonate the charges. The train obviously was the primary target. If we were spotted at either bridge, our mission would be compromised. If half the team were spotted mining the bridge at Chapa, the other half could proceed with the attack on the Lao Cay bridge with a high chance of success. The NVA would surely pursue the men seen at the Chapa bridge. Okay, I said to myself, we could mine the road bridge first while the rest of the team stayed concealed in our field CP in the mountains between the two TAs. If the guys were seen at the Chapa bridge, they would break to the southwest, pulling any pursuit off of the other team, leaving it free to attack Lao Cay.

I stood to stretch and glanced at my watch. We had been in the briefing room six straight hours, engrossed in the intelligence material.

"Hey, anybody for some grub?" I asked.

It broke the trance the others were in. They all agreed and we decided to go outside for a while. I rapped on the door. The guard had to send for Harry, who collected all the packets and secured them before we could leave. Then he took our notebooks and secured them with the packets and covered the briefing map and the photos. Placing a guard inside the room and another at the door, he walked us out.

"I know I don't have to tell you guys this, but *do not* let any of this out, even to other RT people. Is that clear?" he said.

"Clear, sir," Randall replied.

We knew how to keep our mouths shut. Harry knew that, but he was as geared up over this mission as we were. It was the most important operation that I had ever been on and probably would be *the* big one for me. I didn't see any of us coming out of North Vietnam.

"Do we get a replacement for Sergeant Trail?" Griz asked Harry as we parted ways.

"Uh huh. He'll be here in the morning. He has been working with Command and Control South and is en route now," Harry told us, grinning. "Nothing but the best for you guys."

We ate, then bought some cold six-packs and retired to our barracks, but Randall took us out onto the beach. When we got there, he spread our Nungs out around us to make sure that no one could get too close.

"We stage in Thailand, HALO into the mountains between Lao Cay and Chapa," Griz said, breaking the ice.

"Yeah. I found what looks like a deserted ville in that general area. We might be able to use it as an LZ," I chimed in.

Randall and Blake both nodded. Bender sipped at his beer.

"A HALO jump in is our best shot at getting in undetected. We'll let the fly boys work out a route since they'll know more about a safe course in than we can piece together. I noticed that ville too, Hammer. We'll use it as a tentative LZ until we can get better photos of it at different times of the day, see if it really is deserted," Randall said.

"There is a cave up on a hill I think we could use for a field CP. There aren't any trails leading to it anymore. I checked the recon photos carefully and there aren't any villes around it either, so there wouldn't be any activity in the area," Griz said.

"A cave? Where did you see that at?" I asked. I'd scoured the photos and hadn't seen anything that vaguely resembled a cave.

Griz grinned at me. "I'll show you later. I know *where* it is because I was there in '53 and the photos confirm it is still there."

"Big enough for the whole team?" Bender asked, putting his empty can in a sack.

Griz nodded while Marty popped another beer. "It's a natural cave that the Viet Minh expanded and used for a field HQ until we found them in '53. After that, they never went back."

"How far from the tentative LZ?" Blake asked.

"Less than two miles. From the cave the Chapa bridge is roughly four miles. The railroad bridge at Lao Cay is around nine," Griz told us. It was well located and Griz had obviously gone over it carefully to map out the distances.

Griz had fought with a guerrilla force made up of Legionnaires and the indigs of various Yard tribes. Most of the French units hadn't operated too far out of their star-shaped forts, but Griz's unit had roamed the bush, hunting and killing the Viet Minh, living off the land like the Minh. They had been effective, but the concept had been a case of too little, too late to save the French forces and then had come Dien Bien Phu. Griz saw this as his chance to even the score a little for the good men who had gone before us, his old comrades who died valiantly in Indochina fighting communists. It was more personal to Griz than it was to Paul

Gustav. It wasn't a way of avenging his homeland on the communists or to keep another country from suffering as his own had done under communist domination. It was more a matter of paying the enemy back for friends he had lost along the way. That was how Griz took it. This mission offered him a chance to pay back the puppeteers, the men who pulled the strings of the foot soldiers we normally encountered, and that made Griz very happy.

"Sounds good to me, Griz. We'll eyeball it on the photos tonight and get a contour map from Harry tomorrow. That is unless any of you have a pressing date with Danang Daisy tonight," Randall said after we thought about Griz's cave for a few minutes.

There were several grins from the guys, but Griz turned a fiery red. Danang Daisy was a fifty-year-old Viet hooker who specialized in exotic sex, if anyone could stand to look at her naked. She had never had her checkups either and didn't have the shot card to prove she was free of VD. Anyone who didn't mind looking at her had to chance a dose of exotic venereal disease also. Griz had gotten drunk while we were between missions and taken Daisy out on the town. They had been seen together in all of the usual GI bars and word had gotten around. Since then, everyone had been ragging Griz about his date with the Prom Queen of 1927, ol' Rosie Rotten Crotch herself. Then he had refused to go to the clinic for a VD test, claiming he never had any more than a date with her.

"Aren't you worried about the clap eating your brain up, like it did Capone?" Blake had asked him.

"Don't be ridiculous," Griz said, smiling, "Would I be doing this for a living if I was worried about my brain?"

After we had been out on the beach for about an hour, I looked at my watch. It was early afternoon. We would go back to the briefing room for more planning later that day, setting our own schedule. We had that option.

"The way it looks to me, sarge, we should move on the Chapa bridge first, leave a small demo team, then mine the Lao Cay bridge. If we use the cave as a CP, then the demo team from Chapa can fall back to it after they blow their bridge. It'll make a good rendezvous position for all of us after we drop our bridges," I said.

Randall nodded an assent.

That went on until we had spec'ed out a rough plan, each of us tossing in ideas or picking at them until we had a pretty good idea of what to look for when we returned to our material. We would fill in the details over the next seven days until we had ironed out every step each man would take, and a plan for every contingency. It was a fascinating process to me, like a chess game. We had the advantage in that the NVA didn't know we were coming and we were better trained, better equipped and faster on our feet than they were. Or so we liked to believe anyway.

When we did go back to the briefing room to resume work on the program, we had eaten supper and were concentrating on the tentative plan we worked out on the beach to fill in any gaps that might have been left. All of us worked late into the night, not having any dates with Danang Daisy lined up.

The following morning after breakfast, an Oriental man in jungle fatigues joined us in the briefing room, introducing himself as Mike Feng. He was my height with light brown skin, long straight shiny black hair and a bad overbite. At first, I thought he was the indigenous agent Harry had told us to expect.

"Chinese?" Randall asked.

Feng smiled. "Taiwan. I speak Viet and several dialects of Chinese. I've been briefed on troop placement around the primary TA, maybe better than what is in your packets. I know the area, the language and what troops are where. Can I go?" he asked us, still smiling.

Randall grinned back at him. "Well, have a seat, Mike."

"Oh, I am a demolition specialist too," Feng said and all of us grinned.

He fit right in with our team. We learned that he was from the Taiwan Special Forces and had been to almost all of the U.S. Army Special Warfare courses. He was in Nam working for the Agency at the request of the Taiwan government. They wanted experienced people to train their cadres at home. Feng had been working with SOG and Agency PM teams in the south, which we knew meant Cambodia. When we began working on our operational plan again, he joined right in with us, making it obvious that he had been in on planning sessions like this one before. He made several very workable and practical suggestions that spoke well of his experience in the bush. In the six days that we were in the planning stage, all of us came to like and respect him. He had none of the shyness of the typical Oriental, a result, perhaps, of his having worked with American teams in the bush and proving himself capable with them. I had a very good feeling about the guy. The mission itself didn't seem to faze him or intimidate him either.

Finally, we had the whole operation spec'ed out. When we called for Harry, we briefed him on how we would insert, where we would establish a field base camp, what we needed for commo gear, how we would mine the Chapa road bridge and how we would waste the train. If the Chapa team was spotted, they would blow the bridge and run for the border, aborting their part of the mission, and leading pursuit away from Lao Cay. The Lao Cay team would use them for a distraction and complete their mission, then move back into the mountains.

If the Lao Cay team was spotted, they would take out anyone who spotted them. If not, they would mine the bridge using shaped charges with command detonators. The first charges would take the engine out. Further charges, arranged in a series, would vaporize the chemical carrying cars, taking large portions of the upper span of the bridge with them. The final charges would take out the officers' coach and drop the entire upper span of the bridge into the river. The team would be stationed on a hill northeast of the city of Lao Cay and the bridge with the command detonators. Two Nungs and I would be closer to the bridge with an RPG to make sure that the chemical cars and the officers coach were vaporized if the shaped charges didn't do the job, while the team covered me from above. Then, with the train and its cargo successfully destroyed, we would make a run for the mountains, rendezvousing with the Chapa demo team at the cave we selected as a field CP. Then we covered our extraction with several alternate plans.

We outlined what equipment we needed, both mission related and personal, things each of us wanted and didn't like to be in the bush without. Since it was a sterile operation, some of the things we asked for were going to be hard to find, but Harry promised to do his best. He said he would have all our equipment together for us in Thailand at our staging area in two days. Then he gathered all our briefing packets, files, notes, photos and maps into a large steel case and took off. He had taped our briefing. We sat around the rest of the day until supper, each of us lost in our own thoughts now that we didn't have the mission to occupy our immediate attention.

During that entire week, I didn't get drunk or high once. I slept well, ate well, and didn't have any dreams about Dane's open head wound or Tex somersaulting through the air past me, part of his leg missing and spurting blood. I actually felt good for a change. Alive and useful. I still didn't see any way for us to pull off our mission and get out of North Vietnam alive, but that didn't really bother me that much. If I died in pursuit of a goal that I felt was a good one, that was okay. I accomplished something.

Harry had said total unit closure. That meant that if we couldn't get each other out alive, there were to be no POWs taken from our team. We were to grease anyone who we couldn't carry or drag out. I didn't mind that either. If I died, it would be in pursuit of my ideals, what little there were of them. This wasn't humping the rice paddies, waiting to be ambushed. It seemed like I had been living all my life for this one operation. Over the course of the six planning days, Harry had mentioned to each of us, individually, that mission success would be amply rewarded by his agency. Like the prospect of dying, that didn't affect me much either. I wasn't in Nam for the money as Cat had pointed out. Of course I would take whatever the reward would be, but that wasn't much in the way of motivation to me. I was so wrapped up in the mission that everything not directly related to our performance of it was completely alien to me.

The next afternoon, Harry reappeared. He loaded our whole team into an Air America C123 and flew us to a staging area in Thailand.

We had given Harry our list of wants that specified personal weapons as well as specialty items for the mission and they were all waiting for us at the little camp we were to use as a staging area. Blake and Bender found the radios we would be using, a pair of East German field units. They also had a high freak (high frequency) burst transmitter for satellite communication. Our abort signal would come from that, if the situation arose. The burst transmitter would not give the enemy electronic surveillance people time to triangulate our position if they were able to detect it.

Randall and I dug out the weapons and began inspecting them. Each of us would be armed with folding stock Czech-made AKs. We field stripped them all, inspected, cleaned and oiled them. We went through the crate of Czech frags, dismantling them and inspecting the fuses. We found some Combloc frags that had variable length fuses, from zero on up to six seconds. All of ours were five-second delay fuses.

We inspected the ammo next, checking for corrosion or any other possible faults. The magazines were next, checking them for spring tension and to see if the lips of any of them were bent. Then we stripped and cleaned the suppressed Moisin-Nagant sniper rifle we requested. It was an old model, chambered in the World War II era 7.92mm Mauser caliber. The telescopic sight was one that I had never seen before, but Randall said he had used them years ago while stationed in Germany. He showed me how to calibrate it while we worked. The last pieces of equipment that we worked over were two RPGs.

While we were busy with the personal weapons, Griz and Feng worked over the RPG warheads. If we had to use them on the train, we all wanted to be sure that they worked. Harry had promised us modified, extremely powerful rocket warheads for them and Griz wanted to see just what the spook armory had come up with. Feng was more familiar with the modified warheads and he showed Griz how they worked. They approved the modifications as workable and buttoned them back up.

None of our personal weapons were allowed. We had to use all sterile gear down to our socks and knives. A stack of Yard bush knives were in one crate and some Combloc field knives. Then we came to the sidearms. They were Czech 9mm auto pistols, enough for every man on the team. The Colt .45 auto had spoiled me for any other handgun, but since I couldn't have one, I checked out all of the little 9mm pistols. We stripped and cleaned them. Several of them had attachments for suppressors. I found the cans

or suppressors, threaded them on, removed them again and pulled
them apart to check their packing. I found more suppressors for
the rifles and did the same inspection on them.

While I inspected the small arms, I was somewhat surprised to
find that every piece of equipment was brand new. These weren't
captured pieces, no war booty that had been seized off the battle-
field. No, these weapons had never been fired. The Agency had
one hell of a source somewhere. For all I knew the Agency manufactured them somewhere just for occasions like this.

Griz and Feng had gone from the RPG warheads to the demo
equipment, working until dark with the detonators. When they
broke, we went and ate supper, then retired for the night to the
hootch we had been told to use as a team house. Our uniforms
and web gear as well as load-bearing gear for the mission were
all stacked there in neat piles, with little cards identifying whose
gear was whose. All of the Nungs had black pajamas, sandals and
black VC-style web gear. Our uniforms were a splinter pattern I'd
never seen before. Feng had an NVA officer's field uniform.

"What kinda pattern is this?" I asked, holding up a shirt. It
vaguely resembled our tiger stripe pattern.

"East German," Harry answered from the open door of the
team house. "So are your boots, which are mountain boots by
the way."

"How secure is this base, Harry?" Randall asked.

"You can start breaking your boots in anytime. Don't wear the
uniforms until your insertion briefing. Did you finish inspecting
and clearing your equipment yet?"

"Weapons, radios and demolitions checked out fine. We'll do
the 'chutes in the morning and then test fire the weapons. The
rest of it'll be worked out by day after tomorrow," Randall said.

Harry nodded, obviously pleased. "I brought your strap hangers
along too."

The Cat and a young, tough-looking Oriental strolled in. Both
of them had AKs dangling from one hand, their web gear in the
other, and were wearing old, faded jungle fatigues. I nodded to
the Cat and he returned it with a half grin.

"We have been briefed on your op plan, Randall," The Cat

said, not making any attempt to introduce the Oriental, who stepped into the room.

I thought it was a little late to add an unknown element to the mission, but I didn't say anything. We all knew and had operated with the Cat. There would be no hesitation on our part in accepting him as one of the team for this mission. The Oriental agent who had arrived with him was a different story, however.

I guess Harry read my mind because he motioned us to be seated. "The Cat and Sho here are both demolition specialists. They will add a new dimension to your team. I am sorry to bring new operatives in at this late stage, but it is something that we had to do. Sho was on assignment and unavailable until now," he told us.

Sho, the Oriental, tossed his web gear onto a bunk and moved further into the room. He went to Blake, the closest one of us to him, and shook his hand, bowing as he did so. I watched him move, curious. He seemed to glide, the same way the Cat moved. He was lean, almost as dark as a Yard and close to my height. I thought he might be a Khmer, a Cambodian. Sho went to every one of us and performed his handshake-bow ceremony. Then he sat with us as Harry ran through the briefing he prepared for us.

Cat and Sho were not under our unit closure order. That meant that they were on their own if the shit got deep and that we could depend on them to do themselves if it came down to that. We would have update briefings right up until we loaded the aircraft for insertion. If anything changed, we would know about it instantly. After the briefing, Cat and I talked for a while, then we all turned in.

Early the next morning, I issued the individual weapons and we all trotted out to the range to test fire and zero them in. We spent half the day getting the feel of them. All of us were familiar with Combloc weapons, but none of us on the team had used them much recently so we needed time to become really familiar with them. Feng, Sho and the Cat zeroed theirs, fired a few magazines to check the trigger action and then cleaned their weapons. I guess they were more used to them than we were. After we burned up all the allocated ammo for the test firing and break in, we stripped, cleaned and reinspected the weapons again. All of us were satisfied that the weapons we had would function in the field. Then we broke for lunch.

After we had eaten, we opened, inspected and repacked our parachutes. They were paracommander-type wings that were extremely maneuverable. I had over a dozen jumps with them and really liked them. Then we checked the tags on the reserve chutes and the bail-out oxygen bottles that we would need for the high altitude exit from the plane. We had thermal underwear and one-piece jumpsuits that we would wear, changing into our foreign camo suits on the ground. At thirty-six thousand feet, the air was both thin and cold.

The next morning, Cat, Griz, Sho and Feng went out with some of the explosives to test their charges, caps and detonators. I went out with Blake to be sure the radios worked. I heard a series of explosions crack off an hour or so after we left the compound, so Blake and I followed the sound to its source. We watched the four men place their charge around the base of a tree, lay a line, then detonate it. The tree jumped straight up about a foot, then toppled over.

We walked down to join them. They were using C4 in OD green bags, but Cat and Griz had some metal canisters out and were molding the C4 around the canisters.

"What's that?" I asked, pointing to the canisters.

"Gas," Cat said, "made from pig shit."

"Uh huh," I mumbled.

"No, really. It's an ammonia gas that enhances the power of the explosive by tens," Griz told me.

He demonstrated by blowing one of the fallen trees into pieces with a charge of C4 without any gas attached. It did a job. Then he wrapped another tree with segments of C4 and the gas canisters, detonated them and there was nothing left but toothpick-sized splinters. I was impressed.

"Nice," I said, ears ringing from the explosions.

"Yeah, not bad. You making up the charges for the bridges now?" Blake asked.

Griz nodded. "The Cat and I are making them up now. They'll be in packets for better load distribution. I guess Randall will distribute them tomorrow."

We packed and repacked our gear, distributed everything that we had to carry several times until we had it worked out who would carry what. Harry briefed us every evening, but nothing changed. We were still on our original schedule and plan. Finally, there was nothing left for us to do but wait. I filled my time by practicing karate and rehearsing my role in the mission in my mind over and over.

Finally, Harry gave us our final briefing. We changed into our HALO outfits, shuffled aboard a waiting C130 and were in the air, heading for North Vietnam.

As ever, stepping out into space was a rush for me. I was the second man out. The night was clear and bright. I could see the earth below as we hurtled toward it in an arms-back aerodynamic tracking position. Following Griz, the lead man, I scanned the terrain below for our landmarks. There were three, the final one signaling us to open our chutes. Watching Griz, then my altimeter, compass and the terrain below, I made the first turn as we came over the little village that served as our first landmark and course change. Bringing one arm forward, I arched, feeling my body slip sideways through space, being careful not to move too much and spin out of control. The slightest wrong movement would put me in a spin where I would lose altitude. In itself, that would not be fatal, if I corrected the spin before I hit the ground, but I would lose a lot of altitude and set down well short of the DZ. That was totally unacceptable for this mission.

Griz made a second, wider curve to the north and I adjusted to follow him. We were falling at a terminal velocity of one hundred thirty plus miles per hour, floating free above the world, wind roaring in our ears. All of our course changes made, I relaxed and just enjoyed the ride. After sex and completing a mission successfully, jumping was my third most favorite pleasure. I spotted the DZ and began tracking toward it.

Above the deserted village, we changed our body configurations to alter our angle of descent, dropping straight down instead of at the thirty-five degree angle we used for tracking. At one thousand feet, I pulled the release ring of my parachute. The paracommander main chute deployed above me with a soft "pop" and lifted me slightly as it filled with air. I swung beneath the parabolic wing canopy, watching Griz go in slightly below me. Turning my head, I saw other parachutes deploying too. I was slightly deaf after the roar of the wind and the rapid change in altitude, but I knew that would clear up soon. Pulling the risers of my parachute, I came down in a tight spiral into a perfect stand-up landing in the center of the village.

The rest of the team landed all around me with barely a sound as I collapsed and gathered my canopy, shucked the parachute harness and oxygen bottle and then got out of my jumpsuit and thermals. I quickly pulled on my camo uniform and boots, broke out the AK, threaded the can on it, then locked and loaded. Griz and I stashed our jump gear, then checked the rest of the team.

Randall counted us off. We all did a quick equipment check, then moved out. That was the first time I discovered that I couldn't use a compass anymore. It pointed at me when I opened it to take a bearing. All the shrapnel that had been left embedded in my body for so long attracted the magnetic compass needle. I was bummed.

We moved at a fast pace up into the hills. Krang and Griz led the way. We didn't have to worry about boobytraps or NVA patrols that deep in enemy country and as high in the mountains as we were, so we made rapid progress. Forty-five minutes after we landed, Griz halted us under cover near the cave he wanted to use as a field CP. Randall sent several of us forward with suppressed pistols and rifles to reconnoiter it.

I didn't like caves. They were the same as tunnels to me, only vertical, which didn't make them any better. You couldn't melt me and pour me into a tunnel. I'd taken an Article Fifteen once for refusing to go down one. Fuck that. I let Feng and two Nungs explore the cave while I covered them. When they came out several minutes later, I signaled the team forward and we moved into the huge hole in the side of the hill. It was about thirty feet long, sloping from the opening height of seven feet back to nothing. It was about fifteen feet wide. It was a tight fit for all of us, but we managed. Randall put an LP above the roof of the cave and the rest of us nodded until daylight.

At dawn, we ate, Bender checked the burst transmitter, then

the Chapa team checked its gear one more time and got ready to move out. Griz, Blake, who was assigned as their RTO, Feng, Cat and four Nungs saddled up for the march south. I shook hands with all of them. There really wasn't much to say. "Good luck" seemed stupid. We all just shook hands, slapped shoulders, nodded and went our way. I grinned at Blake as he shouldered his radio.

"Git some, asshole," he hissed.

"You too, dude," I replied.

I heard him chuckle as he turned away to join his group.

Our group saddled up. Krang took point with me walking his slack and we moved off for Lao Cay, nine miles away.

Our progress was slow, but after four hours of quiet, careful, slow movement through mostly mountainous terrain, we sat on the low hill northeast of the Lao Cay bridge that we selected in our premission planning as our forward operations site. Gooks were everywhere around us. It was the first time I was really aware of being in North Vietnam. There were boats all up and down the river, people walking around below us, trucks, jeeps, cars and bicycles everywhere. I could not believe that we had penetrated so deeply into the enemy's home ground without having been seen. It blew me away, so I just sat and enjoyed the feeling for a few minutes. Looking around, I saw that the others had the same expressions of awe on their faces. After we let it sink in for a while, we crawled around the top of the little hill to get a better look at the bridge and China across the river.

Sho seemed to take the whole thing a little less seriously than the rest of us. Even our Nungs were somewhat subdued for a change. Sho watched us for a moment, smiled, then began stripping off his black pajamas. Pulling an NVA officer's field uniform out of his load bearing gear, he pulled it on and walked over to Randall. After a brief conference with him, Sho walked down the back of the hill disappearing below my line of sight.

Randall briefed us all individually. "He's going to check out the routes that we planned on taking down to the bridge, see if anything has changed. Then he'll recon the bridge itself. Don't shoot the guy when he comes back up."

"We still going to snatch the sampan tonight?" I asked before he could move off.

Randall just shrugged and left me alone with my thoughts. I began readying the RPGs that would be my responsibility when the time came. The two Nungs who would load for me unstrapped the rockets they wore in a harness on their back and laid them out around us.

The plan had been to snatch a small sampan from the fishing dock of a little village northeast of us, float downriver with the charges, scale the bridge supports from directly beneath the bridge, place the charges at the preselected spots, drop back down to the sampan and take it back to the village before the sun was up. If that worked, all we would have to do then was sit and wait for the train. If that was impossible, for whatever reason, we would have to try another approach to the bridge. A lot of it depended on how the security forces around the bridge acted. We predicted that they would be beefed up just before the train came through, but the only way to know for certain was an on-site recon.

Pulling my field glasses out, I scanned the bridge, all of the approaches that I could see, the river and the area around us. By midafternoon, I was sleepy, so I alerted Randall and took a nap.

Krang woke me just before dark. Sho had rejoined us, a smear of blood across the front of his uniform shirt.

"If we cross the river there is a blind approach along the bank and none of us will have to crawl the length of the bridge to place charges," he told us, pointing across the river into China.

What the hell? Since we are only a stone's throw away from it now, we may as well cross the river.

"It'll take approximately twenty-four minutes to place the charges once we are on the bridge, sarge," I said, reminding Randall that whatever approach we used would take us right in front of sentries on both sides of the river and that we would have to be in place for at least a half hour to complete the placement of the explosives.

He grunted and turned back to the river.

"What happened?" I asked Sho, indicating the blood smear on his tunic.

"A sentry at the bridge. He is submerged in those reeds near the bridge." Sho told me, pointing to a marshy area on the southwest corner of the bridge. "I wasn't seen or heard."

I nodded. If he had been, we would have noticed the uproar from our position.

"We take a sampan at the fishing dock, cross the river and deliver you two to the far bank. We'll float downriver to the bridge and scale it from the other side. Krang and I will place the charges on our side, the south span, you two will place the charges on the north. One of you place the charges under the tracks, and the other work the supports. When we are finished, we'll lower ourselves to the sampan and pick you up from the opposite bank. Marty'll cover us from here with the long gun and two Nungs will give us close support from the sampan. Clear?" Randall said, briefing us.

We all nodded. Krang briefed the two Nungs who were going into the water with us and they screwed suppressors onto their rifles. I dropped all of my gear except my pistol, affixed its suppressor to it, then strapped on the ten bags that contained the charges I was to place. We painted our faces and hands, left Marty with the Russian sniper rifle to cover us on the bridge and moved down the east slope of the hill an hour after sunset.

The dock had been built for local fishermen. Nets hung around it. There were several sampans moored there. We chose the largest of the three, which wasn't very big at all. The Nungs climbed in while Sho and I slid into the water on one side of it, hanging onto the net lines that hung partially over the sides. Randall and Krang did the same on the opposite side. Krang directed the Nung crew.

I stayed as low in the water as possible, expecting a searchlight to hit us at any second as we rowed diagonally across the river. Krang, at Randall's direction, hissed at us and we let go of the net lines and began a slow dog paddle toward the shore. Behind us the sampan veered off and headed slowly downriver for the bridge. When we reached the opposite shore, we stayed low in the water, slithering up onto the mud bank so that we wouldn't make noise dripping water that was draining out of our clothing.

Looking up I saw why we had a blind approach. We were below an overhanging ledge of tree roots and mud bank that ran all the way up to the bridge itself. Sho smiled at me and nodded toward

the bridge, then led the way, crawling on all fours, placing each
hand and knee carefully. It was just possible that the Chinese had
some kind of alarm devices around the bridge. I followed Sho,
being especially careful, feeling every inch ahead of me before I
committed my weight forward. When we reached the base of the
bridge's foundation, Sho unrolled a line and a padded hook, swung
it a few times, then tossed it upward. It caught on his first throw.
We were concealed from the sentries' view from either side of the
river by the span of the bridge itself. Taking a hold on the line,
I followed Sho quickly up it.

The charge placement had already been worked out. All we had
to do was count off a certain number of pilings or ties, attach the
explosive packets to one of the pilings or under the central span
with the right side turned to the surface that we were attaching
it to, activate the electronic command detonator and go to the next
predetermined location. Simple. Sho and I decided to work up
opposite sides, switch over at the center of the span and work our
way back to the north bank that way. Other than not liking heights,
a bizarre fear for a paratrooper who liked to jump as much as
I did, the job turned out to be easy. I couldn't see too far ahead,
so I actually ran into several of the pilings and then into Randall
at the center of the span as I inched along below the bridge. I knew
I'd hear about that later.

I whispered that half of my charges were in place and activated.
He repeated the same to me and told me to rejoin Sho on the north
bank when we were finished. If I tried to follow Randall to his
side of the span, I might have dislodged some of the charges that
he had placed. I began the traverse to the opposite side of the span,
trading places with Sho. Working my way back to the north end
of the bridge, I found the padded grappling hook after I placed
the last of my packets and began a slow, controlled descent down
the line. About halfway down, I heard voices speaking Chinese.
I froze on the line and tried to pull myself in behind a piling, but
I couldn't reach one without swinging, so I just hung about twenty
feet off the ground.

Two Chinese soldiers walked under the bridge from Sho's side,
one smoking a cigarette and carrying a bottle. Stopping a few feet

away from the line, which was invisible in the darkness unless one of them walked into it, they passed the bottle back and forth, speaking in low voices. Every once in a while one or the other would walk to the far side of the bridge, barely missing the line each time, and look up the bank. My shoulders were beginning to ache from the strain of hanging from the thin line. Both of my hands were going numb. It looked to me like these two clowns were on guard duty and had snuck off to drink a little wine. I figured and really hoped that they would go away soon.

Then I slipped a foot down the line. I couldn't feel with my hands, but I must have let go and not realized it until I felt myself drop. I braked with my boots and hands, knowing I was burning my hands raw by gripping the line tighter as it slipped through my bare hands. Still, I couldn't feel that right then.

One of the guards heard something and looked up. He apparently saw the line as it swayed below me. Using my boots to brake my fall had set it swaying. I silently cursed my luck. I knew what I had to do now, if I could. When the guard was directly below me, holding the line and looking up into the darkness where I hung, I let go and dropped straight down on his upturned face with both boots. It drove him head first to the ground. I performed a reasonably smooth PLF or parachute landing fall, rolled to my feet and charged the second, surprised soldier. He wasn't there.

Sho stood over his corpse, wiping a blade on the dead man's shirt. He motioned to the other guard and I broke his neck as Sho retrieved his hook and line. We cleaned up the scene of the killings quickly and carried the two bodies into the river. Wading out chest deep, we submerged until only our heads were above water and waited for the sampan to pick us up.

As the sun rose, Bender told us that Griz had reported in. All his charges were in place. He was waiting for the fire command from us, freeing him to choose his target when it crossed the bridge. The plan we laid out had us blowing our bridge and then giving Griz a free fire signal. While we pulled back for the cave we would use as a field CP, Griz would wait for a target of opportunity and then drop his bridge. They would haul ass for the cave then too, rendezvousing with us after we secured the cave. No one would be looking for a team that went into ground and hid out after dropping a bridge that far north or so we hoped.

We lay, waiting. Marty sent off a confirmation of our readiness on the burst transmitter. As soon as a Black Bird told Harry that the train was headed our way, he would burst that information to us and we would lock and load. I cleaned all of my equipment again, just to be sure that everything I had was ready to fire. Then I ate, laid out my RPG rounds again, went over the loading sequence with the Nungs who would act as my loaders, rolled into some shade and nodded out.

Randall woke me in the late afternoon.

"Train's movin'. ETA in two five," he told me.

The twenty-five minutes flew past. Randall and I spotted the smoke first, then the train itself through our binoculars. The Nungs and I moved off the hill to our actual firing location in a clump of bamboo near the river. If the charges failed to vaporize the cars, then it was up to the three of us to do it with the RPG. We settled into place as the train halted at the small border checkpoint on the Chinese side. I knew Bender was flashing messages to Harry and Griz right about then. I wondered if I would make it off this hill alive, but that was just a fleeting thought as the train engine belched smoke, blew its whistle and got up steam.

What the hell. No guts, no glory.

The train pulled forward, gaining momentum, chugging onto the bridge. As we predicted, the engineer kept it slow. I signaled one Nung to load my RPG tube as I shouldered it. The engine was nearly across the bridge. I mentally calculated that it should have been over the first charge right about now.

An explosion lifted the engine straight up with a short, flat crack of sound. Pieces of the engine flew outward, away from it, as the boiler ruptured and steam went everywhere. A blast wave rolled over us seconds later as some of the debris started to settle, but it wasn't too severe. Most of the force of the blast had been directed upward by the shaped charge into the engine. Before the other cars had a chance to react to the engine's destruction, a series of rapid explosions came all along the tracks. The cars were blown apart like match sticks. Sections of the bridge span and rails were tossed high into the air.

Our planning paid off. Every single car had been totally destroyed. All that was left of them were still flying through the air, small pieces of debris that couldn't be identified as having once belonged to a train. I laid the RPG tube down on the ground and signaled the Nungs to go back to the team. I followed them seconds later, just as the second set of charges went off. I missed the main span's fall into the river as I circled around to the east side of the hill, rejoining the team. Everyone there, except Sho, was grinning ear to ear.

Marty was encoding a message to Harry right then. The rest of the team was packing up. It was time to boogie. Glancing over my shoulder at where the bridge had been, I saw only jagged support pillars. Even the wreckage in the river was shredded, just bits and pieces of wood, steel and concrete, certainly nothing recognizable as having been a train or a bridge. I grinned down at the wreckage, then Randall was calling us, leading us off the little hill.

"Kill anything that sees you," he told Krang, who took point. We all had our suppressors attached. It was vital that we clear the area as fast as we could before the NVA moved a reaction force in and cut us off.

Our extraction route had been carefully planned. I could have followed it damn near blindfolded, except that I couldn't use a compass. I ran slack for Krang. We moved along a ridge away from the hill we had used for our fire base, down into a small, thin forest and back into more hills. So far we hadn't seen a single person, though we could still hear air raid sirens going off behind us in Lao Cay. They must have thought that an air strike hit the bridge. It wouldn't take them long to find out from their radar bases that no high altitude bombers had been there.

We moved at a flat run where we could. Marty told Griz and his team that we were on the move and then passed a mission complete from Griz to Randall. Both bridges had been dropped. We had made it in and done our job.

Two hours later, we reached the cave, secured it, posted an LP and waited for Griz and his team. They reached us two hours later. We spent the night in the cave, rotating the LP every two hours.

It was warm and dry in the cave and I discovered that after you got used to the idea of all that rock and dirt over your head, it wasn't bad to live underground. It didn't however, change my feelings about running into any tunnels though.

The next morning, we moved cautiously south, working our way through the mountains and hills, staying to the high ground. Reaching the first RON we had preselected during our planning stage, we laagered there for the night. The RON was in the high ground also and it wasn't as comfortable or warm as the cave. While in the cave, I dug around a little in the corners, where the walls joined the floor, just to see if I could find something that had belonged to a former occupant. As I lay under the stars that next night, I wondered who lived in that cave twenty years ago before Griz and his team had attacked it or who had been there two thousand years ago. Some of the distant ancestors of the people we were now fighting? Of the Yards more than likely, if anyone had been there at all. The Yards said that they were the original inhabitants of Southeast Asia, that the Khmer and Viets had chased them into the mountains. I wondered if I were sleeping where a Yard tribe had once slept or perhaps a band of hunters had RONed before moving off.

I fell asleep with those thoughts. Nam was an ancient land, old and civilized when Europeans were young and rowdy nomadics. I wondered if our version of civilization would end up like theirs over the centuries. Corrupt and tyrannical. Or was ours already there and we just didn't know it?

The next morning, we began working our way down out of the hills toward an extraction LZ south and west of where we were. If we didn't have to make any stops or detours, we planned to reach it before dark. We ate on the march, both breakfast and the little bit of lunch that everyone took. I was walking slack again, with Griz on point. We made good time through the mountains, but by late afternoon Randall knew we wouldn't make our LZ in time for an extraction. The slicks couldn't reach us before it got dark from their staging area in Laos. We climbed back up into the mountains and found another RON. This one was even less comfortable than the other. It was just a cut in the rocks that we squeezed our bodies into for concealment in case any NVA wandered past us in the night. I was pretty wired up from the day's march, so I volunteered for the first watch. When it was over, the march had caught up to me and I nodded right out.

When the sun came up the next morning, we were on the move again right away. All of the guys took benzedrine for the first time in the mission. We had to. We had run out of food the night before. We had only brought in enough rations to last four days on the ground, which was what our plan called for, and to lighten our loads a little. The weapons and explosives had been a lot of weight to carry. I could see a look of grim determination settle over the guys' faces as we hit the trail that morning.

When we were less than a mile away from the LZ, Griz stopped us. We pulled back up onto a hill for cover. An NVA heavy patrol cut across our line of march without spotting any sign of us and kept going. It was a tense moment as they paused right below the hill we were on before they moved down the trail. Letting them get well past us, we came out of hiding and moved on.

The LZ was a small clearing, just big enough for a slick to land, in a mountain valley. We stopped in the hills above it and sent out our extraction request by burst. When it was confirmed, we moved very slowly and cautiously down into the valley where a thin forest surrounded it. Settling into cover, we watched the LZ and the area around it for movement. We were in a loose laager. I glanced around at the guys, watching them in admiration for what we had done together as a team, when I noticed one of us was missing.

"Where the fuck's Sho?" I asked Griz, who was sitting next to me.

Griz looked around too. Sho was nowhere to be seen. I couldn't remember exactly when I had seen him last either. Right after we had dropped the bridge, I thought.

"He's gone," Griz said.

The Cat heard me and edged over to us. "He is on assignment," he said.

"Doing what?" I asked.

"He is not extracting with us. The search for us will cover his infiltration into his target area," Cat explained.

"Huh," I said, crawling back to my position next to Griz.

That was slick. Harry was good. I had to give him credit for that. Using our strike to insert an agent was very slick and very gutsy. I wished Sho luck mentally while I waited for the slicks. They came in soon, the familiar whop-whop-whop of their rotors preceding their appearance. Marty was on the radio, talking them in. When they were in sight, Blake ran out onto the LZ and popped a smoke canister and the rest of us moved out.

It hadn't taken the slicks long to reach us. They were staged just across the Lao border at a H'Mong village that a green hat team ran. It didn't take us long to load up. We were flown to a launch site in Thailand where the spooks debriefed us for two straight days. All of our foreign gear was confiscated and our own uniforms returned, though I managed to keep the little Czech pistol with the can. It might come in handy one day.

After we were debriefed, I got Griz drunk and got him to tell me about his bridge in return for a blow-by-blow description of what happened with ours. About a half hour after we dropped our bridge, four deuce-and-a-half trucks full of NVA soldiers came flying down the road, led by an open command car. The bridge Griz had mined stretched over a tremendous gorge, so it was long enough to allow all of the vehicles on it before he dropped it. That was what he had done. Four truckloads of NVA and their unit commander in the car went into the gorge. He was glowing when he told the story.

We had done a hell of a job. Our team had snuck deep into the enemy's home and given him a serious bloody nose. One that they wouldn't forget either. We were treated to Black Bird recon photos of the wreckage of both bridges after our debriefing. It was part of the reward. The Lao Cay bridge was already under repair, a swarm of coolies working on it. Well, we had expected that. The train had been our real target.

Harry let us go to Bangkok or wherever we wanted for two weeks. At the end of that time, we all rendezvoused in Danang. Harry greeted us there and explained how the benefits we had been promised were being paid to us and gave us an unofficial "official'' well done from his superiors. That was all the thanks we would get and we knew it, but just having done the job successfully was thanks enough. That was what it was all about for us. Having it written on paper didn't mean shit. We had done it, gone there and come back. I wondered what Harry would think up for an encore.

Chapter Eleven
The Kill

Harry had us run several agents named Smith or Jones, who looked more like Nguyen or Tranh, into various areas of North Vietnam. We would insert by slick to an area near our TA, then guide the spooks in overland to a predesignated rendezvous site. Then we would leave, sneaking out overland to an extraction site. On several of the missions, we escorted two spooks in, dropped one off, picked up some intel from CAS agents already in place and then exfiltrated. Our main responsibility on those missions was the agent's welfare. That basically meant that we were guides and bodyguards. We had no operational responsibilities or objectives other than that, the safety of the spooks.

I began to zone out while on missions. I'd have nightmares while awake, walking along or laagering deep in Indian or enemy country. That was a bad sign and I knew it. I wasn't sure if the others noticed or not since I hadn't caused any particular problems yet. I was afraid to ask for help. If I did, whoever I asked would take me off operational status. I couldn't make it in a REMF job. I'd zone out and kill the wrong person the first time some other REMF ran his lip to me. No, the only place I was really safe was in the bush.

We didn't make much contact on those insertion ops. Our sneak-around-the-NVA abilities had been finely honed over the months. Things were going smoothly for us too, no REMFs were fucking with us and no idiot officers were trying to get us killed with stupid ops. Harry ran us well. On the average, we pulled one five-day op every three weeks.

When we came in from one particularly smooth insertion, Harry came over to our quarters after we had been debriefed and had a chance to unwind a little. Even if we didn't make contact on those missions, just operating that deep in enemy territory was nerve-wracking. So when Harry came in, we thought he was alerting us for another mission.

"Lay chilly men. I came to see Hammer," he told us, seeing our expressions.

Walking over, he sat on the end of my footlocker. "Your extension is up this next week."

"Huh," I said. I hadn't been keeping track. My eighteen month tour had gone by in a blur.

"Are you going to stay?" Harry asked.

All the guys, except Blake, had stopped whatever they were doing, waiting to hear my answer.

I shrugged. "I dunno Harry. Probably. Can you push the paperwork through?"

"Why don't you take a walk with me?"

I followed him out of the compound and along the beach. It was a good, private place to talk. There were a lot of people on it during the day though, so we walked until we were alone.

"Randall told me you're having problems sleeping and you're getting high a lot," he said, looking out at the sea.

"Yeah," I snapped. It sounded like implied criticism and I didn't want to hear it from him.

"I can get you help, man. But you'll have to DEROS to get it. I checked with some people I know back in the U.S. We can get you into one of the hospitals our agency runs. The shrinks there deal with agent burnout all the time. They can bring you back."

I didn't say anything. I was thinking over his offer. Leave the team, but only because I needed to, or stay and maybe not ever get the chance to detune, get this all out of my system. Or worse, zone out in the bush and get myself or some of the fellas greased. My pride said to stay and see the war through. Common sense told me it was time to walk away from it, if I could.

I explained some of that to Harry. He nodded. "Your team will understand. I'm going to make all of them the same offer sooner or later. I'll get the paperwork started. You are exempt from duty as of today."

He left me alone on the beach. I pulled a joint out of my tiger suit pocket, sat on the sand and lit it. After a few minutes, I felt like a tremendous weight had been lifted off me. I was going home. Alive. I got up and trotted back to the barracks.

When I told the guys, they all nodded. Randall grinned at me. "Yer doin' the right thing, son," he said, clapping me on the shoulder.

Blake grunted something. "You'll be back," he said.

"Not to this war. I'm outta here," I told him.

We said our goodbyes two days later. I didn't know what to say and I guess the guys didn't either, so we clasped hands, embraced and parted. As simple as that. I was sent to the SOG building in Saigon for debriefing and it lasted several days. After that, I would catch the Freedom Bird home to a CIA-run hospital in Virginia. I had the same hollow feeling that had struck me when I flew back to Nam for this tour. I thought that was pretty bizarre. I wondered how I'd feel when I actually got back to the world.

My DEROS date was only a day away when they told me I had an emergency call on a land line from Danang. Rushing to the commo center, I snatched the receiver from the guy's hand.

"Yeah?" I asked, knowing that it was some kind of bad news about the team, that it had happened because I wasn't there with them when they needed me. I got an instant and overpowering case of the guilties.

"This's Randall. We've found Truong. I wanted you to know."

I was dazed. Truong. They were going after the bastard without me. He was the reason I had stayed in Nam as long as I had, to find and kill him. He was the man who cost Tex and Brick their lives, Hardin and Dane their blood.

"When?" I barked.

"This isn't a secure line," Randall replied, "I just wanted you to know, son. Good luck."

"Hey sarge, I'll be right there. Wait."

According to the Army, I went AWOL, but all I did was kidnap an REMF with a jeep to get out to our compound. I ran to the war, not away from it. When I stepped through the door of the room containing our team's billets, two MPs were inside waiting for me. I left them laying in the room and went to find Harry and the guys in the secure briefing room. No one tried to stop me from going in there. I guess they were used to seeing me go in and out.

When I opened the door and stepped into the room, all of the guys' faces lit up. Harry paused with what he was saying, staring at me in disbelief. "What are *you* doing here?" he barked at me.

"What do you think? Harry, I'm going. Get the dogs off my ass or I'll go alone, maybe leave some bodies behind me," I growled.

Blake cracked up. He couldn't control himself. Randall was having a hard time keeping a straight face too. "Now you see what we've had to put up with," he said.

"All right, I'll fix it. But this is it," Harry said, storming out. The briefing broke up with that. When I looked around the room, I saw that Mike Feng was sitting with the team and that Janca and his spotter Caulderson were sitting alone in the back. We nodded to each other in recognition.

"Hell of an entrance," Janca growled, his normal way of speaking, as he swung his booted feet off the chair they were propped up on.

I spotted his rifle leaning against the wall behind him. I shrugged at Janca.

"Where's yer partner at?" Caulderson asked.

"Big Dane?"

"The big guy that was with us down south," Janca said.

"Yeah, that was Dane. He got blown up man."

"Shit. Too bad, I liked working with him."

"We all did," Randall said, stepping up beside me. "I didn't know you two had worked together before."

I filled Randall in briefly on our stint with Fire Bird. He had heard part of it before, about Church setting up Caffrey to be hit. Neither Dane nor I had mentioned any names of the men we had worked with on that operation.

"I need to talk to you," Randall said to me, leading me out of the secure building and down to the beach.

"I came back for Truong," I said as we walked toward the beach.

"Yeah. That's why I called and told you about it. You were there at the beginning, I thought you'd at least want the chance to be there at the end," Randall said, his voice tight, as though he wasn't sure he had done the right thing for once.

I thumped him on the arm with my fist. "Like I told Hardin, I ain't leavin' 'til the job's done."

"Son, I know you've got problems and I know you were on your way out of this."

I cut him off. I knew where he was headed. I wanted Randall to know for certain that I was both able and willing to go on the mission.

"Sarge, this'll be my last operation. But I've gotta go on this one, the same as you. Ya know? So, no matter what happens, if we grease Truong it's a good deal."

Randall studied me a moment, then nodded. "Okay."

Harry did whatever he had to do to keep me from being arrested. I signed another extension, but Harry said he would get me out of it after this one operation whether I liked it or not. I grinned and agreed. Then we went on with the briefing.

The whole operation wasn't about Truong. He was just a bystander some agent in Harry's CAS net up north had mentioned was handling security at a meeting the agent was reporting on. The meeting was the principal event we were supposed to be interested in.

An East German intelligence officer, a big blond communist, was joining an NVA intelligence cadre at a little village ten klicks in from the Lao border to debrief several returning NLF agents. These agents had been doubled by our Fire Bird people. They were a lure to bring the East German within easy reach of a hit team. The Agency wanted this guy terminated with *extreme* prejudice for a reason that they weren't telling us. So we were offered Truong as an incentive.

Our mission roll was to bodyguard the actual kill team, Janca and Caulderson, into the TA, and then cover their extraction. But Harry gave us some leeway on that by telling us right away that he wanted the kill confirmed.

Janca just sat and took it all in. He knew what was going on, that there was some personal payback involved with us and Truong, and that Harry had just given us a license to go in and kill him.

After Harry left us with our briefing packets, Randall asked Janca what he needed from us by way of support.

Janca cut him off. "Sarge, this's nuttin' personal, but I don't like working with a team. If it wasn't for yer boy Truong, me 'n' Caulderson and maybe two gunslingers would go in and do the job. You get us there, then stay outta the way 'til I do my thing. Then your headhunters can do theirs."

It seemed fair to me.

"You tell us where you want to shoot from and we'll spec out our attack," Randall told him after thinking it over a minute.

Janca nodded.

We had three days to get that one together, then a day on the ground to get in place. That wasn't long.

Our TA was a small village ten klicks inside the North Viet border, just above the 18th parallel. The prime target, Colonel Wilhelm Pruest, would arrive in a black Russian-made Zil staff car from Hanoi between 0800 and 1000 hours on a specific date. The weather forecast was good for us, clear and calm. Janca would have good light to shoot by. Pruest would be accompanied by a truckload of bodyguards, possibly Europeans. A footnote in the packet listed them as possibly East German or even Russian elite troops.

Their destination in the little village was an old French Provincial Governor's villa. It would be surrounded by a company of NVA who had seen combat in the south, not home guard troops. Truong was head of security at the site, with a footnote that said he recruited the three agents who were coming in when he was a member of the ARVN Special Forces. It made me grit my teeth.

A small village that was near the colonial house had been emptied of its inhabitants to make room for the NVA security forces. The villa was located at the end of the village's main street. The TA was located in a chain of mountains that marched along the Lao-Viet border, not far from the Charles Seven area we had worked in Laos. The village itself was down in a partially forested valley with high ground around it on three sides.

The agents would be escorted in from Laos, riding in trucks back into North Vietnam. We were to hit the village before they arrived.

We decided to insert into the mountains by slicks two days in advance of the hit, then work our way down to the valley. Then we would spend a day watching the place and hit it the following morning when Pruest arrived. We would need that time to determine troop placement, weapons emplacements and so forth since the full NVA company hadn't moved in at the time of our briefing.

When we ran our insertion and movement plan by Janca, he nodded in agreement.

"I've found a place, here," he said, tapping an aerial recon photo from a Black Bird of the TA, "where I can see the front of the villa clearly. I'll set up in these rocks, since Pruest'll use the front door and dust him when he gets outta the car."

"You need support from us at your fire site?" Randall asked him.

Janca shook his head no.

"Okay. We'll go in loaded for bear, pack all the weapons and ammo that we can. After we have reconnoitered the hit site, we'll split into fire teams and take the village from three sides. It's a free fire zone. We wipe everything in there.

"When Janca hits Pruest we take out whatever troops and vehicles are near the villa with LAWs. Hammer, that'll be you. The fire team will hit their assigned targets with LAWs, grenades and small arms fire. Taking advantage of the shock value of our attack, all fire teams will then sweep the village and inflict massive casualties on whatever is left of the security force.

"We want Truong located before the action starts. Whichever team is closest to him will close with and terminate him. Clear?" Randall briefed us.

There weren't any questions. Our extraction plan was pretty simple and direct. We would be ten klicks inside the border. Slicks could stage nearby in Laos. As soon as we hit the village, we would call for extraction. The extraction point would be a clearing in a valley five klicks southwest of our TA.

The nearest NVA base to the TA was northeast of it, so we should be able to avoid any reaction force that might be sent to the village. We would alert the slicks while we were on the move, secure the LZ and extract, mission complete. Everyone was satisfied with the operation plan, so we broke for the night.

Janca stopped me on the way to our billets. "Whatever hap-

THE KILL 239

pened to that spook?''

"What spook?''

"The one who set up Caffrey.''

I gave him a brief version of how Church had been rotated out of Southeast Asia. "Why?''

Janca shook his head. "I just wondered. You, me, 'n' Caulderson are the only ones left from that op, ya know. Kile got greased in a bar in Saigon, a bomber got him. Now if this whole team got whacked, well son, there wouldn't be any witnesses to anything, would there?''

"Jeez, thanks Janca,'' I said. My paranoia clamped down on me like a vice.

I searched the compound until I found Stone. He was in the NCO club by himself.

"I need that favor man,'' I said, sitting on the bar stool next to him.

"What?''

"If my team gets whacked on this mission, kill our handler. He set us up.''

Stone's face never changed its expression. "Sure.''

Then he swung around to face me. "You carrying a high freak on this op?''

I nodded.

"If you get hit hard, send out my name on the high freak in ten second intervals. I'll have a Hatchet team in the air ASAP. If you're sure it's a setup, send my name and then number ten behind it. If we can't pull you out, I'll send your handler down the highway right behind ya.''

"Thanks Stone.''

"I owe ya.''

As I headed out the door, Stone caught up to me. "Is it Church?''

"No, but it may be about him. It may be I'm just paranoid too.''

Stone grunted. "Just 'cause ya are don't mean there ain't nobody out to git ya.''

"There it is.''

We drew our gear the next morning, which was all the weapons and ammo we could carry, and hopped a C130 to Thailand. From there, the slicks ran us in late in the afternoon. Crossing Laos in slicks was really a sight, especially when I knew it was the last time I would see Laos. The high, green, misty mountains were awesome. I bid them farewell mentally as we flew through the valleys. To keep as low a profile as possible, the slick jockeys flew low, zooming up valleys just above treetops and dodging around mountains. It was a rough ride for us.

When we came over our LZ, I was on the lead slick. I hit the ground and rolled, praying that there weren't any mines under the thin soil. When the second and third slicks emptied, we regrouped and moved higher into the mountains to a RON.

The next morning, we worked our way down to the village, being very careful. We assumed that there would be NVA patrols around the village itself and possibly further around the TA. When we reached the area Janca wanted to use as a firing position, we got our first clear view of the entire village.

It was a picturesque place, surrounded on two sides by open rice paddies. At the end of the village, separated by a short distance from the nearest buildings and hootches, was the villa. It was an old, white, two-story building. Several concrete block buildings were near it. We assumed that one of them was a school or a town meeting house and the other was a clinic or hospital. They were long and low.

We settled in, using our field glasses to reconnoiter the place for the rest of the day. Just after dark, Randall, Krang and Griz went down near the village for a closer recon. When they returned several hours later, we spec'ed out our assault plan.

I would take three Nungs and several LAWs, sneak down to a ditch about thirty meters from the front of the villa and use the LAWs to take out Pruest's bodyguard and any vehicles. We would also have an M79 and our rifles. Then my fire team would assault the two block buildings nearest us, clearing them. Griz and one Nung would take up a position in the paddies northeast of the village and take out any NVA troops from there, then close that route to escape. Blake and two Nungs would take out a hootch the NVA were using as their commo post, then fire Blake's 203 at targets of opportunity from the northwest paddies. They would assault the village and clear any hootches that were occupied on their side of the village. Feng and three other Nungs would move into the village from the east and Randall and Krang would assault the villa from the west. We would all close the jaws of a trap like a steel vice on the security force.

Just before dawn, the fire teams moved to their jump-off points, nodding farewells as we saddled up. I paused to tell Janca about my deal with Stone and to brief Marty, who was staying with Janca with his radio, about the emergency distress call Stone had given me. He just nodded, not questioning me about it. Janca was making his preparations for the hit, communicating silently with his weapon, checking the loads one more time.

"I'll cover you from up here when you make your move on the village," Janca said after I told him about Stone. "But always remember, ya gotta cover yer own ass."

"'Preciate it. Good huntin'."

"Git some, dude," Caulderson called to me as I left them.

As I turned to look at them one last time, Janca was filling two of the sandbags he carried with him, laying the heavy barreled M21 rifle on them. Caulderson was laying out his spotting glasses and his canned M16 rifle. It wasn't full dawn yet, but they had enough light to see by. My fire team went down to its ambush positions around the edge of the little village, hiding in the ditch and waiting.

The black Zil staff car pulled up to the front of the old colonial house, escorted by two trucks full of NVA. A tall blond man stepped out of the car, turned to say something to an Oriental officer with him as he got out and then put his cap on. I thought that was nice of him, to take his hat off so that Janca could see his shiny yellow hair. I watched them from the little ditch behind a stand of weeds, my adrenalin pumping. When the Oriental officer stood upright, he turned to bawl orders to his men in the trucks. My rapid breathing from the adrenalin pump choked off. Grabbing my field glasses I zoomed in on his face. It was Truong.

Crawling to the Nung with the radio, I broke squelch once, signaling Randall.

"What?" came his terse reply.

"Truong just stepped outta the car."

There was a pause in the entire tableau. Time seemed to disconnect for a moment. Then, suddenly, the East German's head came apart like a watermelon that had been hit with a hammer. Janca had put a round right through his head. The man's body spun seconds after his head had and he pirouetted to the ground. That was our signal. I came up to one knee, firing a LAW into the first truck full of soldiers. As it exploded, I tossed the empty tube aside and dropped down into the ditch. A Nung handed me a second tube, already opened and ready to fire. I popped back up and fired it into the second truck only seconds after the first one went off. The soldiers were diving out of it as the second rocket impacted and sent them hurtling through the air.

I heard Griz open fire with his M60 and several other explosions from the other end of the village. Small arms began to crackle. 40mm grenades began to detonate in the village also. NVA soldiers were chopped to pieces as they ran for cover. Raising my CAR, I led the three Nungs forward in a charge down the street to the first of the block buildings we were to clear, firing into the fallen NVA as we went to make sure they didn't come up behind us. One Nung booted in the door of the first building and I tossed a frag in, then we all rushed in firing behind the explosion. One NVA soldier had been inside the single room building and the frag had taken him apart. While we headed for the second building, the rest of the fire teams were sweeping forward from the east and west, covered by Griz and his M60 as well as Janca and his rifle. Randall and Krang made straight for the old colonial house.

"Left, to one o'clock. In the house, a window," Caulderson called out, glasses glued to his face.

Janca grunted, swung the barrel a few degrees, paused and fired. Below him, the object of his attention pirouetted and fell out of sight into the colonial house, blood spurting from the head wound.

"Head shot confirmed. Okay, right, three-thirty, on the move in the street."

As Randall and Krang reached the village, nearly half of it was aflame, the result of Blake and his M203. There were sporadic shots from the confused NVA who were trying to mount a defense, but Feng and his Nungs were closing on them fast, getting behind them as they tried to form little groups and wiping them out with frags and rifle fire. My fire team cleared the second building and swept through several smaller hootches, also setting them on fire as our frags cleared them. It drove the surviving NVA from what little shelter they had right into Griz's M60 or Janca's rifle. We cleared our end of the village and looked around for more targets.

A bunker opened up on Blake and his team, pinning him in the paddies as he moved in. Feng moved for it. I headed for the old colonial house. As I approached it, a long burst from an AK pinned us behind an already burning hootch. One of the Nungs fired a return burst from his M2 carbine, the other popped an M79 buckshot round at the house. I ran for the building under their covering fire. Just as I reached the side of the house, the AK gunner inside popped up to fire again, right in front of me. We were almost nose-to-nose as he raised his AK to fire out the window. I sprayed a wild burst at him that shredded the wooden sill. He leveled his AK at my chest and then flipped backward away from the window, spurting blood from a head wound. Janca had gotten him.

Randall darted from cover to stand beside me, his K sweeping back and forth on the second-story windows as he moved, Krang firing cover for him. We moved toward the back door. I heard grenades pop off at one corner of the village where Feng had gone after the bunker and the rattle of small arms fire from another corner where I guessed Blake was moving in with the Nung assigned to him.

Randall and I entered the house. I booted the door open. He flipped in a frag, then we went in together, spraying the room. He stepped in, I reloaded and followed him. Krang joined us, firing at the second-story windows as he rushed to the house, reloading his K as he entered it. The three of us paused, looking around. We had come in a back door. The dead NVA lay near the window where Janca had saved me and another was sprawled across the room from us.

Stairs led to a second floor landing and a narrow hall led toward the front of the house on the ground floor. Randall motioned me toward the hall and then he and Krang took the stairs. I moved slowly along the hall. There was one door on each side of it, set diagonally across from one another, the nearest one on my left. Taking a frag, I booted the closer door open, tossed the frag into the room, fell back to one side of the door and covered the other door as the frag went off.

Stepping in quickly, I sprayed the room. It was empty. I peeked around the door sill and caught the other door opening as I did. There was a brief exclamation in Viet from the opening door, then an AK barrel poked out between the door and the sill. I emptied my magazine into the partially opened door, just beside the rifle barrel that was poking out of it, hearing a bark of pain. Something heavy thumped to the floor. Reloading quickly I charged, firing, spraying the door and blowing it the rest of the way open.

As I entered the room, an NVA soldier lay sprawled across my path. A second soldier, a round-eye in OD fatigues, lunged at me from my right, AK extended for a shot. He fired behind me. I pivoted, slamming my CAR into his AK in a vertical parry, knocking his barrel away. I kneed him in the groin with my left knee, pinning his AK to the wall with my CAR.

He released his rifle, one hand grabbing the barrel of my CAR. I struck him across the bridge of the nose with the blade edge of my left hand, dropped the CAR and grabbed the hair at the back of his head with my right hand, his chin with my left. With a savage heave, I snapped his chin over his left shoulder. It touched his spine. He went limp and fell away from me. I searched him for any ID but there was none.

As I bent to lift my CAR, the NVA in the door came off the floor and stabbed me in the right forearm with a bayonet. He drew back to stab me again. I hooked a boot behind his lead foot, pulled and foot swept him down. As he tried to rise, I kicked him in the throat. He gurgled, choked and died. I picked up my CAR and moved on. The front of the house was clear.

Randall and Krang moved to the second floor landing without any resistance. Three doors greeted them, one on either side of the hall diagonally, and one facing them at the very end. All three of the doors were closed. Each man moved to opposite sides of the hall and readied frags. At a nod from Randall, they booted the doors open, tossed the frags in and stepped in behind the explosions, spraying the rooms. Both rooms contained only dead men, most of them NVA officers.

Krang stepped into the hall, K trained on the last door, as Randall did the same. The door exploded outward, AK rounds hammering through it, spraying the hall. Krang jerked from their impact. A killer to the end, he triggered a burst from his K into the door as he fell. Randall fired from the cover of the door sill.

Krang landed face forward. Randall charged the door, but to his surprise it was open when he slammed his shoulder into it. His forward momentum carried him into the room.

Truong stood off to one side of the door, facing it, an AK raised to his shoulder. Three dead men in NVA uniforms and one white man in ODs, lay sprawled around the room. Randall saw Truong's finger tighten on the trigger, but the AK only clicked, empty or jammed.

Randall slowly swung the K to Truong.

"Time to die, cocksucker," he hissed.

Truong dropped the AK and drew his knife, the Gerber Hardin had presented him at the A Team camp.

"Man to man, Randall? Do you have the nerve?"

Randall smiled.

Holding my CAR, I took a step with my right foot, spun, slammed the heel of my left boot into the door, kicking it open. It was unlocked. As my boot touched down, I lunged into the room, CAR up.

Randall and Truong were facing each other in fighting crouches, knives in their hands. I aimed the CAR but Randall yelled, "No! He's mine!" I lowered my CAR.

The two began their dance. Truong took the fight to Randall right away. He used his needle-pointed, double-edge dagger in an inverted grip and he came at Randall slashing for his knife arm.

Randall held his knife low and close, blade out, dipping his arm to avoid the slash, leaning back slightly to avoid the return backhand that went for his throat. Truong slid forward and came down with an ice pick attack for the subclavian artery, the attack a smooth three-move combination that should have caught Randall leaning backward, off balance.

Randall slid to his right, parrying the downward attack away with his left hand, then drove his left knee upward into Truong's bladder. He hit the Viet with a solid right cross in the jaw, punching with the hand that held the knife. He was making a point with Truong. I could have killed you, but instead I am just punching you with my fist. Punk. He continued with a right hammer-fist blow with the butt of his knife to Truong's forehead. Skin split, blood spurted. The Viet staggered away from Randall.

Truong recovered quickly despite the blood pouring into both of his eyes. He drew back, grinning at Randall. They made a few tentative circles, then Truong came at Randall again, a high slashing attack hooking in for the eyes. Truong immediately followed that with a low-level hammer-type thrust to disembowel. Randall ducked below the slash, then tried to sidestep the low thrust, but it caught his hip. The needle-pointed dagger raked his flesh, drawing blood.

Randall grunted and Truong moved in. Randall kicked his lead leg knee with a side kick, slamming Truong's knee straight. The Viet grunted in pain. Randall spun, slashing for Truong's neck with the blade-heavy knife. Truong ducked and both men backed away again, Truong limping.

Truong came forward suddenly with a rapid series of slashes. Randall ducked two, then caught the third by slashing Truong's wrist with the edge of his knife. Truong's hand fell off his arm as the razor-sharp blade severed flesh and bone. In a return move, Randall slashed Truong's throat, the front opening in a gruesome smile. Truong staggered back as blood sprayed, his knees buckling.

Randall stepped into him, his left hand catching the hair at the back of Truong's head. For a second, the two locked eyes. Randall hissed, "Mess with the best, die like the rest," into Truong's face, then drove his knife to the hilt into Truong's abdomen. Twisting it once, he held the Viet up with it as Truong's spirit fled his body.

Finally he stepped back, freeing his blade. Randall was in that faraway state I had been in after my duel with the sniper in the Zone. Randall just stood, staring at Truong. I bandaged his hip wound and pulled him out of the room. In the hall, I bent over Krang to pick up his body, but Randall stopped me.

"Let him lie among the enemy he killed. He deserves that much," he said.

A pile of dead NVA was indeed a fitting last tribute for Krang.

Outside, the team had swept the entire village and were coming in to regroup. Blake looked at me and I nodded toward the villa.

"You get him?" Blake asked me.

"Randall."

Blake nodded, then spat toward the house. "Long's someone did."

Randall ordered us to search all the bodies and buildings that hadn't burnt for intel, then torch the place. When it was burning nicely, we moved out.

We picked Janca up on the way out. The sniper looked at Randall's blood-soaked uniform, noticing the minor limp and read what had happened. "Finally evened the score, huh?" he barked.

Randall nodded, eying the scoped and suppressed M21 in the big man's hands. "You?"

Caulderson grinned, "Ten rounds, ten kills. Confirmed dudes."

Three NVA lay twisted near the rise Janca had been firing from, mute testimony to Caulderson's skill with the suppressed M16 he carried.

We picked up what gear we had grounded before the attack, bandaged the few wounds that the team sustained during the attack, and moved out at a fast pace for our extraction LZ. Marty sent a mission complete burst and called for the slicks. A reaction force would be headed toward the village soon and we needed to put distance between us and them fast. Our main concern now was that we might run into NVA troops moving through the area and drawn by the sound of the gunfight.

About halfway to our extraction point, Griz, on point, stopped us. We went to cover quickly. A heavy NVA patrol moved past us, headed north toward the village. We let them pass and moved out. Feng took over on the point and walked us into an NVA ambush.

We had been walking along a forested ridge line, below the crest and staying in deep cover. Feng moved out of cover into an exposed clearing. When he did, there was an NVA unit hanging out in the opposite tree line. They spotted him. Feng took two rounds through the gut right away as the NVA opened fire too soon, not letting the rest of us come into the open. If they had, they would have gotten most of us. Feng fell and rolled down the side of the ridge, laying exposed. Griz tried to lay suppressing fire on the opposite tree line with his M60, but he took a round in the shoulder too.

I went after Feng. Stripping his web gear off him, I put a pressure bandage over his stomach. I couldn't close the exit wounds in his back and he was in terrible pain. While I worked on him, he screamed and cried. I didn't have any morphine either.

I tried to haul him back up the ridge line, but the NVA brought heavy fire on me as soon as I moved. Bark and leaves were piling up on top of us as bullets clipped the foliage around us. I couldn't even rise up to return fire.

The team was doing a fair job of returning fire though. I heard a "bloop" as Blake cut loose with his M203 and then an explosion in the far tree line. There was a scream of pain. He and a Nung with an M79 began laying a barrage of grenades, alternating their fire so that there was almost a constant stream of high explosive rounds going out. The M60 opened fire again and all of the M16s were at work. The intensity of fire from the tree line abated a little. About then, I heard a crackle of AK fire from behind the team.

The NVA patrol that had passed us earlier had heard the firing and returned. I heard Randall yelling orders and men crashing through the foliage toward me. Randall paused when he spotted me trying to hoist Feng over my shoulder and Feng screaming in agony. Bullets were whip-cracking past us. He helped me put Feng on my back and then we ran, Randall firing cover for me.

We outdistanced one group, the ones who had come up behind us, but the blocking force we had run into cut diagonally across our path and we ran into them again less than a klick from our LZ. Blake, on point, spotted them moving into position and waved us down just before they opened fire. I laid Feng behind a tree and rolled out beside a fallen log that gave me cover. As I did,

I saw the Nung with the M79 fire a grenade and blow three NVA out of their covered position. I rose over the log and shot the three bodies, then fell back behind cover. Glancing at the Nung again, I saw him lean out for another shot. Just as he fired, he took a burst in the face and shoulder that threw him out in the open. His body bounced as they kept firing into him.

Randall rose up and ripped a long burst off from his K. I went up to add to his firepower. I saw him fly over backward too. I snarled and rose up again just as an NVA assault wave burst from the tree line. Blake hit them with his M16 and his M203 at the same time, blowing a hole in their ranks. I lit up two, watched them drop, reloaded, dropped two more right in front of my log, then glanced over at Feng where he lay behind the tree. He wasn't screaming anymore. I think he had gone into shock.

An NVA soldier stood over him, smiling. He shot Feng in the head as I raised my CAR to stop him. I was too late. I shot the NVA anyway, in the face. Then I heard a dull thump at one end of the log. It was a Chicom grenade, about a foot away from my feet. I had to lunge at it from my prone position, grab it and flip it over the log I lay behind. I kept my head down and that was the only thing that saved me. It detonated in the air on the opposite side of the log just after it left my hand. The blast and the shrapnel shredded my right hand. My prime hand, the hand that pulled the trigger.

The grenade blew me over onto my back. I was going into shock fast, nausea twisting my stomach, blood pouring out of my hand. I laid on my back, waiting to die. I'd seen Randall go down and I figured I was next. There wasn't much pain, but I was going out fast, a fuzzy blackness closing in on my vision. I saw an indistinct figure loom over me.

The shape of the helmet gave him away. I ripped him from groin to throat with my CAR, firing left-handed, a miracle. It had been instinct. The NVA soldier hesitated to kill me because I looked so fucked up, but I hadn't hesitated to do him. My reflexes had taken over even in a semiconscious state. I knew, someday, if I lived, those reflexes would get me in trouble. At that moment, it had saved my life. The effort of firing that weapon took my reserve supply of will and I passed out.

I opened my eyes and the jungle was moving past me at an odd angle. I was being carried. I tried to move, groaning as I did. I wanted to know who was carrying me.

"Lay chilly," someone hissed.

I stopped the small movements I was making and just hung there. Pain wracked me and I let a groan slip out. There was a sudden sting in my leg and I slipped back into unconsciousness. It reminded me of a Doors' song, but as I went out, I couldn't remember which one. Someone had hit me with a morphine syrette. I knew that.

A shock to the earth tossed me from my left side onto my back. The noise of the explosion focused my consciousness to an alert stage, despite the pain in my hand. I was in a field or a large clearing actually, surrounded on all sides by forest, mountains rearing up behind the trees. Then it clicked in my mind. We were at the extraction LZ. As I swam upward from the drug and pain-induced lethargy, I heard long bursts of full auto fire. Then the plop of a mortar round coming out of its tube, the whine of the round in flight and the flat boom of its detonation. The shock wave rippled over me and with it clods of dirt came pelting down on me. A sharp cry of pain followed it.

Looking around for my CAR, I couldn't find it so I tugged out my Colt pistol left-handed, a chore from a shoulder holster. The team was spread out in a 360-degree perimeter, but there were large gaps in it. I couldn't tell who was missing and who was there. My first thought was of Randall. Then I saw Marty Bender laying next to me, his radio between the two of us, blood matting his curly black hair. I crawled over to him.

He looked at me, eyes wild.

"Slicks are in-bound with a Hatchet team! I used that code you gave me," he yelled at me. Stone and his reaction force were on the way.

Suddenly the NVA broke cover and rushed us. I saw Randall rise and toss two frags one after the other, then a Nung did the same thing near him. They blew gaping holes in the assault line, but the NVA still moved forward. Marty rose and ripped a long burst from his CAR at them and I lay beside him, waiting. My weak-hand pistol shooting was for close range only.

The assault troops rolled over one edge of the perimeter. I shot one off Marty as he ripped another NVA up the middle with his CAR. Turning, I shot a second NVA in the eye at point blank range. We were in tall grass and they couldn't see us until they were right on top of us. Randall had one down and was doing him with his knife. A pair of NVA ran over top of us, firing at the far side of our perimeter. I emptied my clip into one's back and Bender took the other one out by leaping on his back and then pulling him backward over his knee, breaking his back.

"Reload!" I yelled, tossing my pistol to Marty.

He tossed me his Colt after chambering a round for me, then reloaded all his weapons while I covered him.

The mortars fell on us again. I saw a body tossed into the air by one blast. Shrapnel dusted my legs but I only felt the impact, not the pain. My nervous system was shorted out from my hand wound.

Marty talked into his PRC 25. I guessed Blake had the high freak PRC 77. He tossed a yellow smoke grenade into the center of our clearing. Then he leaned over to me.

"Tell Randall that we've got air coming in close. They've got that fucking mortar tube spotted."

I nodded and began crawling toward Randall. I noticed that his left hand was swathed in bandages. When I got to him, I relayed Marty's message. He nodded. "Tell Marty to get the evacs on station. Let the guns cover them."

I nodded to him and crawled back to Marty. As I was telling him what to tell the slick jockeys, he spun away from me, blood flying from his face. I pulled him to me. A round had hit him in the jaw, exiting on the opposite side. It had blown a gaping hole in the side of his face. The whip-crack of bullets sounded all around me. I dug my face into the dirt, reaching for the radio, pulling it closer. I heard return fire going out, then the hollow pop of mortar rounds leaving the tube.

Putting the headphones on, I raised the mike just as the first rounds began dropping over us.

"Airborne guns, do you read, over?" I yelled over the booming of mortar rounds. "This is Iron Six."

"Iron Six, this is Covey Leader. We have four guns and two slicks on station. We have the tubes spotted in the tree line. Heads down boys, we're comin' in."

"Covey leader, we have yellow smoke on our LZ. Get those fuckin' tubes!" I screamed.

"I copy yellow smoke on the LZ. We're making our run. Over." the lead gunship told me.

"Heads down! Guns are coming in!" I yelled to the guys, but none of them heard.

Two Huey Cobra gunships dove from out of nowhere onto the tree line directly opposite me. The whole tree line seemed to detonate simultaneously as the Cobras emptied their rocket pods. The mortar fire stopped abruptly. Tracers reached up toward the fast-moving Cobras.

A second pair dove on the source of the ground fire. Rockets turned another section of the jungle to cinder as the first pair made another sweep, nose-mounted miniguns tearing up the foliage in the lush, green forest all around us. The ground fire slackened considerably.

"Iron Six, this is Bluejay One. Pop smoke for extraction. Over."

I couldn't do it with one hand. Marty was out cold or dead. "Randall, somebody, pop smoke," I yelled.

Too much noise had damaged everyone's ears. I kept yelling, but to no avail. Finally, I threw a smoke grenade at Randall. It hit his foot. He rolled and snatched it and started to toss it away. Then he realized what he had and looked over at me. I held up my shredded hand. He nodded and tossed the marker grenade out into the center of the clearing. Red smoke swirled.

"Iron Six, this is Bluejay One. I have red smoke, over," the slick leader told me on the radio.

"Bluejay One, roger the red smoke. C'mon down. The LZ is hot. Over."

I heard a chuckle from Bluejay One. "Iron Six, roger that ol' son. Get your people ready. We're comin' in."

The black Huey slick swooped in. Immediately, small arms fire roared out of the tree line. The cobras dipped and made gun runs, miniguns singing their high-pitched whine of death. It was a sweet sound to me. I grabbed Marty by his patrol harness and tried to drag him toward the slick.

The NVA mounted another ground assault. I couldn't believe it when they broke out of the shredded smoldering tree line. I saw Griz come up on one knee with his M60, pouring fire into the lead elements of the assault force. Then a Nung came up with an M79 and popped off several grenades in rapid fire, hitting them with HE, high explosives. Griz and the Nung both flew over backward as they took hits. Randall ran to them and tried to drag both toward the slick. All of us carried someone else as we ran for the slick. The NVA screamed and fired as they came for us, while the Cobras dove on them.

I hadn't made it very far with Marty when a grenade landed near me. I heard it thump as it landed. Turning to snatch it, I saw it was too far away, laying near the radio. I grabbed Marty for a sudden heave away from the frag. It detonated. Pain lanced through my head. I was down, half across Marty. There was a loud, painful roaring in both of my ears. I tried to stand, but fell, unable to balance.

NVA were all around us. Looking at the slick, I saw all the wounded were loaded, and the slick swayed up and away. Another one settled in behind it. NVA were standing over me, but I was helpless this time, unable to lift my pistol. I didn't even know where it was. One kicked me off Marty and shot him, then turned his AK on me.

Gouts of flesh and blood erupted from the NVA's chest, splattering me. He staggered forward, then fell over me. Randall had me covered, Griz beside him firing. Randall grabbed me and Marty and then a Nung was with us, grabbing Marty and firing cover with an M16 at the same time. Griz staggered, hit a third time, then straightened and resumed firing his M60. They dragged us to the slick with the door gunner firing over our heads with his M60 until we were all loaded. The slick hopped, did a power take-off and we were airborne. The Cobras dove on the LZ again, shooting the shit out of the NVA who were trying to shoot the slick down. I saw the door gunner jerk in his harness and slump forward, bullets holing the skin of the slick. Finally we were out of there. As soon as they stopped shooting at us, I passed out again.

I was debriefed in-hospital at Danang before they evaced me to Japan. My right eardrum was ruptured, various tissues were damaged, bones were broken in my hand and shrapnel was embedded in 80% of my body. I wouldn't talk to the first spook debriefers until Harry showed up. He gave me an accurate account of what had gone on after we pulled out, but he wouldn't tell me what happened to the rest of the guys. I knew, of course, that Krang, Marty Bender and Mike Feng were KIA, killed in action. I let Harry debrief me and asked him to find Stone and send him to see me. I said it was an emergency. A matter of life and death. Harry gave me a funny look, but promised he would do it.

The Army debriefers who followed the spooks in to hear our version of the mission told me that I would not be going back to Nam. I smiled at them. No shit. I couldn't pull a trigger, couldn't use a compass, couldn't hear at all out of one ear and only with a hearing aid from the other.

During the debriefing, I realized that I hadn't seen Janca since we left the actual hit site. The Army and the spooks both asked me about Janca and Caulderson several times, but none of them would tell me why. As I lay in the hospital thinking about the mission, it came to me. Janca and his spotter were missing. They hadn't been on the LZ at all. The big guy split on us either before the initial contact with the NVA, when Feng had been hit, or right after. As I thought about it, I suspected that it was right after, when we had E&Eed down the side of the ridge through the foliage. It would have been in his character to do that, break away from the team and go for it on his own. I was sure from the questions that the debriefers asked that Janca wasn't on some kind of operation like Sho had been when he came up missing. No, Janca just didn't like working with a team and felt that he could make it better with just his partner Caulderson. I didn't share any of my thoughts on that with Harry. If that was what Janca had done, that was his business. I mentally wished the big guy luck.

Randall staggered into my room one day, grinning at me. He had smuggled a bottle of bourbon into the hospital somehow. Sitting on the edge of my bed in his bathrobe, he opened it and handed it to me. A round had taken two fingers off his left hand as it hit the magazine of his K. That was when I'd seem him go over backward. He had also been hit repeatedly with shrapnel from the mortar rounds on the LZ and stabbed in the hip fighting Truong. As we shared the bottle, we just sat silently, drinking.

When it was empty, he turned to look at me and grinned a small smile. "Well, son, it's over."

I nodded. "Yeah, hell of a way to end it all. Sarge, it's been a real slice, man."

Randall grinned at me and slapped my leg. "Look me up on Bragg when you come through."

After he left, Griz conned one of the nurses into wheeling him into the room too. He had been shot three times and hit with shrapnel. Blake came hobbling in on crutches a few minutes later. He had been hit in the leg with an AK round and dusted with shrapnel pretty good. We talked about the mission a little, but I wanted to know about Janca. Neither of them had seem him after we left the village. We just shrugged it off. He might be out in the bush right then, sniping gooks with his partner, caressing the big rifle that he dug so much. I'd asked to touch it once, reaching for it as I did, and he barked at me.

"Don't!"

I grinned at the memory of him.

Blake filled me in on the Nungs. Only two of them survived the mission. We had evaced all of their bodies, living and dead. Two died on the evac slicks and another died in the hospital. One of the two who survived was one of our original men who came from our Nung platoon on the A Team camp. I wondered what would happen to him now that we were leaving. All of us were being rotated out of Southeast Asia.

I was through anyway. I'd done the slow dance on the killing grounds of Southeast Asia that the Army had choreographed for us until I couldn't take another step. Whatever I had gone back to Nam for after that first tour had been seared into my soul, etched permanently into my skin and bones with heated blades and I still didn't know exactly what it was. The cuts went deep. I had lived though, despite all my efforts and those of the enemy to change that fact. I was unsure then, and even more so now, if I was among the blessed or the cursed, whether life was the wiser choice.

Epilogue

I spent four months in a hospital in Japan being repaired and convalescing. The doctors there did a good job on me. After surgically implanting a new eardrum, I regained most of my hearing in my right ear, but less than half returned in the left. If that eardrum had been ruptured, they could have replaced it. Since it wasn't, they let it heal itself and it didn't. They operated on my hand twice, fusing bones, grafting skin, tying tendons. After several weeks, I was able to close it into a fist again, although my trigger finger never did work right again.

The rest of me took a series of plastic surgeries to fix, but left me with curiously few scars. A few odd lumps betrayed torn muscles or pieces of shrapnel that they told me would work out on their own eventually. Pockmarks from jungle rot and shrapnel were left too. A man needed *some* scars as a reminder, after all.

One day I got up out of bed and prowled around the private ward I was on. I saw myself in the mirror and recoiled from my own reflection. My eyes were sunken, cheeks hollow and nose thicker than before from multiple breaks. A livid scar still creased my forehead and burn scars mottled my cheeks. I was down in weight too, maybe weighing in at one hundred ten pounds from my normal weight of one-forty. At five-ten, I was a walking skeleton.

Shortly after that, I asked the hospital staff for therapy. As soon as they found out I could and would walk, they okayed it. I worked out on a weight machine, swam, jogged a little. At my request, they allowed me to practice with the on-base karate club. A psych saw me three times a week too. He kept me at the hospital after I was more or less fit for duty. He found out that I still had four years left on my enlistment and he wanted to be *sure* he wasn't turning a homicidal nut loose on an unsuspecting society.

I got a part-time job in the gym helping the rehab guys because I found that I liked working with other combat vets. They were the only people I felt comfortable with. One day they sent me to get a guy out of his room. He had just come from Nam and he was crazy, they told me. It turned out to be Stone.

We grinned at each other. "What happened to *you*, man?" I asked, helping him into a wheelchair. That was policy in the hospital. He didn't need it. He had been shot through the hip and leg though and was undergoing therapy for the wounds.

Stone just shook his head.

"How's Lee Wong doing? Is he here too?" I asked, wheeling him along the hall.

He lowered his head and his shoulders hunched up. I stopped the chair and went around to face him. He had a thousand-yard glare in his eyes. I knew the news was bad.

"His whole team got greased over in Laos man. I led a reaction force of PMs and green hats, but it was over before we got there. The bodies were so cut up we couldn't tell who was who."

We both looked down.

"Shit," I muttered.

"Yeah," he quietly agreed.

After a moment, he looked up at me and grinned, "Guess you ain't heard about our old friend Church either, have ya?"

"No. What happened to him? Somethin' bad I hope."

Stone's grin widened. "He was found in his hotel room in Danang with his throat opened. They figure it was someone he was dealing with. He was busted for skimming Agency funds and brought back in-country for a hearing or whatever those people do."

"That's too bad," I said, smiling to myself.

"I owed ya one, son," Stone said.

I flew home a few weeks later, leaving Stone my home address. He told me what had happened after his Hatchet team arrived. We were lifting out when they landed right behind the NVA. While all of their attention was on us and the evac slicks, the Hatchet team kicked their ass real good. They had gotten a body count of close to two hundred. I asked him about Janca and Stone told me that he had heard the sniper was still in the bush. Every once in a while, an RT would come across signs of his presence, in the form of a dead NVA officer with a fist-sized exit wound in his head.

The Army gave me a two-week delay-en-route to Fort Bragg,

but I didn't really know where to go or what to do. Buying some jeans, I changed, carefully packed up all of my Army gear and tried to hitchhike across the country.

It was really weird. A lot of really different people gave me rides. The "right wing" conservative types like the cowboys, truckers, people like that, saw my short hair and gave me rides. They would ask if I was just back from Nam, then give me some speech about how we should nuke the north and then give me excuses why they hadn't gone. When I got tired of hearing that shit, I told them I had just gotten out of prison, not Nam.

Sometimes hippies would pick me up, get me high and ask if I was a deserter. I'd tell them I was a Republican.

All of the people that I caught a ride with seemed really concerned with things that I just couldn't relate to. If it was less than life or death, why sweat it? The worst was a hippy girl driving a flowery Volkswagen bug. She talked for over a hundred miles straight about drugs and women's lib and on and on.

"Say, do you like to fuck?" I asked.

"What?"

"Do you like to *fuck*?"

Apparently she didn't. At least my question shut her up for a while. She was just getting started on the war.

The place that I hitchhiked to wasn't my home anymore. I looked at some of the things I thought I really missed, but they just didn't seem important anymore. All of the things that many of the people I met were so concerned about didn't add up to anything either. If it wasn't a matter of life or death, why sweat it? I made people feel guilty I guess when they asked me about Nam. It gave them a feeling of inadequacy and that made them mad. They took it out on me. That pissed me off. It didn't take much to set me off, but when they would, I'd flip on them, not feeling that they were good enough in any respect to judge me anyway. All of the people who supported the war, the politicians who were the cheerleaders for us when it began and then didn't have the guts for the long fight it took, were embarrassed by us, the men who fought their war.

I was a soldier, so I went where they sent me and shot who they said was the enemy. Was I wrong for that? I thought not. As my hero, Popeye, often said, "I yam what I yam and dat's all that I yam." Still having to wear the uniform, I quickly realized that I couldn't stay in the U.S. I'd end up killing someone. So when I got to Bragg, I begged them for any overseas assignment. After a brief reunion with Randall, I was sent to the 10th SFG in West Germany, where I ran into Stone again. We worked for an intelligence outfit there for a year and I was more or less thrown out of the Army with a medical discharge. Intelligence work in Europe was almost as dangerous as field work in Southeast Asia. Especially working with Stone.

Part of the deal for my discharge was that I had to spend time in a VA hospital. I lucked out and was assigned into a new, clean one in Miami. They put me on the nut ward with mostly other Nam vets and that wasn't bad either. I wasn't strung out on drugs or having a nervous breakdown like most of the other guys on the ward. My problem was with my dreams and lack of sleep, the zone outs and flashbacks. Every time I closed my eyes, something bad surfaced and I'd have a technicolor dream about a brother dying. Usually, it was things that I had felt pretty emotionless about when they had happened. The woman that I had just finished making love to being blown all over a wall. Captain Hardin laying on his back, looking up at me, with two huge holes in his chest. It had been too much, too fast, for too long. I'd overdosed on it.

So they put me on dummy dope until I refused to take it. One of the male nurses ordered me to take it and I ordered him to perform oral sex on himself. They sent for two more male nurses to force me to take the thorazine. I hurt all three of them and would have killed them if one of the other vets on the ward hadn't said just the right thing at the right time to calm me down.

That was how I met my future guru, a Japanese veteran of "their" side during World War II. He taught meditation and a kind of yoga at the hospital for physical rehabilitation. The nurses had run to him to subdue me if I flipped again, but instead of fighting, we just talked. One day he saw me performing a karate form and we began a long, sweat-filled relationship during which he taught me his family's martial art, in between my various wanderings. I spent the rest of the time at the hospital getting my body back into shape.

To this day, I haven't put the war behind me nor have I really been able to work out my feelings about it either. I still feel guilty about a lot of things, but I have learned over the years that I can live with it, accepting the pain as just a part of life. I guess that is about as good a deal as I'll get.

The Final Roll Call

Captain Hardin — Medically retired as a full bird colonel, he lives with his family in Virginia. He works as a security consultant for a government agency.

Master Sergeant Randall — He retired with twenty-five years in the Army as a Command Sergeant Major and a legend among the Special Forces operatives of our era. Since his retirement, he has been active with veterans' groups and with the POW/MIA issue.

Sergeant First Class Dane Trail — Big Dane eventually recovered from his head wound and was medically discharged. He worked for a government intelligence agency on contract, serving with Stoney and some of the other men from this novel in Angola. He went private sector after that fiasco, serving primarily as an advisor. In 1982 he worked in El Salvador for a private intelligence/security outfit. He was found KIA. Someone on his own side, another former green hat from Nam, did the job.

Staff Sergeant Brick Andrews — KIA Rung Sat Special Zone, 1969.

Sergeant First Class Marty Bender — KIA North Vietnam, 1970.

Sergeant First Class John "Tex" Kileen — KIA Laos, 1970.

Sergeant Billy Holcomb — KIA Laos, 1970.

Sergeant Mike Feng — KIA North Vietnam, 1970.

Sergeant First Class Janca — MIA (and still listed that way) North Vietnam, 1970.

Sergeant Caulderson — MIA (and still listed that way) North Vietnam, 1970.

Staff Sergeant Blake — True to his word, he went private sector, serving in Angola and several other African wars. While on a raid into Angola in 1978 with a South African Defense Force unit, he was KIA in an ambush.

Sergeant First Class Griz — After retiring from the Army, he was last seen in 1979 in Thailand at Bear's, a green hat to the last.

Staff Sergeant Stone — Retiring from the Army after eighteen years, another legend among Nam era vets, he fought on. He was in Angola, Rhodesia and several other "bush wars." Rumor has him everywhere, involved with everything. He still does appear from time to time, usually in the company of other old green hats, coming from an op and on his way to another. His current status is unknown.

Staff Sergeant Lee Wong — KIA Laos, 1971.

The Cat — The last time that I saw him was with Stoney, Blake and a band of freebooters in Angola, 1975. The rumor is that he is still working for an intelligence agency somewhere in South/Central America. The other rumor is that he is a private sector assassin who is now semi-retired.

Harry the Spook — Disillusioned by the failure in Angola, he left the Agency. As a freelancer, he was reputed to be a top-grade political assassin based out of Japan. In 1982 he was captured in the United States and faced a death sentence. With the help of a lone accomplice, he escaped custody. Two days later he was found, hands clenched around the hilt of a short Japanese sword, the three cuts of a samurai's ritual suicide complete in his abdomen. A second person had then decapitated him in the traditional manner. The accomplice was never found.

Church — KIA Danang, RVN, 1971. It was rumored that he let Stone catch him in the wrong place at the wrong time.

Madame Xhian — She lives in San Diego, California, where she nears her 100th birthday.

Bear — He, Momma Bear and Baby Bear still run the Lair in Bangkok.

General Ving Tao — After the fall of Laos, he moved to Thailand and still runs a Montagnard resistance program from somewhere in the Orient, still sponsored by the Agency. He has become a premiere warlord in the mountains of Laos, sometimes with Red Chinese help.

Team Leaders After Action Report   REPORT DECLASSIFIED
▆▆▆9July,1970   22 December, 1982
Reconnaissance Team   REF: FIA/607-9
MACV/SOG/CCN
Dtd▆▆▆July, 1970

At that point RT▆▆▆ consisted of four USASF and three Indigenous personnel, was completely encircled by an estimated company of NVA, determined by the amount of fire that we were receiving. The NVA was concentrating both small arms and mortar fire on our position. Every member of the RT was WIA during this time, some of them for the second or third time. SFC ▆▆▆ was delirious from a head wound he had recieved prior the RTs encirclement, and was unable to participate in the defense of the RTs defensive position. An NVA I2.5mm HMG took our position under fire from a low hill to our immediate west, while squad size NVA probing attacks were commenced from the south and north, simultaneously. Pooling our remaining claymore mines we used them and rifle fire to break up the probes.

Sgt. Cramer and the senior indigenous personnel, Sgt. ▆▆▆, a Nung, having sustained the fewest wounds of the RT, took it upon themselves to assault the NVA I2.5mm HMG postion. When they broke out of the RT position, SSGT ▆▆▆ , one other indigenous trooper and myself layed down suppressing fire on the NVA directly opposite us. After engaging several NVA riflemen in hand to hand combat, Sgts Cramer and Krung broke through the NVA lines and were successful in destroying the HMG with hand grenades.

Returning to the RTs position, Sgt Cramer then hoisted SFC ▆▆▆ over his shoulder and carried him out of the RTs position to cover under intense small arms fire all the way. Returning to the RTs position a second time he led the RT in a break out of the encirclement and guided the RT out of the area, sustaining shrapnel wounds from hand grenades twice that knocked him off his feet, and engaging NVA troops in hand to hand combat after his rifle malfunctioned. At that time, he relinquished the "point" position to Nung Sgt ▆▆▆ .

SFC ▆▆▆ died during the move away from the NVA, and we were forced to leave his body. The entire team was weak from loss of blood and unable to outrun the pursuing NVA while carrying SFC ▆▆▆ body. It was hidden in some foliage. We continued moving toward the primary extraction LZ in a SE direction. SSGT ▆▆▆ regained contact with the FAC as we broke out into less heavy foliage. The FAC then guided us to a secondary extraction LZ after having spotted NVA movement around the primary LZ, and relayed our call for extraction helicopters. The RT reached the secondary LZ at approximately I4:30, secured the area, and moved into the center of the clearing the FAC had directed us to. it was a small clearing that had been a Montagnard villa ges farm area, evidenced by the uneven growth of the foliage in the clearing itself, and burnt areas on the tree line surrounding the clearing, suggesting the traditional Montagnard method of clearing prospective farm land; slash and burn. Elephant grass had grown back in the clearing to roughly waist height. As we moved across the clearing, Sgt Cramer utilizing the Marine Foot Sweep Mine Clearing technique, we determined that the clearing was not booby trapped. We formed a 360° defensive perimeter in a depression in the center of the clearing and attempted to bandage our wounds.

While we awaited the extraction helicopters, the NVA pursuit force arrived in the area and set up a perimeter around the clearing in the tree line, and took the RT under fire with small arms initially, The first probe began at approximately I5:00. SSGT ▆▆▆ apprised the FAC of our situation and requested ARA air support. At I5:05 the first NVA assault wave was broken up by our last claymores and small arms fire from the RT. At I5:09 the second NVA assault line moved toward us. Sgt Cramer, Sgt ▆▆▆ , and myself then moved slightly forward of the RTs position, covering one another, and brought M60, M79, and rifle fire on the main portion of the assault line, turning it back.

The NVs seemed content to bring the team under sniper and harrassing fire until they could either be reinforced or bring mortars forward. At approximately I5:15 mortars began falling on the RT, and they were quickly followed by a third assault wave. This attack succeeded in over running the team position. SSGT ▆▆▆ recieved multiple GSW while he

GLOSSARY

1er Rep 1st Regiment of Foreign Parachutists (Regiment Etranger Parachutists) of the French Foreign Legion

Agency The Central Intelligence Agency (CIA)

A-gunner Assistant machine gunner

AIT Advanced Individual Training; where a soldier learns his individual job skill.

AK The standard assault rifle of the Soviet Army at one time and the main arm of Communist insurgents everywhere. It fires a 7.62mm Combloc (or Short) round and is select fire. It is noted for its durability.

AMF Adios, MotherFucker

AO Area of Operation

Arty Artillery

ARVN Army of Republic of Vietnam; the South Vietnamese Army, the "good guys"

ASAP As Soon As Possible

A Team The basic twelve-man team of the United States Special Forces.

AWOL bag Absent WithOut Leave bags were small black vinyl bags sold in every Post Exchange (PX). They earned their nickname because of their size. They were small enough to carry the essentials someone leaving post in a hurry would carry, as opposed to the much larger duffel bags that uniforms were carried in.

bandoleer An OD canvas belt with pockets for holding ammunition, worn over the shoulder.

betelnut A seed from a palm that grows in Southeast Asia.

block As in "on the block;" back on the street, being a civilian

boonie hat A medium brimmed floppy hat

Boocoo A corruption of the French beaucoup, which means "many."

BOQ Bachelors Officers Quarters

Bragg Fort Bragg, North Carolina, home of the Special Warfare School

brief back A command briefing. Once given an assignment objective and having planned the mission, the controller was briefed back on what the team intended to do to carry out the mission objective.

bust a cap To shoot

Cs C Rations

C4 A plastic explosive

C123   A twin engine prop-driven cargo plane

C130   A four engine prop-driven cargo plane

can   A silencer (suppressor)

C & C   Command and Control (see CCN)

CAR 15   A carbine version of the M16

CAS   Controlled American Source; an indigenous agent run by American Intelligence agent handlers.

CCN   Command Control North. SOG was divided into three Command and Control segments. CCN was headquartered in Danang.

cherry   A new soldier

Chicom   Chinese Communist; a person or thing

CIB   Combat Infantry Badge

CIDG   Civilian Irregular Defense Group; the armed civilians Special Forces A Teams trained for village defense.

clacker   A hand-held electronic detonator

claymore   An anti-personnel mine loaded with C4 and steel shot

CO   Commanding Officer

Cobra   A deadly snake and an even deadlier two-man helicopter gunship armed with miniguns and rocket pods.

Combloc   Warsaw Pact Nations; a person or thing

commo   Communications of any kind

CP   Command Post

cyclo   Three-wheeled contraptions with motorcycle motors that were cheaper to rent than a taxi in all of the cities in South Vietnam.

Dai Uy   Vietnamese for "captain"

Delta   A B Team Special Project which was the forerunner of SOG; or the Mekong Delta region.

demo   Demolitions of any kind

DEROS   Date of Estimated Return from OverSeas; the day a soldier returns to the United States from overseas.

det cord   Detonation cord; an explosive cord used for a variety of demolition and other needs.

deuce and a half   An Army two-and-a-half ton truck

Didi mau   Vietnamese for "go away, fast"

dinky dau   Vietnamese for "crazy in the head"

Do (wipe, grease, zap, terminate)   To kill

DZ   Drop Zone

E&E   Escape and Evasion

Eighty Deuce   The 82nd Airborne Division, based in Fort Bragg, North Carolina.

EM Club   Enlisted Men's Club

ETA   Estimated Time of Arrival

ETS   Estimated Termination of Service; the date a soldier is discharged from the service.

FAC   Forward Air Control; usually a small prop-driven aircraft armed only with a pair of phosphorous marker rockets.

fast movers   Jets; usually F4 Phantoms

fence jumpers   Any men or units that operated across international boundaries outside the specific confines of the theater of war.

fire base   A temporary artillery encampment used for fire support of forward ground operations.

fire fight   Exchange of small-arms fire with the enemy

First Cav   First Cavalry Division

FNG   Fucking New Guy

FOB   Forward Operating Base

Forces   The Special Forces

frag   A fragmentation grenade

fragged   To kill with a frag

FULRO   A nationalist organization for the Montagnard tribespeople, composed primarily of the Rhade and Jarai tribes; the words for this acronym are French.

gook   The enemy

GP   General Principle

green hat   A green beret or the man who wears one

Green Machine   The Army or the Armed Forces in general

Group   A Special Forces Group

grunt   An infantry soldier

gunship   A heavily armed aircraft; fixed wing (plane) or rotary (helicopter)

HALO   High Altitude Low Opening parachute jump

ham and MFers   Ham and lima beans; a particularly noxious C-ration meal

HE   High Explosives

High freak   High frequency

hootch   Any small dwelling

HQ   HeadQuarters

Huey   A generic term for a troop carrying, Medevac or gunship helicopter made by Bell

hump   To march

ID   Identify

in-country   In Vietnam

indig   Any indigenous person or people to a specific location

KGB   Komitet Gosudarstvennoe Bezopasnosti; the current name of the Soviet Directorate of Intelligence

KIA   Killed In Action

klick   Kilometer

Kuomintang   The nationalist army of the Chinese warlord Chaing Kai Sheck during his reign in China.

laager   A circular position established at night for security

laissez-faire   laid back, do nothing, let the situation sort itself out, hands off

land nav   Land navigation; the ability to read a map and compass and use them to find a specific location, guiding yourself to it.

land of the big PX   The United States

LAW   Light Anti-Tank Weapon

LLDB   Luc Long Dac Biet, the ARVN Special Forces

LP   Listening Post

LRRP   Long Range Reconnaissance Patrol

Lurp   What a LRRP does, or is

LZ   Landing Zone

M2   A World War II/Korean War era .30 caliber select fire carbine

M3   A World War II/Korean War era .45 caliber SMG

M16   The main battle rifle of the United States military and her client states. It is a light, select fire 5.56mm (.223 cal.) NATO rifle.

M21   A modified M14 rifle; it features a heavier barrel, powerful telescopic sight, lightened trigger action and often a suppressor. In 7.62mm NATO, it is a superb sniper weapon.

M60   A 7.62mm NATO (.308 cal.) belt-fed light machine gun and the standard squad automatic weapon of the U.S. Armed Forces and her client states.

M72 LAW   Light Anti-tank Weapon; a 66mm shoulder-fired, disposable rocket launcher that was mainly used in Southeast Asia as a bunker buster, though it could be used for anything.

M79 Blooper   A 40mm shoulder-fired single barrel grenade launcher

M203 A 40mm grenade launcher that mounted under the barrel of an M16. It replaced the M79.

MACV Military Assistance Command Vietnam

Medevac Medical evacuation by helicopter

medcaps Medical missions into remote villages where free medical treatment was offered to everyone in the village, usually performed on a regular basis.

MG Machine Gun; usually referring to a heavy gun like a .50

MIA Missing In Action

MIG base A base where Russian-made jet fighter planes are flown from

Mike Force Mobile Strike Force; composed of 12 U.S. Army green hats and a company of indigs, often Nungs, who were often used as a reaction force.

Montagnard Indigenous hill-dwelling people of Indochina

MP Military Police

mufti Civilian clothes

napalm A jellylike mixture that was combined with gasoline to form a very flammable compound and loaded into canisters to be dropped from aircraft into enemy positions.

NCO NonCommissioned Officer; a sergeant

NLF National Liberation Front; the communist party in South Vietnam

NSA National Security Agency

Nungs A Chinese ethnic group who lived in both South and North Vietnam. The U.S. Army Special Forces employed many of them as mercenaries. They were considered a tribe, but were not classed as Montagnards. Many people thought that they were the best indigenous troops in that arena.

Nuoc mam Tangy Vietnamese sauce

NVA North Vietnamese Army

OAS A French acronym for the secret terrorist organization formed within the French Army in Algeria that led a mutiny in the early '60's.

OCS Officers Candidate School

OD Olive Drab

one one Radio code for the leader of a SOG Recon Team

OSS Office of Strategic Services; forerunner of the CIA

PAL Police Athletic League

PLF Parachute Landing Fall as taught at Fort Benning, Georgia

PM ParaMilitary; a civilian serving in a military roll or capacity

point   The lead man in a patrol or column

POW   Prisoner of War

PRC 10   A man-portable field radio

PRC 25   A newer man-portable field radio

PRC 77   An encoding man-portable burst transmitter for sending or receiving

PRU   Provincial Reconnaissance Unit

PSP   Perforated Steel Plate; used for temporary field airstrips, among other things

Puff   A four engine prop-driven cargo plane that mounted several multi-barreled cannon of various calibers (they varied from model to model)

PX   Post Exchange

R&R   Rest and Recreation; a leave

Recon   Reconnaissance

REMF   Rear Echelon MotherFucker; anyone stationed in a support position; it usually meant anyone who was stationed on one of the big, relatively safe base camps and was not exposed to combat.

ROK   Republic of Korea; a person or thing from Korea

RON   Remain OverNight position

ROTC   Reserve Officer Training Candidate; usually a college training program with a guaranteed commission in the U.S. Army Reserve upon graduation from college. During the Nam war many Reservists were activated for service in Southeast Asia, especially young officers.

RPD   A Russian light machine gun, their equivalent to the U.S. M60

RPG   Rocket Propelled Grenade; a Combloc shoulder fired rocket similar to a LAW or a bazooka.

RT   Reconnaissance Team

RTO   Radio Telephone Operator; a radio man

Sac mau   The Vietnamese equivalent to "eat offal"

sampan   A generic term for any small boat with a covering on some portion

SAS   Special Air Service, the British/Canadian/Australian/New Zealand version of the U.S. Special Forces and Rangers rolled into one.

SFG   Special Forces Group

short   Being close to the end of a tour of duty

shrapnel   Shell fragments from a hand grenade, mortar round, artillery shell, or other weapon, which caused severe injuries or death.

sifu   The title of an instructor of a Chinese martial art

sit rep   Situation report

skied   Left or got out of there, doing so in a hurry

SKS   A Russian carbine that was replaced as the main battle rifle of the Soviet Army by the AK47.

slack   The second man in a patrol or column

slick   A generic term applied to any lightly armed troop-carrying helicopter, but usually referring to a Huey

SMG   SubMachine Gun; a small select fire or full automatic weapon of pistol caliber.

smoke   The smoke grenade used for signaling

SOG   Special Operation Group; later renamed Studies and Observations Group to fool the press. As the original name implies, it was a "go anywhere, do anything" outfit.

SOP   Standard Operating Procedure

spec   To "spec" something was to formulate a specific plan

Spectre   An AC 130 four engine prop-driven gunship mounting a variety of multi-barreled cannon of varying number and calibers (it varied from model to model and even ship to ship).

spooks   A generic term for any intelligence agent; spies

sterile   Equipment that could not be traced positively back to the sponsoring nation; for Americans that would be non-U.S. equipment or outdated equipment that had been sold abroad like the M2 or M3.

strac   Used to mean a soldier who was always well turned out; one who adheres to military rules and regulations

strap hanger   Any person not a regular part of a team who goes along on an operation

suppressed   Silenced; having a sound suppressor attached (which is different than a flash suppressor).

Swedish K   A small 9mm SMG made in Sweden

syrette   A collapsible tube of morphine attached to a hypodermic needle. The contents of the tube were injected by squeezing it like a toothpaste tube.

T 10 Army Parachute   Standard Army issue parachutes used by all paratroopers

TA   Target Area

Team six   Radio code for the leader of an A Team

tiger suit   A unique pattern of camouflage exclusive to elite forces (U.S. Special Forces, Seals, USMC Force Recon, etc.) and their indig troops in Southeast Asia.

Tong   Chinese secret societies dealing in illicit pleasures. To this day they remain one of the most shadowy, and deadly, groups in the world.

USAID   United States Agency for International Development

unassed   To leave

Uzi   A small 9mm SMG made in Israel

VC   Viet Cong; the black clad guerrillas and terrorists

VCI   Viet Cong Infrastructure; the command control military/political heads of VC cells throughout Vietnam

ville   Any village

World   The United States

WP   White Phosphorous

XO   Executive Officer

Yard   Any member of any Montagnard tribe

zoomies   Jets or jet pilots